DOKESHI MARCH

Year of the Sword Book Three

DAKOTA KROUT

ACKNOWLEDGMENTS

I will never stop being amazed by my wonderful readers. You all make my life so much more fulfilled and awesome.

A massive thanks to all of my Patreons, who help me make this book the best it can be, and a specific thanks to William Merrick, Samuel Landrie, Garett Loosen, and Zeeb!

PROLOGUE

A man bearing a sealed envelope with the violet-hued wax seal of House Sunday hurried down a dark hallway, his uniform a combination of garish colors and sparkling sequins. His balding head was beaded with sweat, and a look of fear crossed his features. As he opened the door to the room overlooking the main gambling floor, he had to shield his eyes from the glare of the brightly flashing lights that shone through the one-way glass. He took a deep breath to steel himself, and walked through the semi-crowded room to approach the masked figure sitting on the throne.

"Lord March! I come with news from the border of February. Your agents from House Sunday have sent a missive through their artifacts, claiming that the man responsible for the death of Lord January has now kidnapped Lady February and is headed this way!" He passed the letter to the exceedingly large man standing near the Lord's right hand. The huge man wearing a mask covered in hearts and bubbles didn't move, instead remaining focused on the table where several men and women were playing cards below. He *did* lightly wince as the Lord of the Month next to him stiffened slightly. "They passed through the barrier three days ago and haven't been seen since. What would you like us to do, Lord March?"

Not getting the reaction he was expecting, the messenger leaned forward to see what held the focus of the most powerful man in the entire district. "*Lord March*, we can mobilize your forces within the hour and bring them to you. All you need to do is say the word!"

Shock rippled through the advisors and sycophants spread around the room like lightning. They gasped, murmuring in raised whispers… but not about the news. They were silenced by the flash of rainbow light emitting from the diamond set into the scepter held by the Lord of the Month, and regarded the messenger with pity in their eyes.

"Three times." The mad smile was the only facial feature visible on the ruler of District March's face, the rest hidden by a mask with a pattern that shifted and swayed according to the wearer's mood. "Three. *Times*. You called me by a name I have banned!"

"Oh. Oh, no. I didn't-" The man doubled over in pain, unable to speak after another flash of light erupted from the scepter. The sound of flesh being impacted by the invisible fists that pounded the man was the only interruption in the sudden silence.

"I am not a *traditionalist*, stuck in my ways. Some dusty *old man*!" A flash of light, and the sound of another blast striking the prone messenger accompanied his words. "Don't forget *The Rules*!" Another flash of light, another blow to the poor man's body. "You will call me by my *title*: Dokeshi March!"

A final blow struck the man in the temple, sending him into an unconscious heap on the floor. Dokeshi March focused his gaze upon the rest of the room to ensure that *everyone* got the message… before turning back to observe the table below.

"Dokeshi, would you… *heehee*… like me to prepare the troops?" The enormous masked man waved for the pitiful messenger to be carried off by the Dicemen, the new name of the Royal Guard. "He was correct about one thing: we could bring the interlopers to you quickly."

The mask shifted to display the painted face of a bored and irritated jester. "Don't bother, Cuddles. Even if he does come after me…" He pushed a button on a small console near the arm of the throne and watched as one of the cards in the hands of the players below switched from a three of diamonds to an ace of spades. "The house *always* wins."

"As you know…" The mad smile crept back to the Dokeshi's face. "I *am* the House."

CHAPTER ONE

Two people stepped out of the barrier dividing the districts of February and March, bringing a storm of energy along with them. Their impressive silhouettes stood firm against the sparks of static electricity that danced around them, for a bare moment. Suddenly, the one in banded armor fell to his knees with a yelp of surprise as one last jolt of energy shoved him forward. His companion—a young woman with shockingly pink hair who was garbed in workout clothes and bright elbow-length white gloves—raised an elegantly curved eyebrow at her companion.

"That isn't how the Lord of January *and* February should make an entrance, you know." Suki, formerly known as Lady February or Pugilist Friday—depending on who you asked—bent down and helped Grant to his feet. "You're lucky I was the only person to see it, or you would have lost all face. We should announce ourselves and get escorted to Lord March."

"How was that *my* fault? That could have taken off my face? Has that happened before? Wait, you think we can just get right to...?" Grant spluttered in protest before spotting the upturned corners of Suki's mouth. "You're joking with me?"

<*Wow*, Grant. It looks like that big surge in mental cultivation is already paying off.> Sarge, the sword spirit bound within February Twenty Nine—Grant's Wielded Weapon—just *had* to add insult to injury. Adding injury was probably the thing he was best at, which made sense… as he was a sword. <I guess I'll have to come up with some new ways to train your mental cultivation… hmm. Since you can barely read, keeping you awake for a week or two is probably the fastest way to increase that characteristic!>

Grant opened his mouth to argue, but Sarge didn't give him a chance to speak. <You're already down to ten months of life left, and it only gets *harder* from here on out. You're going to have to be even more focused on improving yourself, now that you're finally in the Late Spring District. Monsters will be stronger here, and so will the people you have to fight. On the plus side, greater danger means greater *growth*.>

The young Lord was pulled from the one-sided mental conversation by Suki playfully thumping him with her fist on his armored shoulder. "Yes, I'm messing with you."

He clammed up, still unused to any kind of friendly… anything. Certainly not from a beautiful woman who planned to marry him after only interacting with him for less than a day of total time. Suki blew a burst of air from her nostrils and carefully inspected the bright lights and fancy buildings of the area they had landed in. "It appears we've entered into one of the neighborhoods of March."

Grant peered around, truly noticing his surroundings for the first time. They had emerged in a dark alleyway, just off what looked like some kind of entertainment area. He could see vendors behind stalls loaded down with goods, lined up next to buildings that appeared to be theaters and fancy hotels. He shifted his gaze to Suki. "Do you know where we are? As Lady February, I'm sure you traveled into March all the time."

"Wait, no. Hold that thought." He pointed at a particular stall covered in sweet treats, with a beautiful three-tiered cake as the centerpiece. "I see something I need to buy."

Suki reached out and grabbed Grant by the collar, hauling him back to her side and pulling a strangled **ulp** from him. "*Wait.* Before we go out there, we need to go over a few things."

She held up a finger and waggled it in his face. "One: don't *ever* refer to me as Lady February while we are in March. Only traders from House Thursday have been allowed entrance to here for hundreds of years, and the rumors I have heard about this place haven't been good in the slightest. I don't want to think about what might happen if they find out who I really am. Besides, I'm not *technically* Lady February anymore; not until we get married. Then you can call me Lady February again. After you unite the twelve districts and bring down the barriers, you can call me *Queen*."

"You're still on that-" Grant gulped as she glared at him, and he thought over her demands for marriage. As *interested* as he was in making that happen, it was vastly secondary. His eyes flickered over to a screen that displayed his true reason for being here: a Legendary Quest that would kill him in just ten months if he didn't finish it. A drop of cold sweat dripped down his spine as he read.

Quest: Heal the World (Lvl 100. Legendary.)

Grant Leap, by picking up the Wielded Weapon 'February Twenty Nine', you will be henceforth known as Grant Monday and will gain one cultivation level automatically, no matter how much cultivation would otherwise be required.

Important Information: The Wielder of February Twenty Nine, Grant Monday, has one year to gather the power of the Lords of the Month and return February Twenty Nine to the status of a completed Wielded Weapon. (Current Progress: 2/12)

Rewards: Completion of the quest, Heal the World, will result in the reward of the title 'Calendar King' and all wealth and responsibilities associated with that position, along with the ability to wield the most powerful weapon in the world.

Failure Conditions: Failure to complete the mandatory quest 'Heal the

World' within one year will result in the loss of all cultivation levels gained since the acquisition of February Twenty Nine, plus the loss of an additional one level.

Since Grant had been at cultivation level zero when he picked up the weapon, it meant he would drop below zero and die a most terrible death. How terrible, he wasn't sure, but he was convinced it would be an awful way to go. Suki poked him in the nose, forcing him to dismiss the screen in front of him. "Focus, Grant. This is important."

A second finger was raised in front of his nose. "Second thing to remember: This District isn't anything like January or February. People here cannot be trusted. As shocking as it was for you to come to February... think about how terrible this place could be."

"Look, I have some experience dealing with culture shock. I'm sure they can't *all* be as bad as Fe... January." He changed his words at Suki's inquisitive glare, then pointed to the woman selling the cake in the distance. "I mean, they at least eat *cake* here, unlike the cultivation maniac, err, Physical Cultivators you've raised to eat nothing but wheatgrass smoothies and granola."

She pressed her lips into a firm line, her eyes boring into him before holding up a third finger. "Third, try not to start any fights. I have only read reports from the few people that pass between the districts, but they all say the same thing. Fighting in March is a *very* bad idea."

"That's it? No details beyond 'it's bad to fight'? I don't *like* fighting people." He shrugged, shifting his new armor on his shoulders. "I only need to defeat Lord March. That's the fight that really matters. I'll try not to fight anyone else if I can avoid it."

Grant pulled up his status, reviewing the recent gains he had earned in District February.

Name: Grant Monday
Rank: Lord of The Month (January, February)
Class: Foundation Cultivator
Cultivation Achievement Level: 17
Cultivation Stage: Mid Summer
Inherent Abilities: Swirling Seasons Cultivation
Health: 352/352
Mana: 19/19

<u>Characteristics</u>
Physical: 201
Mental: 76
Armor Proficiency: 111
Weapon Proficiency: 149

Late Spring Medium Ornate Banded Mail armor. Full set: Head, Torso, Legs.
Total Physical Damage Decrease per set item (Includes Cultivation bonus): 50.
Total Magical Damage Decrease per set item (Includes Cultivation bonus): 50

February Twenty Nine (Considered as a Late Spring Medium weapon due to Weapon/Armor synergy)
Total Damage increase: 61. (Base weapon increase: 14. Weapon Cultivation increase: 47.)
Critical hit maximum damage: 93

At least with those numbers, he had a chance to do some real damage to his opponents. Sarge seemed excited to be here, but hid it behind a thin veil of insults. <She clearly doesn't know you very well. I bet we get in a fight within the first hour. You are the best, the pinnacle, the *acme* of attracting bad luck. Better than anyone I've ever even *heard* of, and that's including in tall tales.>

"Sarge, it isn't my fault that I'm a calamity attractor." Grant frowned down at the sword sheathed on his hip. "*I* don't start fights with other people; they go out of their way to-"

<I think it's your face. You have a very punchable face.> Sarge's musings were too much for Grant. Before he could ask if there was a way to fix that particular issue, his stomach growled at the scent of baking bread and grilled meat drifting down the alley. He started walking toward the smells, dragging Suki behind him. Her heels were dug in, but it did no good. His stomach wouldn't take 'no' for an answer, and his physical cultivation had reached a point where she could only stop him by using real force against him.

Grant hadn't had anything but rabbit food for a month, and he was willing to stab someone in the face for a steak.

CHAPTER TWO

Grant and Suki stumbled through the alley and into a kaleidoscope of colorful lights that dazzled and amazed them. What Grant had thought were inns turned out to be some kind of game store emblazoned with signs declaring that 'patrons won't be disappointed if they try their luck'. People seemed happy, their laughter echoing about the town square and from nearly every building. As Grant followed his nose and approached the nearest food stall, he noticed a gaunt man wearing the white uniform of a professional chef standing behind a grill.

The smell of cooking beef made him dizzy, and he couldn't hold in his drool; a thin stream escaped the corner of his mouth. As the two approached, Grant managed to get a better look at the man behind the counter. He didn't look like any cook Grant had seen before. In January, any chef under three hundred pounds would be laughed out of business, but this man was somehow even skinnier than the people of February! The hems of his cook whites were slightly frayed, and more than one faded stain was still visible on the front of the thin jacket.

"Step right up, folks! Come try the fancy fare at Fancy

Frank's Fantastic *Foodstuffs*!" His sunken cheeks didn't diminish the smile he cast at the sight of potential customers, and he waved his spatula about like a true showman. "This sustenance station is certainly suitable for special souls such as yourselves!"

Grant still had a few misgivings, but he was already here, and the two steaks sizzling on the grill made his stomach growl like an angry puma. "How much for the steaks… Frank?"

"Frank's my name; frankly, frying's my favorite game!" Grant stared in confusion at the grill. There definitely wasn't any kind of frying equipment or pans in sight.

"Okay…? Frank, how much Time for the steaks?" He dug out the coin pouch hidden in his waistband and jingled it in front of the odd man to accentuate his point.

"Oh, such a silly side to show simple servers!" The cook plopped down a wheel in front of Grant. "Donate a duo of Days to drive the disk! Let Lady Luck locate the luncheon you lick!"

"What? What's happening right now?" Grant glared at the man, confused and starting to feel slightly angry. "I don't *want* to spin a wheel. I want to buy those steaks!"

<I'd laugh at your mental cultivation again, but this is something else entirely. Still…> A bright orange rock that only Grant could see came out of nowhere and smacked him in the head. <The man is saying you need to pay to spin the wheel before you can buy the food.>

<How am I supposed to know that?> Grant mentally retorted, not wanting to be seen muttering into the air. He had been told it made him look crazy. He rubbed his forehead where the rock had struck him, which the others mistook for irritation. <Since when can you throw rocks at me?>

<Grant, if I can throw a spider the size of a horse at you, I can *certainly* pelt you with rocks.> Sarge snorted a new threat just as Grant opened his mouth to speak again, <I'm looking forward to this new iron maiden module I've been tossing around for a while->

Grant's face paled. The cook was starting to lose his smile, so Suki elbowed Grant in the ribs and hissed, "You're making a *scene.* Just pay the man, and let's get out of here."

Begrudgingly handing over two Days, Grant grimaced as the cook's smile returned to its former glory.

"*Delectable* decision, my dangerous disputant." It was obvious that Grant's patience was nearing its end, so the man scooted the wheel closer to him. "Spin, sir, and see such succulent and savory-"

He was cut off by Grant spinning the wheel hard enough that it almost tipped off the counter and onto the flames of the grill. It rocked back to safety, but the motion threw off the rotation of the wheel. The circle was marked with four equal colors, red, yellow, green, and blue. The vendor had nearly lunged for it, but let out a slow sigh of relief as it stabilized and slowly rotated until the pointer at the base landed on green.

"Ah, *green*! What a fun game this was." Grant deadpanned as he held out his hands, ready to finally get the beef his body so strongly desired. "Now that I played with the wheel, can I *please* get the steaks? You don't even have to put mine on a plate. I can probably finish it in three bites."

"The color callous chance chose for cook's customers means I can't cook the choice cuts of cattle claimed by the client." Frank plopped down two plates of wilted salad; Grant was pretty sure he saw a bug in one of them. The vendor gave them a wink and made a shooing motion, telling them to go. "Better luck next time!"

"What just happened." Grant's deadpan growl made the phrase a statement instead of a question. Suki eyed the white-knuckled grip he had on his sword and placed her hand on top of his hand, forcing him to stop before he could kill the food vendor.

"Just *take* the food and go," she stated through a forced smile, nodding toward a pair of men wearing the orange tabards of House Tuesday. "We don't want to make a scene in front of the Peacekeepers."

Grant grabbed the plates off the counter, secretly plotting

the demise of the man that had just charged him a ridiculous sum for *more* rabbit food. "I'm going to kill him."

He whispered the words to Suki like a mantra as they walked over to a table and chairs on the opposite side of the square. She awkwardly patted his hand, hoping that they could get out of sight. "I have *never* wanted to fight someone so much in my entire life. Is getting a steak really too much to ask?"

<Just eat the salad with the bug in it. Free protein! Didn't' get that in February unless you worked your butt off the whole day long!> Sarge laughed at the entire situation, pleased that Grant was being forced to eat healthy even in this District. <Lean meat, good fiber->

Grant seriously contemplated throwing his one-of-a-kind uchigatana into the trash. He wasn't going to eat a bug while *surrounded* by real food! Sarge caught an inkling of what was going through Grant's mind, so he dropped the humor and gave an order. <I know it's hard for you to learn, but stop this thought process and take a look around. Really *look* this time, and tell me what you see.>

Grant understood that it wasn't a *request*, so he sat down and glanced around the square, taking the time to pay close attention to the details that had slipped through. The vendors standing behind the stalls all wore shining smiles as people walked by, but those without potential customers seemed... scared. Hungry. Suddenly, the laughter of the patrons didn't sound carefree and joyous. It had an edge to it, like they were all on the cusp of madness. The hair on the back of Grant's neck started standing on end, and it dawned on him that this wasn't a happy place. It was a *desperate* place.

A woman holding her child's hand was rolling some dice in front of a baker, a huge loaf of bread on the counter up for grabs if she won. As the cubes tumbled to a stop, a tear fell from her cheek, and the man behind the counter handed over a moldy heel of bread. She passed it to her daughter, who immediately scarfed it down like she hadn't eaten in a week. It finally clicked for him. "These people... are they all *starving*?"

<Now you see it. I don't know why, *yet*, since there is plenty of food on display, but everyone in this town is on the edge. All it would take is one spark, and this place would go up like it was soaked in lamp oil.> Sarge's words painted a grim picture that Grant had no choice but to acknowledge.

"We need to get out of here." Suki's subvocalization brought Grant's focus back to what was in front of him. "Hurry up and finish. We *really* need to get out of here."

The look on her face meant she had noticed it, too. Something was wrong here, and they didn't yet know enough about society in March to figure it out. Grant pointed to a man sitting a few tables down from them. "Maybe we should ask someone what is going on? I'll see if that guy knows anything."

Suki hesitated visibly, but she reluctantly allowed Grant to do as he wished. "Fine, but be careful. We don't want to stand out too much, and the wrong question could bring the kind of attention we don't need right now."

Grant stood, and strolled over to speak to the other diner with an exploratory smile on his face.

"Seat's taken, kid." The name tag over the man said he was 'Lucky Luca'. Grant ignored him and took the seat anyway. "Heh, seein' as how ya don' know when a man wants to be left alone, why don' ya just get to it? Tell Lucky Luca what it is ya want, yeah?"

Grant gave the man a once-over, taking in his ragged clothing and unwashed features. The obvious bulge in his coin pouch hinted that the man had plenty of Time, but he wasn't using it to better himself very much. Grant leaned forward, lowering his voice conspiratorially. "I was hoping I could ask you some questions. I'm new here, and there are some things going on that I don't understand."

"Ah, it's information ya want." Lucky Luca pulled out a deck of cards and started shuffling them. "If ya can pick out the high card, I'll tell ya what ya wanna know, see?"

Three cards were quickly laid out on the table. "If I win, ya pay me Time for my time, an' I tell ya what I wanna tell ya. Get me?"

"You'll tell me what *I* want to know," Grant firmly stated. He was having problems with the man's accent; it wasn't anything like he had heard before. "If I need to play your game to make that happen, let's do it."

"If ya win, sure. If I win, we do things my way. Either way… ya gotta pick ya card then, see." Luca gestured to the three cards. "I'll let ya go first, ta make sure things is on the up and up, see."

Grant reached forward, awkwardly choosing the middle card. He flipped it over to see a ten with a large red diamond under it. The other man flipped the card on Grant's right, somehow making the third card disappear in the same motion. His card bore the figure of a scepter, with a 'J' in the corners.

"Looks like I won that one." Lucky Luca held out his hand. "How's about ya hand over an Hour, and I'll tell ya some things I think ya should know?"

Grant still had no idea what was going on, but he passed over an Hour coin. "First thing ya gotta know is ya gotta win *everything*, see? Chance rules this place, so ya betta find ya'self a way to tilt things ya direction."

"What?" Grant was more confused by the information than enlightened. "How does that make any sense? Is that why I couldn't just buy a steak?"

"Nah, see. Ya probably couldn't buy a steak 'cause of the food shortage." He pointed to his own plate. "Somethin' messed up the food comin' from the border, so now we all gotta go hungry, see."

"But he was grilling the steaks right in front of me!" If Grant hadn't been wearing his helmet, he would have pulled out his hair in frustration. "Why wouldn't he just charge me for them?"

"Ya ever heard of advertisin'?" Lucky Luka chortled and took a bite of his food. "Look, kid, ya seem like an alright sort, so I got a piece of advice for ya."

He shuffled the deck of cards that seemed to appear in his hands, as if by magic. "Go back ta wherever ya came from, 'cause I don't think ya got what it takes ta make it in a place like this. When ya gamble for everythin', ya gotta be willin' ta take chances, see. I don't think ya are the sort ta like that kinda thing. You have an unlucky face."

"You *cheated*!" Before Grant could say another word, their discussion was interrupted by an angry shout from across the square. "I saw you tilt the table! Gimme my money back!"

"I'm *no* cheater! You lost fair and square!" The bread vendor's face was livid, and he quickly scooped up a small cudgel from behind his stall. "Take it back!"

"Oh, that's gonna be real bad, see. We gotta get outta here before the carrots start wavin' their sticks." Lucky Luca quickly stood, knocking over his chair in the process. He tipped his hat in Grant's direction before disappearing between two buildings in an instant.

<He might be right. Grab your girlfriend, and let's get out of here. You should be training, not getting mixed up in *that* kind of trouble.> Sarge was talking about the mob of people that had sprung up out of nowhere, surrounding the two men shouting at one another.

Grant took a closer look at the man who had accused the bread maker of cheating. He was almost skeletally thin, his hollow cheeks and shrunken eyes feverish with the beginnings of starvation. It was hard to tell, but it looked like the mob was angrier at the accusation of the food vendor being a cheat than the close-to-death man standing in front of them.

"He's skin and bones. The man just needs food." Grant weighed the options of leaving the man to the mercies of the mob or stepping in to attempt to break it up. Then, Grant looked over at Suki. "Sarge, what would she think if the new Lord February just watched a starving man get beaten, or worse, killed? I can't just walk away."

<You should *absolutely*-> Grant got to his feet, ready to head over and stop the fight. As he prepared to draw his uchigatana,

Sarge chuckled in his mind. <You know what? Fine. I told you it would take less than an hour for you to find trouble.>

"In a place like this, you should have bet on it." Grant approached the mob with powerful strides, his hand on the hilt of February Twenty Nine.

CHAPTER THREE

The crowd surrounding the starving man had reached well over a dozen people by the time Grant got close enough to try to break things up, but by then, it was too late. Someone kicked the man in the back of the leg, dropping him to one knee. Then, in the oddest fashion Grant had ever seen, the people started beating the man.

It was like the kick was some kind of signal for the entire throng. They formed an almost perfect circle around him, taking individual turns to land a punch or kick on the fallen man. He did almost nothing to try and protect himself, beyond curling up an inch at a time between hits in an effort to somehow lessen the blows.

When Grant finally stepped in, he quickly discovered why he had received all those warnings about not fighting; he grabbed the shoulder of a hefty woman he had seen selling cakes and pulled her back before she could hit the downed man with a surprisingly sharp-looking spatula.

. . .

Warning: *You have initiated combat with* ***Peasants of Gambling Center 7.*** *As the instigator, your ability to defend will be reduced to every second turn used to attack.*

"What is even happening?" Grant tried to move, but for some reason, he was stuck in place like a fly in amber. An invisible force was holding him in place, making it impossible for him to do anything beyond strain back and forth. "Why can't I move? *Sarge!*"

Actions: *Please select one option from the following list*

  Attack: *Lethal, Non-lethal, Spell.*

  Defend: *With Weapon, Without Weapon.*

  Run: *Attempt Escape.*

"Sarge! What's going on?" He wasn't sure what to do, but he did notice that everyone else was moving just like he was, lightly bobbing back and forth in place. "Why can't I move?"

The nonchalant council he received was not the direct order he had been hoping for. <Well, kid, you've really stepped in it now. I don't know how he did it, but it looks like Lord March figured out some way to add to the barrier system. You better pick something fast; I think things are about to get interesting.>

"Pick something? What should I pick?" The man directly across from Grant sprang forward, striking him across the face with a bag of onions. Grant hoped that was what it was; otherwise explaining that smell wasn't going to be something he wanted to deeply investigate. "That didn't even hurt!"

Damage taken: 0 blunt (4 mitigated)

<Of course it didn't hurt, ya simpleton! You're wearing *armor*. Getting hit with a sack of laundry *better* not hurt.>

"I *really* wanted that to be onions." The person standing next to the bag-wielder was a different story. They jumped forward and hit Grant with a steel-spiked cudgel, smashing him across the stomach hard enough to double him over; but he couldn't even move enough to make that happen.

Damage taken: 0 blunt (24 mitigated)

Grant tried to unsheathe his sword to deflect the blow, but a red message flashed across his vision, preventing him from moving.

Please select an action-

<Select 'Defend: With Weapon,' and *hurry*! These weaklings are going to finish you faster than your mother finishes a buffet table!> Grant did as he was told, and his sword seemed to practically jump into his hand just as the next person in the circle flashed forward to attack. By reflex, Grant lifted his sword into a high guard, and the man attacking him slammed his fist onto the edge of February Twenty Nine hard enough to risk losing fingers. Unfortunately, it also resulted in shooting blood straight into Grant's eyes and open mouth.

Action: *Defend: With Weapon*

Result: *Critical Success, attacker takes 13 slashing damage—bleed effect active, defender momentarily blinded.*

Actions: *Please select one option from the following list*

Attack: *Lethal, Non-lethal, Spell.*

Defend: *With Weapon, Without Weapon.*

Run: *Attempt Escape.*

<I recommend doing that again.> Sarge paused as Grant once again selected 'Defend: With Weapon'. <Now, try to see if you

can do more damage to the next one. These are just peasants; it won't take much for them to turn tail and run away. If they hit you, they'll literally start to kill themselves.>

"Stop this!" Grant shouted at the next person in line, a muscular young man barely older than Grant himself, garbed in the leather apron of a blacksmith. "I don't want to hurt you!"

"Then you shouldn't try to defend someone accusing another of cheating!" The young blacksmith swung a heavy hammer at Grant's chest, clearly holding nothing back. "Now take this! In your next life, maybe you will be able to see Mount Tai!"

Grant couldn't move his feet, but he could lean to the side. He perfectly positioned his uchigatana to deflect the hammer, while simultaneously allowing the other man's momentum and force to guide the first two inches of its chisel-tipped point into his attacker's thigh. The man gasped in pain and fell backwards off of Grant's sword.

"The Tuesdays are comin'! Everyone get outta here, see!" The shout from the nearby alley sounded suspiciously familiar. Just as the warning ended, the sound of booted feet stomping in unison and chainmail armor jingling in time were clear indicators of an organized force approaching the square.

Congratulations! *Your new battle count moves from* [0 Wins / 0 Losses] *to* [1 Wins / 0 Losses]. *Remember, the lucky rise to the challenge!*

"What is *wrong* with this place?" Grant sheathed his sword. "Sarge, did my cultivation improve at all?"

<I'm upset to admit the fact that you did cultivate some time in your Armor cultivation.> He seemed to grumble a bit, as if Grant was the cause of all the problems. <It shouldn't have jumped at all, given how weak they were. There wasn't

even a Vassal in the whole bunch! Maybe it was the fact that you were resisting a barrier effect the entire->

"Don't just stand there; *help* me!" Suki had already made it over to the man still lying on the ground, and she was doing her best to get him on his feet. Even with her prodigious strength, an unconscious body could be awkward to carry. "We need to get out of here before they see you!"

Suki nodded at a faded and worn poster nailed to the side of a nearby building. It was weather-stained, difficult to make out, but Grant still recognized himself.

Wanted by House Monday

Dead or Alive

Grant Monday

For the murder of Lord January

Reward: 5 Decades

"Five *Decades*!" Grant felt like someone had struck him between the eyes, because he was certainly dazed and confused. "Who would pay that much for me? That's enough Time that I'm almost tempted to turn *myself* in! I didn't even kill Lord January. All I did was take his position! This is *bonkers*! No place will be safe for us now… Suki, you need to get away from me before you get arrested too."

<Why would they draw your teeth like that? You look like a horse.>

"Calm down." She raised an eyebrow at him and motioned for him to grab the other man's arm so they could carry him away. "Look at that picture again. It doesn't look *anything* like you. That version of Grant Monday looks like an overstuffed sausage. You must have lost almost a hundred pounds since that was drawn? No one could possibly recognize you."

She patted her pack with her free hand. "We'll both even

take a potion to hide our identities. We should be safe after that."

<If you don't hurry, it won't matter what you do. Those guards are getting close.> Reminded of their situation, Grant picked up the pace. They quickly disappeared into the twisty alleyways and dark side streets of the poor district, only a few buildings away from the apparent largesse of the market district.

Even with the assurances from Suki, and Sarge analyzing the combat situation, Grant couldn't help but feel like a noose was growing ever tighter around his neck.

CHAPTER FOUR

"What should we do?" Grant began pacing up and down the hallway of the abandoned house they had found. The lack of a roof over most of the building, due to some long-ago fire, was probably the main reason why not even the extremely destitute of the small city had moved in. "If they ask around, I'm sure House Tuesday can figure it out. They'll be tracking us down in no time!"

"We already took the potions to hide our names. Now isn't the time to worry about things we can't change." The name above Suki had changed from *Pugilist Friday* to *Suki Saturday.* Grant had changed his from *Grant Monday* to *Grant Friday*. He wasn't very good at coming up with new names. "What we need to figure out now is what to do with *this* guy."

The man they had saved was looking pretty rough. He was bleeding from his nose, and the shift to his back had made him spit up more blood from his mouth.

"What else did House Saturday give you before we left?" Grant shuffled through his own pack, gifted to him by the people of District February. He hadn't had time to look at everything inside it yet. "I think I saw some bandages in here."

"I can do better than a bandage." Suki pulled a small wooden box from her much smaller pack. Grant, being the winner of their last battle, had been forced to carry the heavier of the two. She pulled free a light pink vial and held it up for his inspection. "We have ten healing potions, five for each of us. I think we should give him one of the weaker ones."

Grant nodded his agreement, and she poured it down their prone charge's throat. The weak man coughed a bit, but he was too damaged to do anything other than drink the thick fluid.

<It's going to take a few minutes for that to work. No sense in sitting idly by while some stranger you have never met absorbs an extremely valuable item you certainly could have used for yourself later.> An orange-tinted bird dropped from the sky, talons aimed for Grant's eyes. <Time to train!>

The reflexes drilled into Grant's muscle memory meant it was almost effortless to dispatch the imaginary bird with the lightning-quick use of Iaijutsu, the quick-draw sword technique which Grant had recently gained a rank in. As the next bird darted for his back, Grant rolled backwards into the room across the hall to give himself some space to maneuver. "Sarge, don't you think it would be a better idea for me to go outside before you start attacking me?"

A blob of orange slime dropped onto his face, burning his eyes. "*Bwharagha*!"

<You need to practice fighting in tight quarters. It's only a matter of time until you get trapped in a confined space and need to defend yourself. Can't always jump out of trees to impale spiders the size of ex-Lord January.> Sarge continued explaining over Grant's grunting struggles. <So don't you worry one little bit; this environment is a *great* training space!>

Grant knew that the acidic slime trying to crawl down his throat wasn't corporeal, but that didn't make the burning on his face feel any less real. While it was still attacking him, a glowing orange man came around the corner and jabbed at him with a spear. Grant managed to interpose his sword between the spear and his body, but that moment of distraction allowed the slime to go straight up his nose. He collapsed to his knees, his sinuses in agony. The shaft of the spear smashing into his head ended his pain.

"By the Regent, what was *that*?" Grant blinked his eyes open and got up on all fours. He shook his head in an attempt to clear it from the jarring effects of his false death. "How am I supposed to fight a *slime* with a sword?"

<I guess that fancy new lightning spell you got is just going to sit around and do nothing? Or is using the side of your blade to knock an enemy away too much to ask?> Grant paused in shame when he realized he had completely forgotten about the new spell he had gained after becoming the new Lord February. <You need to remember to use *all* the tools at your disposal. A true samurai never neglects such a simple thing. Never forget a sword is but a tool, and it can be used for more than just cutting.>

"Sarge, I'm *not* a samurai." Grant rubbed at his face, still feeling the phantom sting of the acidic slime. "I never even *agreed* to becoming a samurai. I'm just a Wielder, and-"

<*Just*-? Listen here, you're not a samurai *yet*. If you want to live to see your next birthday, you had better do your level best to *become* one.>

"I don't even know what that *means*." Grant had heard Sarge angry before, but his current tone was something different: the sword was truly upset with him. In an attempt to distract himself, Grant pulled up his spell description.

Elemental Spell: Thundering Step

Prerequisites: 65 Mind. Two feet. Metal weapon.

Active Mode: Create a static field in a five foot radius around you that damages others when they move through the area. Does not move from the point it was set. Lasts five seconds.

Mana cost: 10 per use.

Damage (Self): 0% Mental cultivation.

Damage (Other): 100% Mental cultivation per second.

. . .

Training Mode: Increase movement speed by 50% while out of combat. Combat is defined as not dealing or taking damage from an opponent for five seconds.

Mana cost: 10% per second. Mana regen halted while active.

"If I had activated that spell, it would have done seventy three damage per second? Isn't that a little overpowered?" Grant reviewed his stats to verify his calculation. "I could kill all kinds of enemies with this spell!"

<Ha! You wish. It takes ten mana just to *activate* it, and you only have nineteen. You can only activate this spell once before having to wait to activate it again. Plus, you are completely forgetting that you aren't the only person with spell damage reduction.> Sarge let out a small sigh, <This is the Late Spring District. Even 'regular' clothing provides a slight amount of armor. Our enemies will be harder to kill, even as we become able to kill them more easily. Oh, and it'll deal just a hair over eighty damage per second. You forgot to add in your ten percent increase from Lightning Attunement.>

"Oh. So I did. Even better. Do you think I shouldn't use the spell?" Grant forced himself to his feet, spitting to get the residual taste of slime off his tongue. "At least it provides a speed boost when we are training."

Instead of getting an immediate answer, another orange-tinted slime dropped onto Grant. This time, it was large enough to encase his entire body. <Did I say don't use it, you foolish mortal? *No*! All I'm saying is don't expect to go around blastin' all your enemies with a thunderstorm like some pansy wizard from bedtime stories! *Use* your tools!>

Grant couldn't say anything in reply, otherwise the acidic slime would crawl into his mouth. Instead, he concentrated through the pain and activated *Thundering Step* in active mode. Power rolled off him, and a five-foot column of brown lightning radiated outward. The effects were immediate, causing the slime to spasm with the electric shock.

Unfortunately for Grant, the 'zero damage done to the spell caster' effect didn't negate the lightning traveling through the slime. He was squeezed, burned, and shocked all at the same time. After the five-second spell timer wore off, the slime collapsed into a puddle, freeing Grant from its embrace. If the slime had been real, and the lightning rebound hadn't been a simulation from Sarge, Grant would have just turned himself into a charred husk. Even with his armor and cultivation reducing the magical damage by fifty, Grant would have still lost one hundred and fifty health: nearly half his total.

<Lesson understood?>

"Sarge, I have a question for you." Grant was gasping in a futile attempt to catch his breath. "What day is it today?"

<I believe it's past midnight, so that would make today a Monday,> Sarge told him after a brief pause to determine where the line of questioning was coming from.

"Well then, it's official." He got back to his feet, shaking out his limbs to try to relieve some of the pain from the shocks. "I *really* hate Mondays."

CHAPTER FIVE

"Grant, he's waking up! Get in here!" Suki called from the other room. Her tone told him that he'd better hurry. The man they had saved was awake and clearly bewildered at his situation. Before he had been knocked out, he was in the market square, surrounded by angry strangers beating him to death; now he was in an abandoned building with strangers.

The now-twenty-year old could sympathize. He had been through some similar situations himself. In his mind, this guy had it easy: there weren't even any spiders trying to eat him.

"Who are you people?" The confused villager rubbed his head, trying to massage away the memory of almost dying. "Where am I?"

The name tag above his head said 'Phil the Peasant', so Suki addressed him by name.

"Well, Phil, this is Grant, and my name is Suki." She handed him a canteen of water. "We managed to get you away from the mob, but you were pretty banged up. We used a very expensive healing potion on you, so we were hoping you could return the favor by answering some questions for us. We just came from District February, and any information on this place would really help."

He thought for a minute, clearly weighing the idea in his mind before speaking. His words, when they came, were slow and careful. "Since you did a life-saving service for me, I think I can get away with telling you things without involving gambling."

"Explain. What do you mean?" Suki leaned forward, her short hair falling across her forehead and nearly reaching her intense eyes. "Why would you need to involve gambling just to *talk* to us?"

"It's… it's *Dokeshi March*. He makes the rules, and we have to follow them." Phil sat up and handed back the canteen after taking a long drink. "He says that the rules are there for our protection, to make sure we don't hurt ourselves in our confusion. We… *I* think the real reason is to keep people from assassinating him. All fighting is done in turns. Since he likes gambling, you have to play a game of chance to buy just about anything."

"Wait." Grant stepped forward and knelt next to the man, his armor creaking with the motion. "Who is 'Dokeshi' March? Does he work for Lord March?"

"No, Dokeshi March *is* Lord March." Phil made a noise of deep frustration as he read the confusion on Grant's face. He spoke his next words slowly, to make sure Grant could *understand*. "He thinks the title Lord sounds too… stuffy? He makes people call him 'Dokeshi'. You know, the word for clown… I mean, *jester*! By the Regent, *never* call him a clown!"

The man was so distressed that Grant rocked back on his knees in shock. "It's okay, you don't need to-"

"His *Vassals*! You need to stay *away*! All his Vassals are named after the greatest jesters in history. Plinko, Blinko, Floof, Fluffy Fingers, Fluffy Buns, Buns the Bear, Boo, Goof, Gank, Yank, Yoinkers, Boinkers, Beans, Taters, Tatters, Frank; you get the idea. But… I'd go against… against any *two* of them before

I upset Cuddles. C-Cuddles is the scary one. I heard he eats people who make Dokeshi March angry."

"He *eats* people?" Suki was aghast at the notion, and her face took on a slight tinge of green. "He can't *actually* eat people, right?"

"Well, miss, we all aren't far from that now." He held up his baggy clothes, proof of how much weight he had lost. "If those food shipments don't start coming back through the border soon, people are going to have to do *something* to feed themselves."

Grant grimaced at the news and locked eyes with Suki. He was partially responsible for the food shortages. Sarge made a grunting sound, as if he were shrugging his non-existent shoulders. <No, you are definitely *entirely* responsible for that. Meh. Not like you had a choice.>

"What else can you tell us about Dokeshi March?" Suki passed the man one of her 'healthy' granola bars. He eyed it skeptically as he gave it a sniff. Grant knew exactly how the man felt. "Anything you have to say would certainly be a help."

"Well, the big thing to remember is to *never* gamble with him." He tried a bite of the granola, made a face, and put it in a pocket for later. "I don't know if he has ever lost a game. Unless he wanted to, maybe? Everyone knows he is either the luckiest man alive… or he can cheat without ever getting caught. But *never* call someone a cheater, not *anyone*. I shouldn't have even said it, and certainly not about the L-*Dokeshi*. You never know when the walls have ears."

He looked around furtively, checking to make sure they were alone. "Why do you guys want to know so much about him, anyway?"

"Is that why the people in the square attacked you?" Suki deflected his question, asking one of her own instead. "You accused that man of cheating?"

"Cheating is severely punished, depending on the stakes of the bet. You never call out a cheater unless you can *prove* it." Phil grimaced, clearly remembering something terrible that had happened in the past. "Some have even been executed, if it was bad enough. That's why people care so much."

<With every bit of their lives dominated by gambling, there is no doubt that everyone in this District cheats somehow. Getting caught is the real problem, so we need to figure out the best way to make that happen.>

"Sarge, I don't like this place." Grant recalled Lucky Luca, how his hands were so fast with the cards, and how the man selling steaks hadn't seemed surprised at where the wheel had landed. "They take advantage of one another."

<Sneaky little *ninja*. They have no *honor*!> Sarge's shout inside Grant's brain made his eyeballs vibrate. <They do not know the way of the samurai!>

<One of these days, you are going to tell me more about this 'samurai' stuff.> Grant rubbed his temples in a futile attempt to stave off the headache. <Could you *not* shout like that? It isn't like I can ignore what you are saying.>

A crash from outside made them all freeze. A quiet chittering sound quickly faded into the distance, and they slowly relaxed. Suki peeked out a window but didn't see anything. "What was that? It didn't sound human."

"That was probably one of the monsters that lives underground, in the sewers." Phil shivered, apparently from another bad memory, and looked down at himself. "They've gotten bolder—and more desperate—ever since the food shortage. No one is throwing out anything edible anymore, so they must be starving. Like the rest of us."

"We need to hurry and defeat Dokeshi March." Suki turned to look at Grant, determination in her eyes. "Once we do, the food shortage here needs to become top priority. It's only a matter of time before the creatures of this District start thinking of the people as their next meal."

She placed a hand on Phil's shoulder, trying to convey a sense of comfort and stability. "With the silly turn-based fighting system in place, even a swarm of weak monsters would quickly overcome any warrior, no matter their strength. Putting an end to it will save lives."

Grant opened his mouth to answer, but Phil turned and bit Suki on the hand with an animalistic snarl. She shrieked in surprise, falling back from her attacker. The screen indicating they were in combat popped up in his vision, and he quickly selected 'Defend: With Weapon'. His body jerked into motion, interposing himself between Suki and Phil, with February Twenty Nine held in a low guard.

"What is *wrong* with you? Why would you attack us?" Suki quickly sprang to her feet, her gloves morphing into giant gauntlets. "We saved you!"

"I'm… sorry… have… no choice…" Phil seemed to be fighting with himself, and his movements were jerking and erratic. He picked up a hunk of wood, cocking it back over his shoulder. "Must… follow *The Rules*…!"

Suki took too long to select an option, so the system rotated to Phil. He let loose a scream, charging at Grant. The makeshift club shattered against his sword, and he impaled himself through the chest. As the man slid to the floor, Grant stepped back and stared at the rapidly-growing sanguine puddle. The notification that blinked in front of his eyes wasn't a welcome vision.

Congratulations! *Your new battle count moves from* [1 Wins / 0 Losses] *to* [2 Wins / 0 Losses]. *Remember, the lucky rise to the challenge!*

<Well, *that* escalated quickly.> Sarge paused for a moment. <Also, your weapon cultivation improved by a very small amount. Whatever this system is, it seems to supplant the normal methods of cultivation.>

"*Why*? Phil, why would you attack us?" Suki rushed forward

and leaned over the man, wiping away the blood frothing from his lips. "We were just *talking*!"

"Dokeshi made us a deal, and everyone had to take it." He paused, wincing in pain. "To live in his lands, we swore on our lives to protect him. If he dies, and a person knows about the plot to kill him... *they* die too."

A coughing fit produced more blood, spraying Suki with the red mist. Phil grabbed Grant's ankle; his grip far stronger than should have been possible. "Promise me you won't do it. If you kill him, *everyone* could die."

Grant's heart seemed to stop beating in his chest. "Kill everyone? What do you mean? Are Wielded Weapons truly strong enough to kill an entire District like that?"

<I don't know if they can wipe out that many people in one fell swoop, but a thousand years ago, Regent December used his Wielded Weapon to divide the entire world into twelve Districts and installed the system screens that everyone sees.> Before Grant could panic, Sarge sent a rock into the side of his head, causing his ears to ring. <But I have never heard of a Wielded Weapon with the power to kill based on a *deal.* Especially one people were forced into taking.> He paused thoughtfully. <I would give you even odds on it enforcing the oaths. Fifty-fifty chance you either kill everyone or free them entirely.>

"He's gone. He... he *died.*" Suki interrupted Grant's train of thought before he could reply to Sarge. "I can't... I can't believe how bad this went."

"Do you think what he said is true?" Grant's fears were plainly visible. "Could I really kill everyone by defeating Lord March?"

"I don't know." Suki took a few moments to think. "He did say that only those who *knew* about a plot to kill him would die. You aren't trying to *kill* him, you're just going to *defeat* him, right?"

"That's the *plan.* I just have to be careful not to kill him...?" He let out a sigh of relief. He hadn't killed Lord January or Suki, so he could surely do the same once again.

<Don't get cocky, kid.> Sarge, true to form, had to crush his hopes and dreams. <You are in Late Spring now, and pulling your punches won't be an option. You may have to choose between going all out and killing Dokeshi, or giving up and letting him kill you. I don't envy you the choice.>

Grant sat down next to the body of the man he had just killed while merely defending himself. It was a perfect reminder that a real fight might not go the way he wanted. He could always stop here, or go back to February and live out his last ten months with Suki. Or, he could push forward and save himself. <Not just save *yourself*, kid. Once you know what you want, you must be prepared to sacrifice everything to get it. You have the chance to heal the world; that isn't something to take lightly.>

"But *can* I? Really?" He looked down at the sheathed sword on his hip. "Healing the World is a quest, but is healing the world worth anything if there's no one left to save?"

The sword didn't have an answer. For once, silence was the exact answer Grant was looking for.

CHAPTER SIX

Grant and Suki were at a loss regarding what to do with Phil's body, so they simply moved to the room across the hall to get some rest. It had been a long day, and things looked like they would only get worse. This entire District was more than either of them had been expecting. They took turns getting sleep, with only a few mild complaints from Suki about the accommodations. She was used to living in spartan conditions, after all: she had long ago given up all accoutrements of wealth willingly.

"Wake up!" Not long after Grant had finally fallen asleep, a tap on his shoulder woke him. Sleeping in armor was far from comfortable, and he had yet to fall into a deep slumber. Suki hissed loudly into his ear, jolting him fully awake. "There's something in the room with Phil."

They shuffled over to the door, peeking out into the hallway. Grant muttered, "It sounds like slurping?"

He tiptoed over to see for himself, trying his best to keep the rattling of his armor to a minimum. The sounds of grunting and fabric tearing reached his ears, and he poked his head around the doorframe, squinting to see in the dim moonlight. In a shaft of light passing through the broken roof, he could faintly make out the back of a furred creature the size of a large dog hunched over the corpse in the room across the narrow hallway. A hairless tail swirling through the coagulated blood on the splintered floorboards told him it was no dog.

Instantly disgusted, Grant drew his uchigatana; the righteous ring of steel echoed into the dilapidated building. Phil didn't deserve to have his corpse desecrated by some monster. With a jumping slide, the sword plunged into the back of the giant rat feasting on the innards of the recently dead.

The creature let loose a screech that set his ears ringing, and he whipped his sword free of the dying beast. Before he could turn to speak to Suki, his vision filled with the already reviled combat screen.

Combat initiated

Action: *Attack With Weapon*

Result: *First opponent defeated*

Opponents remaining: 22

Actions: *Please select one option from the following list*

Attack: *Lethal, Non-lethal, Spell*

Defend: *With Weapon, Without Weapon*

Run: *Attempt Escape*

"What?" Grant was confused, clearly not prepared for more than one enemy. The creak of the wooden floor behind him forced him to spin around to confront the approaching mischief. There was a missing floorboard, and a steady stream of the monsters had begun pouring through the gap into the small room.

<Well, I guess it was a good thing we did that training, huh? >

The swarm of rats rushed Grant, who hurriedly selected to defend with his weapon. The next few seconds were a flurry of activity that left him heaving and exhausted. The strain of trying to strike with his sword made his arms ache with the effort. Whatever was enforcing the turns made it impossible for him to make any move that might be interpreted as offense, and his reflexes were fighting it.

Unfortunately for Grant, the rats must have had plenty of practice fighting in the odd style the district enforced. They had timed their attacks so he could only block one or two attackers, leaving him open to the sharp teeth of their putrid brethren. They were abnormally adept at finding the gaps in his armor, and the runnels of blood covering his legs and lower back accompanied a stream of damage notifications that stormed through his vision.

The swarm contained monsters; that much was easy to tell by the sheer fact that they were able to deal damage to his body.

At least he had given as good as he had received. The bodies of six more rats joined the first, and now it was Grant's turn. He aimed for the larger ones, hoping that they were the monsters.

Action: *Defend With Weapon*

Result: *Seven opponents defeated*

Opponents remaining: 39

Actions: *Please select one option from the following list*

Attack: *Lethal, Non-lethal, Spell.*

Defend: *With Weapon, Without Weapon.*

Run: *Attempt Escape.*

"Hold on, Grant!" Suki finally made her presence known by sweeping into the room in a storm of limbs and metal-coated fists. The whirlwind attack left another eight furry corpses on the ground. Her arrival meant he could no longer use his spell without injuring her as well, and she had disrupted the turn-based system, giving the rats another chance to attack. Suki was unprepared for the swarm of teeth and claws that assaulted her, and her lack of armor was especially noticeable. "My legs! Why can't I *move*? Die, pests!"

Grant selected 'Attack: Lethal,' and his sword slashed through the beasts still clinging to the ragged flesh of her exposed legs. Suki fell back into him, and Grant selected the 'Run' option that appeared in his vision while sheathing his sword so he could lift her off her feet. Meanwhile, the number of remaining rats had increased to fifty and was still climbing. The small room was quickly filling with the bodies of the slain creatures, making footing a problem. It was only a matter of time until they fell, and the swarm would leave them as nothing but a pile of bones.

As he scooped Suki off her feet to run, the attempt was like running into a brick wall. He had used his considerable strength with the intent to hop over the creatures blocking the way, but the woman in his arms had run into something invisible. Grant had been clotheslined off his feet by her body, and she landed on top of him, adding insult to injury.

Both of them were still groaning in pain when the rats pounced, tearing into Grant and Suki with abandon. Getting the breath knocked out of him had made his head feel woozy, and he was convinced he might actually be dying. He glanced at his health, dismayed to find that he was down from over three hundred to just above one hundred. One more attack like that, and they were both dead.

<Tell Suki to select 'Run,' so you can both get away!> Sarge's voice thundered in his mind, clearing up his thoughts. <This system is a corruption of the natural order! Whoever came up with it has no idea what it means to walk the martial way!>

"Suki, select 'Run,' or we die here!" By selecting the 'Run' option himself, Grant no longer had the chance to fight or defend, leaving him unable to even use his spell. From the condition Suki appeared to be in, it would have killed her instantly anyway.

The pressure holding Suki down on him disappeared, and

he clambered back to his feet, rats hanging off of him like a macabre suit of lumpy fur. He sprinted down the hallway, purposefully smashing against the walls as he ran. The momentum demolished both rats and walls, and soon the only thing holding the house up was the layers of dirt encrusted on the outside.

Grant was a little woozy from the blood loss, so he didn't see how or when Suki managed to grab their packs, but when they stumbled into the alley out the back door, she had both of them flung over her back. They were both covered in bloody wounds and coated in filth and hair from the rats. He shivered at the thought of the infection they would face without the healing potions in the packs.

Luckily, the rats didn't follow them outside. He guessed the system deemed the house as the battlefield, and escaping its confines counted as an end to the battle. From the sounds of squealing beasts and tearing flesh, they were distracted by the fresh meat their battle had provided.

Condolences! *Your new battle count moves from* [2 Wins / 0 Losses] *to* [2 Wins / 1 Losses]. *Remember, fate favors the bold!*

It was the only good thing Grant had found within the system. At the moment, the loss was secondary to the relief he felt at getting out alive. If he had been free of the system, that would have been an easy fight. He might have won regardless, if Suki hadn't walked in at the worst possible time, but she hadn't understood just how awful the controlled manner of fighting in the area could be. Now that she had experienced it first-hand, they would be better at planning any future battles.

<I have some good news, at least.> Sarge brought him out of his thoughts, forcing him back into the present. <Your armor and mental cultivation both saw a minor increase in numbers

after the battle. Even in a loss, you gain strength. A true samurai in the making.>

He pulled up a truncated version of his stats, checking the changes for himself.

Name: Grant Monday
Rank: Lord of The Month (January, February)
Class: Foundation Cultivator
Cultivation Achievement Level: 17
Cultivation Stage: Mid Summer
Inherent Abilities: Swirling Seasons Cultivation
Health: 112/352
Mana: 19/19

Characteristics
Physical: 201
Mental: 76
Armor Proficiency: 111
Weapon Proficiency: 149

"An increase in my mental cultivation? I don't see… right. Cultivation is slow, and you don't let me see those numbers." He could understand an increase in armor, but mental cultivation?

<I'd let you see them if you asked *nicely*, but I feel like that'll just bog you down. As to why fighting these is increasing your mental cultivation… well, there are benefits to fighting through the pain. It was more survival instinct than focused control, but that's something we can work on.> Grant shuddered at the grim joy emitting from the sword spirit's thought. <Now, get to a safe place and use your *Live by the Sword* ability to heal some. There is too much damage for a simple potion to heal by itself.>

They quickly put actions to words and climbed onto the roof of a flat-topped building a few streets over. As Grant settled in for the meditation necessary for his healing to activate, his thoughts focused on how much he disliked this 'Dokeshi

March'. Grant muttered, "This Lord has to be *insane* to implement such a terrible system on his people."

<You think so? Here's something to chew on then,> Sarge informed Grant grimly, <It seems that every creature you killed back there was a monster. There's some *real* fear for you: If I'm right, every single one of those was a true monster. That swarm of rats should have obliterated you, and the combat system allowed you to escape. Dokeshi March indirectly saved you. Who's to say this 'terrible' system hasn't saved countless others? >

CHAPTER SEVEN

The replay of the events with the rats ran through Grant's mind. His choice to not use his lightning spell when Suki had come into the room was his biggest mistake. She had been uninjured at the time, and it would have ended with her less injured than the end result of directly fighting the swarm. As always, there were wasted movements and missed blocks his memory told him were glaring mistakes. After the necessary minute of concentration—which felt more like an hour of watching his errors over and over again—he reviewed his health.

Health: 112/352 -> 216/352. Critical areas focused. Soft tissue repaired to 70%. Organs repaired. Infection removed.

Suki wordlessly passed him a healing potion, and both of them laid down on the hard roof to let the mixture work. Without realizing it, they had collapsed close enough to one another that their shoulders touched. It might have been his imagination, but he could practically feel her body heat through the metal of his armor. Fighting the rush of blood to his cheeks, he tilted his head sideways to look at her.

"If we don't put an end to this system, we're going to get killed." His grave tone gave her the energy to turn her head and meet his eyes. Grant watched the healing potion visibly closing a small scratch on her jaw as he traced her face with his eyes. "This time, we were lucky. All it would have taken was one or two more turns, and we would be rat food right now."

"He must be tapping into the power of the barriers. Maybe that's why the barrier between February and March was failing." Suki took a moment to think over that possibility, and her features turned sharply into a frown. "If that's the case, Dokeshi is responsible for all the deaths along the border in February over the past few weeks."

"Not only that, but the barrier turned regular creatures into monsters when it interacted with them. It could be his fault that all the rats are monsters… the system designed to save people might instead be raising creatures too strong for the citizens to fight." They lay in silence for a few minutes, each of them lost in thought. Grant eased himself to a sitting position and rummaged through their bags, pulling free a few of the brick-like granola bars. He passed half over to Suki, and both quickly scarfed them down. The bars may have been little better than enriched sawdust, but healing took a lot of energy from the body.

"I know you're tired, but we really should get out of here." He peered over the edge of the roof in time to spot a pair of guards marching past, clearly searching for something. "We can take a break at the next town."

"I'm fine to leave now. The healing potion is just about done." She glanced over the two of them. "We might want to clean up some first. It looks like we were both rolling on the floor of a slaughterhouse."

After washing up the best they could with some rags and the water from a canteen, the two of them climbed down and headed east, making their way deeper into the District. They had been walking for over half an hour when Grant stopped them; he had a terrible realization. "Just how big *is* this town?"

They had yet to leave the cobbled streets and closely-built buildings. The houses and businesses just seemed to go through alternating phases of nice and dilapidated, but there was no discernible end to them. "Does this just go on forever?"

"I had heard of this, but I didn't think it could be true." Suki began peering into the darkened alleyways as they walked. "Almost the entire District is built up and paved over. There are still pockets of wilderness and a few fields here and there, but they're *made* that way." She gestured in front of them, where another market square was located. "The towns here just bleed over into one another. They say you know when you get to the next one by the clusters of casinos and gambling houses."

"But… how do they grow food?" An entirely urban District was so far outside Grant's experience that he thought it couldn't possibly be real. "Where do they go for walks, or to travel through nature?"

"They get their food from January, and the people here *don't* take walks through nature." Suki led Grant around the market, avoiding the few people 'shopping' at such an early hour. "They get their entertainment from gambling, shows, and plays. It's completely different from what both January and February find important."

"That sounds *horrible*!" He took a moment to inspect the dirty streets and worn buildings. "A District focused on nothing but entertainment and spending money seems like a draining place to live."

They fell back into silence as they moved past the next square. Grant found more posters with his heavier face on them, and he made sure not to make eye contact with anyone near one of them. It took over an hour before they eventually reached another region that was largely abandoned. The sun had risen over the peaks of the roofs and was casting long shadows across the streets. Their tired feet dragged along the ground as they stumbled into what seemed to be an abandoned warehouse.

"You get some sleep first." Suki pulled out a sleeping mat and laid it on the ground. "I'll take the first watch. Ugh... I can't wait to break into the Autumn physical cultivation ranks. Sleep becomes completely optional."

"That sounds nice." Grant didn't bother arguing. The past few hours had been exhausting, and the healing potion had sapped whatever reserves he'd had remaining. He waited to fall asleep until Suki got in a comfortable position, then passed out. His dreams were filled with flashing images of rat teeth, claws glinting in the moonlight, and moldering bodies being devoured with reckless abandon.

When a light touch brushed his shoulder, it was a relief to be brought out of the nightmares. Body protesting, he sat up and took stock of their small abandoned shelter. Suki had silently laid down with a finger across her lips to indicate that he should be quiet. Peeking outside the nearest empty window frame revealed the occasional listless person making their way down the main road, but no House Tuesday guards or Vassals of Dokeshi March.

<Great news! You need to stay silent, and you can practice fighting in an enclosed space again.> Grant held in the groan that tried to escape his lips, instead preparing himself for an attacker from any direction. <Since you have to be quiet so Suki can sleep, we should try to get your Iaijutsu to rank up to Beginner. I feel like you're close.>

An orange-tinted rock the size of his fist flew straight at his face, forcing him to dodge while simultaneously unsheathing his sword and deflecting the projectile off to the side. <Good. Again. *Faster* this time!>

They spent the next hour with Grant getting pelted by rocks and slowly increasing his mastery of Iaijutsu. It was already a skill he thought he understood, but the more he practiced, the more he realized he was far from perfecting it. When Sarge threw more than one rock at a time, he found that he had problems timing the strikes to ward off both at once. Three were entirely too many for him to handle. He did his best, but sheathing and unsheathing the sword without a break was making his shoulder shake with the repeated exertions, and both his aim and form were starting to suffer.

<By the time we reach Dokeshi March, I want you to be able to hit five targets in one swing. With this turn-based combat, you could put down way more enemies at once.> He waited a slight moment for Grant to catch his breath; luckily, recovery came much faster than it used to with his Summer-ranked physical cultivation. <We can take a break. If District February showed us anything, it's that too much training can hurt you just as much as not enough.>

"That's for sure. Some of those people could have been blown away by a stiff breeze. Heh… actually, going against the wind was the reason I won that downhill race." Rotating his sore shoulder, he pulled up his status to check if he had made any progress on his skills.

Skill: Iaijutsu (1/5). This skill is designed for instant strikes, a way to take an opponent off-guard or defend against sudden attacks.

Tier one effect: When prepared to attack, a sword instantly leaves a sheath and slashes or penetrates the target, increasing on-hit damage by 10%.

"Still no change, but I think I'm getting close." Placing his hand on the hilt of February Twenty Nine, he could feel a sense of agreement from it. "Just a little better understanding, and I will get there."

<Since Iaijutsu is a five-rank skill, the highest it can go is Journeyman. Your level two skill is Kenjutsu, which is a ten-rank that can reach Deity, should make it easier to gain mastery in any subskills.> Grant could feel the sword inspecting him with what he could only call a spiritual sense. <You need to eat

something, and then the two of you should be on your way. It's only a matter of time until those creepy clowns catch up to you.>

"Not clowns. Jesters, right?" Grant's words made Sarge harrumph, but the spirit didn't countermand him. Pulling out a depressingly small chunk of dry jerky and even drier granola, Grant sat and did exactly what Sarge suggested. His physique might have drastically improved, but it hadn't taken away his memory of the delicious foods and treats he had eaten in District January. Fantasies of smashing the rhyming food vendor with the hilt of his sword and taking the steaks he'd paid for but hadn't gotten danced through his imagination as he crunched on the parchment-flavored food.

He went through some stretches after eating, purposefully making some noise to allow Suki to wake up on her own. The sun was past its peak, so if they left soon, the next town square would be at a busy time, making it easier for them to slip through the crowds of hungry people looking for an evening meal. Suki bolted up as soon as her eyes cracked open. "What time is it? Anything happen while I was asleep?"

She didn't wait for Grant to reply, instead clambering to her feet and packing her few items in her pack. "Let's get moving. We can eat while we walk."

A little amazed at how quickly she had gone from completely asleep to ready to go, Grant quickly prepared his own pack, and in moments, they were sneaking out the back alley. They eventually came to an intersection that forced them back out on the main road, but it was crowded enough that they were able to easily blend in with the people headed toward the casinos and food stalls in the distance.

"What do all of these people do when they aren't gambling?" Grant studied the people around them, most of whom looked exhausted and downtrodden. "How would an economy focused on nothing but gambling even work?"

Suki didn't get a chance to answer as another voice shattered the air and caused the crowd to scatter.

"They serve the Houses and the Dokeshi, whatever he might ask of them." As the crowd in front of them vanished like morning fog, a polka-dot-bedecked clown brandishing a scepter gestured in their direction. A name tag with a ridiculous font informed them that his name… was *Fluffy Fingers*. "Much like you will, soon enough! Honk if you're happy!"

He reached up and grabbed his oversized red nose, squeezing it twice.

Honk Honk!

CHAPTER EIGHT

The Vassal facing them was tall and skinny, and it appeared he was wearing stilts under his pants, bringing him up to easily nine feet tall. How the two of them hadn't noticed his bright green hair poking up over the crowd was a mystery. The clear stone at the end of his short metal-banded wooden scepter produced a faint purple glow that seemed to pulse with his heartbeat.

The pace of the pulsing increased as Grant took a step forward to face him. The clown, and this one was *certainly* a clown, angled the scepter across his body, pointing it diagonally toward Grant and Suki. "You know, it's lucky for you that *I* found you instead of Cuddles. He's still searching the village where you caused a scene. I will be much gentler when I present you to the grand Dokeshi."

"Ooh hoo *hoo*!" His eyes shot sideways and landed on Suki, and a tongue at least a full foot in length shot out of his mouth and slurped around the entirety of his mask. "*Much* gentler."

"I will never serve someone that treats the people they are meant to protect with such… *flippancy*." Grant wrapped a hand around the hilt of February Twenty Nine and stepped in front of Suki. If *he* was this creeped out, he didn't want to know what was going through her mind. "I recommend you get out of our way before something bad happens to you. I would just *hate* to see a terrible consequence for someone such as yourself."

<Ooh, good one. I could feel the sarcasm through my sheath,> Sarge chuckled in Grant's head. <I like how you got in front of her, as if she can't take care of herself. I suppose that's love for you. Just remember, it's *magic* when it's good. When it's bad, it just pees in your soup.>

"What-? I don't-" Grant sputtered at Sarge, only to get cut off as Fluffy Fingers twirled his scepter in a mildly impressive display of martial prowess.

"How about… Let's Make a Deal?" The clown danced back and forth on his stilts, looking for all the world like a painted scarecrow. "You walk away after swearing an oath that you'll leave Dokeshi March alone. If you break that deal, you die."

"I have a better idea, Fluffy." Grant used his thumb to pop the first inch of his sword out of its sheath. "We fight, and if I lose, I swear your oath. If I win, I get to destroy your Wielded Weapon."

"Ha! They call *me* a clown!" Fluffy tapped his staff to his head and chanted in a creepy high-pitched sing-song voice. "*A deal is presented, a deal is made. The bargain's struck, now your* fate *is made.*"

A prompt popped up in Grant's vision. It looked different from any he had seen before. The edges were frayed, reminiscent of the malfunctioning border wall that had warped the beasts in District February.

Congratulations! *You have struck a deal with the famously fantastic, sarcastically spastic, bombastically gymnastic, never puffy or scruffy, Fluffy Fingers!*

Details: *Grant Friday (Monday) will either abandon any attempts at defeating Dokeshi March, or Destroy the Scepter of Fluffy Fingers.*

Conditions: *A Duel between the mighty Eighth Vassal of March First and the Wielder of February Twenty Nine will decide the outcome.*

Note: *This deal uses the daily allotment of one offered agreement per day. Vassal weapons do not have the inherent power to kill an oathbreaker —terms of the agreement will have to shift authority from Vassal to Wielder upon earliest convenience to fulfill the full scope of punitive actions.*

<It looks like you stepped in it this time, Grant.> Sarge pulsed in anger. <If you can't defeat this clown, your journey—and your life—end here. *Never* make a deal like this again… if you get out of here.>

"Don't worry, I got this." Grant unsheathed his sword, leaping forward with a perfect display of Iaijutsu that would have made any master proud. Between his movement speed and the reach of February Twenty Nine, his blade easily cleared the distance created by the stilts the clown was wearing. A moment before impact, Grant was frozen in place, the tip of his uchigatana drawing a drop of blood from the shaking laryngeal prominence on Fluffy Fingers' neck.

Combat initiated—Duel

Action: *Attack With Weapon.*

Result: *Duel format requires proper acknowledgment from both parties. Attack stopped. Turn surrendered due to improper actions.*

Actions: *Please select one option from the following list.*

Attack: *Lethal, Non-lethal, Spell.*

Defend: *With Weapon, Without Weapon.*

Run: *Attempt Escape.*

"*What?*" Grant felt like he had pulled a muscle in his shoulder from such a sudden stop, and the confusion from the abrupt rule change in the system caused him to pause before selecting an action. It left him open, and Fluffy Fingers smashed him in the temple with the glowing crystal at the end of his scepter. Stars exploded across his vision, and a damage notification appeared in front of his dazed eyes.

Damage taken: 19 blunt (51 mitigated)

"Oh, hoh hoh *hooo*!" Fluffy Fingers screamed a laugh over his head as Grant dropped toward the ground. "That was a close one!"

<Adapt and overcome, Grant!> Sarge's shout brought him back into focus, allowing him to quickly select 'Attack: Spell.' <That's what I'm talking about! Remember your training!>

The sudden impact of *Thundering Step* on Fluffy Fingers bought Grant enough time to create some space between the two of them. The clown was almost hopping in place, a dome of brown-tinted lightning surrounding his colorful form.

*Damage dealt: 40 lightning (80 * 2 turns. 60 * 2 magic damage mitigated!)*

"That's not right! My spell should have lasted for five seconds!" Grant's indignation at the situation was another distraction, and he once again missed the chance to select his next action. The orb thrown by Fluffy Fingers impacted against his breastplate, and a blinding smoke erupted in his face. "Bah! It burns!"

<*Focus*, Grant!> Sarge was interrupted by the giggles of Fluffy Fingers. <Quit acting like this is your first fight and get your head in the game! The system must have limited your spell somehow, but now isn't the time to dwell on it. Teach that overblown sideshow a lesson!>

With a growl, Grant selected 'Attack: Lethal' and used his turn to leap forward and slam his uchigatana into the upraised scepter of his opponent. February Twenty Nine let out a grinding squeal as the two weapons slid along each other in a shower of sparks. As he jumped away from the failed strike, Grant noticed a small curl of wood coming off of the side of the scepter. His sword must have caught a bit of the Vassal's weapon, peeling a strip off like a banana.

"It looks like I am already working on breaking your

weapon, Fluffy!" Grant gave his sword a flourishing twirl, flaunting his aptitude. "Are you sure you don't want to just give up now and save yourself the pain?"

His words did have some merit. While Grant only had puffy eyes from the gas used on him, the clown was looking a little frazzled from the lightning spell, and the end of his scepter was flickering after the damage it had received.

"Okay, kid." Fluffy Fingers flicked his hand, and a throwing knife appeared between each of his digits. "I think it's time to show you how I got my name."

His arm whipped forward in a blur, and all thoughts of further taunting went the way of all natural greenery in the District: extinct. Grant was barely able to select 'Defend: With Weapon' in time to stop one of the knives. The other three impacted hard enough to knock him back a step.

*Damage taken: 39 piercing (3 * 30. 51 mitigated.)*

Health: 308/352

"Regent's *blade*, that hurt! Wait, that counted as a single attack?" Somehow, the knives had all managed to find weak points in his leg armor, and the blood flowing down his calves felt hot against his suddenly clammy skin. "I can't afford to take many more hits like that!"

<Then stop your trash-talking and *destroy* this fool!> Sarge threw another orange-tinted stone that struck him in the head. <You trained for thi3; now act likc it!>

The shift in the tempo of the duel wasn't a good one. Grant had used his turn to defend, so he had to weather a storm of knives and glass orbs filled with all kinds of various substances designed to distract and harm. All he could do was shift his focus toward defense, constantly selecting the 'Defend: With Weapon' option on reflex.

His health points steadily trickled away, but he fought through the pain and disorientation, finding within himself the skill that allowed him to deflect even the smallest of objects thrown his direction.

Each move became a part of a flowing dance, his uchigatana an extension of his will. The second shift in the fight came slowly, but Grant allowed the harmony of his movements to guide him. He went from deflecting one or two of Fluffy Fingers' projectiles per turn, to executing a single movement that kept himself free of any damage.

"How!" Grant was broken out of his trance by the shouted exclamation of the clown. "I threw everything I had at you, and you're still standing! Want a job? I have an opening-"

<I didn't want to interrupt you there, but take a look around.> Grant did as Sarge ordered, discovering a surprisingly large ring of objects lying around him. <You've been at this for nearly ten minutes.>

Grant checked his health and saw that it was still above two hundred points. The blood once again coating his body was all his, but it was time to change that. This turn, Grant selected 'Attack: With Weapon'.

The uchigatana practically leapt from his hands as he took a deep lunge at the Vassal of Dokeshi March. The clown used his scepter to once again deflect the strike; however, the block wasn't as clean as the last time their weapons had clashed. Grant's sword was able to slide along the groove of the scepter shaft and diamond, allowing him to stab into the upper arm of Fluffy Fingers.

<Good! Don't lose your focus. Strike while the iron is hot!> Sarge's voice showed his excitement. He must have been very concerned about Grant losing. <He's all out of tricks now. Time to use your Kenjutsu to its utmost!>

Taking action to words, Grant drove his uchigatana down the shaft of the scepter and almost took off the clown's oversized nose. As the blood ratio on Grant's armor changed in his favor, he jumped in place and planted his sword through Fluffy Fingers's actual foot while using an elbow strike to his chest to push him backwards. The embedded sword sliced the foot in half, and the enemy Vassal screamed in pain.

"I yield! I *yield*!" Grant *barely* stopped himself from stomping on Fluffy's throat with the heel of his boot. "Please, don't kill me!"

Before he had to guess whether the clown was lying or not, the system confirmed his surrender.

Congratulations! *Your new battle count moves from* [2 Wins / 1 Losses] *to* [3 Wins / 1 Losses]. *Remember, the lucky rise to the challenge!*

<Get away from him! *Move*!> Grant pried his sword free from the blood-slicked cobblestones just as the scepter in Fluffy Fingers' hand exploded with a massive blast of heat and light.

"Gah!" Grant was blown away, slamming to the ground flat on his back. The wind was knocked out of his lungs, and he couldn't help but gasp like a fish on dry land. After a few moments, he managed to wheeze out a question. "What just happened? I thought I was supposed to have the chance to absorb his weapon's power?"

<First off, *no;* he's a Vassal, not a Wielder. Secondly, I think you have a concussion. It'll heal soon.> Sarge switched his tone from consoling to commanding. <Get up off the ground and see how bad the damage is.>

Before he could comply, Suki appeared suddenly by his side. "Grant, that was one of the craziest fights I have ever seen!"

She leveraged him back to his feet, managing to somehow keep her clothes free from the blood and dirt he was covered in. "It took entirely too long for you to defeat him, but I guess forcing him to run out of things to throw at you is a good way to train yourself while fighting. Not sure if you noticed, but I think toward the end, he was down to flinging utensils at you."

She pointed at a spoon to support her point.

"You… fools!" The groan that came from the prone form of the clown stopped Grant short of answering. "You have no *idea* what you have done!"

Suddenly, everyone that had been standing around on the street to watch the fight froze. Grant instantly understood why, because the screen they must have been reading popped up in front of his vision as well.

. . .

Warning: *System failure. Agreement, Deal, and Oath enforcement has been halted. Please remain calm. A Vassal will be dispatched to your location to reinstate deals. Remember, events arou aaaa are aaaaa aatnearathen…*

The edges of the screen blurred, then disappeared in a burst of static. The bystanders remained stationary for a moment, gaping at one another in amazement. Then, with shouts of joy, they collectively ran toward the market square in the distance. Shouts and screams soon followed, and plumes of smoke rose from several buildings.

<I think it would be best if we got off the street.> Sarge let loose a sigh inside Grant's head. <If the Dokeshi's system really did just go down, things are going to get bad. No gambling, no barrier-style protection. Oh… those rat monsters are gonna rampage through here like a swarm of locust in a wheat field.>

CHAPTER NINE

It was a scramble to collect their gear and move off the street. The abundance of dilapidated and abandoned buildings gave them countless places to hide, and they settled on a two-story storefront with almost an inch of dust coating the floor.

"I still don't understand why you grabbed *him*." Suki kept glancing back at the prone form of Fluffy Fingers, who would have to change his name after the fight. His scepter's explosion had done severe damage to the hand wielding it. "You should have just left him for his people to deal with."

"I want him to answer some questions." Grant grunted with the effort of dragging the man up the stairs. He knew the clown was still alive, because his cultivation had only received credit for defeating a Vassal—not killing one. "If the system really is down, maybe we can get a straight answer for once."

The two of them had to clear out a space in one of the cluttered rooms so all three of them could lay down. It was filled with broken furniture parts and rotten bolts of cloth, hinting at some form of upholstery store that had fallen on hard times.

Since the clown was still unconscious, Grant used a layer of the deteriorating fabric to form a makeshift bed. A spool of thick twine that had survived relatively intact was turned into bindings for the enemy Vassal. He didn't look like much of a threat, but there was no sense in taking unnecessary chances.

After a few hours, the rioting outside started to die down. Grant had used the time to clean himself and his armor as best he could, but without a proper bath, he still felt gross. The self-awareness of what others might think about his smell was relatively new. His increase in mental cultivation, along with spending time around people and not farm animals, was evidently changing more than just his ability to cast spells.

"Here, take this." Suki handed him one of the weaker healing potions from their stores. "You weren't able to heal yourself this time, since it took so long to get the clown settled."

She gave him a once-over, inspecting all the scratches and scrapes that had been bandaged quickly. "It wouldn't do for you to get an infection at a time like this."

She was right. Getting sick at any point this year would be detrimental to Grant's mission, so he drained the vial with no argument. It was lower quality, so the gritty taste wasn't nearly as pleasant as the last potion he had taken. He glanced over at Fluffy Fingers, trying to figure out what to do with the unconscious figure. "What's the next step you want to take? Do you think we should stay in one spot for a while, or do you want to go searching for some food?"

"I will try to find something to eat out there. If I left it up to you, we'd end up eating a wedding cake or a whole pig." Suki was halfway down the stairs before he could think of a reply. "You try to recuperate. That clown isn't going anywhere."

Grant turned to appraise the man's condition. He was badly injured, and his arm was still bleeding from the stab wound Grant had inflicted during the fight. The mangled hand and arm had been cauterized by the heat of the explosion, but it would take more healing knowledge than he possessed to fix the broken clown. His current anatomical knowledge was surprisingly high, but it was used exclusively for dealing greater and more lethal wounds. Since he didn't want the clown to bleed out before he could question him, he wrapped the hemorrhaging limb and applied a salve from his stores to the worst of the burns. It should be enough to keep the man alive.

<Don't even think about sleeping for the next few days. Gotta get that mental cultivation boosted. You did a decent job fighting this clown, and I think you reached partial enlightenment with Iaijutsu. Let's push that to the limit.> As soon as Sarge finished, a cloud of orange debris appeared in Grant's vision. Not just rocks, but arrows, knives, orbs filled with irritants, even spoons—anything that Sarge could think of that the Vassals might be sending his way. <Here. We. *Go*!>

February Twenty Nine cleared the scabbard in a smooth motion that seamlessly deflected four of the sharper objects launched in his direction. It wasn't enough to stop everything, but the fluid parry demonstrated his improvement from the last time they had trained. The impact from the other objects hurt, but he had managed to divert the ones aimed for his most vulnerable places, like his face.

<Good! Now, I want to adjust your thinking. There is more than just the edge of your sword. If you had angled your sword upwards a bit more, you could have deflected that spoon with the side of the blade, and a little more follow-through with your swing would have deflected the tail end of the arrow that hit you in your thigh.> Sarge paused to let Grant think about it for a moment.

<I *know* you're tired, but this is necessary. Training your body to keep pushing through the exhaustion is a great way to improve you as a person in all respects. I know it's hard right now, but everything is hard at the start. Everything worth having is difficult. By the time we're done, you should be able to keep fighting for as long as the battle continues; be that a minute or a full day.>

"Sarge, what about proper recovery after a fight?" Grant rolled his shoulder to relieve some of the tension from swinging around his sword so much. He had just fought the Vassal, and the short break hadn't been nearly long enough to recover. "I thought the lessons we learned in District February taught us that *rest* was important?"

<At your level then, yes. You're no longer a mere mortal; you're not even a cultivator. You're a *Wielder* in the Summer cultivation ranks. Pushing yourself past your normal limits is required to ascend to the next level.> Sarge forced a new wave of objects to appear. <We can talk while you train. A master should be able to concentrate on his current fight while also being able to think of other things.>

The orange onslaught of miscellaneous ammunition darted at Grant, and this time, he deflected seven of the more dangerous items. A fork hit him in the nose, which hurt, but it was far better than what the dagger the width of his hand would have done to him.

He automatically re-sheathed his sword on reflex, and another wave appeared before he had an opportunity to catch his breath. He managed a sweeping motion with the blade tilted, knocking aside only six objects due to his exhaustion. The orb of caustic acid that impacted against his calf was reminiscent of the slime that had fallen on his face the last time they had trained, making it hard to concentrate when the orange-tinted spider the size of a large dog sprang at him out of the shadows.

<Don't lose your concentration! In a real fight, you'll still face opponents while people are throwing or shooting things at you!> Sarge couldn't hold in the chuckle as Grant was quickly wrapped in a cocoon of silk and fell on his side. <Get up, and let's try again.>

The next half an hour was filled with more training, with Grant getting more exhausted with each swing of his uchigatana. His body protested with each movement, but the pain slowly became background noise as he focused on where he wanted his sword to go. A constant barrage of objects flew at him, forcing Grant to adjust his movements around the various spiders, spear-wielders, and giant rats that pounced on him from the shadows. He used the attackers to block what he couldn't deflect, and managed to even deflect some of the things toward the people and monsters attacking his flanks.

<Yes! That's it! Use their own weapons against them!> Sarge increased the intensity, forcing Grant to speed up his movements until his sword was a blur of steel that swept around him like a wave of metal. <Good! Feel the Kenjutsu flow through you->

"That isn't resting, you know." Suki's voice broke his concentration, but Sarge took pity on him and dissipated the constructs trying to kill him. "If you keep this up, you'll be too exhausted to see straight."

"I'm not allowed to sleep." Grant stumbled a bit before sheathing his sword and sitting down. "The more I can put it off, and the more I can work on my mental cultivation, the better off I'll be in the long run. If I don't push myself, I will never be able to defeat Regent December, let alone all the other Lords and Ladies."

Suki didn't have an argument against that. Instead, she held up two brown burlap sacks before handing one over to Grant. "This is all I could find. The riots have calmed down some, but it doesn't look like there was much to choose from in the first place."

The shabby sacks contained a pitiful assortment of vegetables. Grant could barely contain the groan that fought to escape his lips when he pulled out a head of cauliflower. A few wilted carrots, a segment of a cabbage, and a surprisingly small potato rounded out the contents.

"You couldn't find any… *meat*?" Grant looked rather ridiculous when he stuck his head inside the bag, searching for more contents. "I am going to wither away if I can't get some kind of meat soon."

"You're *welcome* for bringing you anything at all." She grabbed the vegetables back from Grant and rummaged around for a bit, gathering the necessary items from their packs. "I can make us a soup from these that will make you forget there isn't any meat in it. I'll just need a fire. The back room has a small stove we can use; you go find us some firewood."

Grant shuffled through the building, collecting hunks of wood to burn inside the stove. In less than ten minutes, Suki had a pot boiling. Not knowing how to help, Grant went back to the room that held the clown. His breathing was still ragged, but some color had returned to his cheeks.

"Hey, wake up. It's been long enough. I have questions, and you have answers." Grant poked the clown in the nose. The prone man stirred and his eyelids cracked open, revealing bloodshot eyes. Fluffy Fingers jerked when he realized where he was, and that he was tied up. "Finally. Now that you are awake, we need to go over a few things."

"Why should I tell you anything?" The Vassal's voice was raspy, and he seemed to wince when he talked. "Do you have any water?"

"You can have some water if you answer some questions." Grant grabbed his water skin and set it down next to the clown's head. "I bandaged the worst of your wounds, but the sooner we are done here, the sooner you can get to a healer."

"Gah! My hands!" Grant's comment brought the damaged Vassal's attention to his injuries. "What have you *done*? My fingers, my lovely fingers!"

"At least you realize how important it is for you to answer quickly. The faster you answer, the faster we can be on our way." The clown gave Grant a shaky nod of agreement. "Good. Time to tell me how the Dokeshi's powers work. First, I want to know if I would have really died in the event that you had won and I broke the deal you tried to force on me."

"I couldn't *force* you to do anything." The Vassal winced again, trying to wiggle what fingers he still had. "Everyone who makes a deal has to agree to it. If we try to force it on you or stipulate something silly, like 'If you breathe, you agree', it will rebound on us. It isn't a *fun* feeling if the power rebounds."

"That's good to know, but you didn't answer my question." Grant shook the water skin near the clown's head. "Would I actually have died? Do the deals you make truly hold that much power?"

A long moment of silence was his only answer, so Grant shrugged and started walking away with the water. He returned to the clown's side as he broke down and started talking.

"...No. Only a deal made by the Dokeshi can kill." Fluffy Fingers shifted so he could look at Grant. "Even that is a... recent addition. It wasn't always that way; he figured out how to tap into the power of the barriers. He altered the system, but there was still enough power left over to enforce the agreements people entered into with him. The rest of us can only make deals that cause pain if you break them."

He coughed, and a few flecks of blood splattered the old fabric next to the Vassal's face. Grant took pity on him and gave him a few sips of water. "Now, why did everyone turn rabid when your scepter broke? I expect that kind of shift from *animals*, not people."

"The people in District March are little better than vermin in the first place. They agreed to follow The Rules to live here, and *this* is how they act when we can't *make* them do it," Fluffy complained bitterly, gesturing with his broken hands. "The power required to enforce the system is too much for one Wielded Weapon to cover the whole District by itself. The Dokeshi broke up the District between all sixty of his Vassals. Our weapons enforce the system in whatever area we were assigned."

Grant allowed him another sip of water. "When my weapon broke, everyone felt their agreements break, and they knew they didn't *have* to fulfill their end of the bargain. For *now*, anyway. It won't be long before the Dokeshi makes another weapon, or spreads the responsibility among those that are still functioning."

"What you are telling me is that if I can destroy the weapons of the Vassals, I don't have to follow the stupid turn-based fighting system?" Grant almost broke into a dance of joy.

He *hated* being restricted like that. "At least I know what to do when I run into the range of another Vassal."

"You *can't*!" Fluffy Fingers coughed at his outburst. "It would throw the whole District into chaos!"

"Your mad jester has already doomed this District. Haven't you noticed how *terrible* it is here?" Grant fingered a small tear in his pants where a rat had rent the fabric with its teeth. "The beasts and monsters of this whole area will eventually sweep over the entire area, and no one will be left alive."

"It isn't *that* bad." The Vassal gazed into Grant's eyes and realized how sure he was of his words. "Is it *really* that bad?"

"It's even worse than *Grant* knows." Suki must have been eavesdropping from just outside the room, because when she walked in, her face was set in stone. "Your fun and games have this District teetering on the precipice of doom. The people are starving, the monsters grow ever bolder, and no one can properly protect themselves under the strictures put forward by your leader. This place is an oil-soaked tinderbox, and anything could spark the end for all of you."

Her voice grew passionate, and she started gesturing with the bowls of soup in her hands. "All of you have forgotten your *purpose.* The role of the Houses, Wielders, and Vassals isn't to constrain or limit your people. You are the foundation to uplift them in the good times, their shield when they need protection, their sword when they need deliverance, and their judge when they stray from the path of the righteous."

"Suki-" Grant tried to appeal to her, but she ignored him and the soup that splattered over the edges of the bowls in her furor.

"Instead, you grind these people under your heels until they *are* little better than animals: trapped like rats in a corner. No wonder they rebel as soon as humanly possible. It's time for a *sword* to cut out the sickness of this diseased District." Her eyes darted to Grant but quickly shot back to the face of the clown. "Now, we should eat before this gets cold."

Grant took the reduced portion of soup from her and sat to

eat in silence. Suki's words had struck a nerve inside him, and he wasn't sure what to think about it. Was that his true purpose? Had the Leap Sorcerers of yore made February Twenty Nine to be the sword that cut the cruel bindings choking the life out of the people?

If his true calling in life was to make the world better for everyone, he was willing and *excited* to accept that fate.

CHAPTER TEN

They finished eating hastily, then started packing up without exchanging a word. Grant was even nice enough to give some broth to Fluffy Fingers, though he had to ignore the disapproval coming from both Suki and Sarge. The enemy Vassal was quiet, clearly contemplating what Suki had explained to him. It was clear the clown was conflicted about hearing that his District was fundamentally broken, but Grant didn't have any clue about what to say to the man.

<She's right, you know.> Sarge interrupted his thoughts, and he glanced down at the sword on his hip. <It's something you need to remember going forward. The people and cultivators in the Districts we will travel through depend on Wielders and their Vassals for many things, and their defense and protection are the most important role those offices must fulfill.>

"I agree; of course I do..." Grant paused to gather his thoughts. "It just feels odd, you know? Having people depend on me. Saving Leapkind in District January was one thing, but that was a relatively small number of people. It kind of just fell in my lap. To think that there are even more people out there who depend on me is... well, almost scary."

<That's why you train. You must be prepared for the role you must fill.> Sarge sent a pulse of reassurance through their mental bond. <Don't worry too much. I will help you where I can, and Suki clearly understands the importance of a Wielder. You won't have to fight alone.>

"What should we do with him?" Suki interrupted their internal conversation, lifting her chin to indicate the clown tied up on the floor. "If he doesn't get to a healer soon, he isn't going to last much longer."

"The main road should have some patrols pass through here eventually." Grant knelt to untie the ridiculous amounts of twine holding the Vassal in place. "We can drop him off there, and they will see to him quickly."

"Sounds like a good plan to me." She hefted her pack onto her back and twisted her pink hair up into a coil. "The broth you fed him should provide the energy he needs to keep him alive until then."

"Yeah, I meant to ask you about that." Grant looked at her out of the corner of his eye while struggling with the knots. "Where did you learn to cook like that? The soup you made was the best thing I have eaten since District January."

"Who do you think was responsible for determining which recipes and foods were acceptable for the people in District February?" Suki put her hands on her hips in a proud stance. "I was heavily involved with the process, and I learned to cook from several master chefs."

Grant couldn't help it. His heart skipped a beat, and his cheeks reddened until they felt like they were on fire. The woman he was supposedly betrothed to was a master chef? Maybe he should rethink his reluctance about courting her…?

<Looks like your knowledge of knots is not a lot. The twine will rot before we can trot.> Grant stared at his sword in shock. Sarge was quiet for a second, and a distinct note of discomfort tinged his voice. <Grant, we need to get out of this District. It's beginning to affect my speech patterns.>

"I was going to ask you what that rhyming was about, but I

certainly can't argue with that. I got this." He gave up with the twine and stood over the prone figure. His sword cleared its scabbard in one smooth motion, then flashed out in swift succession, slicing through the fibrous strands without breaking the clown's skin. "There. Now we can go."

Suki's eyes had definitely widened at the show of skill; Grant had already shown improvement from just the small amount of training he had accomplished while she had gone searching for food. It wasn't the same level of impressiveness that the fight against Fluffy Fingers had shown. The whirling blade that had deflected the majority of the items thrown at him was one thing, as his skill had been enhanced by the obvious battle trance he had been in. By contrast, the control he had shown in cutting the twine was without the aid of adrenaline. She couldn't help but be reminded that she had seen her own defeat at the hands of the man as well. "*Beginner*…?"

"Get up. I don't want to drag you down the stairs if I don't have to." Grant helped the still-pensive Vassal to his feet, trying to avoid injuring the damaged man any further. His focus on their foe made him oblivious to Suki's surprise toward his capabilities. "The sooner we get you in the street, the sooner you can get back to your crazy boss."

The three of them tromped down the stairs and onto the empty streets. The smoky haze covering the area was thick; Grant could smell more than just wood burning in the air. He had to concentrate to keep his meal of soup from escaping when he realized he wasn't getting a whiff of cooked pork. The expressions of horror on the faces of the clown and Suki confirmed that he wasn't the only one who had made the terrible realization.

"It wasn't this bad earlier. Something must have changed." Suki peeked around the corner and glimpsed a mass of shadows blur across the main road into an alley. "I think the monsters from the sewers got stirred up by the fires."

"Regent's sharpened teeth!" Fluffy Fingers took an involuntary step back in fear. "You can't leave me on the streets if those things are swarming! They go after people until the only thing left is bones-!"

"Are you saying you are *aware* of the threat?" Grant turned with a growl, grabbing the man by the front of his shirt, his knuckles cracking from squeezing so hard. "You people *know* how dangerous it is out here for your citizens because of your system of control, and you did *nothing*?"

Grant saw red at the corners of his vision as he slammed the clown against the wall. "How many innocent people have died so you can continue your power games?"

He battered the Vassal against the wall once again before tossing him into the middle of the road. "I *doubt* you'll really see how stupid your choices are without facing the dangers personally. If I see you within ten seconds, I'll kill you myself."

The clown turned pleading eyes to Suki for support, but her stony countenance was no place to find it. Cowering, he turned and limped in the opposite direction, quickly disappearing down an alleyway between two abandoned buildings, still clutching his broken hands to his chest.

<Now you begin to act like a true Lord of the Month.> Sarge's utterly content voice in his head broke Grant out of his fuming rage. <Even so, remember not to let your emotions control your actions. If you don't rule them, they will rule you. Don't be a raging barbarian, be->

"If you tell me to be a samurai *one* more time..." Instead of finishing his threat, Grant turned to walk down the middle of the empty street, the haze making it hard to see farther than a dozen yards in front of them. Suki was also silent, her face expressing no emotion beyond the anger that had to be mirrored on Grant's own features.

They continued quietly, both of them trying to keep the noise of their passing to a minimum. It wasn't discussed, but it was a unanimous decision to avoid walking down the darker streets. The sun was still far from the horizon; however, the smoke from the incinerated buildings made the shadows nearly as deep as twilight.

Desolation from uncontrolled fires, the riots of starving people, and the already rundown appearance of the District set a pall over their moods. This was no place for someone to live. Grant was filled with the determination to put an end to the reign of terror which the mad jester was perpetuating on his people.

"What was that?" Suki perked up, peering into the darkened alley in the distance. Grant was scanning their immediate surroundings, searching the rooftops of the dilapidated buildings around them. She pointed toward the left of the approaching intersection, where their path intersected with a wider side street running perpendicular to the main road. "Down there. I think I heard something step on glass."

"I'll cut through this building and come out on the other side." Grant nodded over his shoulder at the ramshackle storefront one doorway back from where they stood. "You stay in the middle of the intersection and try to draw the attention of whatever is waiting over there. That way, I can sneak up on them."

"Will do. Just don't take too long." Her gloves morphed into the giant metal gauntlets she used to pummel any opponents stupid enough to confront her. "I don't relish the idea of facing another rat swarm without someone to watch my ankles."

Grant gave her a sharp nod and took off, doing his best to stay quiet. He had traded his stealth for the *Reflective Skin* skill, but his lack of a proper ability didn't mean he couldn't keep his noise down.

<Don't skulk in the shadows and sneak up on enemies. Just go defeat them properly.> Grant opened his mouth to argue with Sarge, but the spirit kept talking over any objections. <Wait… no. A good general knows the importance of surprising a foe. Just make sure you know the difference between a tactic and cowardice.>

Grant had absolutely no idea what a general would do in

that situation, so he just followed his plan. He was already about to exit from the back door of the empty building anyway. The narrow street behind the shop was littered with the debris common to the poorer regions of most Districts. This one was choked with more smoking rubble than most others they had passed, so he picked his steps carefully, doing his best to avoid alerting anyone that he was approaching.

As Grant rounded the corner, he instantly realized the monumental mistake he had just made. There weren't people lurking at the intersection to attack passersby. Instead, a trio of large beasts lay waiting to ambush anyone foolish enough to enter their hunting grounds.

<This is *great*!> Grant flinched when Sarge shouted in joy upon sighting the creatures. <I didn't know an Ushi-Oni would ever leave their water source! The Dokeshi must have paved over their home, and they have been living in the sewers or something. This will be a *fantastic* way to test your skills!>

"Ummm…" Grant had never seen this kind of monster. The grotesque creatures each had the head of a bull and the body of a giant spider. Their horns curved up and forward, perfect for charging straight into anyone stupid enough to find themselves in range. He couldn't hold in the shudder at the sight of their hairy spider bodies. "What is an Ushi-Oni?"

<Well, specifically, that is a 'gyuki'. An ox demon, found only in the most remote areas of the world.> Sarge chuckled a bit, which didn't make Grant feel any better about his situation. <I wouldn't call them a 'demon', personally; just a monster that people fear, due to their ferocious temperament and ability to kill quickly and without remorse. Now that I think about it… that's probably why people call them demons.>

"Well, *I'm* not going to fight those things. There is only one of me, but there are three of them." Grant took a cautious step back, already planning a way around them. "All I need to do is stop Suki from attacking them, and then we-"

"Die, evil creatures!" The pink-haired streak that was Suki left a corridor through the smoky haze as she sprinted through it, ending her battlecry by slamming an uppercut into the jaw of the Uchi-Oni nearest her.

"Never mind. Die, foul beasts!" Sarge's shout of joy blended with Grant's bellow as he ran into the fray, uchigatana leading the way. "No backing out now!"

CHAPTER ELEVEN

The Ushi-Oni ignored Grant's approach, judging the gauntlet-wielding pink-haired prodigy as the greater threat. He was more than happy to teach them the error of their ways. Dropping his shoulder, Grant slammed into the nearest gyuki and planted his pauldron in its thorax, while his sword stabbed at the base of its bull ear. The impact pitched the freaky spider monster to its side, allowing his sword to slice deeply across its throat.

One-hit kill! Weapon cultivation increased by 30% for 10 minutes!

"One down, two to go!" He was able to dodge the spray of blood that shot out of the monster, but he wasn't able to avoid the spear-like tip of the monster's chitinous leg. It was more bad luck than on purpose, as the Ushi-Oni spasmed in its death throes. Grant shouted as the lethal appendage pierced his forearm. Damage notifications flashed through his eyes, momentarily blinding him. "*Bwah*!"

Damage taken: 31 piercing (31 mitigated.)

<Focus! That yokai is dead, but it isn't done yet!> Sarge's shout was all the warning Grant needed. He rolled backwards, away from the monster attacking him. His arm tore away from the leg attempting to impale him, but he ignored the shooting

pain making his hand numb. The bleeding yokai was desperately trying to get back to its feet, its spidery limbs clattering on the cobblestoned street. <Sword and mind must be united!>

Once again, Grant had no idea what that meant, so he just knelt in a sprinter's stance and darted under the oversized creature as it regained its footing. He ran resolutely through the curtain of blood still pouring from the gaping neck wound, dragging the uchigatana across the length of the bulbous abdomen. It was a wonderfully destructive attack, forcing the monster to plummet to the ground, its insides now on the outside.

"Oh, that's *awful*!" The smell was like a punch in the face to his senses, and he retched in disgust. "I need to figure out something else for the next one."

Now that his first opponent was *staying* down, he could focus on what the other two were doing. Suki was facing both of the remaining Ushi-Oni at once, and the fight appeared to be pretty evenly balanced. She was too fast for even the dashing movements of the oxen-spider-creatures to keep up with, though her giant gauntlets weren't doing much visible damage to the monsters. It was an endurance game to see who would tire first. Given what he knew about Suki, he would gamble all he had on her winning.

The obvious move was for Grant to jump in right away to help, but he was facing the difficult decision of when *exactly* to do it. They were fighting as if almost in a choreographed dance, and he was worried about timing his intervention poorly—it could distract Suki's rhythm and end in disaster.

<Engage in combat fully determined to die, and you will be alive; wish to survive in the battle, and you will surely meet death!> Sarge's howl sparked Grant into action. He knew the sword spirit was right; overthinking things would only slow his reflexes, and he needed to be in top form.

Getting stabbed just once from the ox-spider monster, even with blocking all the damage from the glancing blow, left his arm so numb that he wondered if the creature had been covered in a contact poison. He needed to be careful, or it would be a short fight. The blood from his defeated foe was dripping off his elbow, seeming to fall in slow motion as he sprinted toward the cow-sized monsters attacking the petite girl.

Suki saw him coming and timed a punch to land on the horn of the gyuki he was charging. It positioned the head so the creature didn't see his approach, allowing him to amputate the rear left leg where it met the thorax.

The Ushi-Oni began lowing in a mix of pain and anger, quickly spinning in place to confront the new combatant. Unfortunately for Suki, that meant its bulbous rear slammed into her just as she was turning back to face the other monster. She went flying straight into the waiting claws of the third gyuki.

Grant was dealing with his own struggles; the surprisingly quick spin of the ox-spider indicated that the monster he had killed at first must have been the weakest and slowest of the trio. His hypothesis was reinforced when the front legs of the yokai darted toward his face in an uneven staccato, their sharpened tips like spearpoints aimed at his most vital areas.

Training to deflect incoming threats served him well. February Twenty Nine seemed to block the incoming limbs with a will of its own. Grant didn't even have to think about angling his blade to force them out of alignment; the hardened chitin of the spidery legs created an eruption of squealing metal as their length ran along the edge of the sword.

When the creature reared back to gore Grant with its horns, he ducked forward into a roll that put him within easy striking distance of the gyuki's right eye. He stabbed deep but found he didn't have the leverage to push through the back of the eye socket into the brain. Fortunately, the blow did manage to force the monster to scuttle backwards in pain. Taking the opportunity to glance around, Grant noticed the predicament Suki was in. She had grasped a spider limb in each hand and was twisting and dodging the butting head as it tried to pummel her.

<Let her fight her own battle! You worry about your own

opponent, *then* help her.> Grant's focus snapped back to the gyuki in front of him. <Get in there and finish this!>

He put action behind Sarge's orders, leaping over an outflung limb on the creature's blind side and stabbing his sword through the side of the thorax. He twisted his grip, widening the wound before ripping free and rolling under the downward-striking limbs. The ichor dripping from the wounds he had inflicted made the footing slippery on the cobblestone street, so he jumped backwards into the more open area of the intersection.

The monster fighting Suki must have reacted to Grant moving closer, because a sudden shout of victory from her was immediately followed by the sound of pained lowing. Grant's opponent seemed reluctant to move into the more open area, its spidery instincts convincing it that the more confined space of the narrow street provided more protection.

<You have it scared!> Sarge's shout was excited, and he urged Grant back into the fight. <This is your chance. Go show that demon creature who's boss!>

Grant lunged forward; his sword brandished in a two-handed grip that was aimed at the blind side of the creature's neck. The technique had taken down the first one, so he hoped the same technique would work twice.

It didn't.

The yokai was blinded, so it swept its horn sideways in an attempt to keep Grant back. The bony protrusion smashed into his shoulder, throwing him across the road until he bounced off the street sign on the corner. His breath exploded outward, and his ribs made a crackling sound like crumpled parchment. The whole right side of his body went numb, and he tumbled to the ground in a heap.

"*Uhh…*" Grant groaned as he forced himself to get back on his feet, every inhale stabbing like a spear to the lungs. Even though his right side lacked all sensation, he could still move it. His hand tightened on his sword, and he wobbled forward a step while bracing against the bent street sign. The agony that shot through him almost made him pass out, but somehow he managed to stay on his feet.

<Yeah, no matter how strong you are, busted ribs are their own special kind of pain.> Sarge politely waited for Grant to steady himself. <I don't think you punctured a lung, but at least one rib is definitely broken. I would recommend you finish this fight without doing a bunch of jumping around.>

"Easier… said… than done…!" Grant was struggling to talk, but he was able to get back in position to engage the yokai in combat. The injured monster still looked game to fight, so he tried to appear as though he was too; then he noted his health. "By the *Regent*, they hit hard!"

Health: 143/352
Mana: 19/19

<Like an ox, you might say?> Sarge snorted dryly. Grant had missed the damage notifications when he had hit the pole—hitting the sign was a pretty big distraction—but the shock of seeing half his health disappear was a sobering moment: he couldn't afford to take another blow. Thoughts of retreating to heal ran through his head for a moment before a wave of determination swept over him.

<Good. Losing is acceptable; giving up is not.> Grant could feel the approval coming from the sword in his hands. <Get back in there.>

This time, Grant had a plan. It was time to finish the fight, and he needed to end it in one fell swoop. He shuffled more than ran at the yokai, waiting until it was preparing to kill him with another swing of its horns. He ignited his spell with a shout and outpouring of mana, shocking the ox-spider and causing it to curl up on itself while he recalled the effects of the spell.

. . .

Thundering Step: Create a static field in a five foot radius around you that damages others when they move through the area. Does not move from the point it was set. Lasts five seconds.

Mana cost: 10 per use.

Damage (Self): 0% Mental cultivation.

Damage (Other): 100% Mental cultivation per second (76+ 10%) increase from Lightning Attunement: 83 lightning damage per second for 5 seconds.

A deep belly laugh erupted from him. The devastation the spell inflicted on the monster was instant, blasting the gyuki with four hundred and fifteen damage in total; *well* more than needed. The creatures clearly had no spell resistance—or perhaps they were water-attuned beasts—because the Ushi-Oni was unable to back out of the spell radius, shriveling down to a smoking husk as the spell ended. A downward stab through the skull of the yokai guaranteed it wasn't going to get back up.

<Excellent. Now, go help Suki before she gets hurt.> Sarge urged, leaving him no chance to catch his breath.

A glance at the brawl told him it was for good reason. Suki had crushed most of the limbs on one side of the yokai she was fighting, but the monster still had plenty of mobility left. The pugilistic properties of Suki's gauntlets meant she had to get in close to do any damage, and the spear-like spider legs were making it hard for her to finish off the creature.

Grant waited for an opening and managed another shuffle-run at the monster when it was forced to focus on a thundering blow from Suki. He landed a perfect downward arc onto the base of its neck, almost severing the head in one strike. Exhausted, he immediately plopped down on the ground, not caring about the disgusting paste of monster blood and dusty debris churned together on the street.

The numbness was starting to fade, and shooting pains were slowly replacing the deadened feeling along his right side. He was trying to concentrate on breathing through the pain when a very angry Suki came over and punched him in the chest.

"That one was mine!" Suki kicked the dead creature's head, finishing off the decapitation and sending it tumbling down the empty street. "I had it right where I wanted it!"

Grant wasn't able to reply, since his broken ribs were pushing against his lung. Instead of responding, he dropped into the meditative state that allowed him to replay the fight and heal some of his damage.

Live by the Sword: Pause and meditate on the failures of your combat ability, healing up to 35% of all damage taken within the last ten minutes over one full minute. This ability will increase with physical cultivation.

He was forced to relive every blow and mistake, and contemplate how to improve. The biggest flaw was his poor timing: if he had used his spell at the start of the fight, it would have ended without him being injured at all. The creatures' weakness to spells wasn't something he had known about at the start of the fight, and he had no knowledge of any creature like the Ushi-Oni to fall back on. Next time, he would maximize the radius of his spell.

Health: 143/352 -> 217/352. Critical areas focused. Broken bones repaired to 90%. Organs repaired. Soft tissue repaired to 80%.

It felt like waking up from a long sleep when Grant opened his eyes after the full minute of rest. Suki was smashing the corpse he had electrocuted with steady and measured punches, her blows sending sharp cracks echoing through the area. He gingerly rose to his feet, wincing at the pain it caused him.

Wasn't he supposed to be healed enough by now that it didn't hurt so bad?

<Oh, feeling a little sore, are we?> Sarge seemed angry about something, which confused Grant. He had won, hadn't he? <You didn't see the skill you *earned* yet, did you? Sorry to say, it looks like the system decided to start working against you.>

Skill gained: Bodily awareness (1/3). Your mind has learned what is real, and what is not. Now you will always know for sure.

Tier one effect: the pain of all real damage taken is increased by 10%.

"*What?*" Grant was incredibly angry about the new skill. He'd never even considered that a self-damaging skill could exist, "Sarge, I thought skills were supposed to *help* me, not literally hurt me!"

<If you had fought the way you should have, you wouldn't be in this situation.> Sarge's tone softened, and he sounded a little less angry. <You know… maybe it's partially my fault. I shouldn't have made things orange for you, but it's too late now. I guess it is a good thing you gained this skill. Your mental cultivation is going to go through the roof in no time.>

All Grant could do was sigh as his wounds *throbbed.*

CHAPTER TWELVE

"What are you doing, Suki?" The rhythmic cracking sounds of her gauntleted fists smashing the gyuki's carapace to smithereens distracted Grant from the ridiculous system. "Why are you beating up the dead monsters?"

"Something this big has to have a unique heart inside it. We don't have an infinite amount of coin, and I am sure someone from House Wednesday or Saturday would pay top Time for something so rare." Suki pointed to the creature Grant had beheaded. "You get to dig around in that one. Since you stole my monster kill, you can deal with the mess."

Grant opened his mouth to argue, but her sharp glare was enough to stop him from saying anything. He didn't think it was worth fighting over, so he just got to work. Lifting February Twenty Nine, he hacked down at the tough armor. He heard Suki shout in disgust as she broke through the shell of the partially cooked monster, and he grinned. He had been about to warn her that the smell of a cooked monster might be worse than a raw one, but he wasn't about to go out of his way when she was busy yelling at him. Instead, he tried to take his mind off the grisly work by scanning his status.

Name: Grant Monday
Rank: Lord of The Month (January, February)
Class: Foundation Cultivator
Cultivation Achievement Level: 17
Cultivation Stage: Mid Summer
Inherent Abilities: Swirling Seasons Cultivation
Health: 217/352
Mana: 9/19

Characteristics
Physical: 201
Mental: 76
Armor Proficiency: 111
Weapon Proficiency: 149

"Wait." Grant gave his uchigatana a slightly forlorn glance. "I didn't gain anything from that fight? I feel like I should have gotten a Cultivation Achievement Level at *least*."

<Don't look at me like that. I don't make the rules here; Regent December did. One monster counts as *one*. Size doesn't matter; saving people from monsters does.> Sarge paused as if he was also looking over the stats himself. <Another thing: don't forget that you *did* earn a new skill. Lastly, every fight increases your abilities and cultivation time, even if you don't see immediate results. *I* would say you gained plenty from that fight.>

"At least I was able to beat those things. If I had been restricted to the turn-based system, I would have died from the power of their hits," Grant grumbled as he frowned at his forearm, where the skin was still pink from its healing puncture wound. "Especially since there were three of them."

<*Stop*!> Sarge's shout made Grant jump back by instinct. <You almost cut into the heart! You won't get nearly what it is worth if you damage it.>

Grant looked down to find a seafoam-tinted organ the size of his head poking out from the meaty remains of the yokai. He carefully cut it free, picked it up, and discovered it was much heavier than its head-sized appearance should have allowed.

<Oh, that's a good one. You should be able to get a Month or two for a monster material of that size and quality.> The sword on Grant's hip seemed to vibrate with happiness. <A King needs a treasury. It's good that you are starting early.>

"I'm just trying to survive here, Sarge." Grant wrapped the wet and still faintly-beating heart in a spare cloth and tucked it inside his pack. "I don't have time to plan for becoming the Calendar King. I need to *get* there first."

<Act like a man of thought, think like a man of action.> Sarge perked up when he realized that his Wielder was listening closely. <Victory is reserved for those who are willing to pay its price.>

"Sarge, are you trying to teach me something here, or just reciting pithy sayings?" Pushing Sarge's sputtering out of his mind, Grant abandoned the remains of the gutted yokai to check on Suki. His steps weren't steady, thanks to his exhaustion and lack of sleep, so he took his time getting over to her. "Did you find the heart in that one yet?"

"Did I *find* it?" Suki looked up at him, her face splattered in gore. She irritably flourished a mangled and charred heart. "What am I supposed to do with this thing, Grant? You ruined it with that spell of yours."

"Well, they are ridiculously heavy anyway, so that's one less weight for me to lug around." Grant rolled his shoulders, the pack on his back forcing the edges of his armor to dig into him. "That's a small positive."

"Oh, I didn't say we weren't bringing it." Suki stomped over and stuffed it into his already bulging pack, forcing him to stumble backwards when the weight settled onto his back. "We can probably still get a few Weeks for it."

"Great, I'm so *happy* it isn't completely ruined," Grant managed to get out through gritted teeth. "We should probably get moving. Sunset isn't too far away, and even though the

March system is broken, I don't relish the thought of facing a bunch of giant rats in the dark."

"Oh, I agree." Instead of walking toward the intersection, she turned and took off in the opposite direction. "*Right* after we get the heart from the first monster you killed."

Grant couldn't suppress the groan that escaped from his lips. "But they're *hea~vy*!"

CHAPTER THIRTEEN

The two eventually made their way deeper into the District, allowing Grant to spend some time rethinking the events that had led him to this point in his life. The gaudy desolation of the region only drove home the importance of continuing his quest. The world needed to change, and he knew that was what February Twenty Nine represented: a way to remake everything. The fear of failure was the thing pushing down on him.

That, and the stupidly heavy monster hearts in his pack.

<I don't understand why you are complaining about the extra weight. It's free training! With your levels of extreme exhaustion, it only helps advance your physical and mental cultivation toward the cusp of the next level!> Sarge interrupted his downward-spiral thinking, causing Grant to realize his ruminations weren't helping, which was probably Sarge's goal. While the sword's spirit was strict, Grant recognized that Sarge was certainly the help he needed right now. <Aw, thanks kid. Now lift your legs while you walk. It's called 'high knees', and you are about to do them for the next hour. *Every* day is leg day! Ask Suki; she knows!>

"What are you doing?" Suki glanced over at Grant, doing a double take as he marched down the center of the pothole-ridden road. "Fisticuffing fiends, you're getting ahead of me in training!"

Grant shook his head in astonishment as she started lunging between sets of high knees. For a moment, he had almost forgotten that he was traveling with a cultivation maniac. He didn't feel much strain at present, but he knew his legs would feel like jelly soon enough. "I have to get stronger, otherwise I won't be able to… do what I really want in the future! Gotta beat all the Lords and Ladies of the Month!"

"You have lofty goals, Grant." Suki picked up the pace a bit, weaving artfully through the ruined streets and never-ending dilapidated buildings. There were subtle signs of life here and there, but most areas seemed abandoned, and *all* of them looked like they had seen better days. "It's one of the reasons why I thought a match between you and I was such a good idea. Tell me, what is it you see for the future?"

"It's all about this." Grant used his Iaijutsu to unsheathe his sword and whip it through a passing fly. The buzzing pests had been more prevalent ever since he'd started carrying around the hearts of the yokai. "Ever since I picked it up, everything has changed for me."

"Your Wielded Weapon? I know they are important, but why would being lifted into the Nobility make you want to become the Calendar King?" Suki activated her gauntlets, allowing the dim light of the sinking sun to play over the gleaming metal. "I am—*was*—Lady February, one of the twelve most powerful people in the world, and I never thought about trying to break past the barriers to go challenge Regent December. It sounds like an incredible amount of work to me."

"If I don't defeat all the Lords and Ladies of the Month by the end of the year… I die." Grant killed a few more flies before resheathing his sword. "It's a quest. A Legendary Quest, and I think its true purpose is to just torture the Wielder to death."

Grant pulled up the short version of his quest so he could read it to Suki.

Quest: Heal the World (Lvl 100. Legendary.)

Important Information: The Wielder of February Twenty Nine, Grant Monday, has one year to gather the power of the Lords of the Month and return February Twenty Nine to the status of a completed Wielded Weapon. (Current Progress: 2/12)

Rewards: Completion of the quest, Heal the World, will result in the reward of the title 'Calendar King' and all wealth and responsibilities associated with that position, along with the ability to wield the most powerful weapon in the world.

Failure Conditions: Failure to complete the mandatory quest 'Heal the World' within one year will result in the loss of all cultivation levels gained since the acquisition of February Twenty Nine, plus the loss of an additional one level.

Suki was speechless at first, silently trekking forward, while her sharp gaze continuously roved to ensure they weren't walking into an ambush. Grant belatedly realized he should be doing the same and started doing a better job of paying attention to his surroundings. It was hard, given the level of exhaustion he was feeling. That, and his legs were starting to get tired from the high-knees. They walked without further conversation until the sun disappeared over the rooftops that crowded the edges of the street.

"I can't believe you're only doing this because you're being forced. I… there." Suki broke the silence somewhat judgmentally, cutting herself off and pointing at a building with a half-collapsed front before he could speak to defend himself. "This was probably an inn. We might get lucky and find a few beds still in one piece. Kitchens are usually built into the back, so we might also be able to use their stove."

Grant gave her a sharp nod in agreement, and they picked

their way through the rubble to the relatively undamaged section in the rear. He was wracking his brain to find an answer to her accusatory statement, but eventually gave up. Win or die: why was winning so he didn't have to die something that he needed to justify to anyone?

"It looks like you were right." Grant pointed at the arched stone oven and brick chimney lining the back of the first room they entered. He lifted some rotting boards out of the way and felt relief to discover the fixtures were still intact. "I can break up some of the wood that used to be tables and chairs in the common room."

"I'll get the ingredients for some stew ready." Suki pulled off her much smaller pack and rifled through the items inside. "Since we didn't find anything fresh, it is going to be trail stew. I hope that's okay. When you get back, we are talking more about your quest."

Grant's stomach growled at the thought of *any* food; answer enough for her. He lowered his pack to the floor with a sigh of relief and left to gather the wood. He didn't make it five steps before Sarge started chatting into his head.

<You need to be careful. Suki might not like all the answers to the questions she is about to ask,> Sarge warned as Grant picked through the remains of the common room. <I think you can trust her, but a leader is always thinking of the future. If she says the wrong thing about you in front of the wrong person, it could lead to big problems for you. Perhaps even for her, if someone wants to keep her quiet.>

"I can trust her. Suki was a Lady of the Month. She knows when to keep secrets to herself." Grant had a good pile of fuel in short order, so he went back into the kitchen and got a fire going with flint and steel. Suki exited into the yard as he tended the flames and let him know she was going to search for a well. "Besides, you have to trust people… or life becomes very lonely."

She soon returned with a leaking bucket of water, and the smells of rehydrated meat and vegetables filled the damaged space in short order. She handed him a steaming bowl, and they stood across from each other, leaning on the stone preparation counter in the center of the kitchen. "Okay. It's time for you to start talking. Don't leave out anything."

Grant started haltingly, explaining about being raised as one of the Leapkind in District January. He described finding February Twenty Nine, and how it had changed him from a lowly commoner to a Wielder in an instant. Finding his first real friends, how he killed a Noble—hard for him to get through at first. Suki turned out to be a companionable listener, and describing everything quickly became easier. Eventually, he told her about meeting Auld Leap, and the prophecy that had foretold his coming.

Grant didn't mention the pain of seeing how his fellow Leaps were treated, but Suki could hear it in his voice, and see it through the reflected firelight flickering in his eyes. She was so wrapped up in his retelling that she almost shouted in relief when he told her about saving his friends from execution, and his subsequent defeat of the tricky Lord January.

When he recounted his trials in District February, Suki winced more than once at how the people of her District must have seen him at first. She laughed when he described trying the food, and gained a better understanding of why he had fought so hard to save his friend that was fighting along the border. When he finally finished, their food was long gone, and the fire had burned down to a few glowing embers.

"So, your sword can steal powers, talks to you, and hits you with things only you can see." She leaned over and patted the sheathed uchigatana. "It's nice to finally be introduced to you, Sarge."

<See? I told you that she could be trusted. It's a good thing you listened to me.> Grant eyed his sword with a raised eyebrow, then casually swung it into a rock. <*Ow*! What?>

"You'll die if you don't defeat the leader of each District and bring down the barriers?" Grant brought his gaze back up at Suki's inquiry and nodded. "Okay then, we have a lot of work to do."

"That's it?" Grant was shocked at her reaction. He had expected more… something. Surprise, maybe? Disbelief? "I told you I am trying to change the world, and all you have to say is that we have work to do?"

"No; we have a *lot* of work to do. Unless you have some other ridiculous quest I don't know about, what else am I supposed to say?" Grant coughed and pulled up another quest screen. It was Suki's turn to raise an eyebrow and level a pointed stare. "Don't tell me, you have *another* Legendary quest?"

"Ha! No, it's just… Epic." He pulled up the quest screen and read it off to her. He was pretty sure he'd failed it anyway, since he wasn't in the city of Valentine anymore.

Quest: Ties that Bind (Epic Level)

Information: You have discovered that the onyx idol is an ancient relic from the Wielder Wars. Proceed to Valentine to learn more.

Reward: Unknown.

"What is this relic?" Suki was already heading over to Grant's pack to start digging through it. "There are more than a few relics from the Wielder Wars in the palace. Maybe I can help you figure it out?"

"Really?" Grant rushed over and groped for the item, surprised to find that the rare mushroom he'd previously stored in his pack had somehow stuck itself to the burnt monster heart. Shrugging it off, he pulled free the onyx figurine and carefully handed it over to her. Suki took it with reverence, brushing off some lint that had collected in the crevasses.

"I recognize this." She took the carving closer to the glowing embers of the fire to get a better look. "My father used to have one very similar, but he sold it to House Thursday. They were used to mark troop positions on a living map during the wars. When a unit would move in real life, the map would move the figure to match."

She passed it back to him and brushed her hands off on her shirt. "I think they were originally meant to be a part of some fancy game set, but the wars turned them to a... darker purpose: helping leaders position troops like pawns to be slaughtered. Some historians even claim that it was items like those that made the wars worse. It enabled the Lords and Ladies to see their subjects as pieces on a game board, and not people."

Before Grant could say anything, his vision was filled with the purple screen of an epic quest.

Quest Update: Ties that Bind (Epic Level)

Information: You have discovered that the onyx idol is an ancient relic from the Wielder Wars, used by the leaders of the time to track troop movements during combat, and as a piece to play the noble game of chess. Find and collect the remaining pieces of the black set. (1/16)

Reward: Half of a full chess set. Unknown.

"I guess I didn't fail the quest after all." Grant shrugged and stowed it back in his pack. "But what am I supposed to do with half of a chess set? How am I supposed to find the other pieces?"

<It's still an Epic quest. No time limit on it, right? All you can do is keep your eyes open and hope you can find the rest.> Sarge paused as Grant wavered when he rose up from putting his quest item away. <Okay, I think that's enough. You can sleep.>

Grant almost shouted with joy, but he stopped when Sarge finished his sentence. <For three hours. Then, we get back to training.>

The young man let out a sigh and immediately laid down on the floor. Three hours was better than nothing.

Suki had observed Grant almost falling over. She was deeply relieved: all of the instances of talking to himself and spontaneous jumping around at weird times made sense now. "We can talk more later. I'll take first watch."

Grant didn't even hear her.

CHAPTER FOURTEEN

Grant was awakened by the sound of something frying in a pan. It was probably the most effective way to wake him up from a dead sleep, next to a giant spider attacking him.

<Move!> An orange spider dropped down from the ceiling rafters, and Grant sliced it in half by reflex using Iaijutsu. He didn't even open his eyes, merely pulling, slicing, and putting the sword away in one smooth motion by instinct.

Prerequisite met: 10,000 successful uses of Iaijutsu!

Skill increase: Iaijutsu Novice -> Beginner! Beginner bonus: Perfect Aim. If you can use any sense to detect something coming for you, your sword will be there.

<Wow. Maybe I *have* been throwing a lot of stuff at you.>

"I take it Sarge is already starting your daily training?" Suki was crouched over the grate in the fireplace, flipping what looked like pancakes in a frying pan. "I decided to let you get some rest, so sunrise is only about two hours away. After we eat, I'll take a nap while you clean yourself up outside. The well is by the stables."

"I saw that you have soap." She wrinkled her nose as he got closer. "You need it."

"Thank you." Grant stretched and rolled his shoulders, trying to relieve the soreness from sleeping in armor. "I agree that I need to clean up before we leave. I can smell myself."

He got a little closer to lean over and take a peek at what she was cooking. It looked like pancakes, but it didn't smell like any Grant had eaten before. "What kind of pancakes are those?"

"Oh, these aren't pancakes." She flipped a pancake-shaped food item before grinning up at Grant. "These are dehydrated salmon-oatcakes! I blended them myself. They will give you the energy you need to face the day!"

"I'm sure they will." The dejected tone of his voice went completely over her head.

"The salmon is a variant from District February's northern mountain streams, and it has been proven to have the highest protein content of all non-monster fish ever harvested in February." Suki's excitement at the high quality of the food she had packed was evident in her wavy hand motions and faster speech. She sounded like a person trying to make a sale. "The oats are grown in the deepest valleys of the southern plains, where the soil imparts the best nutrients seen this side of the January border."

"But… pancakes are just supposed to be delicious." His whisper fell on deaf ears.

<I think this explains some of the ridiculous food prices in District February.> Sarge was obviously amused at Grant's continued struggles to find what he thought of as 'good' food. <On the bright side, your body really does need a lot of protein to recover properly from the healing yesterday.>

They ate quickly, with Suki humming happily as she ate the dry, fishy patties. Grant practically ran out to the stable yard so he could drink almost a full bucket of water. The patties somehow managed both to be wet, as well as suck all the moisture out of his mouth at the same time. From there, it took a lot longer than he expected to get clean. The dried blood of the Uchi-Oni had turned into a kind of sticky paste that just didn't want to come out of the creases in his armor. Or his hair, for that matter.

He was contemplating just cutting the congealed mess off when the sound of a snapping twig forced him to look up from his cleaning. The sun had yet to peek over the horizon, and a group of four men in the cut of clothes that House Tuesday traditionally wore were stumbling around in the twilight.

"Are you sure you saw smoke coming from the chimney?" A high-pitched, scratchy voice echoed down the narrow alley into the stable yard where Grant stood.

"Shhh! Keep your voice down, you idiot!" A clunking sound of metal meeting metal soon followed. "If anyone is in there, we don't want them to know where we are."

The second voice sounded like an older man, who carried the tone of someone used to giving orders.

"Why does it matter?" The third voice was much deeper, and obviously came from the biggest of the four. "We stole these uniforms from the Peacekeepers, so anyone we order around should listen."

"Yeah! This should be the easiest robbery in the *history* of robberies!" The fourth voice sounded like someone too young to be associated with bandits, and it set Grant on edge. He had been robbed by the desperate in the past, and he didn't relish the thought of losing his armor and belongings again.

<This group sounds harmless, but you need to treat every battle like your life depends on it.> Sarge paused for effect. <Because it does. I'll cut you.>

"Suki let me get some extra sleep. I think I can take care of these four without disturbing her." He quickly started strapping his still-wet armor on, doing his best to keep it quiet. "I don't want to kill them, but I will if I have to."

<A warrior is useless if he does not rise above others.> Grant took that as encouragement as he buckled his sword over his armor and looked down at it.

"Just so we're clear... what is that supposed to mean? I just said I was going to beat them." He eased out into the narrow alley that led to the street from the stables. "Am I supposed to stand over them after I win?"

<Let's not worry about that. Defeat them quickly, and try to keep it quiet.> Sarge sounded exasperated, which mirrored Grant's emotions perfectly. <We really need to get your mental cultivation higher.>

"Gentlemen, I believe you are looking for me." Grant stepped out of the alley onto the street behind the four bandits. They all jumped and spun around, pointing their weapons at him. It was hard to see, with only the first rays of the sun starting to brighten the sky, but it was immediately clear these men had nothing to do with the Peacekeepers. All four were carrying spears, but they were obviously of low quality; more like broomsticks with a piece of pointy metal nailed on the end. "I have no fight with you. I suggest you take those stolen uniforms off, and end this before something bad happens to you. No one would ever believe men so poorly armed were Vassals of House Tuesday."

"Ha!" The man with the high-pitched voice took a step forward. "There's four of us, and only one of you. I think *you* should be the one to think about… stuff!"

"Yeah, what he said. Just give us your Time, and we'll be on our way. You can't win." The big man with the deep voice planted the butt of his spear on the ground, leaning it forward in a threatening manner. "Numbers make all the difference in District March."

"Let's just stick him and get out of here. We can't be the only ones who saw his smoke." The young bandit was hunting around quickly, as if waiting for someone to sneak up behind him. Which *was* actually what Grant had just done, so maybe he wasn't unnecessarily paranoid. "There are bigger groups than us running around out here."

Instead of continuing the conversation, Grant unsheathed his uchigatana and swiped through three of the four spears pointed in his direction. The young kid was too far back to reach without Grant exposing his side, and his ribs were too sore to take even a light punch from the big guy. All four stumbled back in surprise as their spears became sticks. Grant calmly lifted his sword diagonally across his torso. They all stood in silence for a few heartbeats, the bandits clearly not experienced enough to be used to sudden displays of violence.

"Well boys, I think I'm going to call it a day. It's too early to deal with a Wielder." The older man straightened up and tossed his stick to the ground. "The system must be down still, because we didn't see the combat screens… so. I guess now's the time to get some honest trading done in the market before a Vassal gets out here. This was a stupid idea, anyway." He gave Grant a nod and turned around to walk away.

"Just like that?" The man with the high-pitched voice stomped his foot in anger. "You're just going to give up without even trying?" The other two were already backing away, following in the wake of the older man. "*I'm* no chicken!"

He reached out and snatched the spear from the younger bandit, spinning to stab Grant in the chest with it.

Damage taken: 0 piercing (12 mitigated)

The makeshift spearpoint bent flat against the metal bands that made up Grant's chest armor. It did rock him back a step, and the ache in his ribs intensified with the blow; his new 'skill' caused the pain in his wounds to be even more alarming. Grimacing, he smacked the flat of his blade against the temple of the bandit, dropping him like a stone.

<I *told* you to take every fight seriously! Just because it *looked* like the fight was over didn't mean it was over!> Grant grunted in agreement at Sarge's words. He had let his guard down, and he'd paid for it with some aggravated ribs. He knew that if the bandit had been an actual cultivator, it could have been far worse. <Expect some serious training after this.>

"I know. I'll do better," Grant mumbled under his breath.

"Come get your friend and get out of here. I have a long way to travel today. Perhaps think about giving up banditry! It doesn't suit you!"

The three men scrambled to pick up their unconscious compatriot and quickly started away. Sarge waited for Grant to sheathe his sword and head back to the well to finish cleaning the gunk from his hair. <The sun is up. Time to wake Suki and get moving. Good job not killing them. I'd bet they're not worth a single minute of cultivation.>

"Is that the only reason you're glad I didn't kill random people that couldn't hurt me even if they threw everything they had at me?" Grant scathingly retorted.

<No,> Sarge answered kindly. <Even though that man caused you pain, you held back. No matter how much you hate, or how much you suffer, you can't bring the dead back to life. You're starting to display qualities I would want in the man that will be the King.>

This time, Grant understood *exactly* what Sarge was trying to say. His cheeks were tinged with red as he hurried to rouse Suki.

CHAPTER FIFTEEN

The next two days passed uneventfully. That was… mostly uneventfully. Suki had taken it upon herself to train Grant in the 'Way of the Noble'. To his way of thinking, all that really meant was learning all kinds of different ways to trick people into agreeing to things they never meant to agree to do.

"So, you see? The importance of watching your tongue is no different than keeping watch for attackers, or monsters." Suki laid a consoling hand on his shoulder, which was still sore from the weight of the monster hearts in his pack. "A poor agreement can hurt you more than an assassin's blade. Well, not *more*, but the suffering can last longer."

"I still don't even understand *how* you got me to agree to do your dirty laundry for the next week." Grant gave her a hard stare, but there was no heat of anger in his eyes. "What part of our conversation even brought us to that point? I don't want to do this anymore."

<Oh, you poor man. If you and her actually do marry in the distant future, you're going to be as defenseless as a newborn babe!> Sarge chortled in amusement, the past two days having provided more entertainment than he had seen in

centuries. <The good news is, she *is* trying to help you. I think you've advanced more in your mental cultivation over the past forty-eight hours than you did in the entire month of February!>

"You don't want to do this? How about no more deals, and the next time I get you to agree to something without you noticing, I'll just punch you in the face instead?" He opened his mouth to argue, but she cut him off before he could tell her how much he *didn't* like that plan. "Grant, there is something important I wanted to talk to you about. I've been thinking about your sword's powers, and how it might interact with the citizens of District March."

"I'm… listening." Grant squinted at her as he tried to figure out if it was another trick, following her lead when she stopped in the shade of an abandoned row of townhouses that were leaning out over the street. He made a mental note to talk to her later about the plan to punch him in the face. "What's bothering you?"

"You remember how the contract that Dokeshi March has with his people will cause all of them to die if he is defeated or killed?" Her eyes were fixed on her feet, her right hand nervously fiddling with her ponytail. "The madman has to be stopped, and I think if you can defeat him fast enough, you can steal his powers before it has time to kill everyone. That much power would take time to build up, which should give you a chance to save everyone before whatever he's using is capable of expending the energy all at once."

She abruptly looked up to meet his eye and mimed an expanding sphere with her hands. Without warning, she clapped her hands together, flashing her gauntlets into existence a split second before her hands touched to make the sound louder. "Once you gain control, you should be able to redirect the power surge into something else before it kills everyone. Can you do that?"

"Yeah… I think I know what you mean." Grant placed his hand on his uchigatana. "When I absorb the power of a Lord or Lady, I get a message that pops up with information about what I can do next. Maybe I can select an option to expend the energy quickly?"

"That sounds perfect." Suki let out a sigh of relief. "Just make sure you pick your option quickly; otherwise, the contracts might still be enforced. Oh, and Grant?"

He turned to look at her and caught the flash of light off her left gauntlet just before it crunched into his nose. "Your silence was an acceptable form of agreement. You allowed me to make another deal with you, without thinking about the consequences of agreeing."

Damage taken: 10 blunt (51 mitigated)

Sarge's pealing laughter didn't help Grant feel better when the damage notification popped up in his vision; her light jab had managed to take ten points off of his health, and it felt like his nose was twisted. A second screen appeared, making him forget all about the pain he felt.

Combat initiated

Action: *Defend Without Weapon*
Result: *Total failure, bloody nose to defender*
Opponents remaining: 1
Actions: *Please select one option from the following list*
Attack: *Lethal, Non-lethal, Spell*
Defend: *With Weapon, Without Weapon*
Run: *Attempt escape*

Suki must have seen the same screen, because she froze at the same time he did. Their eyes met, one pair watering a bit, and they bolted for the nearest alley. Beyond the fact that they had no interest in truly fighting each other, the appearance of the screen meant one simple thing: another Vassal of Lord March had entered the area.

"We should figure out how to get onto a roof." Suki was already searching for a method of climbing the buildings on either side; apparently, she was tired of clambering over the debris obstructing the road. "We don't know what kind of range their powers have, but they have to be huge if the entire District is used to living under their rule. They might be far away, or they could be a street over."

"Is there a way to tell how long we've been in range of the system?" Grant still had the screen blocking his vision, and he slowly turned in a circle to see if there was any change. It was impossible to be sure, but the edges of the screen seemed to be the clearest when he was looking to the east: the same direction they needed to go to reach the center of the District, where the Dokeshi's palace waited in the capital of Vernal. "Did you feel any change over the past few hours?"

<I thought I might have felt a tingle of another Wielder's ability shortly after you ate your morning meal; right before I attacked you with that Crazed Murder Goat.> Grant winced at the memory Sarge brought up. The creature had darted out of nowhere and smashed his shin hard enough that it would have certainly broken his leg if it had been real. Just as abruptly, it vanished, and Sarge promised that more of them would be arriving soon. <If that was the system, you have been in range for at least a few hours.>

"Sarge thinks he felt us passing into range after we ate breakfast." Grant hunted around, finding after a moment of rapid searching that Suki was already halfway up the wall of the abandoned temple across the street. "Hey! Wait for me!"

"No!" She called down. "You keep up!"

He ran to the building and found the precarious pile of crates and broken pallets leaning against the temple wall that she must have used as a series of springboards and footing to reach the ledge she was shuffling along. Grant, although his body was as fit and trim as a regular athlete by now, still outweighed her two to one. There was no way that he was going to be replicating her path, especially with his armor and heavy pack on his back. "I'm gonna find a better way up!"

"You have no sense of adventure." Suki's chuckled reply drifted down as she maneuvered herself atop the roof and out of his line of sight.

#ERROR42

Congratulations! *Your new battle count moves from* [3 Wins / 1 Losses] *to* [3 Wins / 1 Losses]. *Remember, the lucky rise to the challenge!*

The strange overlaid system was still malfunctioning, which hopefully meant they hadn't fixed whatever Grant had messed up when he'd destroyed Fluffy Finger's scepter. Either that, or people were better trained to not ignore the system and would just fight after getting punched in the face, or at least select 'Run Away'. "March is strange. I really, *really* dislike how this place works. Why would it throw an error when people don't fight after getting in a single blow?"

<To be fair to the system, I'm rather old, and even *I* haven't seen that very often. When people get hit…> Sarge chuckled, and another Crazed Murder Goat jumped out at Grant. This time, the Wielder sliced its head off using his Iaijutsu skill without even thinking about it. <…they fight back or run. Good job, there. At least when your blood is up, you pay attention to your surroundings. Now, how can I make it so that you fight when you're dead asleep…?>

Grant ignored Sarge's ramblings about how to shape him into a more deadly weapon and used the light reflected from his blade to get Suki's attention. He motioned around to ask if there was anyone nearby, and got a shrug of 'no' in return. She slowly made her way to the steeple of the temple, cautiously picking her way across the slanted roof.

Finding no way to ascend the building, Grant gave up and decided to organize their goods instead of standing idle. He dropped his pack and prepared to move their healing potions within easy reach. There was a small issue with his well-intentioned plan: as soon as he opened the bag's flap, a burst of dust and spores shot out of the opening.

"By Lord January's sausage!" He peeked inside and discovered that the burnt monster heart he had collected was now a dry, desiccated husk. His eyes were drawn to a small mushroom, a fungus he had collected in January that had granted him his first-ever Skill. He had forgotten about it, and now he was paying the price for his negligence. The fungus had practically absorbed the entire organ, and apparently decided that it was time to reproduce. His pack was utterly *choked* with its spores. "So… better clean this up before she sees what it did to our supplies."

Since Suki hadn't spotted anyone among the broken-down buildings, Grant sat on the steps of the ruined temple and took everything out of his pack. He shook it out, flapping the bag until nothing remained to exit the canvas. The breeze carried away the huge plume of spores, looking like nothing so much as black smoke pouring from a burning building. Grant was sure nothing bad would come of it.

He plucked the reinvigorated mushroom off the heart, packing it carefully in a rag so it wouldn't destroy the other two hearts. They were still in surprisingly good shape, considering he hadn't done much to preserve them beyond wrapping them in cloth. After cleaning and repacking everything, Grant made sure to place the box containing the healing potions on the top. If nothing else, it would make it easier to get to them if they needed healing.

"Grant!" Suki whisper-shouted from the roof of the temple down to him, and he looked up and caught her wide-eyed gesticulations to hide. He dove forward and tucked into a roll, springing to his feet in a smooth motion within the empty doorway of the temple. Even as he preened about his body's ability to move, he ducked to the side and tried to blend with the shadows.

His ears perked up as a quiet crunch of footsteps broke the silence. The near-silent approach turned into open walking on the street and steadily grew louder when it became obvious that there was no one out and about in the area. Grant crouched and picked up a piece of broken glass he found on the floor, slowly easing it out of the entrance and tilting it to peer around the doorframe.

The sight nearly made him draw in a sharp gasp, and he barely managed to keep his wits about him. A group of over thirty Peacekeepers were being led by a clown that looked like it had lost a fight with a group of angry cats. If Grant had to make a guess, he would have said it was most likely the Vassal named Tatters. The clown's painted frown was turned upside down, creating a permanent scowl no matter where his emotions might actually lay. The group was walking down the middle of the street, barely paying attention to their surroundings. While not particularly alert, they were certainly disciplined, refraining from speaking and being as quiet as a group that large could manage.

<It looks like a regular patrol, otherwise they would be searching more carefully.> Sarge's quiet assessment was a balm that calmed Grant's sweating palms. He definitely didn't want to face all of those people at once. <There are a lot of them, so they at least must suspect this is the route you'll take to get to the center of the District.>

That didn't make Grant feel much better. He leaned back against the wall and listened nervously as the sound of their passing faded into the distance. When he stood up to leave and check on Suki, Sarge stopped him in his tracks.

<Wait! Don't go out there yet.> Grant froze, his hand

falling to his uchigatana by reflex. <I don't think that was all of them.>

Less than a minute later, Sarge was proven right. A pair of House Tuesday Peacekeepers strode into sight, and this time they were paying much closer attention to their surroundings. A frail-looking woman dressed in a dark indigo robe brought up the rear, her clasped hands swinging a dangling chain censer that leaked bright green smoke.

"A House Saturday assassin…?" Grant managed to curtail his panicked reaction enough that they didn't seem to hear him, but he berated himself nonetheless. The noxious fumes emanating from the bronze orb dissipated quickly, making him think it was the effect of her Wielded Weapon, and not a physical chemical or poison. "We are going to need to find a different road to the capital. If Dokeshi March hired House Saturday, we are in serious trouble."

"I agree." Suki's voice next to his ear almost made him jump out of his armor. She let loose a long sigh and continued in a heavy tone, "There are many roads that lead to Vernal, but I suspect all of them will be heavy with patrols. I think we might be forced to use the labyrinth."

CHAPTER SIXTEEN

"The labyrinth?" Grant had heard the word before, but he didn't know why a hedge maze would be a difficult proposition. "If we have to go through a bunch of bushes, I can just chop them down."

"Shh!" Suki put her finger up to her lips and dragged Grant deeper into the building. "They might still be close by. Keep your voice down."

He ducked his head in shame, paused, and met her eyes, ready to argue against directly agreeing with her. She gave him a glance that told him that she knew what he was about to say, and to just stay quiet. He slowly closed his mouth, internally grumbling against the back-and-forth between training and reality. After a few minutes had passed with no further sounds coming from the street, Suki risked a cautious glance onto the road. "It isn't that kind of labyrinth. Or the regular dungeon kind, either."

"Dungeon labyrinths?" Grant had never heard of one before, but he could guess what it meant. "There are dungeon labyrinths? Non human-made ones? I thought that was a myth."

"Perhaps a myth in a weak place like January—my apologies. That's uncalled for. No, what *is* important is that we have to take a different, unexpected route." Suki crouched down and used a gloved finger to draw a rough map in the dirt on the floor. "Now, I've never seen it in person, but from the maps of the area we had in February, this District is laid out as three layers of gambling houses. The two of us were taking the trade road to avoid them, but it looks like that isn't an option anymore." She glanced up to make sure Grant was paying attention. "We are in the outside layer right now, and the quality of life is apparently far higher as you get closer to the center of the District. The gambling houses are nicer and there are higher payouts for winning, as well as more severe punishments for losing."

Grant nodded slowly as he pieced together the fragmented information he was gleaning. "You're thinking that they guessed that we wouldn't risk going through that way? Probably because of what happened with the food vendor we went to when we first arrived. I'm betting that they completely wrote me off as a gambler… that explains how they're all over us right now. But, how does gambling get us deeper into the District? I'm looking at the ring-shaped layers, and I don't understand why we couldn't just jump over the wall or something?"

"The rings are actual buildings. Instead of just building a wall, the old Lord March had his people build giant casinos that serve the same purpose. The security on them is so tight, so deadly, that there is only one way to avoid them besides the trade road gates." She pointed to the 'wall' drawing. "Three total options. Win enough games at the casinos to buy in to the next area by proving you belong there, get through the trade gates… or test your luck in a more *personal* way. A labyrinth of luck and death."

"Hold up a moment. How could we possibly win enough to get through these places? Won't their guards recognize us?" Grant wasn't convinced that Suki had all the facts. "I still say we try to just climb over the casino walls and make our way to the Dokeshi that way."

"If we get there and we see a way to do it, I'm all for it." Suki held up a bulging purse stuffed with jingling coins. "This may seem like a lot of Time right now, but it will run through our fingers like water if we let you start gambling the way you have been."

"I'm not really *that* bad, am I?" Grant's only answer was a quiet chuckle from Suki, and a not-so-quiet guffaw from Sarge. "Don't want to be good at it, anyway. What's so wrong with just earning your way by merit?"

"That mentality is why you're the Lord of February, and not *March.* Gambling is eighty percent mindset, and that's something we can work on, Grant." Suki stood and brushed the dirt off of her knees from kneeling on the dirty ground. "If you apply the same lessons to life and gambling that I am trying to teach you from the Way of the Noble, you will reach mastery in no time."

They eased their way out the back of the temple and carefully searched the small yard before passing out a back gate. The overgrown cemetery had caused the hair on the back of his neck to stand straight, but he couldn't tell why for sure. Was it all the crows silently watching them from the top of the oversized wrought iron fence? The holes pre-dug in the ground awaiting bodies? The silence that blanketed this area to a degree that nowhere else had seemed to generate?

Suki winced when the gate let out a loud creak as they left, breaking that self-same silence, but no one raised the alarm. The other sound was Suki's stomach gurgling, followed by Grant's less adorable tiger-snarl as his stomach took up the warcry. He abashedly pulled out a couple of the tasteless granola bars and passed one over to Suki so they could chow down while they moved.

Occasionally, Sarge would bark an order for him to execute an exercise, or throw a monster or rock at him to continue to improve his reflexes. The man was tempted to complain that they needed silence and stealth, but he could feel the gradual gains he was making with his Iaijutsu and Kenjutsu skills. While they walked in a zig-zag pattern through abandoned streets and dark alleys in search of a sign to point them toward a casino entrance, Suki also continued to ask him questions, and got him to agree to things he didn't really want to do.

"So, you were raised on a farm, right?" She kept idly rolling a fat gold Week coin across her knuckles. Of course, it just so happened to have her face on it, since the District it came from had been hers. She had said she was 'practicing', but it did a great job of distracting Grant, causing his attention to his surroundings to lower. "Would you be willing to show me how to operate a farm when all of this is over?"

"I'd *love* to!" For the first time, Grant was *excited* at the prospect of spending some time with her, and he wondered why; he would just be giving her lessons in farming and not… other things. Perhaps because it was something he knew how to do, so he could prove his knowledge on the subject, and maybe win her respect? The man flushed at that thought and tried to cover his reaction by speaking. "First, I'll show you how to care for animals. They are my favorite part of farming-"

Suki flipped the Week up into the air, punched him in the face, and caught the coin before it could hit the ground. "Ow! *Why*? What was that for?"

"Just because you want to agree to something, doesn't mean you should." Suki surreptitiously rubbed her knuckles against her hip to relieve the pain from punching him in the jaw. She hadn't activated her gauntlets this time, and she hadn't noticed before that his face was as hard as granite. Next time, he was getting the full-metal treatment, even if it did mean the battle system would be activated again. "By the time this is all over, you will be the *Calendar King*. You have to learn to be a good steward of your time. What do you think the best use of that time would be? Giving farm tours? You'll be managing the farms for the entire planet!"

Grant was once again struck by the size of the task before

him. This mess wasn't going to simply end when he defeated all the Lords and Ladies. That was just the *start.* His pack suddenly felt really heavy again.

<That's why it's so important that you become a Dao Cultivator. Personally, I'm still pushing for the samurai route.> Sarge seemed to at least understand what kind of weight Grant was feeling at the moment. <If you can balance your thoughts and actions, it will help you be a kind and just ruler. One the people of this world need. It also won't hurt that your lifespan becomes 'until killed'. You wanna raise farm animals for a few decades? Why not, when the world is at peace?>

"Thanks, Sarge." Grant rubbed his face to alleviate some of the throbbing pain from getting punched in the face again. "At least you'll be there to help me when I need you."

Sarge didn't answer. Grant took his silence as acceptance. Suki had taught him that: silence in the face of a question, especially an ethical one, was the same as indirectly agreeing.

"There! A sign! I knew we were going the correct direction." In the distance, a glowing advertisement for 'Patty's Perfect Palace, Poolroom, and Pavilion of Perfect-Pick Poker and Pinochle' was poking over the pointed roof of a poorly maintained post office. Suki was almost bouncing with excitement at having finally found something to point them in the right direction. "It's large enough to serve as a wall, I think. How much do you want to bet that place is where we need to go?"

"I don't know… maybe it's just another gambling house? They seem to be a dime a dozen around here." Once again, he didn't see the fist coming. Thankfully, his training brought his weapon into his hands like magic, just in time to stop her from socking him in the cheek. The attack by the metal gauntlet was enough to activate the system, but Grant just ignored it as he glared at her, sparks flying as their weapons ground against each other. "Again with this? I didn't agree to anything, and I hope you know I'm not about to *let* you punch me."

"That's for trying to ruin my good mood." He didn't bother

to argue with her, simply raising an eyebrow that she ignored. "It's good that you're getting better at blocking them. Another lesson from the Way of the Noble: even your companions could attack you at any moment. Before the Wielder Wars, assassinations of Lords and Ladies were commonplace. We are *all* taught from a young age to expect the unexpected. Trust *no one*, and you won't be taken by surprise when they try to betray you."

<I can't argue with that idea.> A slime dropped out of the sky, and Grant stepped to the side to dodge the offending glob, which splattered and disappeared a few moments later. <Maybe it's time to adjust away from the color orange? Hmmm…>

"I think that's a sad way to live, if I'm being honest. As to the casino? There's only one way to find out." Grant took off before the two of them could attack him in some other way he wasn't expecting. Perhaps they'd tell him he needed to wear more colorful clothes, but not *that* color, since he would have been the one to choose it. Who knew? "If we're going to make it to the casino before we're caught, we'd better get a move on."

CHAPTER SEVENTEEN

The structure turned out *not* to be a casino. Instead, Patty's Perfect Palace, Poolroom, and Pavilion of Perfect-Picked Poker and Pinochle was a three-story building that took up a whole city block. They weren't stopped from going inside by the House Friday Vassal guarding the door; the inter-house politics must have kept House Tuesday and House Saturday from easily recruiting aid from the other Noble Houses. A failing on their part for certain, but a definite boon to Grant and Suki.

"Well, it might not be the border, but at least we should be able to gather some supplies. Maybe get some directions?" Grant was shocked to discover how large the building was on the inside. "There's gotta be a store here, right? I mean, this front room alone is a whole market district!"

"I believe they call it a shopping center." Suki was equally impressed, but her training allowed her to hide it like a proper citizen of the District, and not a tourist that would be an easy mark for the unscrupulous. "There is something else they call a 'strip mall', but I don't think we want one of those. I heard they're filled with overpriced goods and consumables."

"Hopefully, this casino won't be like that." Grant headed to a stall that displayed a bunch of fresh fruit and vegetables. Their trail rations had started to run low, and he was hoping to find something to supplement their dwindling supplies. He took a single look at the options for payment and shook his head. "I'm *sure* they have their customers' well-being at the forefront of their priorities."

"Hand me the beast hearts." Suki pointed to a pair of stalls that displayed the flags of House Wednesday and House Saturday next to each other. "I'm going to try to sell them. If I give them a good deal, maybe we can get those directions for free."

Grant passed the swaddled organs over, relieved at finally getting rid of the heavy items. They had started to smell a bit, and he was worried that his little mystery mushroom might find a way to eat those as well. Carrying around food for the tiny fungus felt mildly insulting for some reason.

"Well, sir, how can I help such an esteemed gentleman?" The woman running the food stall seemed much better-fed than most of the people Grant had encountered so far in District March, but her clothing still looked a little more threadbare and worn than was probably the norm for such an establishment. "Would you like to see what your luck can buy?"

"I need some root vegetables, and hard-skinned fruits, if you have any." Grant pointed his thumb back at his pack. "Things that travel well."

"My good sir, all you need to do for a full *crate* of food is place a Day coin in the slot and pull the lever!" She wheeled around a waist-height machine with three spinning wheels connected to a bunch of gears and a lever. "This slot machine is checked for its honesty and accuracy by the Ethics Commission every day!"

<Oh, I'm sure it is.> Sarge's sarcasm was palpable. <Any group named the 'Ethics Commission' *certainly* doesn't involve any corruption.>

"Um, is there some other way we can do this?" Grant had already pulled a Day coin from his pouch before his new training with Suki took over, but he was loath to spend it on a machine he couldn't control. "Like, I just give you this coin, and you give me the food?"

"I'm sorry." The vendor winced, and her eyes darted around to make sure no one was listening. "I just work here. The casino owns the stall."

<I have an idea.> Grant felt a tingle come from Sarge. <Put one hand on my hilt, and use the other to pull the lever. Let's see if we can tap into your *Lightning Attunement* a bit.>

Dropping the coin into the slot, Grant did as Sarge suggested. He felt a strong surge of power come from his sword, and his mana dropped by two points. The handle made a hard clunking sound when he pulled the lever, and a spark of static jumped from his fingers when he pulled his hand away. The vendor was already pulling out a small crate, containing food that had wilted and showed a few spots of mold, when the machine started shaking and the three wheels with little symbols and numbers slammed to a stop.

"How... what happened?" The vendor seemed dumbfounded and unsure of what to do next. She glanced over at a House Friday guard standing near the entrance to the gambling floors. "Um, I don't know what to do now."

"Does it mean something good when I get three of those little pictures in a row like that?" Grant pointed at the symbols of a pile of Time drawn on the wheels. "Do I get extra food or something?"

"What seems to be the problem here?" The uniformed guard had approached, and his eyes locked onto the machine that displayed what Grant had won. He glared sharply over to the woman and stalked over to whisper furiously into her ear. After she shook her head and whispered something back, the guard waved over to the other guard by the door. "Sir, it seems as if there is a problem with this machine. We will be happy to refund you, but you will have to try again to win your prize."

"I don't think so." Grant shook his head, then nodded toward the attendant. "She told me this machine was checked by the Ethics Commission just this morning. I clearly won. Are you saying there is something wrong with their testing? Can I get your name and position so that I can put it in the complaint?"

"No, not that!" The guard blanched and looked for support from the other guard that he had waived over. He was already wheeling away the machine and was no help. "Look, that machine gave you a jackpot, and for any payouts of that size, we have to talk to the floor manager."

"Floor manager?" Grant peered around pointedly, clearly verifying that they were standing in the market section and not the actual gambling floor. "I am just trying to buy some food here."

The guard was angry, but everyone present knew Grant was in the right. No one said anything as they waited for the manager to show up. Eventually, a greasy-looking man wearing a fancy suit and tie approached, his hands wringing as he guided the two casino employees off to the side. After another bout of furious whispering, he finally came over to speak with Grant.

"My, um..." His eyes quickly scanned over Grant's Late Spring armor and sheathed uchigatana. "My *Valued Guest*, what seems to be the problem?"

"Are you joking right now?" Grant gave him a stern glare, allowing his hand to drift closer to the hilt of his Wielded Weapon. "I won, and now I would like to get the fruits of my winnings. Vegetables, too."

"Well, we seem to have had some technical difficulties with our equipment, and we will need you to try again." The man produced a deck of cards from his pocket. "Perhaps we can play a quick game to determine your prize, instead of you having to wait for the machine to undergo repairs?"

"This is ridiculous. Just give me my food, and I will leave." Grant attempted to walk around the man, but he held up his hand to stop him. "I'm willing to report this to the authorities.

You are clearly breaking the rules… *avoiding* paying me my winnings, even?"

Now it was the manager's turn to grimace at the thought of the punishment for being caught. Grant used the momentary distraction to grab a perfectly red apple. As soon as he picked it up, he immediately discovered the problem. "This isn't even real! This food is all made of wax! This whole place is one giant scam!"

"No! It isn't like that!" The manager took an involuntary step back in fear. He tried patting the air with his hands in a motion intended to calm Grant down. "That's just the display we use. It is just a representation of what we offer."

"It's *misleading*, is what it is. Do you do this with other items? *Lie* to your customers?" Grant purposely avoided using the word 'cheater,' but he was slowly building up to it. His hope was that the manager would just give him what he wanted before it got to that point. He was trying to use all of the lessons Suki had given him so far, but he wasn't sure it was going exactly the way he intended. It was too late to stop now, though. "I don't see why an establishment like this would risk their reputation over a crate of food."

"Fine! Please!" The distressed manager waved for Grant to follow him toward a door off to the side of the market. "Come with me, and we will get you the prize."

<Yeah, like that doesn't have 'trap' written all over it.> Grant narrowed his eyes suspiciously just as he was about to take a step. Sarge's comment had likely just saved him, and he was in full agreement.

"I think I'll wait out here." Grant's refusal stopped the greasy man in his tracks. "It's just a single crate of produce. There's no need for me to follow you into a side room where there aren't any witnesses."

<You're laying it on kind of thick, kid.> The look of pure venom the man shot Grant's direction would have melted a block of ice. <Abyss, maybe you *aren't*. I think it would be a

good idea to double-check any of the food that man gives you. He seems the type to poison it, just out of spite.>

"I'll be back with your *winnings*." The manager turned and waved for the guard to follow him. They disappeared into the darkened doorway, and Grant could easily hear shouts that gradually faded away. The lady vendor surreptitiously motioned Grant closer, and pointedly looked to the side so she didn't appear to be speaking to him.

"They are going to have to get the food from the kitchens, since there isn't anything high-quality out here." A shiver went through her body as she glanced at the doorway. "I recommend you get out of here as quickly as possible. Once word of this gets to the main office, it would be better for you by far if you were long gone. The food shortage is affecting even the big guys nowadays."

Grant executed a single, sharp nod, *not* directed at her. He had already had the same thought. The remaining guards were already eyeing him, and the atmosphere in the room had definitely shifted a few degrees away from pleasant. While he waited, Suki finally finished up her business and made her way back over to him.

"What are we waiting on?" Suki quickly picked up on the mood, and Grant caught her flexing her hands, as though she were only a moment away from activating her gauntlets. "Is there a problem?"

"I won a crate of food. They're giving me a hard time about it, almost like they weren't expecting anyone to *ever* win something good." Grant lowered his voice so the vendor couldn't hear. "The game was rigged. They didn't even have anything here to hand over. As soon as they bring it out, we need to leave."

He raised his voice back to a normal level. "How about you? Were you able to sell the beast hearts?"

"Yes." The corners of her mouth turned down sharply. She produced a tattered scroll of parchment from a pocket on the side of her small pack. "I had to take a pittance for what they were really worth, but I was able to get some information we might need, as well as a basic map that shows the entrances we need to find. It isn't the best, but it was all they were willing to part with."

"It's definitely better than what we had before we walked in here." Grant took a quick look over the scroll before handing it back. "I think we can make it to the closest place by this time tomorrow, if we walk late and wake up early."

"We should be fine." They were interrupted by a shout, followed by a chorus of groans that came from the casino floor. Suki instinctively took a half-step toward the flashing lights and cheery sounds before catching herself. "It's too bad, really. I wanted to get some more practice in before you had to face the high-rollers in the major casinos."

"It can't be helped." Grant casually placed his hand on February Twenty Nine and glanced in the direction which the broken—or now not broken, depending on one's perspective—betting machine had been taken. "I think I can manage, though."

Grant heard a squeak of fear from the woman that had been working the produce stall, and he spotted the manager returning from his trip to the back. He wasn't alone.

"Well, it took some searching, but we were able to find the food you won." The oily man was much more confident, considering the five guards accompanying him. One in particular was an incredibly large specimen. The guard's burly hands made the small crate of food look like a tiny square of wood. "Congratulations on your win. I do hope you will avail yourselves of the other games of luck and chance which our fine establishment has to offer!"

<Don't show fear.> Sarge steadied Grant's mental state with his calm tone. <Men like them won't know how to act when the object of their attention doesn't react the way they think they should.> Grant allowed a silent agreement, placidly reaching forward to pluck the crate of food from the human mountain of muscle.

"Thanks!" Tucking the crate of food under his arm, he didn't even bother to check its contents. "We have business elsewhere, unfortunately. Maybe we can swing by to try our luck the next time we are in the area."

He turned his back on the six of them and headed for the exit without missing a beat. The manager's face darkened in anger, clearly upset at having been dismissed while surrounded by the intimidating guards. As for the guards, they seemed more confused than anything. Grant glimpsed the unpleasant man making a few sharp gestures with his hand in the reflection of the shiny gilding on a lamp by the door. The five guards quickly moved off, obviously heading for another exit so they could confront Grant and Suki once they left the safety of the more public areas.

"We are going to have to run." Grant passed the crate of food off to Suki so she could secure it in his pack, and he almost stumbled when she jerked the straps tight to close the covering flap. "I saw him give some kind of order to his guards. They'll probably be right behind us."

"I noticed." Suki tapped the pocket that held the map. "We just need to cross the bridge that's a few blocks away, and we should be able to lose them in the buildings on the other side."

<Or, you could *fight*!> Sarge seemed excited about the prospect of Grant facing the human brick wall. <Just think of the amazing cultivation gains you could get from defeating all those Vassals!>

"Sarge thinks that all of them were Vassals. I think running is the best option." Grant held the door open for Suki, and the two of them walked calmly down the steps as Sarge ranted about engaging in combat. It had started to grow dark while they had been inside, and the tall buildings cast long shadows across the road. The moment the two of them hit a dark spot, they started running.

<If they have more than half a thought between them, you have to know they'll be waiting for you at the bridge.> Grant

grimaced at Sarge's admonition. He had the same concern. He glanced at Suki, who was steadily racing farther ahead of him.

"We'll just have to hope they have less than half a brain, then." Grant lengthened his stride to catch up with Suki. "Otherwise, you'll get your wish soon enough."

CHAPTER EIGHTEEN

The deepening shadows were a great place for more than just Grant and Suki to blend in. Considering the proximity to the casino, far more people were milling around than in other areas of the District they had been through recently. They had to run past several beggars that looked on the edge of starvation, and Grant slowed to hand a fresh tomato from his pack to a particularly skinny little girl.

"I have to change things in this District, one way or another." Grant's determined tone brought a buzz of approval from his uchigatana. "I can't let anything stop me."

<That's the *spirit*!> the Sword Spirit enthusiastically agreed. The fact that he was a sword didn't mean he wanted to see children starving. <You get closer to the proper mindset for growth every day. Only one who devotes himself to a cause with his whole strength and soul can be a true master. For this reason alone, mastery demands *everything* of a person.>

"We need to go right up here." Suki cut in on their conversation, and Grant refocused his rising anger on the thought of people standing in his way. They would regret trying to keep him from bringing this District out of the darkness. Up ahead, the twisty alleyways and curvy roads started to straighten out.

The two Wielders located the bridge in the dwindling evening light. Standing on it were several distinct figures, a fair number more than the five House Friday guards that had left the casino. A gust of wind ruffled the shreds of the lead figure's outfit, and Grant recognized the tattered clothing. This was Dokeshi's Vassal. "Good. He's about to find out what happens to hostile Vassals when they cross a Lord of the Month."

When they reached the edge of the bridge, Suki stayed on his immediate left since he didn't pause. Arrayed against them were the five guards, along with ten of the soldiers that had accompanied Tatters on the patrol they had spotted earlier. The only person Grant was truly concerned about wasn't present: the House Saturday assassin must have continued with the other patrol elsewhere.

"I just *knew* you would have to pass through here eventually." The frowning clown propped his hands on his hips, trying to look dramatic. "When these House Friday sweethearts arrived, imagine my joy when they described who was on their way here! This is far more exciting than toying with the trash inhabiting this region. To be able to bring the head of the man that killed Lord January and defeated Lady February to the Dokeshi? This will bring me more pleasure than watching the light leave the eyes of tenants as they read their eviction notices!"

"First off, Lord January is still alive and… he's alive. I need you to answer a question for me before we get started." Grant completely ignored the other fighters flanking the Vassal. "Are you the only Vassal from Dokeshi in the area?"

"I'm all that's needed." Tatters seemed confused by the question, his narcissism taking a hit when he realized that this wasn't the response he had been expecting. "Why would that matter? Once each of us gets a blow in, you won't be alive to care anyway."

"I challenge you to a duel. If you win, I will go with you

quietly. If I win, your weapon is destroyed." Grant placed his hand on his uchigatana in preparation of the system approving the duel. Instead, the clown started laughing.

"Ha*hah*! Accept a duel from *you*? I don't think so!" Tatters waved his hands expressively at the men waiting behind him. "There are enough of us to guarantee my victory without bothering to make silly deals."

"That works too." Grant crouched, his legs tensing. "I was going to go easy on you, but I don't think that's an option anymore."

Before he could leap into their midst, an arrow flashed out from the rear of the enemy formation. Iaijutsu knocked it out of the air before it could strike him.

Combat initiated

Action: *Defend With Weapon*
Result: *Attack deflected*
Opponents remaining: 26
Actions: *Please select one option from the following list*
Attack: *Lethal, Non-lethal, Spell*
Defend: *With Weapon, Without Weapon*
Run: *Attempt Escape*

Grant selected 'Spell' and jumped forward. He landed in their midst, and Sarge shaped the lightning coursing through his body. The spell activated fully, and lightning jumped from enemy to enemy, disabling and injuring over half of his opponents.

Thundering Step is increased by Lightning attunement! Damage per second is currently: 83.6 per second

. . .

Lightning Strikes Twice: your spell damaged at least ten enemies within a single second! Mental cultivation is increased by 10% for one hour!

Suki was right behind Grant, and she landed a *huge* uppercut on the House Friday guard that was doing his best imitation of a muscled outhouse. The man teetered backwards, teeth and blood spraying out of his mouth as the combat system caught him and made him wait for his own turn to fall over. She dropped back, unable to capitalize on the devastating hit until her turn came around again.

The soldiers and House Friday guards were wearing armor that carried varying degrees of spell mitigation, so they weren't uniformly affected by the lightning sparking through them. Tatters, who had been on the edge of the spell range, appeared to only be a little twitchy from the continuous shock. He raised a scepter in one hand and a potion bottle in the other.

Grant selected 'Defend: With Weapon' and suffered through the attacks of three soldiers in rapid succession. They were regular cultivators, so he couldn't afford to accept their hits directly. He managed to knock the blow of a naginata into the path of a fourth attacker, when a brief pause interrupted the battle as Suki leapt off the railing of the bridge right on top of another House Friday guard who was using a crossbow. Everyone watched in amazement as her flying punch caught the man straight in the top of his head. The unfortunate guard seemed to shrink a few inches, and he tottered around for a moment before falling forward onto his face. There was a collective wince before everyone jumped back into the fight.

Grant was continually selecting 'Defend: With Weapon,' biding his time for the perfect moment to strike. Tatters finally tossed the potion bottle at Grant, who surprised the clown when he used the flat of his blade to redirect it toward the archer that had first fired at him. The man was just getting back to his feet from the spell when the glass vial shattered in front of his face, and the pained screams that quickly followed made Grant *very* happy that he hadn't broken the glass while it was still near him.

"Well, *that* didn't go like I thought it would." Tatters shoved the soldier closest to him at Grant. "Get in there! We can wear him down eventually!"

The entire party targeted Grant, except for the jumbo-sized guard. He was focused on Suki, blood still leaking from his ruined mouth. She was landing punishing blows to his midsection, but this man was clearly able to weather the damage. His retaliatory strikes were nearly as fast, and just as dangerous. Her gauntlets were doing a good job of deflecting the punishing blows from the giant's club, but every time she knocked aside his thundering swings, Grant detected a sharp wince of pain.

Everyone present could clearly see that the clown's assertion had been correct. No matter how skilled or strong the two of them were, a constant stream of cultivators and Vassals would eventually wear them down, and the fight would be over.

Deciding it was time to shift the dynamic, Grant dove forward in a roll right at Tatters the moment his turn to attack came up. He sprang to his feet only a sword-length away and immediately selected 'Attack: With Weapon.' Tatters must have selected 'Defend: With Weapon', because he lifted his scepter to block. It was exactly the response Grant was hoping for.

Kenjutsu (2/10) Skill tier 1: All damage dealt when wielding a sword is increased by 10%.

Skill tier 2: Your sword will never betray you. When a sword is wielded by you, the blade will always land exactly where you intend.

The spot Grant intended to hit was the neck of the scepter, where the crystal head joined with the wooden shaft. A Vassal's weapon was only a copy of the Wielder's weapon it was based on, and unlike a Wielder's weapon, Grant had learned it could be destroyed. He put every bit of power he could muster into the swing, and it struck like a hammerblow straight from the heavens.

A tinkling sound of shattering crystal rang out over the bridge, immediately followed by an explosion that threw everyone on their backs. The stone and mortar bridge shook from the detonation, raining down dust and grit into the filthy polluted water running under the supports.

"Ow." Grant sat up and scanned his limbs to check the damage. He was sore, but didn't feel any broken bones or see any major bleeding. He looked over to see what happened to Tatters, and realized his lack of serious injury wasn't the norm. Grant's opponents had been on the side of the explosion where the crystal shards had been scattered by his sword strike, and all of them were in bad shape. He felt a spike of worry that Suki had been hit, but her shockingly pink hair poking out from under the unconscious form of the human mountain indicated *exactly* where she was. It looked like the big guy had taken the hit on his back, so she was probably okay, if slightly squashed.

The people that had been on Grant's side of the explosion were already starting to rouse, so he jumped to his feet. As he moved to strike the naginata-wielding soldier on the base of the skull with the hilt of his sword, a screen popped up.

Warning: *System failure. Agreement, Deal, and Oath enforcement has been halted. Please remain calm. A Vassal will be dispatched to your location to reinstate deals. Remember, events around a temporary breach will be dealt with-th-thh…*

<System is down! Strike now, while they are still disoriented!> Sarge projected his merciless attitude, and Grant was quick to comply.

He laid about with his sword, sometimes knocking his enemies unconscious, and other times ruthlessly chopping into arms and legs if they continued attempting to rise and fight. He did his best not to cut through bone, but he wasn't willing to let them get to their feet. They hadn't been interested in a fair fight, so neither was he. No one would stop him from fixing this District, especially the kind of people that followed a person like Tatters.

"Speaking of the evil clown…" Grant finished with the cultivators still able to get to their feet, and walked to the side of the bridge where the other half were still laying prostrate. The Vassal was laying on his side against the waist-high railing, his body torn and bleeding. "Wow. It looks like you got torn up pretty bad there, Tatters. I'd be flattered to say you're looking a little battered, if what I said mattered."

<Don't. Don't taunt people.> Sarge cut him off before he could continue. <Not because it's ignoble. It's just that you aren't very good at it. We can add this to the schedule for practice.>

"You think… this *matters*?" Tatters sounded off, smiling hungrily with blood dripping out of the corner of his mouth. "Dokeshi March… will still have… your head… as an *ashtray*!"

<That seems oddly specific. Do you think he already has a head for a hookah? You know, now that I'm thinking about it, I feel like your head would be the perfect size for a footrest.> Grant sheathed his sword and glanced at it with a raised eyebrow. <What? Now that I've mentioned it, the next time you see your reflection, I bet you'll see it too. Really, it's something you can't unsee.>

"When… you die… you will be screaming." Tatters was trying to sit up straight, but his arm wasn't willing to hold his weight; probably because most of it wasn't there. "I-"

February Twenty Nine jumped out of the sheath like it had a mind of its own, smoothly removing Tatters' head from his body. With an extra flick of his sword, the head took a trip over the bridge to explore what lay at the bottom of the stream.

<Behind you!> Sarge's shout was a split second too late, but it meant the crossbow bolt that would have impacted the middle

of his back instead embedded itself in the back of his left arm. <Finish him!>

Grant spun around in time to see the crossbow-wielding House Friday guard scrambling to reload. He forced his sore, battered body to sprint at the man, managing to slam into him just as the twang of another bolt sounded in his ears. His uchigatana had punctured the man's abdomen, but it had deflected far enough to the side that the wound wasn't immediately fatal. Neither was the additional crossbow bolt that now resided in the front side of Grant's left arm. The limb hung uselessly at his side with what looked like a solid wooden stick poking all the way through.

"Abyss! *Again*?" Grant rolled off the man he had stabbed, not exactly being gentle when removing his sword from the man's abdomen one-handed. As he raised his sword over his enemy's head to give him the same treatment that Tatters had received, the guard raised a hand in defeat, the other pressed against his wound.

"I yield! Please, don't kill me." The man sounded too tired to be as scared as he should have been. "This is just a job for me. I swore to do it to the best of my ability, but I didn't swear to die for that stupid casino. Plus, agreements seem to be broken right now? Please?"

Sighing, Grant returned February Twenty Nine to its sheath as a screen he hadn't seen in a long time popped into his vision.

Do you, Grant Monday, wish to absorb the power of March 30: Double Tap? Accepting 'Double Tap' will override any previous Wielded Weapon power absorbed in the current monthly series. If not overridden by another weapon of the same month, this ability will return to its current Wielded Weapon at the end of the year, unless the quest 'Heal The World' has been successfully completed.

Accept / Decline.

. . .

The guard was a Wielder, not a Vassal? Grant accepted. Taking the power was an easy decision. If he survived his grave injuries, the young Lord of the Month would be long gone before the bleeding Wielder was capable of coming after him. He would worry about what the ability actually did later. First, he had a much bigger concern.

How was he supposed to get the unconscious big guy off of Suki with one useless arm?

CHAPTER NINETEEN

"Ow." Suki sat up, rubbing her lightly bleeding head. Grant knew *exactly* how she felt. Looking around, her eyes widened in shock and surprise. Dead, unconscious, and heavily battered people littered the ground. "What *happened*? I can't have been flattened for *that* long."

"When I broke the Vassal's weapon, it exploded." Grant winced as he finished kicking the big guy off of her. He had started by using his hand, but still managed to hurt his injured arm, so he'd switched to using his undamaged legs. "In the confusion, and with the subsystem down, I had the chance to defeat everyone else. I don't think they actually know how to fight when combat isn't turn-based."

"Breaking the scepter blew the clown's head off?" Suki's face turned a little green, and she started dry heaving as she took in the carnage. This left Grant confused. He knew that she had seen dead bodies before, and had even killed monsters right in front of him. She jabbed a finger at the dead man's neck, eyeing Grant with more than a little hostility. "That wound looks like a clean cut with a sharp blade. Not an explosion."

"That's because I cut it off?" Grant started to shrug in

consternation, pausing only when the bolts sticking out of his arm caused him to wince and abort the motion. "He was pure evil. At least Fluffy Fingers didn't delight in the power he had over people. That guy was a menace to everyone, so I took care of him. Like a rabid trash panda on a farm; you have to put them down before they can hurt anything else, or infect those around them."

"But… he was a *person*! You can't just go around cutting people's heads off!" Suki had begun shouting, and Grant couldn't understand why.

"Did you just want me to let the clown go?" He shook his head. "He would have gone on to do terrible things after getting a new scepter. Justice only works when people are punished for their crimes. There's no chance Lord March would have allowed that to happen."

She waved a shaking finger at him. "You don't just get to be an executioner whenever you feel like it! You don't even know if what he was saying was the truth. He could have been lying just to mess with your head!"

"Was I supposed to capture him? Take him with us? Let him go, so he could keep hurting people when the mood struck him? He sure *sounded* like he was telling the truth." Grant's volume began ratcheting up as his tone reflected hers. "I *will* save these people, and I *won't* allow monsters like that to roam free. I'm supposed to become the Calendar King, which means I have to *think* like a King. I've seen you kill monsters before, Suki. Just because he's *shaped* like a human didn't make him any less of a beast."

Grant grabbed the bolt protruding from his bicep and ripped it free with a shout and a spurt of blood. Suki was shocked into silence and dropped her gaze to her feet.

"I've… never had to kill a person before. I've trained as hard as I could so that I could defeat an opponent without having to resort to killing them. It isn't that I think a murderer should be spared, but there are trials and procedures to follow before an execution." Suki was breathing harder, and she raised a burning glare to the killer right in front of her. "I understand that the system has named you both Lord January and Lord February. It still isn't right for you to serve as judge, jury, and executioner. It's a bad mindset for any leader to have, and it worries me to see you adopting such a harsh outlook."

Instead of continuing the conversation, since there was practically nothing he could say against that argument, Grant removed the second crossbow bolt and sat down to meditate. If he waited too long, he wouldn't be able to heal the damage. It was dangerous not to get somewhere safer, but it would only take one full minute for his absorbed healing skill to work. He glanced at his health before he started, calculating how much damage he had taken in the fight.

Health: 311/421
Mana: 22/22

"What?" Grant was flabbergasted when he realized that all of his injuries had only brought him down to what he had practically thought his maximum health was! "Sarge, what happened? The increase in my health is huge; almost seventy points!"

<You have a *lot* of information to look over.> Sarge sounded extremely pleased with himself. <In that battle alone, you defeated one Wielder and five Vassals. Then, you killed one of the defeated Vassals, which counted toward your levels as well. You jumped from cultivation level seventeen to nineteen almost instantly. Like I've told you before: for you, defeating enemies is the fastest path to power. Frankly, it's the only way to make up the difference between you and the people that have been cultivating for years, decades, and centuries. Ignore her whining: be brutal. It's the only way you're gonna survive the year.>

"Wow. That's..." Grant was stunned by both the increases,

as well as the demand. "I'll look everything over when we get to a safe spot and think through what you're saying."

He blocked out the urge to look over his stat sheet immediately, and instead concentrated on healing, as the ten minute time limit was already almost up. Slowing his breathing, he willed the stolen ability to activate, finding himself instantly overwhelmed as the replay of events detailed his mistakes.

The first major error was the fact that he should have waited to use Thundering Step until his second turn to attack, even if the surprise usage had been effective. It would have resulted in a tighter cluster of enemies, allowing him to down more of them at the start and avoid getting injured by others in the first place. His second issue had been the angle at which he had struck the scepter. If Grant had destroyed it after maneuvering the clown away, forcing him to slightly turn, he could have utilized the explosion as an anti-personnel spell and taken out nearly all of the enemies on the bridge at the same time.

Health: 311/421 -> 355/421. Critical areas focused. Soft tissue repaired to 80%. Internal bleeding successfully stopped.

"Grant, we need to move," Suki was crouching next to him and shaking his arm. It was still sore, so he flinched away as the motion registered. He opened his eyes, getting a clear view of a forest of spears moving at speed toward them. They had some time to get away yet, but his blood turned to ice at the faint sight of a short figure oscillating a golden orb leaking green gas.

"Yeah. Let's get outta here." Even with the system down, Grant had no way to fight against what was likely the poison of a House Saturday assassin bearing down on them. "Lose them in the alleys?"

The two intruders to the District scrambled to their feet and started their exhausted escape by heading in the opposite direction of the approaching spears. While neither Wielder was in perfect health or in a great place mentally, the thought of what was behind them kept their pace to a fast jog. In just a few minutes, they had successfully passed out of sight, weaving between and through the abandoned buildings of District March.

While they ran, Grant felt Suki occasionally sneaking looks at him. They hadn't finished their conversation about him killing the clown yet. He was almost certain of it, even if *he* was done speaking about it. The Lord firmed up his jaw, convinced that—at least this time—he hadn't made a bad decision.

The Vassal had declared his intent to kill Grant, so all he had done was respond in kind. He could have killed the others, but he had at least given them a chance to survive. That was more than they would have offered him. He hadn't been in the wrong, and he already knew that he would do it again.

Probably far too soon.

CHAPTER TWENTY

They didn't stop running until late into the night. The two of them had split up, come back together, moved onto rooftops when possible, doubled back a few times, and even set up a fake campsite inside an old bakery. Thick smoke slowly drifting from a partially blocked oven chimney would hopefully make it harder for any tracking animals to follow the trail, especially since they hadn't stuck around long enough to get all smoky.

Suki had eventually found a recently abandoned blacksmith shop for them to hide their actual makeshift camp in. They were even within sight of the casino, which would be necessary for them to move through in order to reach the next area. Once they had laid eyes on the place, it had become readily apparent why no one could just hop over the casino walls.

"He isn't just tapping into the power of the barriers to power his system. Dokeshi March is a madman! He's draining the energy to create his own miniature barriers!" Suki was pacing back and forth, clenching and unclenching her fists. "No wonder the barriers in February were acting up and creating disasters. How many deaths of innocent people can we lay at that monster's feet?"

Her gauntlets flickered in and out of existence, and her voice dropped to a whisper. "Just so he could sift his people, based on how well they gambled in his stupid casinos? He killed *hundreds* for the sole purpose of keeping the unlucky ones away from him?"

"It won't matter much longer." Grant once again felt a wave of determination wash over him. "We're here to remove him from power, and that means making him pay for his crimes."

"Oh, what, will you cut off *his* head, too?" Suki spun to face him, her gauntlets doing more than just flickering. They practically _*clanged*_ into their full form. "Let me guess: killing him is your answer to this issue as well?"

<I'm just a sword spirit, but I wouldn't answer that.> Grant closed his mouth just in time to prevent himself from letting loose the barrage of justifications he had been building in his head since the first time Suki had lashed out at him. Sarge was probably correct, and looking like a fool wasn't going to help him. <Smart choice.>

"Suki. Give me your dirty laundry." Grant held his mostly-healed arms out. "I saw a full rain barrel out back, by the forge."

"What?" The rapid change of subject caused Suki's gauntlets to unconsciously fade back into gloves. "Give you… my laundry? Why would I do that?"

"Remember? We made a deal. I have to do your dirty laundry for the rest of the month." Grant pointedly roamed his eyes over her stained clothing. "We might not get another chance for a while, so I'll scrub clothes while you whip us up something to eat."

"That's… *you*! Changing the subject…? Okay." Suki took a deep breath, seeming to realize just how close she had been to losing control. That fact clearly bothered her. Not only due to the recent deaths, but the control structure in place would be hard for anyone to stomach. As a leader that she hoped others would aspire to be, Suki was used to putting the people first, making sure that potential wrongs in District March either never happened in the first place, or were *severely* punished. "At least you honor the deals you make, even if they're punishments. Also, *I'm* washing my own underclothing."

"Thank you?" Grant smirked at the thought. Personally, he didn't see what the issue was, but it was funny to see her blush more the longer he held his laughter in. "Less work for me. I saw you bending pretty far when you were fighting, I figured I'd need to really *work* to get those clean."

Suki's blush faded slightly, and her face hardened as she remembered how the night had started. Hurriedly turning away, she picked out her more private pieces of clothing, then pushed over a surprisingly large pile to Grant to wash. He sighed as she looked anywhere but at him, and he couldn't help but wonder how she had fit all of these garments inside the tiny pack she carried. He gathered everything and grumbled so softly that only Sarge could hear, "Is it just that I have never interacted with them, a Suki-specific thing, or are women truly *this* strange?"

<Kid, you have no idea. You think they're mysterious now; just wait until they've had hundreds of years of practice befuddling people. You'll think you know what's going on, then… *bam*! You're ripped outta your body and distilled into a sword.>

"What…? Is there more to that story?" Grant's question went unanswered. He shrugged, and after setting up a line from the corner of the main building to the forge to hang the wet clothes on, Grant unwrapped a small package that contained a brick of lye soap and started scrubbing the soiled shirts and pants in the rain barrel. He found a depressingly large number of blood stains, mostly on his stuff. With his hands busy but his mind free, he worked methodically under the starlight and pulled up his stat sheet to study the changes.

Name: Grant Monday
Rank: Lord of The Month (January, February)
Class: Foundation Cultivator

Cultivation Achievement Level: 19
Cultivation Stage: Late Summer
Inherent Abilities: Swirling Seasons Cultivation
Health: 403/421
Mana: 22/22

Characteristics
Physical: 247
Mental: 87
Armor Proficiency: 131
Weapon Proficiency: 166

Weapon Absorbed abilities:
1) Sword Grandmastery: Imbue your weapon with a sword spirit that creates a model that allows for enhanced physical, mental, and weapon cultivation. Restriction: the training plan must be followed, else the ability locks for 24 hours. There is only one warning given per day.
2) Live by the Sword: Pause and meditate on the failures of your combat ability, healing up to ***40%*** *of all damage taken within the last 10 minutes, over one full minute. This ability will increase with physical cultivation.*
3) Double Tap (NEW): After four consecutive hits on the same target, the fifth attack will be perfectly duplicated by an intangible copy of the Wielded Weapon. Damage is unblockable by all forms and types of armor, and effect is randomized between slashing, piercing, and blunt damage. Certain spell effects can potentially mitigate damage.

"I can think of some interesting uses for this." Grant was especially happy to see the new absorbed ability. "It might not be too useful in a group fight, but in a one-on-one duel? They literally won't know what hit them. A new ability is always great, and it looks like Live By the Sword got stronger? Nice! Increasing how much I can heal up is pretty important. I like not being in pain."

<You shouldn't just focus on abilities. You might not always have them, or be able to access them. The only things that are

yours are your cultivation, and growing into the Late Summer stage of cultivation pumped up the damage you can deal out, gave you more mana—that'll allow you to use your spell twice in rapid succession—and produced a huge upswing in health.> Sarge sounded grudgingly pleased to see Grant's rate of growth. <If you keep this up, you just might have a chance to pull this off. Also, you should know that you rubbed a hole through Suki's nice shirt with that rough bar of soap.>

"No!" Grant dropped the soap into the barrel and had to practically take a bath to fish it back out. Quickly inspecting the shirt, he found that he hadn't actually worn all the way through the fabric, but it was close. He hoped Suki wouldn't notice.

<Oh, she *definitely* won't notice. I think you'll be *just* fine.> Grant let out a huge sigh of relief at Sarge's affirmation, stopping short at the subsequent snort. <Remind me to add 'how sarcasm works' to get in the rotation for training sometime soon.>

Ignoring the snooty sword spirit, Grant finished up the laundry and hung it on the line to dry. The slack twine drooped low enough that a casual passerby wouldn't notice it, and the breeze blowing through the small yard should be enough to get the clothes dry enough by sunrise.

"I made stew again." The quiet voice of Suki standing behind him made him jump slightly and take a defensive position by instinct. He'd been so caught up in the simple and familiar task that he hadn't heard her approach. "I hope that's not going to be an issue."

Grant gave her a nod of acknowledgement, and they both returned to the dilapidated building. It was awkward between the two of them, so Grant used the silence to pick through the fruits and vegetables from the crate he had won at the casino. A few items had been bruised by the explosion on the bridge, but overall, the food looked unexpectedly decent. He was surprised to find a lack of poison or powder on them from the casino manager.

<The weasel probably thought he would be gathering the

food right back up, so he didn't want to mess it up.> Grant silently agreed with Sarge's assumption; it made good sense. <Make sure not to overeat. You might have a lot of running to do tomorrow, and being too full will slow you down.>

"Don't worry, I've learned *that* lesson." Grant fished out two apples, tossing the perfectly ripe one to Suki. He kept the green one for himself, figuring that the tartness would complement the stew well, and he didn't think Suki would notice the difference. She actually enjoyed drinking blended *grass*, for Regent December's sake. "Apples for dessert."

She gave him a nod in silent thanks, and they ate their stew rapidly enough that it had no time to cool. That was when Grant realized why she had been hesitant about the meal she'd made; since Suki hadn't used any of the fresh ingredients he had worked so hard to get, it was exactly the same trail stew they had eaten several times before. Anything was better than another granola bar, and Grant honestly didn't mind very much. Still… Suki calling attention to the fact suddenly felt like she was intentionally not using the spoils of the evening as a punishment.

"Do you mind taking first watch?" Suki grabbed his bowl and stretched. "I'm pretty beat."

"Is this another *test*?" There was no reply, so he shook his head in disgruntlement. It had been an exhausting day, and she had done more running than Grant had when they were losing their pursuers, but he was on edge and not afraid to show it. He stood, flexing his sore arm. "I don't mind doing it; I need to practice some sword forms in the yard. Just be sure to bar the front door. I'll be out back."

Suki still didn't answer, so he took her silence as an agreement. After a few extra minutes to unpack his own bedroll, Grant decided it would be better to work through their disagreement… some other time. Perhaps after they had both had some rest.

"Okay, Sarge. Let's do this. Time to train." A veritable whirlwind of orange debris lifted from the ground and started swirling around him. As it encroached, all he did was smile. This was how he made sure his enemies would never be able to beat him just by encircling him.

Nothing would stand in his way. Winning was all that mattered.

CHAPTER TWENTY-ONE

Grant was awakened by a stream of light coming through a crack in the rafters and hitting him in the eyes. The blinding glare made him wax philosophical as his brain kicked into gear. Namely, the thought flowed through his mind like water: How did the sunlight always find a way to get him, no matter how perfectly he tried to hide? It acted like a beam when going through a window, and a wave of water when skirting objects just to annoy him.

He sat up with a groan of pain, his sore body complaining. His left arm still wasn't perfectly healed yet, and the training last night hadn't helped his torn muscles to heal. The ten percent boost in his pain sensations certainly wasn't allowing him to ignore the issue either. At least the training had helped him wake up less stiff than sleeping on the ground usually merited.

"I let you sleep in, in consideration of the fact that we don't have to travel far today." Suki was preparing something with the fresh fruit from Grant's pack, slicing it up with expert motions. "We should probably practice our story and work on a plan for some of the games that are sure to be there."

She hadn't met his eyes the whole time, so his neophyte

social skills informed him she might, just possibly, still be mad at him. He got to his feet and immediately started strapping on his armor. Just in case someone attacked them. Or she punched him. "We should also work on not being mad at one another. Being at odds over making sure he would never be the *head* murdering clown just doesn't make sense to me."

"See, that's the problem." Suki slammed the cooking knife down on the table, and finally looked up at Grant. "The murdering clown is *exactly* the kind of thing we should be at odds over. You walk a slippery slope, one that ends as you filling the role of leader as a *tyrant* your citizens will fear, and not a benevolent ruler people respect."

"What?" Grant couldn't see how making sure Tatters couldn't get a-*head* in life would end with him becoming a tyrant. "How does slaying a *head*strong killer like him turn me into a bad king? We don't even know if I will become the next Calendar King!"

"It's the mindset you have." Suki picked the knife back up and started brutally chopping the fruit into smaller pieces. "Sure, yesterday you murdered a Vassal that was a *known* killer; someone that publicly abused their power. Today, you might kill a Vassal who stands in your way. A year from now, you could be ordering the deaths of hundreds that challenge your right to rule them."

When she looked up into his eyes, hers were red around the edges, as if she was fighting back tears. "Don't you see how this *ends*? The other Wielders responsible for the safety of their people would band together and put you down. Not because they wouldn't want you as king, but because it would be their *duty* to put down a savage dictator! You *can't* become the kind of person who I need to hunt down and stop."

<Just saying, if all the Wielders came after you… you'd get *so* strong when you defeated them.> Sarge was practically salivating in Grant's mind, a distinctly strange sensation. <Can you imagine all those Cultivation Achievement Levels?>

"Hey, calm down." Grant shook off the intrusive thought

and walked over to place his hand on Suki's shoulder. "First off, I will *not* apologize for doing what I've needed to do. That's the only reason I've lived this long. It's *also* why I've been able to defeat not one, but *two* District leaders. Think back, Suki. I could have killed a *lot* more people. I *haven't*, and now I have you to help make sure I never get to that point. *Right*?"

<*Pre~e~ety* sure she's gonna think you just told her to calm down when she's upset because she's worried about you. Then a direct admission that you won't be apologizing?> Sarge sounded like he was choking back laughter. <It was nice knowing you. We had a good run, kid. Try to put up a good fight.>

"Is *that* how you see me? Am I only the moral compass keeping you from shifting from hero to villain?" Suki took a deep breath and let it out slowly, the tension draining out of her. "I know how to do that much, at least. It'll be easier with one person than an entire District, at any rate. Now, this isn't exactly what I had planned, but I shouldn't be terribly surprised. I'll add social norms as a part of your training, and I expect you to ace every single test I give you."

<No. What? How did that work?> Sarge seemed baffled for some reason. <That literally *never* works. You should be in the middle of a fight by now! *Boo~o*!>

"All I've *been* doing for the last few months is training and learning. What's a little more?" Grant was trying not to look down at the now 'finely-diced' food Suki had been preparing. It looked more like a mashed mess than anything, but he was hungry enough to give it a try. "Whatever it is that keeps me from being a monster, and keeps you around... I'm all ears."

It was the perfect time for his stomach to growl like an angry tiger. Suki forced a chuckle and grimaced down at the mess she had made. "Sure. All ears, huh? More like 'all stomach'. This... it was going to be a tart. Let's eat the fruit paste and then try some new things."

"I'd love to bring you to January someday. Then you'll see what 'all stomach' really is." Grant chuckled at the thought of the highly active, incredibly fit District leader encountering January for the first time. The two of them ate quickly, both wanting to move past the awkwardness as rapidly as possible, then got down to learning the business of gambling.

Suki laid out a deck of cards that had been included in the supplies they'd bought, running Grant through the different types of games he could expect to see. It didn't take long for him to realize how much trouble he was in.

"How do you keep all these rules straight in your head?" He pointed at the game they were practicing at the moment. "I am supposed to slap the Jacks and Jokers, but not the others? Then this one: the one where I have to count to twenty one… I don't slap, I *hit*? What am I supposed to hit again? The dealer?"

"*No*. No, don't hit the dealer." Suki massaged her left temple as her eyelid twitched. "You *say* the word 'hit' when you want another card."

"But in this game, I'm supposed to hit." Grant pointed at the pile of cards in front of him. "Do I get to hit the dealer in *this* game, then?"

"No! No hitting actual people!" Suki picked up the cards and shuffled them. "Let's stop worrying about the games where you might get us kicked out, and focus on just one. The most important game to learn is poker. It's known as the gentleman's game, and it focuses more on reading other people than the cards themselves."

"Poker. So, I… poke them with my sword?" Grant placed his hand on the hilt of his uchigatana and leaned forward in excitement. "I can probably win *that* game with my Iaijutsu skill!"

"Oh, may the late Lord February preserve me…" Suki sighed and put the cards down. "You don't poke anyone with your sword. You don't poke them with your finger, or a fork, or a spoon, or anything!"

She hadn't meant to raise her voice at the end, but she was starting to get very frustrated. "The game is *called* poker, but there isn't any actual *poking* at all. Don't worry about the name! It is a game about *trying* to get the best *hand*."

"This sounds gruesome. Now I have to cut people's hands off?" This time Grant genuinely was teasing her, but by the way her hands kept shifting into metal, she didn't seem to think it was funny. "Just… trying to have some fun with this! Ah… who decides what makes the best hand? Is there a hand judge of some kind? Or do we bet on which player has the best hands, and then fight to cut them off?"

"Are you actually trying to make me punch you in the face?" Suki's gauntlets flickered into existence. "Because right now, I would *love* to play your version of poker with you."

<Here's a thought; how about you just listen and stop talking?> Once again, Sarge was having a hard time sending along his thoughts because he was laughing too hard. <Or don't. This can only get better—for me, that is—from here.>

"Okay, how about you just explain the rules, and I stay quiet until you are done telling me which person gets their hands cut off." Grant leaned back, just in case Suki decided to attack him.

"May the Pugilist Deities guide him to a better life… no, no." Suki picked up the cards again after allowing her gauntlets to fade away. "Let's start over. This game is called poker, which doesn't involve any poking *whatsoever*, and the person who wins has the best hand, which is most definitely *not* a literal hand."

<I'm beginning to think Suki really should have woken you up early.> Sarge sounded as though he was heaving for breath. <At this rate, you won't be walking into that casino until dark!>

CHAPTER TWENTY-TWO

It did not, in fact, take until dark before they walked into the casino. Suki had mostly given up on Grant's ability to bluff by lunch, and they had devised a new plan by the time they were done eating.

"Okay, going over it one last time." Suki kept fiddling with the cloth covering the lower half of her face, her nerves on clear display. "I take on the guard to the left, and you take the one on the right. When we get through the door, we stick together and head for the nearest exit on the far side of the casino."

"Making sure that we don't get bogged down in a big fight." Grant was putting on his own mask, making sure it was tight against his face. He didn't want it coming loose while fighting. "If we get separated, we meet up at the third intersection, or the first one with a fountain on the other side, no matter how far away that is."

There was only one person opposed to their current plan. <You look like a filthy ninja, and I won't stand for it.>

"Sarge is unhappy with this plan, since we won't be fighting openly and honorably." Grant relayed the real meaning of the sword's words to his partner.

"Perfect. That's how I know it's a good strategy." Suki pulled the hood lower on her cloak to cover her distinctive hair. "If this goes right, no one will be able to identify us, which means they might keep looking for us on this side of the barrier instead of the other."

"Right. We've got this. What could go wrong?" Grant winced as soon as the words left his mouth. "That is, I'm sure everything will go without a hitch. It's a well-planned idea, and we all get a little bit of what we want out of it."

"Are you trying to get us killed?" Suki gave him a sharp poke in the side. "Stop tempting fate like that! You should know better than anyone that someone might have a Wielded Weapon sensitive to the threads of fate. Talking like that is like throwing meat in front of a Bastard-Beaked Crow!"

"Oh look, a change in topic!" Grant took the opportunity to stop talking, choosing instead to get a better look at the front entrance they were approaching. The two gate guards were both muscular women in full plate armor, hoisting oversized halberds in their right hands, with sheathed short swords on their hips. It was impossible to tell if they were well-armed Armor cultivators, or full-blown Warrior cultivators; dual cultivators focused on both Weapons and Armor.

Even more impressive, the entrance they were guarding appeared fit to deny admittance to an army. The huge wooden doors were banded in thick strips of black iron, with nails the size of Grant's palm holding them in place. A thick locking bar was deeply seated in the reinforced grooves around the extra-thick steel frame. The lack of visible hinges meant it opened inwards, making it easier to block the door from the inside. A small group of people waiting to enter were standing in a huddle at the base of the short set of stairs, the sharp eyes of the guards silently judging their skinny frames, ratty clothing, and dirty faces.

<I suddenly have even less faith in this plan.> Sarge was clearly paying attention to the gate as well. <There are a lot of things that could go very wrong. Strategy without tactics is the

slowest route to victory. Tactics without strategy is the noise before defeat.>

"You could have mentioned that before we made it all this way." Grant subconsciously dropped his hand to the wrapped hilt of his uchigatana. He had layered it in strips of colored cloth to try and hide its appearance, in case a witness tried to describe it later. "Perhaps before we went to all the trouble of coming up with these disguises?"

<You call these getups *disguises*? I thought you were making a joke! You're both still clearly a male and female team, one using a sword and the other giant metal gauntlets. Can you see where you lost me?> Grant chose to ignore Sarge's solid points, instead weaving around the crowd to approach the steps first, in an effort to hide his flushed cheeks from Suki.

"Halt!" The guard on the left held up her hand for them to stop. "This entrance opens only at the ninth bell. Wait with the others, and make sure you have your entry fee ready. No free-loaders allowed in the World's Third Best Casino!"

Instead of answering, Grant rushed up the stairs to confront the guards. He leapt off the first step, feinting toward the guard on the left before engaging with the one on the right. His surprise change of direction worked, which caused the guard to bring her weapon out of position to block the sword headed straight for her head.

The gonging sound of the flat of his blade slapping against the side of her helmet rang out in the small courtyard, and she stumbled instantly. Suki was only a heartbeat behind, landing a heavy blow to the abdomen of the other guard after sweeping her halberd to the side. It lifted the guard off her feet, and she didn't get back up after the mighty hit. Grant chopped down a few times, making sure his opponent was fully unconscious, and Suki did the same. He nodded at her. "Vassal subsystem is still down."

"Good. I hate having to fight in turn-based combat. It's unnatural. Get the door!" Suki was already searching the guards' belt pouches for any special keys or magic items they might need to get through the casino. "Don't watch *me* search, get to it!"

Grant started, not having realized he was staring. Suki was very impressive when she was running things. Or punching them. He went over to the door and grasped the locking bar to lift it free. Instead, the moment he grabbed the bar, a jolt of lightning shot through it, locking his hand on the bar and causing his whole body to clench up.

Lightning Trap Damage is decreased by Lightning attunement by 10%! Damage per second is currently: 1.9 per second (58 Armor Magic Damage Reduction)

Pain from Lightning Damage is increased by 10% from Skill Bodily awareness—Current status: Paralyzed.

While the damage amount was low enough that Grant could take it for over five full minutes, the effect took him out of the fight. Meanwhile, Suki had found a single key in the pouch of the guard she had defeated, but it was far too small to fit the lock for the gate. When she looked up to see if Grant had managed to get it open, all she found was him standing there, staring at the door like it held all the secrets to the universe.

"Hey! What are you doing?" Suki walked over to see what was taking so long. "If the bar is too heavy to lift, all you had to do was-"

As soon as Suki rested her metal-gauntleted hand on Grant's metal-armored shoulder, her own body locked up, forcing her grip to clamp down bruisingly hard. She almost bit the tip of her tongue off when her jaw locked, and all thoughts of hurrying through the door flew out of her mind.

They both stood, locked in position, for over a minute. The only thing that saved them was that the power in the trap ran out. They collapsed in a heap on the steps, and Grant felt internally charred. Even though he would live, since he was looking at less than one hundred damage, the pain increase from his skill made the full-body effect of the trap hurt way more than it would have normally. He eventually rolled to his feet, twitching from the residual effects.

Suki had received a much-reduced version of the trap, but she didn't have the same lightning damage reduction. Her pink hair was frayed, the tips of it poking out from under her hooded cloak. Where her gauntlets met her arm at the shoulder were especially blistered, and she dismissed the weapons with a gasp of pain.

"I think… we should regroup… and try this a different way." Grant helped Suki to her feet, and she gave him a pained nod of silent agreement. "Come on, let's go." The two of them shuffled off, heading in the opposite direction from the blacksmith shop they had camped in the night before. There was another entrance half a day's travel down the wall, and they would have to try their luck again there. The group of people waiting to enter watched them leave in total silence, glee dancing in their eyes at the sight of the guards being taken out for just… no reason at all. It was cathartic.

"Who do you think those people were, Granny?" A boy no older than ten asked the old woman standing next to him. The whole incident had lasted less than five minutes, but it felt like ages to the duo as they moved along at a steadily increasing pace. Both Suki and Grant could hear their conversation as they stumbled away down the street.

"Just people like the rest of us. Hungry, down on their luck, and desperate. You saw that even guards can have unlucky days, but even so… those vagabonds got the worst of it." The old woman pulled her grandson closer, her voice still loud enough to carry down the alley where the two Wielders limped away from their failed attack. "Terrible things are going to happen to those two because of what they did here. Let them serve as a lesson to us both: play by the rules. Don't forget what the Dokeshi says… The House Always Wins."

CHAPTER TWENTY-THREE

"Well, that was a colossal failure." Suki gingerly rubbed some ointment on the burn where her gauntlet touched her shoulder. "I can't believe we fell for such a simple trap."

"I don't know; it doesn't seem that bad." Grant was doing his best to wedge the door to the abandoned leatherworker shop back in its frame while they talked, grunting as the distressed wood finally popped into place. "We couldn't have known there was a trap on a door they must open a bunch of times a day. Besides, you did get that key from the guard. You never know, that might be useful later on."

<On the bright and shiny side, the guard you defeated was a Vassal, so it helped with your cultivation.> Sarge sounded upbeat just so the next part would hit harder, and he dropped his voice to a whisper. <It was pretty embarrassing. You should feel bad for getting laid low like that.>

"Don't try to make this sound like some kind of victory." Suki finished applying the ointment and started laying out their bedrolls. "It was an absolute, complete failure."

"It wasn't. We learned how the doors work, and what to expect as we go in there. They're open at certain times, and you don't touch anything unless you know it isn't a trap." Grant went over to Suki's pack and pulled out the map from its side pocket. "In fact, I think I might have an idea how we can get around this."

"You can't even understand how to play Bridge, but you think you understand how casino security works all of a sudden?" Suki was struggling to run a brush through her frazzled hair, so she waved it at him instead. "Please, enlighten me, oh wise one."

"Hey! I'm smart! It isn't *my* fault there's a game called 'Bridge' that doesn't even involve a single bit of construction." Grant spread their map out on a worn work table, mumbling about people naming things in a way that made no sense. "Just look at the doors marked on the map. This whole thing is a circle, right? Well, we were trying to enter at the nine o'clock position. Do you remember what that guard said? It only opens when the ninth bell rings."

"So, you think that if we go to the ten o'clock position, the door will open at the tenth bell?" Suki took a good look at the map, tracing her finger across all the marked positions. "Okay, let's say you're right. We still have to get you gambling at a high enough level to prove you belong in the next region. How do we do that?"

"Well, maybe all I really need is practice." Grant pointed to a large square on the map only a few blocks from the eleven o'clock position. "How much do you want to bet this is a big market square of some kind? We could make it there before dark tomorrow if we hurry. I should be able to get some practice in, and then we can just enter the casino at the eleventh bell."

"Hmm… it's a bad plan. High chance of us losing everything before we even get through the first casino." Suki contemplated the map a bit longer, still fighting her frazzled hair with the brush. "Yet, I somehow can't think of anything better, and it's probably a good idea to try to enter a bit farther from our failed attempt."

She carefully repacked the tattered parchment before laying down on her bedroll. "If you fail, we can still try fighting our way through. I'm sure it'll be easier once we're already inside."

"Now who's tempting fate?" Grant teased with an arched eyebrow, trying to keep a straight face. It didn't last long. The two of them burst into laughter, relieving some of the tension that had hung over them ever since their failure. "You should get some rest, and try to recover from the shocking events at the gate. I'll head down to the basement and get some training in."

"I have to admit... I'm impressed." Suki pulled her blanket up to her chin and rolled over. "You have enough dedication to training that I think the people in District February would be jealous."

Grant snorted in disbelief. He had seen the way they trained. No thanks. He didn't want to get blown away by a stiff breeze. More importantly, he was determined to find a steak and eat every single bite himself, even if he had to kill the cow personally.

"I'm also pleased by your restraint. Knocking people out without killing them is actually pretty difficult." There was a long moment of silence, then a grunt of displeasure. "Or should I be worried about how many times you needed to practice that before you stopped killing them and started knocking them out?"

<Don't answer that. Just walk away. Tonight, I think it would be a good idea to practice your Iaijutsu from a seated position.> Sarge had clearly been planning the training Grant was about to undertake. <My reasoning: you're going to be sitting around at a lot of card tables, so I think you should be prepared if something goes wrong. Let me rephrase that: when. *When* something goes wrong, because we both know something is going to go wild before this is over, you'll need to know how to kill your way out from any position.>

"That's... fair?" Grant didn't have a reply for that. He couldn't fault Sarge for the assessment, considering how things tended to go. No one liked to lose, and even fewer were willing to part with their lives. Instead of coming up with anything to say, the Lord continued down to the basement.

He stacked a few empty crates left by the former owners to simulate a table and chair, then got to work. Sarge ran him through a gambit of enemies, attacking him from all kinds of different angles. Grant wasn't sure how likely it was that a horned rabbit would attack his legs under the table while he was playing cards, but he went with it anyway.

After spending the first hour testing Grant in every imaginable way to fight while seated, Sarge decided to up the ante. Grant had to stay in a sitting position without the help of a chair, his enhanced body cultivation the only thing keeping his legs from trembling… for the first hour. Eventually the pain of the uncomfortable position forced him to gasp and snarl as he held the pose and fought. To make his training worse, Sarge started dropping slimes on his head to force him to learn overhead awareness.

The semi-liquid bodies required Grant to intercept them perfectly, swatting them away center-mass with the full length of the side of his blade. If he was just a *touch* off, they could still coat him with at least a portion of their caustic goo.

<*Perfect*!> He slapped aside an orange-colored slime, turning the motion into a slash that bisected a faceless man wielding a narrow dagger. <That's it! If you keep this up, you might have a real chance at winning!>

As intended, Sarge's mental shout caused Grant to miss the next object headed his direction, a sharp-edged card that struck him on the end of the nose. He reflexively jerked his head back, throwing off his precarious balance and toppling.

"*Oomph…*!" Landing hard on his backside, he still managed to remove the hand of the second dagger-wielder trying to make his insides become outsides. He raised his legs with the intent to flip his weight forward to help him back to his feet, but the motion caused him to accidentally kick the edge of the old crate functioning as a table. It exploded into a cloud of splinters, making a loud racket that he was certain would cause

Suki to wake up ready for a fight. "Ah, Regent… that isn't good."

<You better get up there and tell Suki you're okay, otherwise you're going to regret it.> Sarge agreed as soon as Grant was back on his feet and had sheathed his uchigatana. <We should probably wrap it up for the day anyway. Now that you have some training with fighting while seated, it's time to practice what you will be doing at the tables in the first place.>

When Grant made it to the top of the stairs, he was shocked to find Suki still asleep. Apparently, the last few days had been enough to wear out even *her* incredible stamina. Or, now that he thought about it, she may have been using her Fragment to boost her recovery even more than he had initially assumed. He quietly walked outside, searching for a well or rain barrel to wash himself with. The smell of such vigorous training wasn't a pleasant one, and he would need to be at least somewhat presentable when they sat down at the high roller tables.

<I'm glad I don't have to threaten you to make you bathe anymore,> Sarge chuckled in Grant's mind. <Farm, moist body, and clogged-pore sweat was not the most pleasing scent. I'm made of *metal*, and it was getting to me.>

"In all fairness, my Mental Cultivation was *four* when we first met, if you remember correctly." Grant flicked his eyes to review his current levels. "I'm at eighty-seven now. The fact that I can hold a conversation about personal hygiene while sore and actively searching for threats probably has something to do with the overall changes you've seen in me."

<Oh, most definitely. Your mind alone has shown improvement of almost twenty-two times over. Just imagine what it will be like when you are in the hundreds… the thousands?> Sarge let that concept sink in for a moment. <If I had any money, I'd bet that at that point, you might even be able to feed yourself without making a mess!>

"Such a *sharp* wit." Grant rolled his eyes as he finally tracked down a well in the back corner of the lot and started washing. He didn't dwell too long on the 'stinky' comment, as he knew the sword spirit was only giving him a hard time. However, the other point was needling him. "In a real way, Sarge... what kind of improvements can I expect when my mental cultivation finally gets into the hundreds?"

<It's... hard to say.> Sarge let his humor drift away, replaced by a strange trepidation. Grant recognized that this might be an opportunity to learn something important ahead of actually needing to experience it. <It should go without saying that your ability to remember things, and your speed of thought will increase, along with your maximum mana and mana regeneration levels. It *should*, but I know you were at a mental cultivation of *four* not long ago.>

"Yes, yes, you are the sword of hilarity." Grant nudged the conversation along.

<The fact is, everyone's mind is different. I have heard that people can do wondrous things with a higher mental cultivation level, but I don't think that's in the cards for you. You're a fighter, a warrior, and that means you will probably just get a flat improvement in those skills.>

"That would at least make sense." Grant had moved on to scrubbing his armor, trying to get the sweat stains out of the leather clasps that held it together. "I just didn't know if there was anything special to look forward to."

<Don't be in a rush to put too much on your plate, Grant. There can also be downsides. It's usually in the changing of cultivation ranks that people's methods will deviate, and something goes terribly wrong. Having sudden, drastic shifts to your mind? Let's just say that it's always good to make sure that change is *careful*.> Sarge let out a long sigh. <Now, don't let this eat up too much of your thoughts. You already have quite a full list of things to do. Besides, you have a different goal right now. Remember: civilize the mind, but make savage the body.>

"That... that's something I can do."

CHAPTER TWENTY-FOUR

After they both had some rest, Suki and Grant got serious about practicing a few select card games. Grant was particularly fond of the strange game 'twenty-one'. It was simple, and he didn't have to worry about whether the other player was being honest or not.

Poker, the one he was told was a 'gentleman's game', was probably his least favorite. He couldn't *believe* it when Suki told him that a player could outright *lie* about the cards they were holding. Not only that, but there was no standard bet! If someone felt like dropping a ridiculously high number of coins on the table, they could just lie! Grant had no dependable way to determine if they were telling the truth or not. Suki, on the other hand, had no problems.

"It's not hard. The only advantage I have is that I've been training since birth to read the intentions of others, no matter how hard they try to hide them." Suki gathered up the large pile of wood chips they were using to mimic bets from the center of the table. Grant looked at her askance, and she shrugged. "What? It's common training that all nobles receive from the cradle. Any person meant to lead should know if people are lying to them."

"I suppose that... makes sense," he stated slowly, "I just think that people in charge shouldn't equate politics to gambling. It might send the wrong idea."

"They have almost the exact same skill sets." Suki pointed at the pile of cards on the worktable between them. "There is something we both want. One of us is in the better position to obtain it, but neither of us knows who it is. So, you posture and bluff your way into winning, even if you *know* you have the winning hand."

"But... it's lying your way into the winner's spot." Grant squirmed a little in his seat. "I don't like *not* telling the truth. A warrior should be honorable, and people will follow them naturally."

"Don't think of it like that." Suki stood up and swung side to side to limber up. "Imagine two fighters in a duel. When you make a feint, the person you are fighting reacts to that action, and you use the opening to strike."

Grant nodded, agreeing with her argument so far, so she drove on, "If they try a feint, and you see through it, often it allows you an opening that you can take advantage of. That's what it's like when you *know* you have the better hand. You can crush them by playing along properly."

"Okay, but how do you *know* you have the better hand?" Grant pointed at the cards she had just picked up. "There are all kinds of combinations that can trump one another."

"Well, there is one way to win for certain every time." Suki paused in her shuffling to flick a card out of her sleeve. "You cheat."

"You wouldn't!" Grant stood up, pointing his finger at the evidence of her double-dealing. "Have you been cheating this whole time? We're supposed to be practicing, and you just ruined it by tricking me instead of training me how to play correctly!"

"Do you really think the people you are going to have to

play against won't do *exactly* the same thing?" Suki made the card disappear with just a simple bending of a finger. "Part of your training should include learning how to spot a person that is cheating. They take that oddly seriously here, so you have to make sure you only call them out on cheating when the timing is right. Don't do it too soon; try to let the best cheaters clear out some of the other players first, *then* you pounce!"

The cards scattered as she punched down on the table for emphasis. Grant stood, scooting the cards back toward her half of the table. "I think I'm done practicing with you right now. For someone that lectures me on being a leader, you sure seem ready to do all sorts of… tricky things. Just, we need to go. The sun is starting to rise."

Suki seemed taken aback by Grant's aversion to cheating, so they walked in silence as she tried to come up with something to say. The two of them were soon weaving in and out of sprawling streets and narrow alleys to throw off any possible pursuit. Once again, the obvious devastation of seeing a District based on a single product was hard to witness. There were practically *hollow* people around almost every corner, and nearly every business except large casinos were either abandoned or on their last legs.

"I don't know if these people can make it much longer." Grant had paused to hand out some of the produce from the crate in his pack to a group of emaciated children with sunken cheeks and cracked lips. "They look close to death."

<This place is practically a war zone,> Sarge chimed in, adding his personal experience to the mix. <If you don't end the reign of this mad jester, none of these people will see the end of next month. They'll riot before then and be wiped out by the clown's Vassals.>

"What was that?" Suki was passing out some of her gross health food bars. Even the starving children seemed to look at them like they were unsure if they should eat them or not, leaving Grant feeling rather vindicated. "Did you say something?"

"Not really. We need to get going." Grant passed out a few more vegetables that looked like they were close to going bad. He was down to less than half of the food he had won in the jackpot. Most of what remained was miscellaneous root vegetables and a few pieces of a spiny fruit which Suki had told him would last for a long time. "The market might be closed before we get there, and we won't get a chance to practice."

Back on the road, the two silently agreed to pick up the pace. Instead of weaving through the abandoned buildings, they stayed on the main road and kept up a steady jog. Handing out the food to the kids had noticeably lightened Grant's pack, enough that he noticed the difference even with his enhanced cultivation numbers.

They made it to the market indicated on their map with roughly an hour to spare, and Grant was less than impressed. Sure, hints of its former glory could be seen under the dirt and grime that covered everything in the District. But now, instead of stalls and carts, permanent pagoda-like structures had been spread in concentric circles around the large fountain that was spewing dirty water in the center of the square.

"What do you think that is?" He gestured to the lumpy shape in the center of the fountain. It was coated too thickly in some kind of scum to identify what it really was. "Some kind of… cow?"

"No, I think it used to be a statue of the Dokeshi's father." Suki squinted at the plaque at the base as they approached, but it was filthy to the point of becoming unreadable. She was clearly unwilling to wipe away the dirt in order to read it. "Maybe his grandfather? I can't even imagine letting an image of my father deteriorate so far."

"Yeah, I remember." Grant's soft chuckle earned him a sharp glare, but he waved her off. "Let's split up, but keep each other in sight. After we practice some games, we meet back up right here when they start to close down. Hopefully, we can add to what we already have, and make it to the gate opening with plenty of time to spare."

He went straight for a meat vendor that seemed to be using twenty-one to determine what his customers won, and Suki drifted over to a dry goods vendor that already had three people sitting at a small table with piles of chips in front of them.

"That's right, good sir!" The man in front of Grant wore a spotless white apron over surprisingly nice clothing. He was one of the first people Grant had seen who didn't look like he had missed more than a few meals. "Mighty Mike's Majestic Meats—we beat the meat of all our competition! Step right up and let us dazzle you with the size and quality of our fine fares!"

Grant didn't know what to say, so he just walked up and placed a Day coin on the counter. He was eyeing a particularly tasty-looking piece of sausage that looked fat and juicy as it sizzled on the hot grill. It was making his mouth water, and he couldn't even remember the last time he had seen such a delicious-looking tube of beef.

"The game is twenty-one. A Day coin is only one chip, though you need at least two to play." The vendor waved to the dealer standing behind a small round table covered in a white tablecloth. "Every ten chips are worth one item of your choice. That's right, you manage your own magnificent meat at Mighty Mike's!"

"How many chips do you want to start with, sir?" The dealer was a much younger, smaller version of the vendor, leading Grant to easily guess it was his son. "You need at least one more Day to play at all."

"Here, take it." Grant was more than a little distracted by the display of wonderfully prepared flesh laid out before him. He handed over a stack of nine more Day coins, drastically reducing the amount in his coin pouch. "I really want that sausage."

"I understand, sir. Here are your chips." The dealer scooted over five chips and made the money disappear with a flourish. He then shuffled the deck of cards with a practiced motion and laid out four cards, two in front of each of them.

"Wait… you didn't give me-"

"Please place your bets!" The vendor hurriedly tapped the table. Grant had no idea what to do in this situation, but he was still aware enough to play it safe. He laid out a single chip, and the dealer flipped over one card in each pile. Grant could see a ten on the top card, and carefully lifted the corner to see what the bottom card was. Another ten.

"Hit or stay?" The dealer was holding up the deck, ready to flick another card on the pile. Grant waved his hand to signify he didn't want another card. The dealer was showing a five, and flipped his other card over to show a nine. "Dealer hits."

The next card was an eight. "Dealer busts. Congratulations, sir."

Four more hands went in a similar fashion, and soon Grant had a pile of chips next to his elbow. He began to feel good about his chances, and he grew comfortable betting taller stacks of the small clay disks. A small crowd started to gather, and eventually a gloved hand grasped his shoulder.

"Grant, what are you doing?" Suki was eyeing the group clustered around the pagoda. "You do realize you are making a scene, right?"

"I'm just practicing, like we planned." Grant motioned toward the stack of over fifty chips precariously balanced on the edge of the small table. "I think I'm doing pretty good!"

"If you're doing well, maybe you should cash in and we should go *somewhere else*?" Suki's eyes flickered around the crowd of people. "There are plenty of other places for you to practice."

"Okay. Just one more hand." The gleam in his eye was almost feverish. He still wanted the meat, but winning so many chips was giving him a thrill a good sausage just couldn't. "I have a feeling about this next one."

"Sir, please place your bet." The dealer interrupted their conversation, and Grant scooted over half of his pile to the center of the table. "Very well; thank you sir." He flipped the cards over, and Grant had a ten on top. The dealer had a six. After checking his other card, it was also a ten.

"I want a split." Grant turned over his hidden ten, and slid the other half of his stack over to cover the additional hand. "I'm feeling lucky!"

"As you wish." The dealer quickly dealt another two cards, one next to each of Grant's tens. One had a six, and the other a nine. "Would you like another card?"

"One card on this hand, please." Grant indicated the hand with sixteen. "I'll stay with the other one."

"Very well." The dealer placed down another card, this one a ten. "Ah, a bust. So sorry sir." The pile of chips was swept away, leaving Grant with the hand showing nineteen. Grant swallowed as the dealer flipped over his second card, showing a ten. "Dealer hits."

The next card was a five, giving the dealer a perfect twenty-one. "Dealer wins."

Just like that, Grant went from top of the world to rock bottom. He gazed longingly at the meat sizzling only a few feet away from him. The speed of the change in fortunes had literally made him dizzy. Suki grabbed his arm and led him away, heading for the dry goods vendor she had approached earlier. "Come on, let's go somewhere else. I could have told you that was going to happen. The dealer kept picking cards from the bottom of the deck."

"*What*?" Grant stopped in his tracks and turned to fiercely glare back at the pagoda where the sign with Mighty Mike's Majestic Meats was hanging. "He was *cheating* me?"

"Of course he was. Frankly, it's a good lesson, since it only cost you money and not your ability to go deeper into the District. The dealer wanted you to get overconfident." Suki stopped a few feet away from a table where a handful of people were playing poker. "That way, when you lost everything, you would blame yourself instead of taking a closer look at the way he was dealing cards."

She nodded toward the poker game, firmly ignoring his crestfallen stare. "Now I want you to learn. Just stand and *watch* for a minute. Pay attention to how they play, how they each work the table. I need to make up for the Time you lost, and we could really use the grand prize the winner gets."

Grant finally noticed the railing of this pagoda was draped with signs displaying the various items players could win. The first-place prize was a large bag of rice, an even larger bag of flour, and a small sack of salt. Somehow, he knew that Suki was going to win. Her arched eyebrow and Sarge's light chuckling confirmed exactly *who* would be carrying the bulky bags around as punishment.

CHAPTER TWENTY-FIVE

The first few rounds of the poker game went to a man with a thin pencil mustache. He always seemed to have cards just *barely* good enough to win, and his bets and grin both started to grow larger as time went on. Grant waited quietly on the sidelines, watching as Suki steadily lost chips. He was getting concerned that she would lose everything, but the corner of her mouth occasionally twitched upward into a knowing smile when none of the other players were watching.

<She's got him right where she wants him.> Sarge let out a low whistle in Grant's head, which always made him cringe. <Any moment now, she's gonna start clearing the table.>

"You're sure about that, Sarge?" Grant grabbed the hilt of February Twenty Nine as he leaned against the railing of the pagoda. He shifted from foot to foot nervously as another Day went to the table favorite. "It looks like she's going to be out in another two or three hands."

<Just watch.> Sarge waited for the dealer to start gathering the cards to shuffle again, then highlighted the mustachioed man's hands a deep orange, leaving a trail of light as the man moved. <There. Did you see that?>

"I see it!" Specifically, Grant had watched the man palm a card from the last hand instead of passing it to the dealer to be reshuffled. "So that's what cheating looks like?!"

<I'm pretty sure he's got two or three cards already saved up his sleeves from earlier hands.> Sarge was practically buzzing in excitement. <Yep, here we go. Suki is about to come out on top.>

Grant wasn't sure what he was talking about, considering she had the least amount of chips at the table. There were four other players—not counting the cheater—and although they barely had more than she did, Suki was in last place. Just as the dealer leaned forward to start passing out cards, she stood slightly and placed her hand up in a stopping motion.

"Excuse me sir, but it looks like the deck is a little *thinner* than it should be." Suki was talking loud enough to ensure everyone in the small observing crowd could hear her. "Would you be so kind as to count them quickly to ensure we have the full amount?"

The whispers about whether or not she was being a sore loser quickly swept through the spectators, but the dealer only raised a questioning eyebrow before deftly counting out the cards on the table. Grant carefully watched the man with the mustache, and he could swear a thick bead of sweat was running down from his temple.

"...Forty-six, seven, eight, and nine. See? There are a full fifty-two-" The dealer did a grand double-take down at the cards. "Wait, what?"

His surprise was clearly forced, as was his anger. A poor actor, but certainly not about to let himself take the fall. The dealer barely paused for a breath before shouting for the uniformed members of House Tuesday stationed in the market. "Guards! We have another one!"

The cheater didn't wait for the guards to come over and start searching sleeves. He jumped up and took off sprinting, leaping over the railing and disappearing into the deepening shadows, a bevy of furious men in the uniform of House Tuesday soon in hot pursuit.

"I must *apologize* for this disruption, ladies and gentlemen." The woman who must have been the owner of the pagoda emerged from behind the counter where the boxes for the winners were displayed. She looked like she could have been the sister to the meat vendor at the pagoda that had swindled Grant. He couldn't help but wonder if all the vendors in this market were from the same family. "To make sincere amends, I shall be increasing the prizes, as well as adding the cash reward to the first and second place contestants."

She sent a sweet smile to the dealer, who appeared more than a little worried. "After all, it's our responsibility to catch any cheaters before they become a problem, and it was *our* dealer that didn't notice the smaller deck."

<I would hate to be that guy right now. Look, these are terror lines. Oh, look at that! Reading an opponent counts as training for your sword, so I can do this without a problem!> Sarge highlighted several points on the dealer's face for a split second, so Grant could see them clearly. <I bet he'll be begging on the streets by this time tomorrow, if my guess is correct. Pairing up with such a terrible card player was a bad idea.>

The Lord inspected the dealer more closely as Sarge took a few moments to point out tiny facial expressions. The man did seem to be sweating a lot, considering the cool breeze of the evening air. "That's so strange to me… why would he try to cheat in the same game that he was dealing?"

<There's no way a professional dealer in *this* District wouldn't know he had a short deck. They practically sleep with a deck of cards in their hands.> The sword spirit sighed and sent along a mental shrug. <As for *why*, sometimes there's no telling why some people do the things they do. But, this time it's pretty obvious. He needs more food than what his job allows him to afford, so he schemed with the other man to win first prize. Like I said, I wouldn't want to be him.>

After things had settled down and the cheater's pile of chips were evenly distributed among the remaining players, the game quickly resumed. The next ten hands went by in a blur, the dealer speeding the rounds up to the point that it seemed the players barely had time to place their bets. Just as Sarge had predicted, Suki completely turned the tables on the other players.

Eventually, it was down to just two people—Suki, and a man so old and hunched that he needed a cane to walk. The old man was eyeballing her much larger pile of chips, and the sweet young lady picked up on his concern.

"It's getting late, and I've somewhere I need to be." She shoved her pile of chips into the center of the table while the dealer shuffled his cards. "How about we just do 'winner take all'? Second place still earns a profit, since that bad man had to run off. It's a win-win for both of us."

After a few seconds of deliberation, the old man proffered a cracked smile and a vigorous nod of agreement. The dealer laid out all the cards face-up, revealing Suki's defeat of the old man's two-pair with a straight. Even though she held her composure, it was obvious she was fighting down a smile. This was a woman that liked winning.

"The generous newcomer wins first prize!" The owner of the place herself approached the table with a pair of small purses, playing to the crowd with the voice of a practiced orator. "Make sure to return tomorrow for another chance at great prizes!"

Grant and Suki quickly gathered their winnings and made their way toward the exit. Their initial concerns of being followed proved to be simple paranoia after they took a twisting path through the surrounding streets and couldn't detect anyone following them. The excitement of the man who had been caught cheating must have helped to keep any potential thieves from trying their luck, considering the increased presence of the guards hunting for the escaped card shark.

"You have to tell me how you did it." Grant had been trying

to hold in his curiosity ever since they had left the marketplace. "How did you know you would win the last hand?"

"Sometimes, you just have to let the cards fall where they may." Suki gave him a knowing smile. "And other times, you just have to trust your luck."

"Well, I need to figure out how to do that." Grant scratched his chin, where a light beard was trying to come in. "Before that, I need to remember which hands beat the others. It's too much for me to remember all at once."

<No, it isn't. You just haven't applied yourself to it like you have other things, like fighting.> Grant tried to ignore the rude sword spirit, so the sarcasm in Sarge's voice thickened. <You just find it boring and don't want to try. You *do* understand that I know you better than you know yourself, yes?>

"I've got a plan to change that, Sarge." The pair finally stopped at the edge of a narrow street, hesitating under the bright light of the rising moon. They also just so happened to find themselves next to the line forming to enter the casino. Suki pulled a card from her pack and handed it to Grant. "This is a card that shows which hands are the strongest. I wrote this up for you, and no matter what anyone else says, you are allowed to have them at the table. Most people don't bother with them, since they're usually only given to children when they're first learning how to play the game."

"Technically I'm only five years old, so I'll just call it good." Grant was extremely thankful for the card, although his non sequitur and cheerful attitude in obtaining it made Suki roll her eyes. "Just to be sure, I can just look at this while I play, and it'll let me know if I've got good cards or not? If people tell me their cards are better, this proves if they're lying?"

"Not exactly." Suki took his hand and placed a thick leather bracer along his wrist. It looked like the ones Grant had previously seen archers use to protect themselves from the bowstring slapping against their forearm. "From now on, never take this off."

"Why?" Grant tried adjusting the straps to get it to fit better, but no matter how he tugged it, the leather was rough and lumpy against his skin. "I don't use a bow, and this thing is uncomfortable."

"Because you need it if you are going to win." Suki slapped his hand away. "Let me see the card I gave you."

Grant handed it back to her and was shocked to watch her sliding it into the hidden slit in the edge of the bracer that ran along his forearm. "There you go. Now you can check it without everyone knowing how inexperienced you are. Later, I'll show you some sleight of hand to help you out of a tight spot."

"But… that would be cheating." Grant practiced slipping the card out of the hidden pocket while he talked. "I don't want to be a cheat. I'd rather take my chances by cutting my way through."

Suki opened her mouth to argue, but they were distracted by a commotion farther up the street. The people waiting in line by torchlight were all pointing at something farther up the road, just out of eyesight.

<Back in the shadows, *now*!> Sarge's shout thundered through Grant's mind, and he quickly jumped to obey. <Hurry, crouch behind those piles of garbage!>

Suki let loose a quiet squawk when Grant pulled her back against the nearest building, but quickly went silent as the sound of stomping boots echoed down the dark streets. They watched, wide-eyed, as a double-line of over forty guards came stomping into view, headed to the entrance of the casino they needed to enter. Bringing up the rear was another of Dokeshi March's Vassals, and the House Saturday assassin they had seen before. The light of the torches glinted off the dangerous censer that the professional killer kept swinging at her side.

"How could they have possibly found out where we were trying to go?" Suki breathed soft, tickling words into Grant's ear, and he tried to pull away, but she gripped his arms and held him tight. "Don't run! We're just going to need to change tactics and try again at another entrance tomorrow. Whatever you do, don't draw their attention. One glance this direction, and we're caught."

Unable to shake her off in time, Grant failed to block the enormous sneeze—which any father of four would have been proud of—from exploding out of his mouth.

CHAPTER TWENTY-SIX

The thunderous exhalation echoed down the alley, forcing both him and Suki to shift into near-panic mode. They huddled together against the filthy wall in the dark alley, waiting for someone to turn and look for the source of the noise. Yet, it didn't happen. The marching of all the soldiers was apparently plenty loud enough to drown out the sound of Grant's ill-timed nasal expulsion, and the squad continued past them without issue.

"Well. Good thing no one heard that." Suki glared at his relieved tone, making grasping motions at his chest as though she were about to reach in and tear out his heart. Unwilling to test her self-control, Grant stepped to the side and out of range, "What? It wasn't like I did it on purpose; you were literally holding my hands to my sides!"

"Just… control yourself?" Suki turned away and started searching for a way to climb up onto the roof of the building they had been leaning against. "We need to get higher, to see what these people are up to. If they go into the casino, we might have a major issue. If they're just passing by…"

"Let's be realistic. We both know they're looking for us."

Grant started piling up a bunch of loose crates. "Why else would they be here? Help me stack these so we can get up to a good vantage point."

Suki quickly tossed him several boxes and crates from further down the alley, since she couldn't find any easier way to the roof. "If they're going into the casino, it means we need to find a different entrance. There's no way we can sneak around with all those people looking for us."

Grant stopped speaking and focused on piling boxes even faster. The thought of having to walk dozens of miles just to get inside a stupidly *massive* casino was incredibly unwelcome. He managed to finish the precarious stack after only a half-minute, just tall enough for them to reach the roof.

"You first." Grant motioned for Suki to get moving. "I'm heavier, and at least one of us needs to make it to the roof. I might bring the whole thing down."

"That's for sure." Suki's eyes ran up and down his body, obviously weighing him with her mind. "That armor by itself weighs as much as I do."

Grant wasn't sure if she was calling him strong or taunting him somehow. Frankly, he didn't know how to handle their relationship. He wasn't used to companionship of any kind, and suddenly he had a potentially-romantic partner with him at all times. That alone was enough to throw him for a loop. He inspected himself, still amazed to see his lean, muscular form instead of the glorious mass he had aspired to his entire life.

"Was that really less than three months ago?" he muttered softly as his mind whirled. Before he could sink too deeply into introspection, Suki was already disappearing onto the roof and whispering for him to hurry up.

"Hey, quit looking at your… oddly satisfying abs, and get up here!" Suki hissed sharply down at Grant, her head peeking over the edge of the rusting gutters for a quick second.

<Ha! She caught you!> Grant blushed furiously at both reprimands, even as his emotional turmoil doubled. <Oh, man, are you in trouble.>

"It isn't *that* weird," Grant mumbled under his breath, trying to hide the grin that was creeping across his face. Sarge started to reply but apparently thought better of it, merely chuckling instead. The young man decided to ignore the sword spirit as he glanced down both sides of the alley he was in. Since they wouldn't be needing the crates after he reached the roof, he had the strangest feeling that he should do something other than climb.

With a short jog, he built up speed and launched himself against the wall, using the momentum to propel himself into a flip and landing halfway up the stack. Another sharp jump brought him the rest of the way up, and he sprang for the roof as the crates collapsed beneath him. Instead of an easy climb to the top, he caught the edge with one hand and dangled for a moment.

As he watched the impromptu tower collapse and shatter into mulch beneath him, he twisted to bring both hands to the edge and leveraged himself up onto the rooftop with a straight-arm pull-up. His smile reappeared as he looked to Suki for a commendation, but he rapidly withered under her scowl. "Could you *possibly* make any more noise? That was *way* worse than the sneeze."

"Oops, I guess?" Grant was embarrassed for a reason he couldn't explain, even beyond having made noise.

"Just be more careful? Please?" She turned and pointed out a few weak spots in the roof tiles, then eased her way up to the peak of the building. "Watch your footing. This whole District is more rot than wood."

Stepping carefully, Grant crept along to crouch next to her. After making sure he wasn't about to fall through the creaking shingles, he peeked over the edge to see the Dokeshi's Vassal and House Saturday Wielder talking to the gate guards. A large clock hung over the doorway, and it showed that less than thirty minutes remained until the entrance would open. The rest of the troops were methodically inspecting the line of people waiting to get into the casino, forcing them to drop hoods and hats alike in order to get a better look at who was trying to gain entry.

"It looks like they're just looking for us, not actually going inside." Grant squinted in an effort to get a better look at the Vassal and assassin, but they were too far away for him to see much of anything. "Why is that? Do you think they can't touch us once we get inside? Wait… what House controls these casinos?"

"I'm… uncertain, but usually House Thursday has a hand in anything that takes a large investment. I can't think of a project that would require more money than constructing a single building that cuts off a huge chunk of a District. That aside, even *if* we are fine once we get in there, how do we make it past all those guards when they're checking everyone?" Suki scooted to the right to get a better angle. "There are too many for us to sneak past."

"How many is too many?" From his angle, Grant could only see a few guards searching everyone. Since he made a larger silhouette, he was forced to crouch lower than Suki. Even in the dark, his broad shoulders might be noticed against the backdrop of stars. "Can you get a good count?"

"Give me a *second*." Suki's voice was strained, and he looked over to see that her foot was stuck between a couple of loose shingles. "This part of the roof is super unstable."

"Yeah, I see that. Do you need some help over there?"

"No, you're too heavy with all that gear and our supplies. You might bring the house down around us." Suki carefully worked her shoe free, then edged her way higher for a better look. "I see at least fifty, not counting the Vassal and Wielder. There's probably triple that number of people waiting to go inside when the door opens."

She crouched back down and turned to face Grant. "What we need is a distraction. Something that will make them abandon the search so we can blend in with the crowd."

"Where are we going to find a distraction big enough to pull *all* those guards away?" Grant motioned to the barren rooftop they were huddled on. “We’re sorely lacking random people that would put their life on the line for us.”

Suki’s eyes drifted to the crumbling chimney at the center of the roof. Without saying anything, she carefully picked her way over to the stack of red brick and mortar. It took a moment, but she was able to pry loose a few bricks where the chimney met the roofline.

<If she pulls too many of those bricks out, that chimney is going to collapse onto the roof and bring this whole building down with it,> Sarge warned Grant as soon as he realized what she was doing.

“Are you trying to knock that over?” Grant started cautiously sliding over to her, making sure to spread his weight out as much as possible. “I don’t want to be up here if that happens.”

“I know this may sound crazy, but I think that’s exactly what we are going to do. If we can get a bunch of them inside, then drop the top half of the chimney onto the roof, I think the whole building will collapse with them inside.” Suki hefted a brick, testing its weight, then peeked over the edge to make sure the situation hadn’t changed. “Any of them not trapped inside will rush in to save the ones we manage to take down.”

“How are we supposed to drop the chimney on them without ending up in the collapse ourselves?” Grant tested the sturdiness by roughly stabbing the rotting wood where it touched brick. “This will come down too fast for us to jump over to the next building, and I have no idea how any construction works. I can’t help with this.”

Suki bit her lower lip in thought. “It’s definitely a problem…”

<What about your lightning spell?> Sarge’s interruption was sudden enough that Grant almost jumped in surprise. <Doesn’t the training version provide a speed boost?> He pulled up the information to check.

. . .

Elemental Spell: Thundering Step

Prerequisites: 65 Mind. Two feet. Metal weapon.

Active Mode: Create a static field in a five-foot radius around you that damages others when they move through the area. Doesn't move from the point it was set. Lasts five seconds.

Mana cost: 10 per use.

Damage (Self): 0% Mental cultivation.

Damage (Other): 100% Mental cultivation per second.

Training Mode: Increase movement speed by 50% while out of combat. Combat is defined as not dealing or taking damage from an opponent for five seconds.

Mana cost: 10% per second. Mana regen halted while active.

"I've got an idea, Suki." Grant's hand drifted to grasp the hilt of his sword, and he slowly drew it, watching as the moonlight glinted off the edge. "It's been a while since I brought down the house with thunderous applause."

"What?" Suki rolled her eyes at his cheesy statement, but Grant's grin only widened as he stared at the Vassals in the distance. "Why are you so *strange*?"

"My best friend for more than a decade was a cow."

CHAPTER TWENTY-SEVEN

After going back and forth on their respective responsibilities, the two of them settled on a plan. Suki took a running leap over to the nearest building to get into position, and Grant pulled free several more bricks in a notch around the section of the chimney that they wanted to fall. He then wrapped a section of rope around it and tied the other end around his waist.

Grant made sure to double-check his work, then moved to the edge of the roof. The rope wasn't long enough for it to reach much farther than that, so he would just have to make do. After lining up several bricks along the peak of the roof, he crouched down to wait. He caught a flash of movement a few buildings away and gripped the hilt of February Twenty Nine in excitement.

This was going to be fun.

Suki was only one rooftop away from the soldiers when she threw the first brick. It smashed into the helmet of a cultivator digging through the bag of an old man, and the impact caused the armored thug to stumble over the clothes he had thrown in the dirt.

The second, third, and fourth bricks were thrown in rapid

succession, the moonlit flash of Suki's gauntleted hands instantly giving her position away. The soldiers started pointing and shouting, with only a few seeking cover. It was a testament to their training that the majority sprinted through the city streets to surround her location.

Considering they were focused on the wrong building for the rest of the plan, it was now Grant's turn to show off his throwing arm. The first brick he tossed went sailing past the guard he was aiming for, and the sound of it shattering against the invisible barrier was accompanied by a flash of azure light from the defenses. The light show caused the remaining guards to duck, and Grant's second projectile flew true.

The House Saturday Wielder seemed more stunned than injured as the brick hit her and just *stopped*. The sheer audacity of someone attacking her with a mundane weapon—a brick—was enough to incite a momentary wave of disbelief, followed by a glare of pure murder that Grant swore he could feel from his rooftop over sixty yards away.

<It's more like seventy yards from where you are to the entrance, and a rather impressive toss. We should consider getting you some throwable weapons.> Sarge's observation caused Grant to blink in surprise. <You still underestimate your new strength. Suki had to use her gauntlets to help with throwing the bricks that far. It isn't necessary for you to use your Wielded Weapon to assist you; your cultivation alone is more than enough to manage such a simple attack.>

Grant didn't have time to answer. The House Saturday assassin was already moving his direction, the vast remainder of the guards following in her wake. He was glad that either the system didn't record the ineffective ambush as the start of combat, or a Vassal wasn't clowning around in the area. It must have been the same for Suki, because she didn't pause when the remaining guards and their leader started toward her. She was already leading them north, away from the rooftop he was hiding on.

The sound of the warped, rotting door exploding from a

massive impact below forced him to focus back on the group coming for him. The Wielder from House Saturday must have used some kind of skill to cross the distance so fast, because the majority of the guards following her weren't even close to the entrance of the alley leading to his building.

<You're going to have to hold her off until they catch up.> Sarge's advice was always welcome, if somewhat obvious. <Remember, the whole plan revolves around getting as many of the guards trapped inside as possible. Whatever you do, don't breathe in that gas. I don't know what it does, but it certainly can't be good.>

"Thanks for that. I would have *never* guessed the obviously poisonous gas wielded by a Saturday would be bad for my-" Grant's sarcasm was cut off by the destruction of the roof only a few feet away. A golden ball spewing clouds of green vapor erupted from the rotting shingles, the light of the stars granting it an ethereal quality that was almost mesmerizing.

When the ball was jerked back down by the thin chain it was connected to, it brought with it a sizable chunk of the surface that Grant was standing on. He was forced to scramble backwards, his spine bouncing against the chimney sticking out of the roof. It teetered in place but luckily settled back when Grant sprang away. The distraction allowed the Saturday assassin to jump up onto the roof uncontested, causing Grant to miss his best opportunity to attack the dark-robed killer who had been hunting him across the District.

"In all my years of hunting a target, I don't think I've ever met one so foolish as to actually try to ambush me with something as ineffective as a *brick*." The assassin's voice was sweet and melodic, almost hypnotizingly beautiful. She was like a viper, dancing before it strikes. It was hard for Grant to tell, due to the lack of lighting, but the frail woman had likely been very beautiful when she was younger. "I should thank you, though. You made completing this contract much easier."

She whipped her weapon at his face, the weighted censer acting more like an extension of her arm than a regular ball and chain. As Grant deflected the attack with his sword, his vision was filled with the much-hated system screen.

Combat initiated—Duel

Action: *Defend With Weapon.*

Result: *Attack deflected. Paralysis poison inhaled. Movements slowed by 5%.*

Actions: *Please select one option from the following list.*

Attack: *Lethal, Non-lethal, Spell.*

Defend: *With Weapon, Without Weapon.*

Run: *Attempt Escape.*

Grant selected 'Attack, Lethal', then 'With Weapon' on the follow-up screen, darting forward in an effort to hit the woman. She swayed backward effortlessly, avoiding his strike and skirting the hole in the roof; her lighter frame allowed her to stand on the edge without the risk of the rotting wood crumbling from under her. Grant didn't have the same luck.

The roof started to disintegrate as soon as he got close. Scrambling backwards, he had to once again deflect the poisonous weapon as it snapped toward his face. The motion caused more of the wooden roof shingles to slide out from under his precarious footing, forcing him to roll backwards. The rope tied around his waist got tangled in his legs and prevented him from getting smoothly back to his feet.

Action: *Attack With Weapon.*

Result: *Attack dodged by opponent. Defend with weapon selected by default. Defense 90% successful. Paralysis poison inhaled. Movements now slowed by 15%.*

Actions: *Please select one option from the following list.*

Attack: *Lethal, Non-lethal, Spell.*

Defend: *With Weapon, Without Weapon.*

Run: *Attempt Escape.*

This time, Grant could feel the effects of the poison. When he tried to shift his position, it was almost like his limbs were underwater. His movements were still smooth and controlled, but they weren't anything like his normal speed.

"It's only a matter of time now." The Saturday mercenary was clearly more relaxed, now that her poison was doing its insidious work. "If you surrender now, I promise to bring you in with a minor reduction in the amount of pain and agony you would normally expect."

"Surrender?" Grant scoffed at her. "I'm just getting started! Haven't had a proper fight since we got to this District."

He risked letting his eyes sweep quickly over the guards who were finally making their way inside the building. "How about you just step aside? I'd rather not get in conflict with House Saturday, even if I've always dreamed of dropping a house on a witch."

<It's been five seconds since she attacked; now's your chance!> Grant used Sarge's shout to select 'Run' while activating the training mode of his lightning spell. The selection created a cascade of messages that threatened to block his vision.

#ERROR16

'Run with spell' is not a valid option.

#ERROR22

Run with spell action is *compatible with the system. Option added to system memory functions.*

#ERROR27

Hold up. This User is not allowed to add options to the system.

. . .

Grant stopped reading, not bothering to consider how his actions violated the Dokeshi's broken controls. Instead, he kept his focus on the pink-tinted lightning dancing across his body, where it settled around his feet.

"Stop!" The shout of the woman held an aura of command that almost stilled his feet, but it passed in the same instant. He sprinted toward the edge of the roof, the spell boosting him enough that she had no chance to catch his escaping form. The rope trailing behind him went taut, and he jumped for the nearest roof with all the power his legs could muster. It wasn't enough.

"*Gwar-agh*!" The shout that escaped Grant's lips was more of a croak, forced out of his chest when the rope slammed him to a stop. He swung down sharply, his body pretending to be a wrecking ball by slamming against the side of the building. He felt something in his hip quietly **pop** as the rope dug into his waist, a sharp pain suddenly making it even harder to breathe.

The face of the assassin peeked over the edge just as he looked up, her grin visible even in the dim light of the stars. She opened her mouth to taunt him, but the rope shuddered, and Grant started to slowly slide. She fired a wordless shout back toward the guards clambering onto the roof behind her, but it was too late.

<Well, I'll be a rusty nail! I think it's about to go!> There was another shudder, and the chimney fell. Unfortunately for Grant, the chimney didn't collapse. It held together, and the rope started dragging him upward as the heavy stack of bricks plunged through the rotting wood of the abandoned structure. He was towed along right behind it, slamming his already injured hip against the edge of the roofline. <Cut the rope! What are you, a fool farm boy or a Foundation Cultivator?>

By pure reflex of listening to Sarge, Grant's sword flashed out of its sheath and sliced through the rough hemp strands. His training saved him again, as he forced himself to position his body for a proper landing automatically. The impact with the ground was pure agony, his Bodily Awareness Skill making an already debilitating injury almost unmanageable. The only silver lining was that he didn't break anything else. Not inside himself, at least.

The shouts and screams of the people inside the building as it collapsed around them like a house of cards brought a momentary flash of guilt, but only for a second. They would have done much worse to him. A few moments after the rumbling of the destruction stopped, Suki's shadowed form poked out from the edge of the roof across from the alley where he was laying on the ground. "Hurry up and get over here!"

"I can't!" He tried to shout loud enough for her to hear him, but the pain made it hard for him to take a full breath. "I think I messed up my hip!"

<Concentrate. You need to meditate through the pain, or you will lose your chance to reduce the damage through your skill.> Grant weakly nodded at Sarge's command, trying to clear his mind enough to activate the ability. It just wasn't going to happen. The shouts of the second group, led by the Dokeshi's Vassal, were quickly growing louder. This was about to get much worse.

Congratulations! *Your new battle count moves from* [3 Wins / 1 Losses] *to* [4 Wins / 1 Losses]. *Remember, the lucky rise to the challenge!*

#ERROR92

Win was achieved while selection Run was active.

#ERROR34

Combatants not directly involved in duel were also defeated. Procedure violated.

<If you keep this up, the system is going to alert the closest Vassal. If it hasn't already, of course.>

"Drink this." Out of nowhere, Suki was standing over Grant, a potion held up to his lips. He had no idea how she had gotten over to him so fast, and it worried him to think that he perhaps wasn't fully aware of time passing. "You did a good job, but we don't have time for you to lay around."

Unable to argue about the definition of lying around, he quickly swallowed the gritty mixture. It must have been one of the lower-tier potions, but it was still powerful enough to shift his hip back into place with a sharp pop, causing his brain to fuzz out for an instant as the pain washed over him.

<You need to move, Grant.> Sarge's voice brought him back into focus. <If you don't get away from the rubble soon, you're going to have to fight the Dokeshi's Vassal, if the Saturday assassin doesn't pop out of that rubble shrieking like a pirate on a ghost ship first.>

"Okay, let's go." He struggled to regain his feet, fighting against the wave of pain that came with moving. "I don't think I can run yet, but I can walk. If I can't, I'll crawl."

"It'll have to be enough." Suki pulled him to standing without his weight managing to shift her a single inch, then led him through the twisting alleys in a roundabout way toward the gate. "The entrance will open in just a few minutes. We need to get in line before they take a headcount of who's going inside. Pretend we belong. They won't be looking right under their noses immediately after all of *that.*"

Grunting in agreement, all Grant could think was how happy he was that they were *finally* moving forward toward their goal once again.

One agonizing step at a time.

CHAPTER TWENTY-EIGHT

Actually getting inside the casino turned out to be very anticlimactic, even if Grant was utterly hollow inside from nerves. The gate guards were more focused on the commotion caused by the fallen building and their trapped compatriots than the downtrodden people trying their luck inside the casino. While they shuffled forward through the arched door, Sarge filled Grant in on the results of their trap.

<According to your cultivation levels, you defeated one Wielder and two Vassals in that trap.> Grant was about to make a pithy comment about his genius when Sarge stopped him. <Oh, and you killed another Vassal. The other guards must have just been regular cultivators, so you didn't get credit for them. Still, killing one and defeating four; that's pretty good for a single fight! You are getting very close to advancing to level twenty.>

"Never tell Suki that I killed some people. I think she was expecting them all to be able to survive a simple falling building. Anyone from February could have, after all." While Grant wasn't exactly distraught over killing one of the guards, he couldn't help but feel bad about being responsible for someone's death without even knowing what they looked like. There was no telling how many of the other guards had died, since they wouldn't show up in his cultivation system.

<A leader doesn't always get to know the faces of those who die because of his orders. A leader just does the next right thing.>

Grant quietly contemplated Sarge's assertion. "Is it really that simple? Just ignore the deaths of those that stand against me?"

<That's *not* what I said.> The venom in Sarge's voice made Grant freeze up. <Leaders determine the fates of thousands because they *must.* The weight of that responsibility shouldn't feel light. Duty is heavier than a mountain, and you'll be holding the entire world on your shoulders one day.>

Grant decided to meditate on that advice when he next had a free moment. For now, he decided to focus on the next phase of their plan. He leaned in close to speak into Suki's ear so he didn't have to shout over the background noise. "You head straight for the poker tables, and I'll go wherever there aren't a lot of people."

"I haven't forgotten." Suki looked Grant over, straightening out his cloak to better hide his rubble-dusted appearance. "You clearly didn't forget that we're supposed to look like poor and starving peasants, not proud warriors ready for battle. You're forgetting to do one thing, though."

Grant raised his eyebrow in confusion, so Suki sent a sharp punch toward his gut, which he managed to lightly slap away. "Hunch over, you lummox!"

Grant obeyed promptly, though he was proud that she hadn't managed to land even a sneak attack on him in several days. Following her advice was easy enough for him: he just pretended that he was back working under Randall. That thought in mind, he sunk in to make himself seem smaller, his slightly distracted and worried expression blending him in with the crowd in an instant. It was actually easier for him than for her, even despite their height differences.

Suki just didn't have the same life experiences to draw on. Even though she was hunched over, it was obvious to anyone looking that she wasn't the same as the Marchurians around them. The former leader of District February had an aura of *weight* about her, a presence that seemed to naturally pull people into her orbit.

As soon as they had made it through the entrance hall, the two separated. Grant slipped into a large group headed for a row of machines covered in spinning colors and chiming bells, blending in as he cast aside every trace of his former proud bearing.

<Don't try your luck with those. They're more like flashy traps meant to catch the unwary than actual ways to gamble.> Agreeing completely with Sarge's assessment, Grant shuffled off toward the back where there weren't as many patrons. He passed by the section containing the tables meant for dice and completely ignored the side rooms, where the clacking of bones being slammed on wooden tables meant that people were playing dominoes or mahjong.

Grant's interest was finally piqued by a small row of tables that were sitting nearly empty. As he approached, a woman shuffled furtively from a corner table, moving to a set of swinging doors in the rear. She stood to the side until a uniformed server walked out holding a tray of drinks. As the door swung back inwards, she darted through the opening. Instead of raising a commotion, the person working the table she had left silently watched her as she disappeared.

"What do you think, Sarge? Didn't that seem a little odd to you?" The presence of guards around the room was heavy, but the tables in the rear had only the dealers as security. "You would think that a place like this would have better safeguards."

<I don't know, kid. Don't forget, this place is the farthest from the center of the District, meaning it is going to have the lowest amount of Time changing hands. I'm not sure what that dealer might be up to in the first place.>

The fact that this was the poorest of the casinos simply

didn't add up in Grant's head. The place seemed plenty nice to him, with the heavy use of what *must* be utility spells. Flashing lights, chiming sounds, gilt, glitter, shine; it was all meant to dazzle the senses and befuddle the mind, and it was *all* magic to him. The thick deep red carpet on the floor muted the sound of people's footsteps, and lent the giant room a sense of closeness.

A cynical mind might have realized the color would make it easy to hide any spilt blood. <You know what? I think we should go check it out.>

Grant spotted Suki sitting at a crowded poker table, already building a bevy of admirers. "She should have enough proof of success to make it into the next area in no time, right? We need to catch up. Just because we might be able to follow along on her coat-tails, doesn't mean I don't want to try to make it on my own."

The tables along the back were much smaller than the ones elsewhere, with room for only two or three people to play against the dealer. Grant made sure to head toward the man who had watched the woman sneak through the doorway. She hadn't come back out, and Grant hadn't heard any commotion from her being discovered.

"Welcome, good sir!" The dealer spread a deck of cards across the table with a flourish, the red and white cards shining in the glow of the fancy lighting overhead. "This section is for people who wish to play a game of great skill and amazing focus. It is called Pai Gow Poker."

"Never heard of it. What kind of name is pie cow? I don't see any cows, nor pie, for that matter." Grant tapped his chin and glanced around to make sure. If there *was* pie involved, he wanted to make sure he knew exactly where it was.

"No, valued guest! Not 'pie cow', Pai *Gow*. It means 'double-hand'." The dealer quickly tossed down seven cards in front of each of them, splitting into one group of two and another group of five. "You have to beat the dealer with both hands to win, but he's required to beat you with both hands for you to lose."

“I’m not sure about this. I’d rather play a game with actual pie. Do you have any of those?” Grant watched as the dealer’s face turned a little red, either from anger or embarrassment, he wasn’t sure. He kept the smirk off his face; this sort of inane chatter really seemed to throw people off their game. It had even accidentally worked on Suki.

“No… sir, the casino doesn’t have any games that involve pie." Grant's face fell, as he was once again disappointed by the ridiculous way people named games. The dealer, recognizing that he was about to lose a potential customer, cleared his throat to get his attention. "But, to help you out, we can play a few rounds for practice before you have to start gambling your Time. How does that sound?"

"Hmmm…" Grant gave the dealer a once-over. The man reminded him of a person from District February. He was in very good shape, but the recent lack of food must have been hard on him. The uniform he was wearing appeared to be looser than it should be, and his cheeks looked a little sunken. The sandy blond hair and dark brown eyes still had plenty of luster to them, though, meaning the man wasn't to the point of starvation yet. "Okay, that sounds fair. Deal me in."

The dealer took his time, shuffling the cards skillfully while explaining the rules. To Grant, it was very much like the game Suki had called ‘seven card stud’—which had zero prize horses—but he had to divide the hand into one hand of two, and another of five. It wasn’t as complicated as he’d thought at first, and he quickly racked up several wins in a row.

“Well, sir, I think you are ready to start betting!” The dealer then laid out the next hand theatrically, and Grant set down a stack of Day coins. As if by magic, a waitress materialized next to Grant’s elbow as soon as the Time appeared.

“Would you like a drink, sir?” The scantily clad woman slid a drink with a tiny paper umbrella sticking out of the top toward him. “It’s complimentary.”

“Complimentary?” Grant grabbed it by reflex, and the woman walked away before he could hand it back.

<It means you don't have to pay for it.> Sarge's voice rumbled through his head, obviously upset at Grant. <Whatever you do, do *not* drink that. It will only end badly. A true warrior treats his body like a well-honed sword. Smashing a sword against the rocks isn't exactly recommended.>

"Sir, your hand?" The dealer forced Grant to focus back on the table. He set the drink down and quickly separated out what he thought would be his best option. The dealer flipped his own hand over, and it ended in a draw. Grant had won the five-card hand, but the two-card hand lost. "The Time stays on the table, and we go another round. Would you like to add any more coins?"

"No, I'm going to… let it ride?" Grant waved his hands to show his ambivalence. "No sense in betting more until I figure this game out."

<Considering the odds, you should be able to play this long enough for Suki to earn enough for your passage through to the next region.> Grant glanced over to where Suki was sitting. Somehow, the young Wielder had already increased the stack of Time in front of her to ridiculous heights. She hadn't glanced in his direction the whole time - he confirmed with Sarge—but he was sure she knew exactly where he was waiting for her. <Just bide your time, and she'll be by to collect you soon.>

"Would you like another drink?" Grant was dragged out of his internal conversation with Sarge by the waitress, who had once again appeared next to his elbow, as if by magic.

"No, thank you, though." Grant held up his still-full glass, showing her he was fine. "Just got this one."

He couldn't be sure, but it appeared as though she seemed a little worried that he hadn't finished the beverage. Sarge highlighted tiny facial movements as her eyes even flashed to the dealer, as if he was the reason she was worried. Before he could comment on it, the woman's reaction was covered up by a bright smile and she silently nodded before walking away. <Yeah, *that* should set in stone the fact that you shouldn't let a drop of that past your lips.>

"Sir, would you like to look at your hand?" While he was distracted, the dealer had once again laid out the cards on the table. Grant quickly separated his cards, knowing he would certainly lose the hand. There was a suspicious lack of high cards this time. Without thinking about it, he brought the glass sitting next to him up to his lips while waiting for the dealer to announce his loss.

<Stop! Don't drink that!> Grant merely faked taking a sip before setting the drink down again. <Oh, lad, you had even *me* certain you were downing that. Nice. I suspect there's more than just cheap alcohol in that glass, and I can even take an educated guess as to what happens to the people who play cards at these tables.>

"Dealer wins. Another hand, good sir?" The man was smiling now that he thought Grant had taken a drink, and it was pretty clear to Grant that this table was bad news. "I'm sure your luck is about to change."

"You know, I think it is too." Grant pretended to hesitate for a long moment, then dropped a heavy silver Month coin on the table, "Let's see how lucky I really am, shall we?"

"Indeed, good sir." The dealer's eyes lingered on Grant's coin purse, obviously trying to estimate how much he had remaining. Considering Suki had given him almost half of the Time she had with her, even the estimate was enough to nearly make the man drool. He snapped himself out of it and quickly shuffled and dealt the cards.

<Finally, some good cards!> Grant couldn't help but agree with Sarge. The two hands he could make were almost unbeatable. A high pair and a straight flush, almost as good as he could get. <You should have bet more.>

"Congratulations on the win, Valued Guest!" The dealer scooted another Month across to Grant, doubling the Time he had on the table. "Would you like to bet again?"

"Sure!" Grant just pushed the two Month coins back into the center. "It worked so well last time, why don't we try it again?"

<Are you sure about that?> The sword spirit was quiet for a second, and Grant felt a tingle in the back of his eyes, a feeling that he had learned to associate with Sarge reviewing his recent thoughts… then the sword started lightly vibrating as he began chuckling. <Oh, that *is* a good plan. I like it!>

The next several hands flew by, with Grant pretending to take sips from the drink. As the pile of Time in the center of the table grew, the grin of the dealer grew with it. The coin stacks weren't anything like the amounts Suki had built up, but Grant was pretty sure he could now qualify to pass into the next part of District March. The win streak he was on defied any form of belief, which clearly meant the dealer had to be cheating.

"Well, Mr. High Roller, congratulations!" The dealer gave a subtle nod to someone standing just out of sight behind Grant. "It looks like you have earned enough to journey into the Labyrinth! Just walk through those doors, and someone will be by to help you shortly."

Grant looked toward the doors the dealer had indicated, which were definitely *not* the doors that other high rollers had gone through. It was, however, the same exit which the other lady had disappeared through, where casino employees had been passing in and out with drinks and plates throughout the evening. Wanting to see things through, Grant stood, gathered his winnings, and headed toward the indicated doorway.

<Looks like you have made enough for them to think it's time to rob you.>

Grant pretended to feel woozy, so he slowed his steps. No one commented, so he assumed this was standard. "Why are they robbing people? Don't they already have access to all the Time they could want working here?"

<The Time here belongs to the casino, not the employees. They have probably been running this scam for a long time. The only question is, how many of them are involved?> Grant stole quick glances around at Sarge's words, noting several eyes following his progress. He purposely stumbled, trying his best to act like the drugged booze he'd pretended to drink was affecting

him. <You're a terrible actor. Luckily, I don't think it is going to matter.>

"Should I tell Suki what's going on?" Grant looked back to where she was still seated, chatting away with the other players. "She might wonder what I'm doing."

Before he could start to wobble over to her, two large men stepped up behind her. Apparently, Suki had also earned enough to go through to the next area. Since she had drawn so much attention, they led her to the doors where people were supposed to cross over. Her eyes flicked past Grant, and she gave him a crisp nod. He had no idea what that meant, but it didn't look like they were going to let Suki come over and collect Grant before leaving.

He had to find his own way.

Walking through the door he had been sent to, Grant entered a large kitchen area. The room wasn't as impressive as the massive cooking stations found in District January, but it was close. On the opposite side, Grant could see another set of doors that resembled the entrance to the casino they had used when entering the barrier. That must be the way out.

"Congratulations on making it this far." The speaker turned out to be a portly man wearing chef whites and gripping a very impressive cleaver. He was standing on the other side of the long preparation table that ran the full length of the room. Grant watched as he expertly chopped up a slab of meat, his thickly muscled arms straining against the sleeves of his uniform. He might have looked portly, but the weight hid an obviously well-muscled frame. "Now, all you have to do is pay the toll, and you can walk through the door to the Labyrinth."

<Yep, here comes the shake-down.> Sarge was obviously excited, pleased that Grant was going to fight. <Defeat this fool and catch up to Suki. There's no telling how long it'll take for you to get to the other side.>

"How much is the toll?" Grant silently agreed with the sword spirit, and his hand drifted casually to the hilt of his uchigatana. Other people were milling around the room, but none of them seemed to be paying the cook or Grant any attention.

"All of your Time. A small price to pay, for safe admittance to the Labyrinth." The cook's eyes flicked over to a pair of waiters standing off to the side. They were both holding serving trays, but the discs could easily double as shields if they wanted to fight. The three men would probably be enough to intimidate a drugged-up and scared person who had been expecting a simple walk to the next area, but they certainly weren't enough to stop Grant. "Just drop your coin purse on the counter, and be on your way."

"Nah." Grant turned to walk toward the door on the other side of the room, deciding to ignore the three. "I'll keep my Time. I'm going to need it if I want to make it through to the center ring."

"Your mistake." The cook's smile didn't reach his eyes. "Boys, handle this guy and dump the body outside. I'm sure there are some hungry rats roaming around."

Expecting this outcome, Grant swayed past the wildly swinging fist of the first waiter to charge him. The system didn't even activate, which indicated that these two didn't pose the slightest threat to him at all.

<Fight, seriously! That's the voice of complacency. Remember that a single grain of rice can cause an avalanche, even if the stupid system doesn't recognize it.>

Grant unsheathed his sword, using the motion to drive the hilt of his sword into the chin of the second waiter. The man's jaw slammed closed in a spray of blood and teeth, causing the first attacker to stumble back in fear. "I hope you remember, you asked for it."

"He's supposed to be drugged!" The cook was also wide-eyed, and he was brandishing his giant cleaver like it was a sword. "What's going on?"

"Do you actually get people to fall for your little operation?" Another quick swing of Grant's blade, and the flat smacked against the temple of the cowering waiter who remained on his feet. "If so, I recommend you stop robbing people. Things are going to be changing in this District soon, and people like you aren't going to be able to get away with this kind of thing anymore."

Instead of answering, the cook slammed his cleaver down on a large bag of flour. The ensuing explosion of white dust blinded Grant, and he was soon choking on the powdered grain.

<Behind you!> Grant reacted instantly, diving forward under the table. The sound of a large cleaver smashing into the metal table made his ears ring, and the system finally acknowledged that he was in a fight.

Combat initiated—Duel

Action: *Defend: Without Weapon.*

Result: *Enemy attack dodged. Stunned from auditory attack for 2 seconds.*

Actions: *Please select one option from the following list.*

Attack: *Lethal, Non-lethal, Spell.*

Defend: *With Weapon, Without Weapon.*

Run: *Attempt Escape.*

Selecting 'Attack: Spell,' caused a storm of lightning to erupt from his blade. Grant had only selected it because he wasn't sure where the insane cook was hiding, but the memory of an incident involving a flour mill and a torch suddenly flashed through his mind. Unfortunately, it was too late to stop the reaction.

The flour dust floating in the air was ignited by the lightning, causing an explosion that blew him straight into unconsciousness.

CHAPTER TWENTY-NINE

The pain in his chest was the first thing that Grant noticed when he jolted awake. Looking down, he discovered a piece of metal sticking out of his chest. His armor had stopped it from penetrating deeply, but it had still stabbed firmly into his pectoral muscle.

<*Finally*! I was wondering how long you were going to be unconscious.> Grant grabbed the sharp triangle-shaped hunk of metal and jerked it out of his chest. <It's been a good ten minutes since you blew through the side of the casino.>

"Ouch." Grant immediately started coughing, the smoke and dust in the air causing his lungs to let him know they weren't happy. "What happened?"

<Well, the explosion originated from me and spread outward from there. It blew you back into that giant table, and you kind of rode it through the back wall into this place.> Wrestling himself into a seated position, Grant inspected his surroundings, noticing all the rubble and small fires burning the ridiculously tall hedges that evidently made up the walls of the labyrinth. He couldn't even see the casino walls from his posi-

tion, which meant he must have flown past the entry area. <Along with most of the contents of the kitchen. I would recommend you get out of here before their search for the culprit reaches this deep into the maze.>

The sound of furious voices echoing from around the corner near his landing spot provided the impetus for him to climb to his feet. He was in no condition to fight at the moment. As he stumbled away, his vision was filled with an unwanted but familiar screen.

Congratulations! *Your new battle count moves from* [4 Wins / 1 Losses] *to* [5 Wins / 1 Losses]. *Remember, the lucky rise to the challenge!*

#ERROR34

Combatants not directly involved in duel defeated. Procedure violated.

#ERROR03

Spell effects didn't conform to standard functions. Parameters exceeded by 129%. Report compiled and submitted to program managers.

"Well, I guess it doesn't really matter. It isn't like the Dokeshi wasn't going to hear about this eventually." Grant shrugged, immediately wincing in pain. The wound in his chest made every motion sting. He glanced at the faint trail of blood he was leaving behind and applied pressure to his chest. The group following him would know exactly where to go if he didn't stop bleeding everywhere.

<No, keep the trail going. You can double back at the next turn in the maze and leave a false path for them to follow.> Grant grunted in response to Sarge's advice, and increased his pace. He found a likely spot to turn down, and paused to dig out another healing potion. After he took it, he would only have

two left. Suki had the rest. <Thinking of Suki, you are going to have to find her soon. I'm sure she was victim to some sort of scam as well, and she might need your help.>

"Do you have any idea how far away she might be? I'm already lost." Looking around, Grant was immediately struck by how difficult this was going to be. "These hedges are so tall and dense, there's no way to know where to go next."

<I agree. You're lucky to have such an amazing sword spirit by your side to help.> Grant quickly choked down the low-quality healing potion before sending a feeling of agreement toward the sword. He truly *was* lucky to have Sarge there to help, and it was strangely liberating to be just the two of them again. He hadn't noticed how worn out he was getting from constant contact with another person.

<Now, I can't be one hundred percent sure, but I think you need to work your way this direction.> An orange arrow flashed into existence in Grant's vision, pointing to the left. <She should have entered that way. If this place makes any sense at all, Suki has to be somewhere to the east, and not far.>

"Sounds good." Grant had already doubled back to the gap in the hedges that was in the general direction he wanted to go. He paused to make sure he wasn't leaving a trail of blood anymore, and started to head deeper into the twisting pathways. "Do you think we'll come across anyone else in this mess?"

<It's only a matter of time. A place like this would be perfect for bandits or thieves to set up shop, and District March is *rife* with bandits and thieves. At least here, they won't be hiding behind rigged games of chance when they try to steal your Time.> Grant snorted in amusement. He certainly couldn't argue with that; ever since entering the district, people had been trying to steal from him. Even having the chef level a knife at him had felt like coming home before Grant blew the place up.

Sarge fell silent, so Grant focused on his surroundings as he made his way east. The Labyrinth turned out to be more than just dense hedgerows. He passed by stone walls, small courtyard-like areas with fountains surrounded by multiple entrances, and more than one makeshift hut built into the walls of the maze. Each one was empty so far, but it was clear from half-hidden bedrolls and garbage littering the area that people had made this confusing place their home. Grant didn't take the time to search for them, instead staying focused on following the arrows Sarge used to tell him where to go as the Labyrinth continued.

<I think I sense something ahead. Be careful.> A section of stone wall near the upcoming intersection was highlighted orange, so Grant moved to the opposite side of the path. This area wasn't as narrow as some of the other places he had already worked his way through, meaning he had more room to maneuver if a fight broke out.

"You might as well come out. I know you're there." Grant put his back to the hedge opposite the wall. "I don't want any trouble, so just let me pass on by, and everyone goes to sleep safe tonight."

Instead of answering, a glob of acid flew straight at his face from the side of the wall.

<Mimic!> Sarge's shout was the only warning he had as the entire wall fell toward him. Instead of fighting, the Wielder dove away. The glob of acid melted through the hedge where he had stood, and the thick stone wall slammed into the ground behind his heels.

Combat initiated

Action: *Defend: Without Weapon.*

Result: *Enemy attack dodged.*

Actions: *Please select one option from the following list.*

Attack: *Lethal, Non-lethal, Spell.*

Defend: *With Weapon, Without Weapon.*

Run: *Attempt Escape.*

. . .

<Run!> Sarge's shout echoed in Grant's mind, and he immediately did as the sword spirit ordered. A mimic was something he had only heard about, and stopping to fight one while people were still searching for him seemed like a bad idea. <Yes, but more importantly, now the Dokeshi's men will have to deal with the mimic!>

Sarge chuckled as Grant put as much distance between himself and the monster as possible.

Condolences! *Your new battle count moves from* [5 Wins / 1 Losses] *to* [5 Wins / 2 Losses]. *Remember, fate favors the bold!*

"That one shouldn't even count!" Grant was mumbling to himself, angry about the way the system graded events. "I don't understand how this system keeps track of things."

<Poorly, clearly. Welp, now that we're in the next area, you should probably prioritize defeating the nearest Vassal in order to bring the system down.> Grant nodded in agreement, mostly because of how much he disliked how restrictive it was for his fighting style. <By the way, I don't think you could have beaten that mimic on your own with the system messing with you. One hit from something that size, and you'd have been done for. You'll need to be able to attack several times in a row and stay completely mobile to stay alive, much less defeat it.>

Grant shuddered, contemplating the impossibility of taking a single hit from the giant wall. Sarge paused to think while Grant made his way deeper into the maze of hedges and right-angled walls. <I think this region is intended to be traversed by a large group, not an individual. That might be why we were seeing such large collections of people standing at each of the gates. They must be planning to pass through here together.>

Grant could only agree. As much as it irked him, the mimic being so close to the entrance meant that he was in serious trouble. If most of the monsters in the maze were meant to be fought with a group… "Yeah, I need to find Suki."

CHAPTER THIRTY

The next few hours were notable only in their confusion: a jumble of turns that left Grant's head spinning. Moving through the Labyrinth was a lesson in frustration; every time he tried to work his way closer to the area where Suki should have entered the maze, he would hit a dead end or find himself body-blocked by a massive monster. He was starting to feel like he was spending more time backtracking than he was moving forward.

Just as he seemed to find a path that allowed him to move deeper, he heard the sound of fighting from the other side of the wall. A loud crash and hard thump caused the ground to rattle, and he dashed toward the noise so he could determine what was happening.

"Move left! Move left!"

"Don't let it block us off! Get those spears braced!"

"What *is* this thing? It keeps changing-" The last voice was cut off with a wet **squelch**, followed by a few cries of alarm.

<Hope those people were after you, because they absolutely found a mimic.> Another earth-vibrating crash shook numerous leaves from the hedges. Both Grant and Sarge went silent to try to listen in on the fight after an ear-splitting wail

echoed over the walls of the Labyrinth. The shouts and screams continued for several minutes, before gradually moving away. By his estimate, either they were in a running retreat, or a second foe had used the mimic's attack to launch their own.

How they could be followed by a wall was a mystery to Grant, so he assumed they were escaping. <Might not be a wall. Couldn't tell you if it's the same mimic or not. They might be endemic to the area. Frankly, I'm just as turned around as you are.>

"Really?" Grant looked down at his sheathed sword in surprise. "I'd have thought you could keep track of all these turns better than I can."

<There must be some kind of magic changing the region around as we move.> Sarge sounded a little angry, as if the trickery of spell users was a personal attack. <It can't cover the whole area. I imagine they have people watching through the walls and shifting things around as we pass through.>

"If that's the case, speed is going to be the name of the game. I can start running, but I don't even know which direction we came from." Peering along the strange hedgerows that grew along dense walls, Grant felt a wave of vertigo. Everything was the same—either shifting greenery or certainly trapped bare wall—and it was very disorienting. "I don't know how much longer I can put up with this."

<The sounds of the fighting came from your left as we walked here.> Grant could agree with that much, at least. <Put the wall with all the leaves on the ground to your left, and get a move on.>

Putting action to Sarge's words, Grant took off at a ground-eating pace. He could keep up a jog for hours now, and he was happy to put his conditioning to use. An orange-tinted monster rat jumped off a hedge onto his back as he rounded a turn, forcing Grant to roll into a wall to dislodge it. <I'll keep an eye out for monsters and people, so we're gonna train while you run.>

"Make it happen." Grant's hand slapped February Twenty

Nine's hilt, and a smile ghosted over his face as he thought about how cool he looked running like this. The fact that he could *do* it never stopped impressing him.

<We should keep an eye on that seed of narcissism you're formulating. That's really not what you should be basing your path on. Looking impressive is fine, but you need to cut people, not amaze them. I can help you keep your thoughts focused.> It took a full hour, but Grant once again heard the sounds of fighting. This time, the commotion came from straight ahead, so all orange constructs in the area faded as reality became more pressing than practice.

Sweat was dripping into his eyes, making his vision blurry, but a few calming breaths and a quick wipe at his face cleared that up. There was a 't'-shaped intersection less than twenty feet away, and Grant wasn't sure which turn would reveal the source of the screams and shouts.

<Stop and prepare yourself. Rushing into battle half-blind is more foolish than shearing sheep with a dull spoon.>

"Already ready to go, Sarge." Grant thought it was strange that the sword hadn't noticed his preparations. He loped forward, and Sarge made a choking noise as Grant explained, "Eyes are clear. Let's-"

A large gorilla creature rounded the corner on Grant's right at a dead sprint, watching behind itself at whatever it had been fighting. Which meant it didn't notice him until after they both went down with a meaty collision. Grant had only managed to get his uchigatana halfway out of its sheath when they collided, his slowest draw ever after reaching Beginner Iaijutsu. The oversized creature's proportions made it deceptively fast, making him misjudge the timing of his Iaijutsu strike. <What could make *this* thing run from combat?>

"Get back here, you stinking apes!" A very familiar voice was almost drowned out by the thundering footsteps of another half-dozen gorillas immediately on the trail of the first, and the sight of pink hair and shining gauntlets as they flashed past his prone form made Grant smile. He had really missed Suki these last few hours. "Don't think I can't catch you! Stand and fight!"

The gorilla on top of Grant didn't bother trying to stand, instead scrambling away from him on all fours as soon as Suki ran past. As he got back to his feet, Grant watched the monster disappear back around the corner. The entire incident hadn't even brought up the system prompts. Spinning to follow in Suki's footsteps, he quickly managed to catch up to her. She was busy pounding the slowest of the beasts into the ground with her fists, the rapid-fire impacts causing the gorilla to quickly fall unconscious.

"Suki! Sword Saints, I finally found you!" His cheerful greeting earned him a glance, and the slightly crazed look in her eyes quickly diminished. "I've been trying to catch up to you for hours!"

"Grant, thank the Regent. This place is a *nightmare*!" Her eyes glazed, obviously reading the screens that only she could see as they popped up in her vision. It only took her a few seconds to clear them away before refocusing on him. "What happened? How did you make it into the maze? The last thing I saw before they tossed me out the door was you still standing by the tables in the back."

"Oh, that's the cow-pie game. I'm actually pretty good at it, even though it doesn't actually involve pie. When we take this place over, let's make gambling for anything but Time illegal." Suki didn't know what to say to that, so she kept her mouth closed as Grant relayed the events of the past few hours to her. After explaining why he and Sarge thought they were getting turned around so easily, and describing the sounds of battle between the people he was pretty sure were following them, Grant finally held up the pouch containing all the Time he had won. "Also, since they couldn't catch up, we now have plenty of coins for our mission."

<Just because you have Time, doesn't mean you have *time* to waste. You two need to get going before someone catches up.>

Sarge's urging caused Grant to scan the area, realizing that they were unwisely relaxing in a very open location.

"Sarge has a good point. Perhaps a four-way intersection isn't the best place to stop and talk. You can tell me what happened to you while we find someplace to rest?" Grant picked Suki's pack up from where she had dropped it during the pummeling of the ape-man-thing. "We need to get our winnings distributed, and get some food in us. Keeping our energy up will be important."

"That's… a good idea." Suki seemed surprised at Grant's decisive directions and sudden increase in competence, but she quickly reconciled reality with her mental image of him. "You do a lot better in situations you're familiar with, don't you? It's strange to me that you're more comfortable in an area teeming with monsters while completely lost than you are around people. I guess, from the little we've discussed of your past… that makes sense."

"Running and training through greenery, while getting jumped at, basically describes my time in District February." Grant chuckled mirthlessly, pulling a wan smile from her.

As they walked, Suki relayed her own version of events, starting with just how *much* she had to cheat to win in the casino. "Absolutely everyone was cheating, even the dealer. I was lucky that everyone was more interested in not getting themselves caught than hunting for other cheaters."

"I don't like how dishonest everyone in this place is. It just…" Grant led the way deeper into the maze as he struggled to articulate his thoughts, his hand on his sword and eyes constantly scanning for signs of mimics and monsters. "I guess I feel that it makes hard work and learning proper skills seem less important? It makes my gut clench with… not anger… indigestion!"

"Indignation," Suki corrected him, taking the initiative to smoothly move the conversation along. "While I agree with you, there isn't much we can do to change things in the here and now. All we can do is adapt to the situation, and make the best of it."

"Don't get me wrong." Grant frowned, unsure how to word his grievance. "I understand that changing this place will take a lot of time, but I don't agree with compromising our integrity by bending to our circumstances. If we want these people to be more honest, don't we have to set the example for them to follow?"

"I… don't know what to say to that, beyond stating that winning in the short term is more important to your actual quest. You could theoretically live forever as a cultivator, not to *mention* as the Calendar King. You'll have the time you need later." Suki's argument left a bad taste in Grant's mouth, but he had no choice other than to stay silent. "Anyway, when I had enough winnings to prove I should move on, they didn't even let me stop to use the bathroom. They practically dragged me to the exit, and tossed me into a pit on the other side."

Suki winced, the memory obviously making her uncomfortable. "I was able to climb out easily, but there was a group of bandits ready for me as soon as I did."

"Bandits?" Grant was a little shocked. He'd thought that the honest way to get through the casino would be the safest way through the Labyrinth. "How many were there?"

"Not enough to stop me." Suki cracked her knuckles to emphasize her point. "It didn't take long to teach them the error of their ways. Then, I just kind of wandered the maze until those gorillas ambushed me. You know the rest."

"I wouldn't say you 'found' me. It was more like we ran into each other." Grant eyed her apprehensively, still trying to bring the conversation back around to the issue of honesty. "Why do you disagree with me so much about cheating to win? Don't you hate it too? Isn't transparency in leadership your whole deal?"

"Grant…" Suki sighed and straightened her spine, clearly fed up with this line of questioning. "It isn't about you being *wrong*. It's about you learning the wrong lesson from this. You haven't experienced the life of Nobles for very long. This is just how things are done. Not to be as rude as I know this is going to sound, but I don't *expect* someone with a commoner background to understand. Not without a *lot* more experience."

Grant opened his mouth to argue, but she cut him off before he could say anything. "Don't worry. When we're married, I'll deal with the other Nobles while you concentrate on ruling the twelve Districts. It's the perfect division of roles. Just another reason why our impending marriage is an excellent transaction."

The reminder made Grant blush furiously as his mind partially shut down. In all the excitement, he had almost forgotten about her desire to wrangle him into marriage. He still wasn't sure how he felt about the idea.

A heavily-armored woman bearing a halberd rounded the corner in front of them, and the two Wielders came to a stop, relaxed but ready to fight. "Oh, did we come across a lover's quarrel? How fun! Dillon, did you hear that? These two are supposed to get married!"

"Congrats on the impendin' nuptials!" An archer, holding a horn bow with a wickedly barbed arrow nocked, stepped out of the foliage behind them. "I'd warn ya against gettin' tied down to jus' one person at your age, but I don't much see the point. Get it? The *point*, cause it's an arrow that's gonna kill ya! That's jus' pure comedy right there, I'm tellin' ya-"

He wasn't able to finish the thought; Grant was already right in front of him. The bow **twanged** as the bandit released the string out of sheer surprise, but it was too late. The uchigatana was already in position to deflect the arrow high into the air. Before the system could even prompt Grant for an action, his sword found and removed the archer's throat.

"Dillon!" The scream from behind him reminded Grant to shift his position and take down the secondary threat. "*No~o!*"

Combat initiated

Action: *Attack: With Weapon.*

Result: *Enemy defeated. Two enemies remaining.*
Actions: *Please select one option from the following list.*
Attack: *Lethal, Non-lethal, Spell.*
Defend: *With Weapon, Without Weapon.*
Run: *Attempt Escape.*

Grant had already spun in place, ready to sprint at the woman holding the halberd. She had rushed forward as well, trying to use the axe head at the end of her polearm to chop down into a surprised and unprepared Suki.

Her gauntlets flickered into existence, and she easily caught the downward swing in one hand. A sharp blow to the diaphragm of the bandit woman forced her to drop to her knees. Grant sheathed his sword as Suki tossed the halberd away.

<The system, Grant!> He halted, trying to figure out what Sarge was trying to say. As a crossbow bolt slammed into the crate of produce still in his pack and rocked him forward, he realized what the sword meant. The system had said there were *two* enemies remaining.

Spinning around once more, Grant spotted the only place the crossbowman could be hiding: a gap in the hedges a few yards back that he was sure hadn't been there before. He was already moving before his conscious mind caught up.

Action: *Defend: With Weapon.*
Result: *Projectile deflected. One enemy remaining.*
Actions: *Please select one option from the following list.*
Attack: *Lethal, Non-lethal, Spell.*
Defend: *With Weapon, Without Weapon.*
Run: *Attempt Escape.*

. . .

By pure reflex, Grant had used his Iaijutsu to deflect a bolt he hadn't even seen until it was already knocked away. Selecting 'Attack: With Weapon,' he stabbed low into the hedge, feeling more resistance than he should have. With a quick twist and flick of his wrist, the system told him the bandit was done.

Congratulations! *Your new battle count moves from* [5 Wins / 2 Losses] *to* [6 Wins / 2 Losses]. *Remember, the lucky rise to the challenge!*

Peeking into the leafy alcove, he found another man that looked similar enough to the first archer that he could have been his twin. Grant guessed they were brothers. The man quickly bled out, joining his sibling in whatever afterlife was waiting for a pair of men who regularly robbed and killed innocent people.

"What have you *done*?" Suki walked over, her eyes lingering on the pools of blood. "I thought we talked about showing true skill by *not* killing our opponents? These are just basic Weapon cultivators!"

Instead of answering, Grant's sword flashed out, blurring so close past Suki's head that a few strands of pink hair floated on the breeze. Behind her, the female bandit was impaled through the wrist, and her dagger clattering to the ground was a loud counterpoint to the second movement in the quiet that followed. As the bandit crumpled to the ground, the hated system gave Grant another update.

Congratulations! *Your new battle count moves from* [6 Wins / 2 Losses] *to* [7 Wins / 2 Losses]. *Remember, the lucky rise to the challenge!*

. . .

"They told us they were going to kill us. They *tried* to kill us, and they would have if *I* hadn't stopped them *all three times*. Treat *every* battle as if it's life or death. It isn't just cultivators, Vassals, and Wielders that can threaten your existence." Grant angrily wiped his sword off on the dead bandit at his feet before sheathing it. "You nearly got us killed to prove a point. I took a crossbow bolt to my *back*, Suki. If I wasn't carrying this crate, that would have gone through my armor like I wasn't even wearing any at this range."

"It still wasn't right for you to kill them." The arrogance in those words finally made Grant snap. As he stalked away, he threw Suki's condescending words in her face.

"It isn't that you have the wrong idea, it's just that you've learned the wrong lesson. Only spending your time on non-lethal training, with enough resources to feed fifty people spent on you every day? I wouldn't expect you, as a Noble, to understand. This is just how commoners do things."

CHAPTER THIRTY-ONE

Finding a place to rest was as simple as tracing the steps of the bandit team they had defeated. Now that he knew to look for them, Grant could detect all kinds of places where residents had carved hidden paths and spaces throughout the hedges. It was strange to find that the walls that he had assumed were solid behind every bit of greenery had so many faults.

<The fact they took such measures to hide them means there have to be some kind of organized patrols through the region. We likely haven't seen any because you're here. The people meant to patrol are busy searching for you and Suki.> Grant agreed, keeping his eyes open but his mouth shut. Neither he nor Suki had said a word to one another since the fight, and he didn't want to be the one to break the silence. Not that he knew what to say in the first place. <Sometimes, not speaking says more than any speech.>

Having found the small camp, they set up shop and Grant got to peeling the small potatoes from his produce crate. The starchy vegetables had taken the brunt of the damage the crossbow bolt had caused, so they needed to be eaten before they spoiled. The fact that they were also the heaviest item remaining in the crate had nothing at all to do with his choice in their meal.

The ramshackle encampment was actually the unfinished portion of a wall section about a mile from where they had fought the bandits. Builders had finished the portion of the barrier which people walking the maze could see, but the corner section was only one or two stones thick on either side. They had made it appear finished, but left plenty of room for a single person to walk between the two parts. The top was even open to the sky, meaning they could manage a small fire if they were careful. The maze was cheaply done, like so much else in the District seemed to be.

<They were probably rushed to complete it by some ridiculous timeline imposed by the insane Wielder in charge of this bonkers District.> Grant poked at the loose mortar holding the large stones together. <Considering the situation, I might have done the same.>

"Grant… I'm sorry." Suki's voice finally broke the silence, making Grant slip and send the knife into his thumb while peeling the potatoes. A quick glance revealed that his Armor cultivation had dulled the knife instead of his flesh taking damage. "You didn't deserve to be treated like that. By me, especially."

"So, does this mean you-"

"I shouldn't have expected a commoner to truly understand how to properly act. It's not your fault that you were raised in a shed and thought that the first thing you should do after getting a sword was to start killing people." Suki cut Grant off with a chopping motion. "It's my job to make you understand. I've been failing in my duties. As your future queen, I need to make you into more than some murderhobo with an incredibly dangerous weapon."

<While a nice compliment to me, I think you should take this opportunity to part ways with this narcissist.>

"Are you actually serious right now?" Grant calmly put the already-peeled potatoes in the pot, taking deep breaths so he didn't lash out. He was so angry that it was hard to think of what to say. "You're… you're like a greenhouse… spider! You have no actual experience. All you know how to do is lie, cheat, and manipulate those around you! You pretend you can fight, but you have no resolve!"

"A greenhouse spider?" Suki appeared genuinely surprised that he was offended by her explanation. She tore up pieces of dried meat and angrily tossed them into the pot. "You think it's *me* that has no life experience? Wasn't it Grant *Leap* who didn't even know to bathe when he smelled like a latrine?"

He didn't have an answer to that. The only defense was that his mind had been that of a child, and the sheer difference to who he was now would be the same as telling her that she had once been a bedwetter at two years old. Not a great thing to toss into conversation, as it would just give her more arrows in her quiver. Biting his tongue as he stewed, Grant just finished peeling the vegetables and silently cooked the meal.

Soon they were eating a meal of boiled potatoes and rehydrated jerky. It somehow managed to be lumpy and dry, even saturated in the thin broth the mixture had made. Without even thinking about his words, Grant spit out a piece of the tough potato skin he must have missed and grumbled, "One of these days, I'm going to have a *real* meal, and it's going to be delicious. These meals make me feel sad inside."

"Oh, *quit* your *whining*. Food is meant to power our bodies, not replace the joy of progressing through life!" Grant stared at Suki like she had grown a second head, barely noticing that her gauntlets were on full display.

"You are a *stereotypical* Februarian of House Friday, aren't you? All personal skill growth and a refusal to do what *really* needs to be done. Every time I speak with you, I understand why the food in District February was so terrible, the people were so desperate and afraid, and why your District was collapsing *just like this one*." Grant slammed his spoon into his empty bowl just as her fist tried to slam into his face.

Too bad for her that Sarge had been making him practice

fighting from a seated position. With a flick of his wrist, February Twenty Nine whipped into the empty air and slapped the metal gauntlet away. He followed up his parry with a kick to her stomach that sent her flying into the hedges, and he winced as he was locked in place as the System activated. They both simply held their positions until it faded away, glaring at each other.

"I'm going to do a little scouting." She punched their small fire, killing it instantly, and moved to leave their hidden alcove. "Don't worry. I won't go far away enough to get lost. Not that the company of monsters would be any different than what I'm dealing with now."

Grant opened his mouth to argue, but she was already gone, disappearing into the hedges.

<She's right about one thing… she's got a great sense of direction.> Sarge paused, as if he was testing his words before speaking. <How ya *do~in'*?>

"I'm *fine*. You know what? She doesn't get the last word in." He followed the traces of broken limbs and disturbed dirt to a gap on the far side of the alcove, and reentered the maze. It wasn't hard to follow in Suki's wake; she was leaving a clear trail by stomping with her cultivation-enhanced strength, and the occasional fist-sized hole in the hedges marked where she had been working out her frustrations.

He picked up his pace, eventually catching up to Suki after almost an hour of tracking her. "I thought you weren't going to go far?"

"Since you make more noise than a moose walking through a crystal forest, I knew you weren't far behind." Suki tossed Grant a piece of broken wall, and he barely caught it before it slammed into his head. "There must be another hiding place nearby. It probably holds more bandits. Do you plan on killing those people too?"

Hot fury ignited in his chest. "I saved your *life*, you ungrateful-"

"Finish that sentence, and I'll show you what your *teeth* taste like!" Suki's gauntlets flickered into view, causing Grant to take a step back. "You didn't *save* me. I'm a *cultivator*. We have healing potions, and there was no way a *dagger* could have done enough damage to kill me!"

"You're a *Berserker* cultivator! Weapon and Body! I'm not hearing *Armor* in that list!" he bellowed in return.

"You think you know what kind of damage I can take because you beat me in a *spar*? Fine! Let me show you *exactly-*" It was Suki's turn to be cut off when a giant tree monster stepped out of the nearest hedge and punted her through the opposite wall.

<Well, that's one way to win an argument.>

Combat initiated

Action: *Defend: Without Weapon.*

Result: *Partner condition unknown. Four enemies remaining.*

Actions: *Please select one option from the following list.*

Attack: *Lethal, Non-lethal, Spell.*

Defend: *With Weapon, Without Weapon.*

Run: *Attempt Escape.*

"This should count as an ambush! What in the Houses is this stupid system even doing?" Grant selected his spell and activated it as three more tree monsters joined the first one. Unfortunately, the coursing lightning didn't seem to do much beyond slowing the sylvan brutes down a bit.

Action: *Attack: With Spell.*

Result: *Enemies slowed for five seconds. Four enemies remaining.*

Actions: *Please select one option from the following list.*

Attack: *Lethal, Non-lethal, Spell.*

Defend: *With Weapon, Without Weapon.*

Run: *Attempt escape.*

. . .

<Well, that didn't work.> Grant rolled backwards to avoid the downward slam of the nearest tree monster, automatically selecting 'Defend: Without Weapon'. <These're called Mangrove Thugs. Dumb. Tough. Strong. I recommend you don't let them hit you.>

The sword spirit's words were prophetic, as the downside of the system finally caught up to Grant. He tried to roll backwards again to dodge another kick from a tree monster, but it wasn't his turn. He took the impact full in the chest, his armor only stopping a small portion of the mighty blow.

Damage: 201 (58 mitigated)
Health: 220/421
Mana: 12/22

His health status was the first thing Grant saw when he opened his eyes. The rubble lying around him told the story of his journey through the same wall that Suki had become acquaintances with a short time ago. Squinting up through the dust hanging in the air, he saw all four of the Mangrove Thugs trying to pick their way through what was left of the barrier. The system must have warned the creatures that the fight wasn't over.

"*Ha*!" Suki's shout was all the warning the fearsome foliage had before she landed on top of the one farthest from Grant's position. She latched onto the head and shoulders of the leafy creature and slammed a gauntlet-covered fist into its bark-covered temple. Instead of being able to follow-up on the successful attack, she was halted by the system. "Gah! Stupid thing! Let me punch this shrub into wood chips!"

The Thug closest to the entwined duo took a swing at Suki, but she managed to shift just enough to dodge. A tree trunk-sized fist pounded into the surprised features of the monster Suki was riding, causing it to fall backwards. Right on top of Suki.

<That's two heavy strikes she's taken. You need to get her out of here if you still have any hopes of going through with your engagement.>

Grant activated his Thundering Step again, but this time, he chose to speed up his movements. As the lightning flowed through his body, his speed increased to what felt like ridiculous levels. He was a blur as he ran past the three trees still standing around the fallen form of their fellow forested friend. Scooping Suki into his arms as the monster struggled to stand, Grant took off for the nearest turn. He knew he needed to lose them while the spell was still active, otherwise they were finished.

Run: *Attempt escape automatically selected!*

<Take the next right!> Sarge's sense of direction was certainly better than his at the moment, especially since the pain shooting through his chest made it harder to focus. <There; now, keep going down this path until you see a place to turn left.> Grant risked a peek over his shoulder as the five-second timer wore off. None of the terrible topiary seemed to have caught up with them, so he slowed his pace a bit. <Those things are slow, but they have plenty of stamina. I'd keep running if I were you.>

Condolences! *Your new battle count moves from* [7 Wins / 2 Losses] *to* [7 Wins / 3 Losses]. *Remember, fate favors the bold!*

Sighing at the stupidity of the system forced on him, Grant could only take the loss in stride. In his mind, he took just *surviving* the attack as a win. With the turn-based system restricting him, any fight involving opponents as fearsome as those energetic evergreens was a recipe for disaster. They really needed to find the Vassal in charge of this place and crush their weapon before the disproportionately strong monsters spelled their end.

Wincing in pain, which was only made worse by the ever-annoying Bodily Awareness enhancing his agony, Grant hefted his unconscious *perhaps*-fiancé and started running again. If he could make another turn before the angry arborists rounded the bend, they wouldn't know which way they had gone.

After what felt like the longest straight sprint of his life, Grant finally found the nearest left-hand turn and took it. Glancing back, he could barely see the tops of the hedgerow back at the last bend moving unnaturally, but the monsters hadn't reached the corner yet. They had made it, just in time.

CHAPTER THIRTY-TWO

"What… happened?" Suki sat up, the healing potion Grant had poured down her throat finally kicking in and bringing her crushing injuries to manageable levels. "Where are we?"

"I don't know where we are exactly, but we got beat down by some angry trees that *absolutely* should not be able to live in a Spring District." Grant flopped to the ground and activated Live by the Sword, regaining eighty health, then quickly relayed the events of the past hour. As he finished, he pulled out his bedroll and flopped onto the thin material. It was getting dark, and they both needed some rest. Their hiding place was a section of the hedge wall that Grant had chopped at until it was hollow enough to fit them both. "You take the first watch. I'm exhausted. Using my spell twice in a row like that, then taking a healing potion… I can barely function."

<Forcing yourself to stay awake would train your mental cultivation.> Sarge heard Grant's whimper, eventually relenting. <You have been through a lot… I can also see the benefits of you getting some rest.>

"Thanks." Grant spent the next few minutes tossing and

turning, trying to get comfortable. While his body was exhausted, his mind was far from tired. Time to check his stats.

Name: Grant Monday
Rank: Lord of The Month (January, February)
Class: Foundation Cultivator
Cultivation Achievement Level: 19
Cultivation Stage: Late Summer
Inherent Abilities: Swirling Seasons Cultivation
Health: 300/421
Mana: 3/22

Characteristics
Physical: 247
Mental: 87
Armor Proficiency: 131
Weapon Proficiency: 166

He read over everything just to practice reading, but the only changes were to his health and mana; even those were just because he had been hurt and used spells. They should refill with just a little rest. There was only one other noticeable change: his damage output increased by a single point. "Sarge… It feels like my progress has stalled. The recent lack of focused training is catching up to me, but I have no idea where I could have fit in more. It's like I've been doing nothing but running, gambling, and arguing since we got to District March."

<Don't be so hard on yourself.> Sarge's sincere tone surprised Grant. The sword spirit was constantly pushing him to do more, and go farther than he ever thought possible. <You aren't far from the truth. You haven't had the same opportunities to train here that you did in January and February. As we progress deeper into the Districts, I imagine that will only become more of an issue. We can only hope that will mean

more actual combat. For now, get some rest. We'll work on training more soon.>

"Thanks, Sarge." Grant curled up in his bedroll and quickly drifted off to sleep. It felt like only a few minutes later when he was nudged awake by Suki. Her boot to his ribs wasn't necessary, and he was about to tell her off when he felt the ground tremble. Her wide eyes told him everything he needed to know.

The Mangrove Thugs had found them.

CHAPTER THIRTY-THREE

The tree monsters had somehow followed their trail, but they hadn't found *exactly* where the two Wielders were concealed. Both remained perfectly still as the sounds of tree-trunk-sized legs shuffled and stomped all around their hiding place. Since they were huddled in a newly-fashioned alcove, the Mangrove Thugs didn't know where to check.

Taking the chance to silently gather their gear, Grant packed everything away in preparation for a hasty escape. Suki was peeking through a small gap in the leaves, but he had no idea what she would even be able to see in the heavy darkness. After what felt like an hour—but was probably no more than fifteen minutes—the animated evergreens finally moved on. Suki was about to step out of the hedge when Sarge bayed into Grant's mind. <*Hold*! That was only three sets of footsteps!>

Grant reached out and caught Suki by the wrist, yanking her back against him. She turned sharply, a fist raised to crush his jaw into powder, but luckily there was just enough light from the stars to reveal him holding a finger against his lips. He breathed instructions so softly that even he could barely hear them. "A moment. The injured one might be trailing behind them."

After another subjective eternity of waiting in the dark—that was probably less than two minutes—the shuffling plod of the last Mangrove Thug gradually shook the leaves of the hedge surrounding them. Suki's eyes widened in surprise, and she gave Grant a bitter smile of thanks for stopping her from throwing them into combat. He tapped the hilt of February Twenty Nine, indicating that it had been Sarge that saved them from becoming fertilizer.

Instead of exiting the hiding place that had worked so well, Grant took out Suki's bedroll and motioned for her to get some rest. He wasn't sure how long he had slept, but she certainly hadn't gotten any at all. Suki didn't even try to argue, which meant she had to be truly exhausted. "Healing potions really take it out of you, don't they?"

<Potions are always a last resort. As for your mental state, you slept for a little over three hours, so you'll be fine. It should be sunrise in three more, giving you both the same amount of rest.> Grant tapped the sword hilt in thanks and positioned himself so he could get more comfortable. <Now that you have some time, I think you should work on your mental cultivation.>

"Work on my mental cultivation? How do I do that?" Grant knew for a fact that they had no books he could read, or any puzzles to figure out. "Wait, are you going to make some issue for me to solve?"

<That is a fine idea!> A snarled mass of twisted metal appeared in front of his crossed legs, its orange tint signifying that it was a construct that only Grant could see. <While you work on untangling this, I want you to answer equational problems I give you.>

"I don't know how to solve Equational's problems. Sarge, I can't even solve my own problems." As soon as Grant finished, Sarge sighed in his mind. Since the sword didn't actually need to breathe, Grant knew he had misinterpreted his trainer's intent. "Okay, just tell me. What did I get wrong?"

<Now, *that's* the right attitude. No complaining, no excuses, just the desire to *change* for the better.> Sarge's genuine pleasure made Grant relax and feel better about the upcoming task. <First, I know you understand addition and subtraction. That's as simple as understanding how to count. Now, we're going to go over multiplication and division. Don't forget to solve that blacksmith puzzle as we work. There should be seven different pieces you need to separate.>

Grant snatched up the puzzle, trying to unsuccessfully pull it apart. <Now, where was I? Oh yeah, multiplication. So, imagine leading an army of twelve heavy Bear Knight cavalry, and they have to fight against seven Troll Shieldbearers. As I'm sure you know, you can't count either your enemies or your allies as a one-for-one exchange on the battlefield. The force multiplier for calvary when working together as a whole is better on flat terrain, so you have to account for…>

The next three hours were a blur in Grant's mind. He was pretty sure Sarge wasn't doing anything but trying to test his mental pain tolerance by analyzing how bad of a headache he could survive. So far, the answer was excruciating, divided by throbbing; all by exhaustion squared.

<Okay, we can take a break. It's time to wake up Suki anyway.> Grant exhaled in relief and gently shook her awake as the first rays of light started to brighten the morning sky.

"What's the plan for today?" Suki was soon slicing a melon from the remaining produce for breakfast, while Grant was busily repacking everything. "I vote for finding the Vassal that keeps the system running and destroying his scepter. That's the only way we're going to be able to survive with just the two of us."

"I couldn't agree more." Grant slung his pack across his back and accepted a large slice of fruit from Suki. "My bet is they're waiting in the center of the maze. It's the only way to make sure their influence can reach the entirety of this section."

<Sound logistical planning.> Sarge paused, and Grant thought he felt his uchigatana vibrate in its sheath for a second. <I think I can help with finding him. All I need you to do is find an enemy to fight, and I can triangulate the strength of the system's hold on the region. That should at least tell us what direction to go.>

"Sarge thinks he's got a way to use triangles to help us find the Vassal." Suki looked at Grant like he was crazy, but all he could do was shrug. "All we need to do is find something to fight. Preferably something we can beat, this time."

"Ah, I see. He wants to triangulate where the system is strongest. Makes sense." Suki turned to leave, even holding apart the branches of the hedge so Grant could squeeze through with the bulky pack on his back. "Let's go."

"Isn't that what I just said?" All Grant could do was shake his head. These people just didn't make sense sometimes. He couldn't be sure, but it seemed to him like they had too much book learning for their own mental well-being. "I think we should go straight. Those tree monsters went left, so going somewhere else seems like a good idea."

"Can't argue with that. Getting booted through a wall wasn't my favorite way to take a nap." Suki started walking, leaving Grant behind and forcing him to rush to catch up. "You do have a strong survival instinct. It makes you clever, if vicious."

"Are we *still* doing this?" Grant was getting *exceptionally* tired of her underhanded compliments. "Is it just so ingrained that you can't help but be insulting to everyone else?"

They spent the next hour sniping back and forth at one another, with long pauses in between to listen for any possible enemies they could fight. There was a large group of the gorilla creatures that they avoided, due to the sheer number of the troop, but otherwise their journey was uneventful.

Finally, they came across a ruined campsite in the middle of the path, with clear signs of a recent battle. The two of them silently separated, one to either side of the wide path. Both paid close attention to the hedges they were hugging, making sure nothing was waiting to pop out and attack.

"Psst!" Suki hissed to catch Grant's attention, pointing to an almost indistinguishable gap between the hedge and stone corner they were approaching. "I think this corner section is hollow, like the other one we saw."

Grant eased over to take a look, carefully stepping over the bloodstains still marking the area. "I'll go first, since I've got better armor."

Suki gave him a silent nod as her gauntlets flickered into existence. As he unsheathed his sword and moved to push aside the few branches blocking him, she sent one last jab at him. "Just try not to kill every human as soon as you see them. It sends the wrong message."

"You-" Grant shook his head, deciding to stay focused on what was hiding in the wall section. As he rounded the corner, it was immediately clear what had happened to whoever had been camping in the middle of the path. The myriad of gnawed-on bones and shredded clothing was a dead giveaway.

Rats.

"Back." Grant didn't turn around, and he made sure to keep his voice low and calm. "We don't want this fight."

Suki peeked around his shoulder to see what had him so concerned, and she blanched as soon as she realized what was waiting for them. Their last fight with the vile creatures was still fresh in her mind, and the thought of facing them again made all the blood drain from her features.

Just as they made it back into the pathway, the sound of a twig snapping behind them forced the two to spin, ready for a fight. Instead of a swarming flood of the disgusting furry creatures, six humans in the uniform of Dokeshi March were just as surprised to see them as they were to find a patrol.

"Ah! The deities of fortune smile on us today, Paulson!" The man wearing the nicest armor of the bunch let a wicked grin cross his face as he shouted to the spear wielder standing right next to him. "The pair we're hunting for in this accursed place just pop out right in front of us! What are the odds?"

"Shh!" The dual shushing from the two Wielders wasn't what they were expecting, and the group actually went silent in confusion. The sound of chattering squeals and gnashing teeth came from behind the pair, and the fear on their faces wasn't feigned.

"*Run*!" Which of the guards broke and shouted first was unclear, but that didn't stop everyone from scattering. As Grant and Suki sprinted around the corner, the patrol was right on their tails.

"Hey! Stop right there, criminal-*ahh*!" The guard in nice armor was the slowest of the bunch, so when he was swarmed by the wave of fur and teeth that appeared from the gap in the hedge, the rest of the patrol only noticed due to his screams of pain. Grant and Suki didn't wait around to see how the fight between their two enemies turned out.

Sometimes, the enemy of your enemy… is still just your enemy.

CHAPTER THIRTY-FOUR

They reached an entirely different section of the maze before they finally stopped running. In this region, the hedges had thorns, and the walls were made of brick, not stone. Panting, they leaned on a vine-covered portion of red brick to catch their breath.

"Who do you think won?" Grant quietly questioned his companion around long, even breaths. "You think any of them lived through that?"

"Does it matter?" She pushed off the wall and stood up straight before peering back the way they had come. "The rats won't leave their hunting grounds to follow us after getting such a big meal, and the patrol won't be able to catch up after getting mauled by such a large group of beasts."

"Doesn't matter. Interesting. The loss of life only matters when the blood is *directly* on our hands." Grant took a good look around at their surroundings, reaching out to touch a nearby thorn. It was sharp, even more than his belt knife, but still failed to draw blood. "At least we shouldn't have to deal with things hiding in the walls anymore. Nothing that isn't an Armor cultivator could deal with these thorns." As soon as he unconsciously put his finger in his mouth to gnaw at a strange itch, an unexpected screen popped into his vision.

Combat initiated

Action: *Defend: Without Weapon*

Result: *Mimic poison entered bloodstream. One point of health lost for the next sixty seconds.*

Opponents remaining: 1

Actions: *Please select one option from the following list*

Attack: *Lethal, Non-lethal, Spell*

Defend: *With Weapon, Without Weapon*

Run: *Attempt Escape*

"What did you *do*?" Suki was already preparing to fight, dropping her pack against the wall as her gauntlets appeared over her closed fists. Grant didn't have time to answer, because a ten foot section of the thorny hedge wall suddenly shuffled into the middle of the path, completely blocking any escape in that direction.

"Stay back!" Grant jumped in front of Suki; his sword already held vertically in front of him. "The thorns are poisonous, and you aren't wearing any armor!"

"I'll try to get around it." She sprinted for the vine-covered wall and started climbing. "Most mimics can't form a shape on both sides. Just keep it distracted!"

"Keep it distracted. Yes. A plan. A good plan. I'm lying to make myself feel better." Grant was just mumbling under his breath, but the wicked smile she tossed back told him she had heard. Deciding the best course of action was full-out attack, Grant selected 'Attack: With Weapon' and slid into range as he slashed downward into a heavy blow in the center of the monster.

Instead of the sensation of breaking branches and the resistance of wood, the blade felt like it was parting leathery flesh.

The spray of ichor and mucus that coated his face was also unexpected. “Gwargah! This thing is disgusting!”

<This one isn’t that bad. You should see what happens when they imitate a Slime Pod. The combination is enough to make even a dragon gag.>

Action: *Attack: With Weapon*

Result: *Critical Success, attacker takes 107 slashing damage—bleed effect active.*

Actions: *Please select one option from the following list*

Attack: *Lethal, Non-lethal, Spell.*

Defend: *With Weapon, Without Weapon.*

Run: *Attempt Escape.*

The mimic didn’t take Grant’s attack standing still. A whip-like appendage appeared from the base of the creature, and he immediately selected ‘Defend: With Weapon’. The thorn-covered limb struck with the speed of a crossbow bolt, aiming straight for his unprotected eyes. Luckily, since Grant had been training his Iaijutsu, the appendage hit the ground in a squirming spray of mimic blood instead of giving him a face full of poisoned thorns.

Action: *Defend: With Weapon*

Result: *Attacker takes 27 slashing damage—bleed effect active, defender momentarily blinded by viscera.*

Actions: *Please select one option from the following list*

Attack: *Lethal, Non-lethal, Spell.*

Defend: *With Weapon, Without Weapon.*

Run: *Attempt Escape.*

"*Hiya*!" Suki's shout echoed over the rows of hedges as she finally jumped from near the top of the wall, the flickering blue shield of the strange, redirected barrier that kept things from climbing over the walls shimmering as her pink hair brushed against it. Her downward punch nearly folded the mimic in half, and Grant timed his choice of 'Attack: With Weapon' perfectly. He used the distraction of her assault to stab the leathery back of the monster while it was exposed.

The combined blows were too much for the disturbing creature, and it completely folded forward into a gloppy mess. Somehow, Grant had managed to become coated in the disgusting miasma, while Suki was spotlessly clean. He took a few moments to review all of his life choices leading up to that point, trying to see where he had gone wrong.

Congratulations! *Your new battle count moves from* [7 Wins / 3 Losses] *to* [8 Wins / 3 Losses]. *Remember, the lucky rise to the challenge!*

<That was a wonderful victory. I'm surprised you were able to defeat such a mighty foe so quickly.> Grant only grunted in reply, doing his best not to get the slime in his mouth. <I wonder why such a strong mimic was in the early part of the Labyrinth, while this weaker one was deeper in. My guess is you're close to the hunting ground of a mighty beast.>

"A mighty beast? How close do you think it is?" As he ignored the slime as well as he could to get clarification on such dire news, a glob of snot-like substance inevitably slid between Grant's lips. It caused a brief moment of furious spitting, and after a few moments, he was able to collect himself. "Seriously, Sarge. How close do you think this 'mighty beast' might be?"

<Well, to be completely honest, the fight let me finally triangulate the Vassal, and he's only a few hundred yards to the west.>

"Seriously?" Grant could feel his blood pressure rise. "You let me get that disgusting goop in my mouth for nothing?"

<Well, it wasn't for nothing. Personally, I thought it was hilarious.> Grant glanced at Suki, who despite being unable to hear both sides of the conversation, was also fighting back a smile.

"You guys are jerks." Grant stormed off, all the while doing his best to shake off the coating of disgusting phlegm.

<Clean yourself off, and get your mind back on the matter at hand.> Sarge's voice deepened, killing intent radiating off the weapon. <Let's go show this Vassal what a proper Lord can do.>

CHAPTER THIRTY-FIVE

"I can't see any enemies." Suki was standing on Grant's shoulders, peeking through a small gap in the thorny hedges. "I can only see a stand with a piece of paper on it by the exit on the other side, but it's pretty much just a clearing; an empty circle."

"Is it surrounded by thorns, or walls?" Grant grunted as Suki shifted to get a better view. The problem wasn't the fact that the Wielder was heavier than she looked; he was *pretty* sure she was digging her toes into him on purpose. "Because if it has walls, they could be hiding enemies."

"The side we're on is full of thorns, but the far side is just one big curved wall." She shifted again, causing Grant to stumble away from the hedge. Suki did a backflip off of his shoulders and landed gracefully behind him. "Here's what we know: this is *obviously* a trap. What we don't know is how serious of a trap it really is, or if we can beat whatever comes out of it."

"There's one way to find out." Grant swung his neck from side-to-side, trying to hide his relief that she was on the ground. "We're gonna look terrifying and unstoppable when we crush this trap. I'll go in first, and you wait to come out until we know what we're facing."

"Don't come crying to me if you end up getting killed the moment you walk in there." Suki realized that Grant was just standing and staring at her, so she waved her hand toward the small opening that led to the center of the maze. "Well, what are you waiting for? Get going."

Grant was fully unsure of what to say. He was tired of arguing with her, but he wasn't sure what to do to fix their situation. The two of them had such different views that he had no idea what they could do to harmonize their seemingly irreconcilable differences.

<Time and experience, Grant. That's the only way to truly learn how to see the world through another's eyes.> Sarge dropped a slice of fresh knowledge on him, and it was exactly what he needed to hear. <Stop delaying and get in there!>

The young Lord stepped through the gap in the hedge. It was *almost* exactly as Suki had described; she had forgotten to mention the white marble-paved depression in the center of the circular-shaped clearing. The unexpected flooring was surrounded by a low ring of solid metal. It looked like either brass or copper, and Grant could tell by the dried water marks that it was supposed to be some kind of pool or fountain. While he was inspecting it, a camouflaged door hidden in the center of the stone wall rolled to the side, and a rather rotund man wearing plate armor painted to look like a clown stepped out.

"A Januarian?" Grant's mouth snapped shut as he realized he was giving away too much personal information.

"I was beginning to wonder when you'd finally show up!" The tinny voice of the terrifying knight-clown echoed in his helmet as he stepped to the opposite side of the fountain. He hefted an oversized sword shaped like a cleaver in one hand, and the familiar scepter of the Dokeshi's Vassals in the other. His scepter-stone glowed a sinister red, making it appear as if he was covered in gore. The enemy Vassal's face was covered by a faceplate painted to look like a grinning clown, with a bulbous red nose that somehow managed to look scary instead of silly.

A colorful rainbow-dyed wig was poorly glued to the top of his helm, and the armor was rusted in places where the clown paint was scraped off. At least, Grant hoped it was rust, and not dried blood. "I've been waiting here for you since I was informed of that fiasco in the casino. Let me tell you a secret about every place beyond the first casino… the closer you get to the heart of March, the higher the stakes become. Right here, you either gamble with your Time, or with your life. I'm glad you came to me. It means you want to bet your life."

"I most certainly do *not* want to bet my life. Who are you?" Grant had been having an understanding of contract-law beaten into his head since he'd stepped in the District, and he wasn't about to let an 'implicit agreement' happen. Not with this level of stakes. His grip on the hilt of his sword was tight enough that it made his knuckles ache. "I haven't heard anyone mention the Dokeshi having an armored Vassal like you."

"That's because people don't live to spread rumors about me." The giant chuckled; the faceplate unable to hide the obvious joy he felt at the idea. "I'm the second most powerful Vassal, behind only Cuddles. You can know me as… Dangerous Dade!"

He waved his scepter, popping another hidden door open. The sound of hooves clopping on paving stones rang through the second door. "Meet my loyal pet, Minamino!"

<Huh. Well, that's… that's a new one, even for me.>

A massive bull, no doubt weighing in at multiple tons, plodded into the makeshift arena, cracking the stones he stepped on. Unfortunately for Grant's future desires to have regular dreams at night, it didn't have a normal bull head. That would have been much preferable to the completely normal human head that sat on the monstrously thick neck of the creature. It made eye contact with Grant, and dropped its head so they were at the same level. It opened its mouth, squinted, and made a sound that he never expected to hear from a creature like this.

"*Moo.*" There was nothing animalistic about the vocalization; it just sounded like a person telling their child what sound a cow makes.

"Sword Saints… what *is* that thing?" Grant unconsciously backed up a few steps, making sure to keep the dry fountain between him and the two opponents.

"Who, Minamino?" Dade rested his sword on the rim of the fountain so he could give the giant man-headed bull a pat and scratch on the back. "He's a *good* boy, yes he is!"

<I'd be shuddering too, if I had a body to do it with. That's disgusting.>

Grant shook his head sharply, getting back into the moment. He raised his gleaming sword, deepened his voice, and prepared to attack. "What do you want me to put on your tombstone?"

"Pepperoni! *Ha*! You have spirit. This should be fun!" The clown knight pulled a massively-horned silver helm from behind the edge of the fountain and buckled it on the man-head. "Let's make this more interesting, shall we?" He landed a heavy slap on Minamino's rear, and it snorted in anger. The fact that it came from the nostrils of a human-sized nose instead of a bull-sized nose didn't make it any less intimidating.

<Whatever you do, don't let that thing hit you.> The four thousand pound creature started to trot around the rim of the dry fountain, crushing even small pebbles to dust with its prodigious weight. <Don't let it step on you, either.>

"Sarge, I'm gonna promote you to Captain soon. Captain *Obvious*." Grant backed up along the rim, trying to keep as much of the fountain between himself and Minamino as possible. The obvious side-effect was that he had to move closer to the stationary figure of the clown wearing plate armor. Considering the two enemies he was facing, Grant decided to try to focus on the Vassal first. At least he knew how to fight against a man with a sword.

"Oh, you think *I'm* the easier opponent, do you?" Dangerous Dade lifted the heavy cleaver off the ground to rest it on his shoulder. "Good luck getting through this armor with that little toothpick you call a sword!"

<Did he just call me a toothpick?> Sarge snarled, and Grant could feel his heartbeat begin to race as man and sword got on the same level. <We'll just have to see about that! Aim for his joints, Grant! Take this creepy clown out at the knees!>

That was exactly what he tried to do. Grant sprinted around the curve of the fountain, rolling under the downward strike of the cleaver aimed for his head. The explosion of rock chips that echoed out behind him when the blade impacted the ground threw off his aim, and Grant's uchigatana bounced harmlessly off the greave covering the monstrous clown's shin.

Combat initiated

Action: *Defend: Without Weapon.*

Result: *Dodged primary attack. Secondary effect, 'Ground Breaker,' causes Disorientation for 3 seconds.*

Actions: *Please select one option from the following list.*

Attack: *Lethal, Non-lethal, Spell.*

Defend: *With Weapon, Without Weapon.*

Run: *Attempt Escape.*

Action: *Attack: With Weapon*

Result: *Disorientation results in inaccurate strike. No damage to opponent.*

Actions: *Please select one option from the following list.*

Attack: *Lethal, Non-lethal, Spell.*

Defend: *With Weapon, Without Weapon.*

Run: *Attempt Escape.*

. . .

The cleaver had stuck in the ground, leaving an opening for Grant to capitalize on Dangerous Dade's vulnerability. He could even see the bloodshot eyes of the evil clown through the holes in his metal mask. Before he could select 'Attack,' the rumbling of the ground warned him of Minamino's rapid approach.

<Look out!> Grant selected 'Defend: Without Weapon,' and dove backwards inside the ring. The screaming sound of the horned helm scraping against the metal rim ran shivers up his spine. The man-bull rumbled the ground as it charged past, barely missing the Vassal standing in the way.

Action: *Defend: Without Weapon.*

Result: *Dodged primary attack. Secondary effect, 'Ground Shaker,' causes unstable footing for 3 seconds.*

Actions: *Please select one option from the following list.*

Attack: *Lethal, Non-lethal, Spell.*

Defend: *With weapon, Without Weapon.*

Run: *Attempt Escape.*

<Good job. Now, do it again.> Confused for a moment, he almost didn't see another smashing swing from the clown. He was forced to select 'Defend' again, and rolled toward the center of the fountain.

"It looks like I was right!" Dangerous Dade pried his cleaver free of the ground. "You're *fun*!"

Action: *Defend: Without Weapon.*

Result: *Dodged primary attack. Secondary effect, 'Ground Breaker,' causes Disorientation for 3 seconds.*

Actions: *Please select one option from the following list.*

Attack: *Lethal, Non-lethal, Spell.*

Defend: *With Weapon, Without Weapon.*

Run: *Attempt Escape.*

"I see how this works." Grant climbed to his feet. "I'm not playing this game, bouncing back and forth between the two of you."

"Oh, really? Then do something about it!" The Vassal used his scepter for the first time, tapping it on the edge of the fountain. Almost instantly, water started bubbling up from the cracks in the tile. "It looks like you won't be able to hide in this ring much longer."

In moments, the fountain was full to Grant's knees. It would reach to his waist before long, and he would be easy pickings for the much larger Vassal. Another very human-sounding snort came from behind him, telling Grant that Minamino was ready and waiting for him to try to climb out of the fountain. The clown giggled wildly. "Time to come play my game, little Wielder."

Grant couldn't help but smile as a familiar shock of pink hair started sneaking up behind the unsuspecting clown. Instead of giving her away, he spun around to face the monster waiting behind him. "I'll just have to take care of your pet first. Then you and I can settle things."

"Ha! You think it'll be easy to-" The gong of metal against metal cut off the verbal jousting, and Grant glanced over to see Dade stumbling forward to lean on the rim of the fountain. "Oh, two of you? Now this isn't just fun… you're making this *interesting*."

The Vassal climbed to his feet, but Grant was too busy to notice what happened next. His attention was taken up by the sharp pain he felt when he tried to lever himself over the edge of the fountain. Grant was shocked to see the man-bull had bitten him on the hand, and was growling at him like a dog as it shook the hand its teeth were clamped onto.

. . .

Action: *Defend: Without Weapon.*

Result: *Attack successful. Completely normal bite does 5 damage (58 mitigated).*

Actions: *Please select one option from the following list.*

Attack: *Lethal, Non-lethal, Spell.*

Defend: *With Weapon, Without Weapon.*

Run: *Attempt Escape.*

<Look on the bright side.> The sword spirit seemed to think Grant's pain was funny as he jerked his hand out of the creature's mouth. <At least you were bitten by something without sharp teeth.>

Minamino snorted in Grant's face, spraying him with a fine mist of snot. Grant splashed a handful of water from the fountain to clean the ick off and glared at his sword. "This District is *weird.*"

CHAPTER THIRTY-SIX

Grant backed up before jumping up onto the rim. Minamino was ready for the move, and swiped his horns at Grant's legs. Anticipating the attempt, Grant maneuvered past the pointy instrument of death and swung his uchigatana downward at the base of the man-bull's neck. Somehow, the creature knew to shift a half-step backward, and his sword clanged off the heavy helm.

He immediately selected 'Defend: With Weapon' and had to block a furious blow when the man-bull spun and kicked out at his chest. The creature moved so fast that Grant suspected it had to be some sort of ability. The sound of the iron-shod hoof impacting his sword made a harsh ringing noise, and he couldn't help but drop to a knee to clear his head.

<I don't think this is the right match for you, Grant.> He decided to ignore the sword spirit, especially considering the fact that there wasn't much he could do, at least while kneeling right in front of Minamino. <Your style is too straight-forward. This one has the cunning of a beast, with the insight of a human.>

. . .

Action: *Defend: With Weapon.*

Result: *Deflected 'Killing Kick' attack. Stunned by impact for 5 seconds.*

Actions: *Please select one option from the following list.*

Attack: *Lethal, Non-lethal, Spell.*

Defend: *With Weapon, Without Weapon.*

Run: *Attempt Escape.*

As he selected 'Defend: With Weapon' again, Grant was barely able to knock away a horn as it tried to gore him. He was able to use the force of the impact to roll backwards against the rim of the fountain, which he used to pull himself back to his feet. This time, he managed to trick Minamino into angling its head down, and the horn attempting to impale him stuck itself in the ground.

Action: *Defend: With Weapon.*

Result: *Deflected attack. Opponent delayed for 3 seconds.*

Actions: *Please select one option from the following list.*

Attack: *Lethal, Non-lethal, Spell.*

Defend: *With Weapon, Without Weapon.*

Run: *Attempt Escape.*

<Try to switch with Suki. Even with her ability to deal damage through armor, her fight is at a stalemate. She has more experience killing monsters than people, so she'd fare much better against this creature.> Grant glanced over to see his companion trading blows with the knight. It looked like her strikes against his plate armor were doing damage, but using her gauntlets to deflect the mighty swings of the cleaver-sword was hurting her as well. <I'd suggest running to her battle against the knight, and using the bull creature to disrupt their fight long enough to switch.>

"If I try that, I'll just get run down and trampled!" Grant's words were emphasized by the monster finally tearing itself free of the ground with a very human-sounding roar. "How am I supposed to outrun a bull the size of a freight wagon?"

<Well, I know I—your sword—am absolutely amazing and you only ever want to use me to solve your problems, but think it's been long enough since you were last hit that you can use your *spell.*> Sarge's scathing retort was a grim reminder that Grant needed to *remember* to use every option at his disposal.

Selecting the 'Spell' option, Grant activated the speed boost it provided in training mode, and took off like a bolt from a crossbow; using his left hand to hold on to the rim of the fountain as he ran around it to the opposite side. Grant was surprised to see the copper ring absorb his lightning and divert it into the water all along the rim, but he had to refocus, as he was approaching the clown, who had already turned to follow his approach.

"Ha-hee! Come to face your end at the edge of my blade instead of the horns of my pet?" The thundering hooves of Minamino approaching from the rear were rippling the water in the fountain, causing the lightning to dance. "Well then, I'd be happy to-"

The clown went mute as Grant slammed his sword into the upraised cleaver. His spell deactivated the moment he returned to combat, but Dade's metal plate armor meant the lightning imparted by Grant's blow through his sword made the Vassal jerk and dance for a moment before grunting in pain and taking three steps back. "Ugh. I see. Elemental spells. Cheap tricks will not bring you victory, little Wielder."

Suki was more than willing to take advantage of the Vassal's distraction and landed a haymaker in his ribs. It rocked him to the side, but he didn't even pause to look back at her. Minamino, seeing his master attacked by the pink-haired Wielder, thundered past the two men and plowed directly into her crossed gauntlets. Her feet dug furrows into the ground as they slowly came to a stop, and she paused to shake her arms out.

The man-bull shook his head to clear it at the same time, revealing that Suki wasn't the only one affected by the impact. Grant's vision was filled with the system screen, telling him how effective his spell had been.

Action: *Attack: Spell.*

Result: *Opponent takes 5 damage (90 mitigated).*

Actions: *Please select one option from the following list.*

Attack: *Lethal, Non-lethal, Spell.*

Defend: *With Weapon, Without Weapon.*

Run: *Attempt Escape.*

<His armor blocks ninety damage. That isn't good.> Sarge paused, as if reading something. <Alright… here's the deal. To be this powerful and hard to kill, I'm positive he has only two areas of focus: Armor and Weapon cultivation, so this is a Warrior cultivator. His health is only going to be whatever pittance his Cultivation Achievement Levels give him, so your best bet is going to be wearing him down and finding his weak points. Now, your base damage is only seventy-one, meaning you could beat on him all day and it wouldn't do a single point of damage to him. However, a *critical* hit does a maximum of one hundred and seven damage. It's time for you to be perfect.>

"You know, I'm glad I get to take you down first." Dangerous Dade waved his scepter, and the ground began to tremble faintly; likely a setup for his earth-based spell to disrupt movement. "The Dokeshi wanted you brought in alive, but that isn't fun for me. Everyone knows clowns love to have *fun*!"

Grant was forced to dance backwards, swinging his sword where he thought the cleaver was going to aim. If he could deflect it into the ground, it would buy him a few moments to make a clean strike on the joints of the armor. Unfortunately for Grant, the ground took that moment to shift, and he was tossed off-balance.

"Ha!" The impact of the cleaver smashing into the sword without Grant being prepared for it caused the back of his own blade to smack him in the face, which Dade found hilarious. "Hee-ha! That was brilliant! Does your plan to defeat me involve beating yourself up first? I don't think anyone has tried that one against me before."

The coppery taste of blood from his split lip didn't put Grant in a laughing mood. He completely ignored the notice telling him about his failure to defend, and instead chose the 'Attack: With Weapon' option. Since the Vassal was just standing there laughing at him, Grant was happy to take advantage of his stationary stance. His uchigatana darted out in a heavy stab, and the impact of his sword tip on his target made his hands vibrate with the impact.

<Ooh, good plan! I like the way you think.>

"*Ow*! That wasn't very *nice*!" The Vassal was shaking his hand while the sound of his scepter splashing into the fountain signaled the end of his elemental spell. "It isn't very polite to attack a man while he's having a laugh."

The Vassal dashed toward the still-rising water to collect his lost Vassal weapon, but Grant wasn't going to let that happen. The Wielder was much lighter than the man in full plate armor, so he was able to get over the rim and back in the water much faster. The clown naturally didn't want him to reach it first, so he finally took his turn. Grant's only warning was the whistling sound of the cleaver as it swung for his ribs, so he wasn't able to get his sword at a good angle. He was *slapped* out of the fountain, somehow managing to hit both his face and the back of his head on the copper rim.

<Now's your chance! Activate your spell!> Still stunned, Grant followed Sarge's directions by reflex. Even though he had certainly been knocked out of his spell's attack range, he selected the option. <Perfect. He *definitely* didn't expect that.>

"What?" Grant squinted up, watching the clown in full plate

armor doing a very odd dance inside the fountain. “What’s wrong with him?”

<That, my young Wielder, is what happens when you apply lightning to water through a copper medium.> The spell lasted a full five seconds, after which the evil Warrior sank bonelessly into the rising waters. <Enough standing around, Grant. Finish him!>

Still groggy from hitting his head, Grant used his sword to help him climb to his feet. As he got up, he glanced over to see how Suki was doing. If she needed his help, now was the only time he might have to give it.

“What’s wrong, little man-bull? Too scared to fight a *girl*?” She definitely didn’t need his help. Somehow, Suki had already knocked the heavy horned helm off the creature’s head, and she was aggressively chasing it around the courtyard.

<Yeah, she’s good. Clown-icide! Go!>

CHAPTER THIRTY-SEVEN

"How does she do that?" Grant was almost mesmerized by Suki dancing around the bulky Minamino. Her fighting style was a mixture of feints and dodges that allowed her to counter-attack every move the man-bull made. "She never fought me like that."

<Suki has been training to fight since she was a child. There's no doubt she's got several different fighting styles.> Sarge paused to watch her latest dodge. <She's fighting the larger opponent like a matador. She probably didn't think it would be necessary to fight you with anything other than a single style. Also, *go kill the clown*!>

"What's a matador?" Grant had never heard the word before.

<It's an ancient kind of warrior that specialized in fighting minotaur and bulls. Their manner of fighting died out when the barriers went up. Now, move your rear! Finish your fight!>

Grant finally looked at the notice trying to pop up in his vision.

. . .

#ERROR030

Damage calculation outside parameters.

Action: *Attack: Spell*

Result: *Critical Success, opponent takes* ***#ERROR111*** *spell damage—opponent stunned for* ***#ERROR187*** *seconds.*

Actions: *Please select one option from the following list*

Attack: *Lethal, Non-lethal, Spell.*

Defend: *With Weapon, Without Weapon.*

Run: *Attempt Escape.*

Grant looked over the rim of the fountain to find Dangerous Dade still underwater, flat on his back a few feet away from where his scepter still glowed. Grant jumped back into the water and sloshed over to the hated device that enforced Dokeshi March's will over the area. He raised his uchigatana over the glowing stone, point-down. As Grant tensed to drive his weapon through the crystal, he was abruptly jerked off his feet.

The crushing grip of a gauntlet around his ankle shot pain all the way up to his hip, which only got worse when the clown stood up and Grant was dragged underwater. Heaving in deep breaths, the armored Vassal yanked the Wielder up and shook him like a wet towel.

"How did you do that?" The knight was having trouble talking, his lungs heaving like blacksmith's bellows as he tried to catch his breath. "How did you hurt me so bad? No one has managed to bring my health so low in *years*. Not talking? Then I guess I should return the favor!"

<Uh-oh. This is going to hurt.>

In a show of utter fury, Dangerous Dade swung the back of his cleaver into Grant like a butcher tenderizing meat, striking the young man like a gristly chuck steak. Each impact blasted the air out of Grant's lungs, and the only thing that likely kept him from being beaten to death was that they were standing in waist-deep water. It managed to both hurt him as well as dispersing the force of the impacts enough to merely leave Grant heavily bruised instead of mangled.

No matter what he did, Grant couldn't find a way free. Damage notifications flooded his vision, but he ignored them, instead trying his best to keep from inhaling water.

Finally, whether it was because the knight was getting tired, or maybe just bored, Grant was released and the clown used a two-hand swing that was hard enough to crack the marble tiles as Grant was driven below water. The impact was so great that he managed a quick moment to suck in a desperate breath of air as the water was knocked away from him in a mighty wave. It rushed back in, splashing over his prone form in a wave of bubbles. Blood-tinted fluid washed over the sides of the fountain, soaking into the ground and lowering the water level to knee-height inside the metal ring.

<Get it together, Grant!> Sarge's voice rang inside Grant's head like a bell, causing him to wince in pain. His whole body was one giant bruise, and he couldn't help but groan, letting out some of his precious air to join the bubbles swirling around him. He had no idea where his sword was, and a quick glance at his stats told him he was down to less than two hundred of his health. <On your left!>

Glancing over, Grant spotted through his blurry vision what his target had been initially. The scepter. Not pausing to think, Grant used *Time is Space* to recall his sword. The uchigatana appeared in a swirl of light, his grip angled so the tip of his blade would form *inside* the crystal atop the scepter. The resulting explosion blew Grant into the copper rim of the fountain so hard that he dented it.

<If you keep this up, there are going to be 'Grant' imprints stamped all across the twelve Districts. It's honestly kind of impressive, when you think about it. Most Lords have statues built of themselves, but you're going with a much faster version. It's honestly very efficient.>

"What have you *done*?" Dangerous Dade wrestled himself out of his own indention in the rim of the fountain, and he seemed to be just a tiny bit upset. "Do you have *any* idea what this means?"

Warning: *System failure. Agreement, Deal, and Oath enforcement has been halted. Please remain calm. Please remain cal-*

The message just cut off this time, instead of glitching out like it had in the past. The thought that Grant might be doing lasting damage to the system brought a smile to his face, despite the pain the movement caused.

"The rabble are free to do what they want! *Years* of work have been undone in a split second of destruction!" Dangerous Dade lumbered over to where his giant cleaver had landed after the explosion, wedged into a cracked marble tile. "The Dokeshi will be furious after this!"

"Ask me…" Grant tried to extract himself from his indentation, but he couldn't get his limbs to properly respond. "If I give a *soggy* Regent's…"

<Grant, you need to get up and fight. Your health is low.>

Grant checked his stats with a flicker of his eyes; less than sixty health remaining.

"You just stroll into March, waving your sword around, and think that means you have the *right* to ignore our laws?" The clown hefted his cleaver and started lurching over to Grant, who was now having to deal with the water rising. It was already up to his shins, and ascending quickly. "I'll truly enjoy killing you, even if it doesn't count toward my victory totals."

Fighting through the pain—which was enhanced by his hated pain skill—Grant managed to leverage himself back to his feet. He tried activating *Time is Space* again, but couldn't find a travel-line in the air to grab it from. His sword hadn't been inside this part of the fountain before, but… Grant swayed back against the copper rim, and leaned back as the Vassal approached. He had run along a portion of the rim earlier, and all he could do was hope that it was this part of the fountain.

"Any last words, little man?" Dangerous Dade hefted his cleaver onto his shoulder, ready to smash it down on the unarmed Grant. Instead of finding fear in the Wielder's eyes, Dade was shocked to see a smile on his face. "Is your death truly that funny to you, boy?"

"*My* last words? You really should have used the sharp side of your cleaver. I have three mana regen per second." A flash of light brought his sword back to Grant's outstretched hand, and his bloody smile only grew. "*Thundering Step.*"

The lightning that shot through his body made Grant clench up, but his Lightning attunement allowed enough freedom of movement for him to fall backward out of the fountain. Dangerous Dade wasn't quite as lucky.

Without the system to keep him from taking a turn, Grant had only needed to wait another five seconds for his mana to replenish enough to ignite the spell a second time. He raised up enough to peek over the edge of the fountain, and watched silently as the clown danced. Steam rose from the seams in the Vassal's armor, and he toppled back onto his back in the rising water for the second time.

"I don't have enough mana for a third spell." Grant heaved himself to his feet and climbed back into the water. "Gotta take my own advice and end this with the sharp side of my weapon."

<Excellent. Get that double dip! Your cultivation now shows a credit for defeating a Vassal. If you keep this up, you'll reach level twenty very soon.>

"Well, this should help." Grant raised his uchigatana over his head, and stabbed it down through the eye slit of the evil clown, pressing until his weapon sank four full inches. He sighed as Sarge mumbled happily, knowing that Suki was going to be mad at him.

A scream of indignation brought his attention to the thundering form of Minamino, who must have seen him bringing an end to his evil master's life. The blurred form of Suki intercepted the creature's charge, a mighty uppercut knocking the man-bull to the side. Its legs gave out, and its massive body slid into the edge of the fountain hard enough to crack the copper ring. Grant struggled to stay on his feet through the impact, and ended up using his sword like a cane to approach the monster.

Suki had been clipped by the shoulder of the massive bull and was still picking herself up off the ground. She watched dejectedly as Grant repeated his performance, stabbing his sword down through the skull of the defenseless opponent she had spent the last several minutes trying to defeat. To her, it was a hollow victory, but not one she could voice a complaint over. Suki was smart enough to realize the threat these two would hold for any group of innocents traveling through the Maze.

Unless Dokeshi March wanted to surrender and make it effortless for them to move into the next Zone, there was no easy option for them to get through. She had also seen what Grant had failed to notice, since he had been fighting in the center of the courtyard the entire time. Suki had been fighting around the edges, and she had discovered the remnants of far, *far* too many people. In fact… there was a chance that no one had *ever* been able to make it into the second ring from the first.

That meant that the hedges in this part of the Labyrinth were watered by the blood of those trying to make their lives better, and the Lord of March had made sure that would never happen. She would never admit it out loud, but Suki let out a sigh of relief as Minamino died.

CHAPTER THIRTY-EIGHT

"You aren't mad at me?" Grant had just stood up from his meditation, using the absorbed ability *Live by the Sword*. It brought his health from the mid-sixties to a little over two hundred and thirty. "I killed both of them, and I know you get all worked up when people die."

"How about we check out that paper on the pedestal instead of talking about my feelings?" Suki pushed up from her seated position, leaning her back against the thoroughly destroyed fountain. "We still have to make it through this maze, and then find our way to where the Dokeshi awaits."

Grant nodded in agreement, slowly stretching as he took account of his body. He was still down over a hundred hit points, and his whole body was throbbing in pain. His Bodily Awareness was really starting to wear on his nerves.

The two of them approached the pedestal, finding it hard to hold in the sigh of relief when they saw it was a map. It clearly showed their current location, and no less than three different ways to an exit. There had to have been some kind of spell on it, because the map also showed several yellow, green, and red dots that moved around the maze.

"I'm not sure, but I think this shows the location of all the monsters, bandits, and travelers inside the Labyrinth." Suki followed a cluster of red dots as they approached a single green dot. They met each other at a blind corner, and the green dot sped away, the cluster of red dots following quickly behind. "My guess is the red are monsters, green are regular people, and the yellow must be bandits, or maybe the Dokeshi's troops. Not that there's a big difference between the two."

"Hmm… I've got an idea." Grant looked over her shoulder to get a better idea of what was in the surrounding area. Suki turned to look at him, and Grant tapped a finger down on the nearest exit. "Now that we know where to go, we *could* make it out of this maze in just a few hours. Or—hear me out—we could take our time, kill off some of these monsters, and make it easier for everyone else to travel through this place. Maybe even save a crowd of people and send them out first to distract the watchers on the other side?"

"I see…" Suki's eyes drifted to the edges of the courtyard, where the remains of those who had worked desperately to find a better life had ended up. "Another thing; we mark each intersection we walk past with directions to the nearest exit. That way, people don't have to wander around lost for weeks at a time."

"That's a great idea." Grant rummaged around in his pack for a moment, his excitement starting to overflow. "Let's split a health potion, and then set up some ambushes of our own."

While they studied the map, waiting for the potion to do its work, Grant cleared his throat. "Suki, there's something I wanted to ask you."

"Look, I already told you we don't need to talk about it now, and-" She paused her tirade as Grant shook his head.

"It isn't that. When I was fighting that man-bull creature, I couldn't do much against it." He took a deep breath and let it out slowly. "Sarge told me it's because my fighting style is too straight-forward. I lack subtlety, and that makes it hard to land critical hits. Would you be willing to teach me how to fight more… gracefully?"

"Sure." Suki thought for a moment, eyeing him curiously. "We can practice your sleight-of-hand while we rest, and I can coach you on how to better anticipate what an enemy can do, as well as how to counter-punch by putting yourself in the right position while we fight the monsters. Now that the system is down, it should be much easier to fight the swarms."

The two Wielders ate a small meal, then made their way to the closest cluster of red dots on the map. It wasn't long before the seething cluster of rats the size of small donkeys was in sight, and a quick spell launched by Grant served as their introduction to the group.

<It's good to see you fighting so smoothly, Grant. I was worried that having to take turns over and over again would have impacted your fighting style by now, like it has these monsters. You know; making your swings jerky or choppy.>

"Thanks, Sarge! …I think!" The severed limb of a giant rat arcing over his shoulder helped to emphasize his motions, as Grant was also able to avoid the stream of blood flying behind it. Both Suki and Grant had laid into the vermin like very angry geese chasing after a child holding a piece of bread. It was pretty close to unfair, really. "I'm just happy to be able to fight like a normal person again."

"Don't forget to anticipate their movement!" Suki was using the superior numbers of the rats against them, dancing from side to side and allowing the disgusting monsters to trip each other up. "Remember, you're supposed to be learning how to counterattack!"

Chagrined, Grant stopped his full-frontal assault. Instead, he backed off and allowed them to bite and snap at him. The shift in momentum put more pressure on Suki, but she was more than up to the task. Her meteor-impact punches laid out rats like a bloody metronome.

<Perfect! Now, do it again, but without letting them bite you

first.> Grant was slowly starting to see the openings that happened when an opponent over-extended. He just needed to ensure he didn't sacrifice himself first.

The next rat in line lunged forward, overbalancing itself onto its front legs. Grant did a half-spin and planted his uchigatana in the monster's ribs. A quick twist freed the sword, and he reset himself for the next attack. He couldn't hold back the smile that was creeping across his face. Grant could feel himself improving, and he knew instinctively that it wouldn't be long until he leveled up his Kenjutsu to the Apprentice tier. He didn't know what level three would bring, but it *had* to be better than the pain increase from *Bodily Awareness*.

That was how their progress went for the next several hours. Grant and Suki prowled the maze, searching for monsters so Grant could practice, and future citizens of District March had a fair chance to make it through the Labyrinth.

<Grant, one more monster kill, and you should have enough absorbed energy to reach cultivation level twenty!> Sarge's outburst caused Grant to miss the dodge he was trying to execute. The spiked vine of the oozing plant monster scraped along his ribs, scoring his armor and forcing him to tear off a piece of his cloak before the acid could eat through anything else.

"That's great and all, Sarge, but there's a time and place for these kinds of things!" Grant was forced to roll to his right, using the momentum to slice through the hamstring of the gorilla creature Suki was fighting. It wasn't enough to bring the monster down, but it would certainly help her finish the fight quickly.

<You should have an iron focus. My voice in your head should never cause you to make a misstep.> Sarge paused, as if he was looking over something. <The jump from level nineteen to twenty isn't very profound, but at least you're advancing.>

"That's great, Sarge. How about you tell me how to beat this vine monster instead of distracting me with levels?" Grant used the bulk of the gorilla to stop a whipping vine that splattered burning acid across its back. The baleful stare it graced him with only gave Suki a chance to land a right cross that crossed its eyes. Grant sprinted around the dazed primate to close with the plant monster after giving Suki a brief salute with his sword. "This thing isn't exactly easy to kill. I can't even get close to it!"

<Bah, I don't see what the problem is. I'm immune to acid. Just use me to kill it.> Grant fired a quick scowl at his uchigatana. <Don't look at me like that. You're the one trying to make things more complicated than they really are. If I were to be in a similar situation, I'd try to focus on trimming back the foliage a bit. Cut down on how much reach it has.>

The next vine came at him like a spear, so Grant held his sword up directly in front of it. The vine split along the edge of the blade, each end shooting off to either side. Even though it didn't have a mouth, the vine monster still managed to make a screaming sound; music to Grant's ears.

"That's right, you overgrown fern! I'll bring the pain!" He leapt forward to slam a mighty blow down on the giant flower in the center, but was swatted out of the air by the thickest vine he'd seen yet. He was knocked straight into the thorns of the hedge on the opposite side of the intersection. It took less than a second for him to climb free, panting from his screaming ribs. "Or you can bring the pain instead. That's fine."

"Quit playing with the plant! Get over here and help me!" Suki's yell snapped Grant's attention to the other side of the intersection, where a second oversized gorilla was now forcing her to retreat from her first opponent.

<The sounds of this fight must be drawing in the creatures from the surrounding area. You need to hurry before you're overwhelmed.>

"Alright, shrub. Time to end this!" Grant drew a deep, bone-splintered breath, and sprinted right at the monster. He sliced through the first three vines that came directly at him, and then got thumped in the head by the big one. This time, he was able to counter, and chopped halfway through the offending greenery before it could withdraw for a second strike. "Ow." Grant was seeing stars from the hit, and he felt more than a little nauseous.

<It's a good thing you have such a thick skull. Now, push through that concussion like any good athlete and finish this!>

Swinging for all he was worth; Grant threw everything he had into the attack aimed for the center of the cluster of vines. He missed.

<Maybe this concussion is worse than I thought. Your skills should have kept that from even being possible. How many blades am I holding up?>

The miss might not have done any damage, but it forced the plant creature to jerk the thick vine in position to block. The sharp movement was too much for the damaged vine, causing it to snap where Grant had cut it earlier. The ensuing flood of acid-like blood was easily dodged even by the dazed Wielder, especially since all he had to do was stumble backward.

"Did I get it?" Grant shook his head in an effort to clear it, which was definitely a mistake. It set the world into a spin, and he sat down hard. "Is there an earthquake or something?"

The loss of blood caused the vine creature to wilt into a gray pulp, and it flopped onto its side. One last flail of its vines signaled the end, and it stilled, never to thump a Wielder on the head again.

<Yep, you got it! No, there isn't an earthquake.> Grant was suffused with a dim light, and his head cleared enough to stop the world from spinning. <But you did just hit level twenty! It wasn't enough to heal you all the way, but it should help you finish this fight.>

"No time to celebrate. I need to help Suki." She was retreating in circles, leading the healthy gorilla on a ponderous chase. As they neared Grant's position, he prepared himself to jump into the monster's path. Which was how he ended up getting punted across the intersection for the second time.

His timing might have still been a little off.

"Thanks!" Suki shouted out to a dazed Grant, whose accidental sacrifice gave her a chance to double back and pounce on the distracted gorilla. She hit it with a straight left jab, tilting the chin back, before a haymaker from a right hook on the temple literally knocked its skull off. A part of it, at least. She was able to dance backwards to avoid the spray of blood and gray matter, but it was impossible to ignore her disgust at the accidental kill.

"Ew." Grant managed to sit up just in time to witness the unintentional beheading, and his nausea from the head injury combined with the gory scene made it hard to keep down his breakfast.

<That was impressive.> Grant shook his head and struggled to his feet. <Go finish off that last monster. Every kill brings you closer to the next level.>

Without saying anything to Suki, Grant walked over and planted his sword through the base of the monster's neck. When he looked up, Grant noticed her standing there, staring at her hands with tears brimming in her eyes.

"What's wrong?" Grant was still feeling the pain from the head injury, but he wasn't nearly as bad off as Suki seemed to be. "Are you hurt?"

"No." Suki's gauntlets flickered back into place. "It's nothing. Let's go to the next bunch."

Grant could only shake his head, which was a mistake. The world tried spinning again, and he could only shuffle along behind Suki as she led the way.

<You should stop and meditate to restore some of your health. That hit to your head may have been worse than I thought. You haven't even had a chance to check your new level! Killing thirty monsters is a great achievement, and you should at least take a moment to look over your gains.>

"I'm fine. Suki wants us to hurry, and I don't want to hold her up." Grant finally sheathed his uchigatana, just then realizing that he was still walking around with it. "Besides, didn't you say that I need to kill more monsters? Meditating isn't killing monsters."

"Are you coming? There's so many dots ahead, and I *will* take them all for myself." Suki didn't wait for Grant to answer, instead speeding up to make it to the turn before him.

An arrow sank into her face.

CHAPTER THIRTY-NINE

Grant rushed to check on Suki, but she had merely taken the shot in stride. The arrow had deflected off of her cheek bone, leaving a wide, bleeding laceration across the middle of her face. From the look of sheer murder on her face, Grant almost felt sorry for whoever the archer was.

Almost.

"*Bandits*!" Suki screamed in rage, then disappeared around the corner. Shouts and screams suddenly echoed down the narrow pathway. As he finally caught up to her, Grant was shocked to see how many people made up the bandit group. This was a *very* well prepared, highly geared team.

<This is closer to the end of the maze. These bandits have to be one of the strongest groups in the area in order to survive here. It also means they get to rob, loot, recruit, and steal from the strongest people that make it this far.>

Even though the world was still trying to spin around him, Grant shuffled into the fray. It was quickly clear that the group wasn't used to fighting without the turn-based system in place. The man wielding a mace seemed to pause longer than necessary after making a swing at Grant's midsection, which gave him an opening to exploit. A quick upward swing removed the fingers holding the mace, even though he was aiming for the hand.

<Definitely worse than I thought. Grant, you need to take a healing potion.> Grant shook his head in denial, then stumbled. Even if he wanted to take one, there was no time. Suki was dancing circles around four different attackers, but she wasn't actually taking any of them out of the fight. Another arrow flashed out of the corner of his eye, and Grant tried deflecting it out of reflex. Instead of knocking it away, Grant just redirected it into the top of his foot.

"Ow." The arrow had gone all the way through, and was now holding him in place. Two more bandits approached Grant, their obvious smiles at his predicament making him mad. "You think my pain is *funny*? *Thundering Step*. How about that? Is other people's suffering still funny?"

The two men had both been dual-wielding daggers, and the spell caused lightning to dance between the upheld blades. While the spell was still functioning, Grant used his uchigatana to remove their heads. The hidden archer must have seen it happen, because another arrow impacted against Grant's armor. It didn't penetrate, but the force sent him stumbling backward, painfully snapping the arrow off inside his impaled foot.

A second wave of bandits burst from around the corner farther down the pathway, making their situation worse. Suki still hadn't taken down a single opponent, and a cultivator he had shocked with his spell was already getting back into the fight.

"Suki! Watch your back! Spear to the rear!" She didn't acknowledge Grant's shout, but it was obvious she had heard him when she managed to angle the thrust from a short-sword into the path of the spear aimed at her back. Before the second wave could reach them, Grant was surprised by the man he had cut the fingers off of. He had picked the heavy weapon back up, squeezing it between his palms. A crunching blow into his knee was the only warning Grant had that the man was marginally back in the fight.

<At least it's the same leg as the arrow injury.>

"Not helping, Sarge." Grant shifted his weight as he turned to face the bandit, and his leg barely held up his weight. "That's going to be a problem."

Grant slapped aside the mace and made a quick stab to the middle of the fewer-phalanged man's chest that finally put him down, but the damage was already done. "There are six more coming, and I'm hurt! Suki, you have to quit playing around, or we're both dead!"

An arrow piercing his left shoulder only emphasized his point. Suki did a double-take when she took a look at Grant, shocked to see how much blood he was covered in.

"Aahh! *Why?* Why are you making me do this!" Suki's next punch folded the elbow of one of her attackers in the wrong direction, making him shout almost as loud as the sound of snapping bone. A follow-up punch rammed the bandit's head back so hard that Grant could hear their neck snap. "I don't want to *be* this kind of person!"

The left hook she laid into the woman who was holding a longsword crunched ribs and caved in the entire side of her chest. "Why are you making me kill you?"

A third attacker was obliterated instantly when Suki jerked the spear out of the hands of the bandit standing behind her, and she shoved the blunt end all the way through their head. A quick spin put the spear point through the second to last bandit's torso, only increasing the amount of viscera splattered over the area.

Whether it was her crazed shouts, or the brutal ending of their friends, the approaching bandits decided to slow their charge. The final enemy still intent on facing Suki darted forward to stab her with their short sword, just in time to get an arrow right between their shoulder blades. They fell with a shout, and the archer finally came out of hiding, shock on her tear-stained face. The approaching six clustered up around the archer, as if passing her down the walkway would put them within range.

<Grant, you need to stop the bleeding from your foot and shoulder. Your health is dropping fast.> Sarge ordered him, forcing Grant to check. He was at one hundred and thirteen; as he watched, it ticked down to one hundred and twelve. Grant tried to take a step to the side, but his injured leg gave out on him. He dropped to his injured knee with a grunt of pain. Suki glanced over in his direction, and her eyes seemed unfocused, like she wasn't even seeing him. A screen popped up in Grant's vision, making his vision swim.

Debuff: Bleeding from multiple wounds. Loss of one HP every three seconds.

"Suki, I've..." Grant paused to do some mental math. It took him longer than normal, considering his condition. "I've got about five and a half minutes until I bleed out."

Her eyes came back into focus, and she winced when she surveyed what she had done. Her face flattened when she looked back at Grant, as if all the emotion was drained out of her. She took a step toward the cluster of bandits, who had been emboldened by Grant taking a knee. "It's okay. It'll all be okay, Grant. I'll take care of things."

As she squared up in a horse stance a little in front of him, the bandits decided to charge. Grant quickly activated his spell again, catching all but two of the charging people in the radius of lightning. They locked up, their momentum bringing them closer even as they fell. Even on one knee, Grant was able to kill the three that landed within range. Suki quickly finished off the two that were closest to her by crushing their throats with deliberate hammer fists. The entire time her face didn't even flicker with emotion, which greatly worried Grant.

The last two bandits were the archer that had started the whole thing, and a large man wearing black leathers and a gray cloak. They began backing up, before Suki squared her shoulders and sprinted at them. Considering her *astounding* sprinting speed, it was obvious they wouldn't be fast enough to get away.

The man stopped running and crouched low, ready to take her charge. It also allowed for the archer to shoot over the bandit's head. The emotionless Suki didn't seem to care, barreling straight at the arrow pointed at her head. Grant didn't have the mana to toss out another spell, so he did the only thing he could think of. He threw his sword.

The uchigatana tumbled through the air before bouncing off the ground hilt-first. It clattered to the ground three feet away from the two bandits, doing absolutely no damage to anyone. Somehow, that was enough.

Distracted by the flashing sword thrown at them, the enemy fighters took their eyes off of Suki just long enough for her to get in close. She used the shoulder of the crouched man to vault over him, executing a chopping axe kick into the top of the archer's head. Even though her feet didn't have the offensive bonus provided by the gauntlets her fists had, Suki's legs were powerful enough to kill the archer with the first hit.

"*No*!" The cloaked man shouted out, his exclamation expressing his emotions better than any discourse could. A swinging backfist caved his face in before he could bring his weapons to bear, killing him just as quickly as the archer.

Seeing that all the enemies were gone, Grant immediately dropped into meditation. It was impossible to sit in the lotus position with his knee, so he just laid down on the blood-soaked ground.

The fight replayed in his mind, showing him how to improve. There was a harsh lesson about finishing off enemies when he had a chance, especially if the enemy carried a weapon that didn't require a full set of fingers to use. It was also painfully, deadly obvious that Grant should have listened to Sarge and tried to heal as much as possible before charging into battle. All he could do was try to lay that blame at the feet of his head injury, but that felt… cheap.

As Grant opened his eyes, he finally took the chance to pull up his stats.

Name: Grant Monday
Rank: Lord of The Month (January, February)
Class: Foundation Cultivator
Cultivation Achievement Level: 20
Cultivation Stage: Late Summer
Inherent Abilities: Swirling Seasons Cultivation
Health: 272/449 (Persistent Head Injury, current maximum health capped at 300.)
Mana: 16/23

Characteristics
Physical: 266
Mental: 92
Armor Proficiency: 141
Weapon Proficiency: 174

The changes were slight, besides the addition of an open spell slot. Grant was more concerned about the notice that he had a persistent injury than anything else. That meant a healing potion wouldn't be enough to fix it. They would have to find a professional healer to fix him, or try to wait it out. Either way, it would be a huge pain to get his injury cured.

He sat up to inspect his knee, relieved to find that it had mostly healed. It was still tender, but he was sure it could handle his weight. The bleeding wounds he had suffered were also healed, which thankfully ended his countdown to death. They were still tender, however, and he could tell that he needed to be careful not to reopen them. As he stood, the world went spinning again. Definitely needed to get his head injury taken care of.

"Suki, I need a professional healer." The pink-haired Wielder had picked up the bow that the archer had dropped, and she was staring at it with watery eyes. "Suki? What's wrong?"

"I... I can't do this." She waved her hands at all the corpses, their blood still soaking into the ground. A single tear rolled down her cheek and got caught on the bloody furrow left on her face by the arrow. "This is just too much. I can't keep watching the light go out of their eyes, their life leaving their bodies. Maybe I can kill from a distance. Taking up the bow would mean I don't have to be *right there* to watch them die. I can give my gauntlets to a person more worthy of Wielding them."

"No. That's not fair to you, or your people." Grant's voice was quiet but firm. Suki looked up at him, the question clear on her features. "Would it be better for them to have a leader that *enjoyed* killing? To have a Wielder that was excited by the idea of watching as a person's eyes faded into darkness?"

He paused to meet her eyes and show her how very serious he was. "You only killed them when you had no choice. There's a good chance that you could have gotten away, but I'd have died after my knee was crushed. You saved my life. While I might not be the smartest Wielder in the District, even I know enough to say that a leader who only kills as a last resort is a good person to have in charge."

"Are you… are you *sure*?" Suki sniffed, trying and failing to hold back her tears. "I still feel like I'm no better than the monsters we killed."

"These *bandits* were no different than those monsters. They just looked like humans." Grant took the bow from her trembling hands and tossed it to the side. She nodded silently, and they started walking for the exit. They left the bow in the dirt, and neither bothered looking back. "You aren't an arrow that kills from afar. I know you better than that. Lady February is a gauntlet-covered fist that beats evil into the dirt."

CHAPTER FORTY

The exit of the maze was—surprisingly—unguarded and completely unwatched, as far as they could tell. The two Wielders approached the gate, only to find it cracked open. Several rising pillars of smoke were visible on the other side of the barrier, and the casino floor they entered was abandoned.

"What do you think happened here?" Suki pulled back a tattered curtain to peek at an area that had clearly been ransacked. It might have been a high roller room, or just a fancy breakroom for the employees. Now, it was mostly splintered wood and torn fabric. Even the gilt and ivory inlay on the walls had been stripped. "Some kind of natural disaster? A beast attack?"

"I'm not sure." Grant kept one hand on his sword, and the other on Suki's shoulder. Holding on to her helped prevent the world from spinning. "Whatever it was, we should get out of here."

"Agreed. This place is giving me the creeps." Suki led them through the debris-strewn rooms, eventually finding another unguarded exit. "Which way do you think we should go for a healer?"

"Sundays can be found almost anywhere, right? Even so, they most likely have shops in nicer areas. We should head toward anywhere the buildings look nicer." He motioned to the right, taking his hand off her and swaying dangerously as he did so. "There has to be one eventually."

"That makes as much sense as anything else." Suki warily eyed the drifting pillars of smoke in the near distance. "As long as we're careful, we should be fine."

They walked with the slowly setting sun to their backs, their shadows leading them forward. After traveling for almost an hour, it was clear this area of the District hadn't suffered from a natural calamity. Unless, of course, you counted Grant as a force of nature. Which most would not.

Almost every intersection they approached was strewn with the bodies of emaciated people, and not-quite-as-emaciated guards. There was even the body of one of Dokeshi March's Vassals at the end of an alley, barely visible beneath the pile of dead that had sacrificed themselves in order to bring down the clown. Across the street from the alley filled with death stood a small casino that looked as if someone had tried to burn it down, but gave up after only a few tries.

"Is that written in blood?" The graffiti scrawled on the charred wall was still visible, despite the fading light and heavy destruction. Suki tried brushing aside some of the ash clinging to the sticky substance. "I can barely read it."

<It says, 'Death to the System' right there, and further down, I'm pretty sure someone wrote, 'Down with the Clown.'> Sarge waited for Grant to get closer, so he could get a better look as well. <Ah, it says, 'Down with the *Mad* Clown'. My guess would be that this area was affected when you killed Dangerous Dade, allowing the citizens to revolt. Either that, or the bonds enforced by the Vassals are weakening as you diminish their numbers. Also, yes, that is most definitely blood.>

"Sarge says it's blood, and this destruction was caused by the system going down." Grant swallowed hard, his wide-eyed stare only partly due to his head injury. “Which means all of this is my fault.”

“Don’t think like that, Grant. It was only a matter of time until the people found a way to revolt against the twisted ruler of this District.” Suki pulled him away from the ruins of the building, turning them toward an area that didn’t have as much overall destruction.

“I don’t feel particularly bad about kicking off an insurrection. *That* needed to happen.” Grant’s shoulders slumped. “What I feel bad about is not being here to help the people stand against the Vassals and guards that have had a boot on their necks for so long. How many could we have saved if we were here to help them fight?”

“There’s no point in thinking about that now. All we can do at the moment is find you a healer, and get to wherever the Dokeshi is hiding.” She purposefully lengthened her stride to force Grant to pick up the pace. “Once he’s taken care of, things should settle down quickly.”

“I hope so. Otherwise, there might not be many people left in District March.” They were silent after Grant’s comment. While it was true, the observation didn’t help raise their spirits. Finally, after the sun had completely disappeared from the sky, and the only light came from the stars and still-burning fires of an oppressed people’s retribution, they came across a building with the violet ‘S’ of House Sunday painted on the door.

“Are you sure this is a good idea?” Grant pulled Suki to a stop before she could knock on the door. “Dokeshi March is from a Noble House, right? Won’t these people be on his side?”

“Most Houses are more divided than people realize, especially if the Dokeshi is from a different one. If this particular branch of House Sunday was in the Dokeshi’s favor, do you think they would be this far away from his seat of power?” She knocked loudly on the door. “Besides, they can either heal you willingly, or I can *explain* why it would be in their best interest to help us.”

Her gauntlets briefly flickered into place before disappearing again, as if to better prove her point. After only a few brief moments, the door cracked open a finger, and a surprisingly young-sounding voice came from within.

"I'm sorry, but the Healing House is closed. Please come back at a later time." The voice cracking halfway through the sentence was a dead giveaway that the speaker was an adolescent boy, barely on the cusp of manhood.

"No." Suki shoved her hand in the narrow crack, and her gauntlets appeared before the boy could smash her fingers with the heavy door. "We don't have time to come back tomorrow. You *will* see us now."

"But the Master said-"

"I don't care what your Master said. He'll most definitely want to help us." She motioned back toward Grant, and her voice dropped to a low whisper. "We're the ones who are going to end the reign of the Dokeshi."

The single visible eye widened at her words, and the sounds of a series of chains clattering against the door caused Suki to take a step back. The boy opened the door just wide enough for the two of them to squeeze through, forcing Grant to turn sideways to get inside. "Wait here while I tell the Master of your arrival? Please?"

"Don't worry, we aren't going anywhere." Grant closed and locked the door before leaning against it. The almost constant spinning had worn on him, and he felt nauseous and more tired than he should have been. "In case you were wondering, I definitely don't recommend head injuries. Skull fractures aren't all they're cracked up to be."

"Was that supposed to be a joke?" Suki turned and held Grant's face in her hands, staring deeply into his eyes. Grimacing, she guided him to a bench that ran the full length of the entry room. "You definitely aren't yourself right now, and one pupil is much larger than the other. Sit down and try not to move."

Not having anything better to do, Grant took in his surroundings. The room was lit by a pair of old-fashioned oil lamps instead of the light orbs he'd expected to see in a House as well-off as House Sunday usually was. They were only able to illuminate half of the room Suki and he were standing in, leaving the far side in deep shadow. Two doors on either wall were barely visible, though both looked like they hadn't been used in some time.

The sparse furniture placed around the room lacked any form of padding and looked worn-down. The paint was chipping in the corners of the ceiling, and the faint smell of old blood and dried vomit made him even more nauseous. It was clear this branch of House Sunday hadn't seen prosperity in quite some time.

A deep voice came from the darkness at the end of the entry hall. "What do we have here? A pair of grandstanding hooligans, or two lions wearing the hide of a sheep?"

"Old man. You're the one making a scene here." Suki was focused on a closed door halfway down the hallway, ignoring the shadows at the end of the hall. "Why don't you give it up and come out here. My friend was hit on the head in the labyrinth several hours ago, and isn't getting better."

"Old man, huh? Who are you to-"

"I'm the one that will tear this disgrace of a healing house down to the studs if you don't get out here right this *minute*!" Suki's gauntlets had flickered into place, and for the first time, Grant thought he could see violet lightning sparking along the edges and grooves of the metal. That was new.

"Lions, it is, then." The door she had been staring at opened inward, and a slight man with dark hair just starting to go gray stepped into the room. His voice didn't change much, which Grant found to be extremely funny. How could such a little man have such a deep voice? "I still take offense at being called old, though. I'm the youngest Master Healer in all of District March, and that isn't even counting-"

"If you don't see to my friend's health, I'll do more than just destroy your *building*." This time, Grant was one hundred percent sure he had seen violet sparks dancing around her arms.

It even raised a few strands of her pink hair, making them stick straight out from her head. Which, of course, only added to the crazed look she was currently embracing.

"Wow, you really are a feisty one, aren't you?" The healer walked over to check Grant, plucking one of the lanterns from its place on the side table as he got closer. "Fine, let me look your boyfriend over, before you make a ruckus that brings the mob down on our heads." As he held the lamp up to get a better look at Grant, he winced as soon as he met his eyes.

"Andy!" The deep bellow made Grant shudder in pain, which seemed to only worry the healer more. "Andy, get your lazy rump out here, now!"

"Yes, master?" The boy from earlier was panting, clearly having sprinted from somewhere deeper within the house.

"We have a level four trauma debuff." The healer squinted, obviously using some ability to look more carefully at Grant. "Persistent Head Injury, manifesting as a slow brain bleed."

He grabbed Grant by the arm and laid him down on the bench. Grant couldn't help but notice that the man was much stronger than he looked. He wondered what Sarge would think about that. Wait, when was the last time Grant had heard from Sarge? It felt like it had been hours since the sword spirit had said something. "Andy, I need a gurney, and tell Murphy I want room seven prepped for surgery. If we don't relieve the pressure on his brain, this young man won't survive the night."

"What? What do you mean, 'won't survive the night'?" Suki was wringing her hands nervously, causing violet sparks to jump out from between her hands.

"Don't worry, I think you got him here in time." The Master Healer pulled out a small vial and pulled the cork before holding it under Grant's nose. "You will need to wait out here. He's going to take a little nap now, and then be by your side before you know it."

"It smells like pancakes. Is someone making pancakes? I'd really, *really* like pancakes." Grant started drifting away, his already unsteady mind finally slipping into sleep. Before he could fully fade, he suddenly sat straight up, staring the healer straight in his surprised face. "Not Suki's pancakes. Those things are made of hate and sadness. I want *happy* pancakes."

The healer gave him a tight smile and nodded in acceptance, so Grant relaxed again, safe in the knowledge that he wouldn't have to eat the hate-cakes.

CHAPTER FORTY-ONE

"Is he okay?" Suki's voice was the first thing Grant heard as he started to wake up. "That is a *lot* of gauze."

"I assure you; he'll be back on his feet in no time. I'm not surprised you're worried about him; I can barely believe he could walk with so many partially-healed injuries." Grant tried to move, but his body wasn't quite ready to listen to him yet. The healer's voice was close, as if he was leaning over Grant as he talked. "We drilled a small hole through his skull, which relieved the pressure, then applied a healing ointment to the surface of his brain to stop the bleeding. His natural Physical cultivation should take care of the rest."

They did *what*! Grant struggled even harder to get up, but his limbs still wouldn't respond.

"Thank you, Master Healer. What do we owe you?" Suki's voice was farther away now, and he could hear her rummaging through something. Probably their packs.

"I think we should go elsewhere to discuss payment. If what you told Andy about ending the reign of the Mad Jester is true, further conversation is necessary." The voices of the two slowly faded as they walked away, leaving Grant by himself. Well, almost by himself.

<Finally decided to wake up, huh?> Sarge's voice was distinctly upset. Somehow, Grant had made him angry. <I don't think I've ever met a man who sleeps more than you!>

"Ugnug." Grant wasn't able to argue that it wasn't exactly his fault that his brain was bleeding on the inside, so some stranger had drilled a hole in his head and spread a mystery substance on his thought ball, but Sarge knew what he meant.

<It most *definitely* was your fault. You're the one who let that plant hit you in the head hard enough to cause all of this.> Grant was fighting to stand, but gave up when he only managed to smack his face off the edge of a table next to his bed. He groaned in pain, but it fell on deaf ears. <Serves you right. Damage your brain so bad that we get cut off again, and you'll never hear the end of it!>

"Ish washint on purposh." It seemed like whacking his face on a solid object was enough to get his brain and body to start talking to one another again. "How long wash I oush?"

<Considering the light coming through the windows, I'd say you were unconscious for at least one full night.> Grant tried stretching to relieve some of the knots in his back from laying down on such an uncomfortable bed for so long, but it was asking too much, too soon. He toppled over again, destroying a table and shattering the clay mug that had been sitting on top of it. Thankfully, the ruckus meant someone finally realized he was awake.

"Grant! What are you doing out of bed?" Suki rushed through the open door and hurried over to pick him up off the floor. "You shouldn't be trying to do anything until the Master Healer clears you!"

"If he's got the energy to try and stand this soon, I'd say you might be able to leave in just a few weeks!" The healer was practically dancing with obvious joy, which concerned Grant. Was seeing a patient up and moving a rare occurrence for him?

"Weeks? Can't wait that long." Grant used Suki to help him

stand. As long as he took his time, forming legible words was possible. "Must. Stop. Dokeshi. Leave. Now."

"That's outlandish, even for a cultivator with twice your power." The healer walked over and used his considerable strength to force Grant to sit back down on the bed. The stubborn frown on Grant's face made the healer sigh. "You can lead a Murder Goat to a cliff, but you can't make it jump."

He was mumbling under his breath, but it was still loud enough for Grant to hear him. The healer looked up and met Grant's stony glare with one of his own. "How about a compromise? I'll run you through some tests this evening, and if you pass them, we can discuss you leaving in the morning. Does that sound fair?"

"Fair." Grant didn't have the strength to push the healer aside, so agreeing with him before he could change his mind was his only real option. "Will. Test. Tonight."

"Great!" The healer stood up and headed for the door. "Why don't you get some more rest, and Lady Suki and I'll return before the day is done."

Taking the hint, Suki moved to join the healer. With a wink, the man was gone, disappearing down the hallway much faster than his short stature should have allowed. "I'll have some food sent up in a bit. Make sure you eat all of it!"

"He's right, you know." Suki looked like she wanted to approach Grant, but instead she gripped the doorframe. "You need some rest, to allow your body to heal. I'll be back in a few hours to check on you."

"See. You." Grant laid back down on the rock-like bed and tried to fluff his pillows enough to get comfortable. It didn't work. "Bring. Food."

Suki gave him a nod and left. For some reason, it felt like the room had lost some of the light it had been bathed in. Deciding to ignore such intrusive thoughts, Grant was quickly asleep. Debilitating pain woke him up a few seconds later. At least, it felt like a few seconds. As he opened his eyes, he saw Suki pulling him up into a sitting position.

"It's time to go. Help me get your armor back on." Grant rubbed at his eyes, clearing away the grainy crust that made them stick together. "They're searching for us, and the system keeps going in and out."

"Why would the system keep going in and out?" Grant almost passed out when he bent down to slip his boots on. Grant's stomach rumbled, and he put a hand on his abdomen. "That hasn't happened before, has it? What about food? I've got the strangest urge to have a fiber bar."

"There are mobs of people roaming the streets, trying to hunt down the Vassals that are searching for us." She cinched down on the ties that held his greaves in place. "It's probably due to them coming in and out of range as they run from the mobs. Which means we don't have time for food."

Just as they finished getting the last parts of his armor in place, a blurred screen fuzzed into his vision. Grant couldn't make out what it said before it dissipated into motes of light, but it drove home the urgency of the situation.

"Last thing is your helm. It won't fit with all the bandages in place." Grant felt at his head, surprised to feel a large cushion of gauze wrapped around the top of his head. "Do you want to take it off, or leave it?"

"Suki, you and I both know I'll stand out like a hunter in a zoo if I have clean white gauze piled on my head. Help me cut it off." With his agreement, she grabbed a small pair of scissors from a tray near the door. Once it was removed, Grant gingerly felt at the area the bandages had covered. There was a bald patch on the side of his head, and a small line that led to the top of his left ear. It was tender, but it wasn't so bad that he couldn't put his helmet on to protect it.

<A wise decision. It won't be comfortable, but not wearing it only invites further injury.> Grant silently agreed with Sarge. He had learned a good lesson about not taking care of his head. One should *always* take care of the thing that protects their brain.

"Okay, now that you're dressed, we need to go." Suki

handed Grant his uchigatana, and he secured it on his belt as they crept down the darkened hallway toward the exit. "As soon as we get our packs, we need to head deeper into the district. The Dokeshi has to be somewhere in the center."

"Don't forget to pull out our cloaks. They might help hide us." Suki nodded at Grant's suggestion, and the two of them pulled on their 'disguises'. Their packs were sitting by the front door, and Grant was surprised when he picked his up. He looked questioningly at Suki. "Why is my pack so much lighter?"

"I had to trade most of our remaining food as payment for your healing." Grant's face fell at her words, but she smiled and laid a hand on his shoulder. "Don't worry, we won't starve anytime soon. It turns out, they're a lot like you were when you got to February. They simply don't appreciate the wonderful food my District makes, so we still have plenty of my specialty health bars! Here, I know you're hungry; why don't you eat this one? It's wheatgrass flavored!"

"Delicious." Grant took a bite of the brick-like substance Suki called food, almost chipping a tooth in the process. "Ah, yes. The textured flavor of health."

#ERROR1414

Too many origin points in one area. Unable to initialize system. Please reduce origin points to proceed.

The message shut Grant's mouth instantly. If an 'origin point' was a Vassal's scepter, then they had a more serious issue than he'd expected.

CHAPTER FORTY-TWO

They left the House Sunday building as the sun was beginning to disappear behind the peaks of the rooftops. Grant was still having a few balance problems, but at least he was no longer dealing with the nausea and dizziness from before.

<Your health status is clear now, so you should be able to go back to full health soon.> Grant checked his health status, and was pleased to see that he was already up to three hundred and sixty. <As soon as you get back to full health, I want you to do one hundred pushups, one hundred sit-ups, one hundred jumping jacks, and a long run.>

"What? Why would you want me to do that?" Grant was confused, considering the fact that he hadn't needed to train in several days.

<Just because you have been too busy to train the past few days, doesn't mean you get to slack off.> Grant could only chuckle at the feisty sword spirit. <Also, I want to make sure there are no lingering effects from the operation, and that much physical activity should be enough for me to identify any issues.>

"Huh. That's a good point." Grant tried stretching his joints as they were walking, getting a better idea of any problems he might be facing. "I think I'm pretty good."

<You still haven't raised your blood pressure, heart rate, or respiration. I want to be completely sure you're back to full strength before you have to fight again.>

"You!" A shout from a group of uniformed soldiers hiding in an alley they had just walked past echoed down the empty street. "Come here and answer some questions!"

"It looks like I don't have time to wait before I fight again, Sarge." Grant placed his hand on the hilt of his sword. "I think these people wouldn't be okay with giving me some time for a workout."

"Oh my, aren't these two just *delicious*." The massive bulk that emerged out of the shadows in front of Suki and Grant would have fit right in with the people of District January. "Don't worry, they won't get far."

"Just who are you supposed to be?" Suki balled up her fists without her gauntlets appearing. "Why are you trying to keep us from getting out of this place?"

"Oh, you just gave yourself away, little Wielder." The giant man sauntered into the light, and his mask covered with hearts and bubbles became visible. He was wearing a silk clown costume and carried no visible weapons. The only oddity was the chain wrapped around his waist like a belt. "I'm… *heehee*… the Prime Vassal of Dokeshi March. The one person in all of District March that everyone knows on sight."

The largest scepter Grant had seen to date appeared in the enormous clown's hand. "My name is *Cuddles*. Who wants a hug?"

"Well, this isn't good." Suki's gauntlets appeared in a flare of purple sparks, somehow appearing larger than they had in the past. "I'll handle the big one, and you deal with the guards."

"Those aren't just guards… *heehee*… those are Dicemen, the elite of the Dokeshi's forces." The gem on the top of Cuddles' scepter flared with a blue light. "I don't think just one of you can simply *deal* with them like you have the others."

"It's fine, Suki. I can take them." Grant nodded at her and started approaching their line. "That overgrown clown doesn't know what we're capable of."

"Oh, I don't doubt that you're capable. I just don't think you will be able to fight all of them at once. Especially... *heehee*... when I do *this*. None of those present will use a lethal attack!" Cuddles raised his scepter and declared a new *rule* in a surprisingly official tone. A screen popped up in front of everyone, and Grant was shocked to read what it had to say.

Congratulations! *Since you're within the radius of the Prime Vassal's scepter, you have been automatically included in the New Rule!*

Rule #15943: No lethal attacks can be used while fighting.

Since this Rule applies to everyone equally, including the Prime Vassal, no acceptance or oaths are necessary! All turn-based combat will be adjusted. This rule only applies while within the radius of the Prime Vassal. Other side effects may include frustration, inability to execute those that deserve it, and near-death experiences. Please ask the nearest Vassal if you have any questions.

Suki pounded her fists together, sending purple sparks shooting in an arc in front of her. "You can't just make up stupid rules like that! We have to agree to your stupid deals before they start working!"

"That's where you're wrong, little Wielder! *Heehee*... that might be the case for my weaker brothers and sisters, but not me! Did you ever *agree* to the turn-based fighting system? No? That's because the Dokeshi's Wielded Weapon is powerful enough to enforce *The Rules*, as long as they apply equally to everyone! As the Prime Vassal, my weapon is closer in power to his than anyone else's!" Cuddles spun his scepter and tapped the glowing gem on the chain wrapped around him like a belt. "Now… how about we get things started?"

Grant wasn't willing to just give up, so he rushed at the line of Dicemen that stretched from one end of the road to the other. They were only one rank deep, meaning he should be able to get past them easily.

<The new *rule* is only that you can't kill. Remember your training. You can use the back edge of your sword, the side of the blade, or hit them in non-lethal areas.> Grant assessed himself as he dashed forward, feeling only a faint hint of pain from the cut on his head. <You can also try for disabling wounds, or just remove a few limbs. None of those would be… *immediately* fatal.>

"Good idea, Sarge. I wouldn't mind seeing these guys try to fight without all their hands and feet!" Grant maneuvered to the left side of the street, where there was more rubble to mess with their footing. "Okay, time to roll these Dicemen!"

Combat initiated

Action: *Attack With Weapon*

Result: *Dicemen bonus in effect, resulting in a reduction of damage by 30%. 22 blunt damage, opponent stunned for 45 seconds.*

Opponents remaining: 11

Actions: *Please select one option from the following list*

Attack: *Lethal (not selectable), Non-lethal, Spell*

Defend: *With Weapon, Without weapon*

Run: *Attempt Escape*

Grant was forced to select *Defend: With Weapon* before the other eleven Dicemen could strike. He dropped to one knee as a spearhead flashed through the space where his neck had just been and deflected another from hitting him in the face.

"I thought the rules were supposed to apply to everyone!" Grant rolled back from another trio of stabs from the Dicemen and sprang back to his feet. "Those would have been lethal!"

"Who said they were even trying to hit you?" Cuddles and Suki had been feeling each other out, neither one fully committed to a solid strike. "Perhaps, they were just trying to get you within range of me! *Heehee.*"

The overly large clown tapped his chain belt again, and the odd accessory unfurled itself from his prodigious waistline. As it dropped, it burrowed underground like some kind of worm, sending dust and dirt flying. As soon as it disappeared, Suki jumped back to stand next to Grant. The place she had been standing immediately erupted as the chain shot out of the ground, missing her completely.

"This is bad. That's a *Summer* weapon!" Suki jumped again, landing on an upside-down rain barrel near the edge of the road. She motioned for Grant to do the same. "Don't stand on the ground! Get somewhere higher; that weapon must have a permanent earth effect!"

"Ah, ah, *ah*... I don't think so!" The Vassal raised his scepter again, this time with both hands. "*Everyone present will keep both feet on the ground at all times.*"

Congratulations! *Since you're within the radius of the Prime Vassal's scepter, you have been automatically included in the New Rule!*

Rule #15944: Both feet must always remain in contact with the earth.

Since this Rule applies to everyone equally, including the Prime Vassal, no acceptance or oaths are necessary! All turn-based combat will be adjusted. This rule only applies while within the radius of the Prime Vassal. Other side effects may include problems dodging attacks, multiple toe injuries, and difficulty in walking, running, or climbing stairs. Please ask the nearest Vassal if you have any questions.

Suki immediately dropped off the rain barrel onto the ground, her face red from straining against the new *rule*.

"*Heehee*, I knew you'd love the new rule! It should make things easier." The chains shot up from the ground and started wrapping around Suki's calves. Grant was able to dodge the first chain, but shuffling backward too far led him right into the spears of the Dicemen. A sharp poke forced him to balance too far forward, and he was quickly wrapped around the legs. "Easier for me, I should say."

"You think this is enough to stop us? We haven't even begun to fight!" Suki punched down at the chain wrapped around her right leg, shattering the first link. She started shuffling to get the Vassal within range of her fists, but another chain replaced the broken one. This time, she was trapped in a more awkward stance, almost doing the splits. "*Fight* me, you coward!"

"There's a reason why they call me *Cuddles*, little Wielder. You were close in your estimate of my weapon." Another flare of his scepter, and the chains started crawling up their bodies, pulling down on Suki and Grant. "It's a Summer weapon, yes, but enchanted with a metal snake's ability to produce endless links and move toward enemies. I've got an earth elemental *spell* that allows me to make my chains as heavy as I want. Either you keep fighting them until their weight breaks your bones, or you lay down and *cuddle* with the ground."

While Suki and Cuddles were talking, Grant had been shattering chains with the edge of his blade over and over, until he was able to shuffle away from the place where they had come out of the ground.

"Ha! You can't catch me, you stupid-" Grant was cut off by a chain sneaking up behind him and wrapping itself around his throat. He was jerked back onto his back, and quickly cocooned in the metal links controlled by Cuddles.

"You were saying?" The clown shuffled over to Grant, who wheezed as the weight of the chains kept increasing. Suki was still refusing to buckle, but her knees were shaking, and sweat rolled down her face. "I don't think the two of you truly understand who you have been dealing with."

Before Cuddles could continue monologuing, the sound of glass shattering caused him to look up. "What's this, then? You three, go and ensure we aren't disturbed."

Three of the Dicemen shuffled off to see what the disturbance was, not bothering to hide now that their prey had been captured… which was why the mob had no problem identifying them when they rounded the corner.

"Look! It's another o' them fancy guards!"

"Hey, they's the ones that be guardin' the Mad Jester's clowns! Follow 'em!"

"Yeah! Off wi' the head o' the system keepers!"

As the three men came spilling back out onto the street, the torch-wielding mob followed right behind. The spot that marked the range of Cuddles' ridiculous rules was readily apparent when the whole mess of people suddenly had to start shuffling forward. There was more than a little cursing as people stubbed toes and slid feet over shards of glass, but it wasn't enough to stop the angry crowd.

"There 'e is! Kill 'em!"

"Off wi' their eggs!"

"Well, you two. What to do? Can't kill you, don't have the time to drag you along… it appears it might be time for me to retreat. This group is interested in removing my… eggs? *Heehee*… I don't truly know what that means, but I certainly don't intend to find out." Cuddles started shuffling away, with his Dicemen Guards bringing up the rear. The three that he had sent out as scouts were swallowed by the mob, who showed them no mercy.

Like some kind of insatiable monster, the villagers paused

long enough to deal with their 'snack' before going right back to chasing down Cuddles. The clown turned his masked face to meet Grant's eyes before he shuffled out of earshot. "Now that I know what you look like, I'll find you again soon. You can run, you can hide… but The House *Always* Wins."

CHAPTER FORTY-THREE

Shortly after the mob ran off Cuddles, the chains surrounding Suki and Grant started acting like normal loops of metal instead of living constrictor snakes. They were able to work themselves free shortly before the last few members of the mob disappeared around a corner in the distance. As they did, the metal rusted and fell away as dust.

"Well, that was embarrassing." Suki was hunched over, massaging the muscles in her legs. "We were almost captured by that ridiculous excuse of a Mind cultivator."

"I don't know if I'd call him all that ridiculous." Grant sheathed his sword after inspecting the edge of the blade for chips. "Scary, maybe. Those chains are *heavy*."

"Whatever. Let's just get out of here." Suki led the way, the two of them quickly losing themselves amongst the alleys and streets of the city. This region of the District was in much better shape than the outside portion, but if they looked close enough, they could see the wear starting to show.

Most businesses that lined the streets displayed a layer of dust on the wares in their windows, meaning no one was buying from them. The front of all the houses still looked good, but the sides and backs of the homes hadn't seen a fresh coat of paint in a long time. Some even had sagging rooflines, or collapsing stables hidden behind the false front of success.

"It looks like the entire District has fallen on hard times." Suki wiped the grime off a window to inspect the money-changer office they had stopped in front of, several hours after their fight with Cuddles. "I don't think anyone has been here for weeks. There are footprints in the dust, but even those are faded."

"Will it work as a hiding place until morning?" Grant was exhausted, feeling that perhaps he had not fully recovered from the surgery. "I could use a few hours' rest before we move on."

"We can try the back. This door is too thick for us to break in, and I don't want to shatter a window." Grant let his shoulders sag in acceptance, and Suki led the way through the narrow alley to the back. "Jackpot. This must be the employee entrance. They didn't bother to make this one as tough." Suki's gauntlets flickered into place, and she ripped the whole doorknob off with one sharp tug.

<Wow. Whatever you do, don't make her mad if you get married.>

"I wasn't planning on it, Sarge." Grant didn't clarify his statement as he led the way inside the building, scanning the bare walls and empty cubicles. "I think we're clear."

"Let's try to find a place to sleep upstairs. That way, anyone just walking by on the streets won't even notice us." Suki peered up the stairs, trying to pierce the darkness with her eyes. "If someone was up there, they would have heard us by now."

The two of them made their way up the staircase. Grant was thankful that he wasn't having any balance problems, because the stairs didn't have a handrail. Finding a room without a window on the outside was also impossible, so they sat on the floor as they chowed down on the granola bars from Suki's pack.

"You go ahead and get some sleep." Grant took off his pack

and moved it out of the way. "I've got some training to do before I can rest."

Suki didn't bother arguing and curled up to go to sleep. Grant moved back into the hallway to perform the exercises Sarge demanded of him. There were no problems, and he was able to get them done quickly; all except for the run. Mercifully, Sarge was understanding enough to count the fight with Cuddles as his cardio.

After two hours, Grant woke Suki and took her place on the floor. She stood guard until the sun started to lighten the horizon. He woke up quickly, and she put a finger over his lips before he could say anything. Motioning to the dirty window, Suki showed Grant what had forced her to wake him early.

<That is a whole *lot* of Wielders.> A group of seven Nobles with visibly high-quality weapons were slowly making their way down the street. <Go look out of the windows out back.> Grant hurried to comply, surprised to see a group of four warriors searching nooks and crannies in the back alley of the buildings. <Just what I thought. This is a search party, and I've got a feeling I know who they're searching for.>

"Why would all these Wielders be searching for us? We didn't do anything to them." Grant made sure to whisper, crouching to stay below the edge of the window. "Where did they even come from?"

<This is a much nicer area, so they probably live around here.> Sarge paused to think for a moment. <As for why they're searching for you? My guess would be debt. They probably owe money, and the reward offered for your capture would go a long way toward balancing nearly anyone's accounts.>

"Psst! We need to get in front of them before they see the broken door." Suki motioned for Grant to follow, and they crept out the back door in a crouch. The narrow alley was still shrouded in shadow, so they were able to travel to the opposite end without being seen. "There's more over here. We'll need to stay low and hurry."

The two of them weaved their way through the streets once

more, doing their best to get closer to the region they knew Dokeshi March lived in. They only had one battle the rest of the day, and it was with a single giant rat they surprised as they cut through a basement to avoid another search party.

As night started to return, Suki and Grant were forced to hunker down in a shack behind an empty city administration building. The building had seen better days, but the shack was in surprisingly good shape. The caretaker that stored his tools inside must have taken some pride in his workplace, because when it started raining, they stayed miraculously dry.

"This hasn't been fun. Like, at all." Suki was massaging her legs, which were sore from running around in a crouch all day. "I'm the scion of a Noble House, not some criminal to be hunted like an animal!"

"It isn't all that bad. Not like I've been doing this for the last two months or anything." Grant was soaking a few of the health bars in a pot of water. His plan was to try to make some kind of oatmeal, but the bars didn't seem to be willing to cooperate. "At least this way, we can see them coming. If they were sneakier about it, we would have never known what hit us."

<This was bound to happen at some point. In a society obsessed with money and gambling, owing money must be a serious issue for the established Houses. They see catching you as a chance to dig themselves out from under a mountain of debt.>

"Sarge says they're chasing us because they want to get out of debt." Grant tried stirring the health bars. They still refused to lose their shape, but he was determined to win this battle. "The Dokeshi must have put out a crazy reward for us."

"It *is* quite a large reward; the canceling of debt for nine generations of your House if you're captured, or five generations if you're killed. But not every House is obsessed with Time." The voice came from right outside the door of the shack, causing the two of them to scramble to their feet. Suki peeked out the window and quietly cursed to herself before turning to Grant and shaking her head. "Why don't the two of you come outside, and we can talk about it?"

"Why would we do that?" Suki motioned for Grant to stop talking, but he ignored her. "What would we even talk about?"

"I think we should play a game." Surprised at the answer, Grant cracked the door open to see who he was dealing with. He gulped at the sight of more than twenty people standing outside. Another group was setting up an awning in the rain, in order to keep the card table underneath it dry. Each one carried a polearm that was as long as a spear, but instead of a sharp point, it ended in a long 'U' shape. Since they were all using the same weapon, it meant they were Vassals, and their leader was a Wielder. A powerful one, to have so many Vassals bound to them.

<That's called a 'Sasumata'. It's a weapon designed to capture instead of kill.> Grant nodded, clearly seeing how it would be difficult to fight against such a weapon. <Considering the weapon type, I'd say he must be from the bounty hunter House: House Friday.>

"As you can see, we have you surrounded. Why don't we try to settle this without violence?" The man from House Friday motioned to the table. "We play until one of us runs out of chips, or forfeits. If I win, you come quietly without a fuss. You will be escorted to the nearest prison, where you will await the judgment of Dokeshi March."

Grant was gripping his uchigatana hard enough that his joints creaked. Getting thrown in prison would be a death sentence. "So, when I win, I just go free and have to deal with the next Wielder hunting us?"

"No, that wouldn't be very sporting." The man flicked his wrist, and two large disks appeared. "I'm holding two passes to the Dokeshi's End-of-Month Tournament. If you win, I'll guide you to his personal casino and ensure you're enrolled in the semi-finals."

"Grant, I don't like this. Let me play him instead." Suki was already trying to move around him, pushing Grant to the side. "There's no way you could beat a Noble in a game of cards."

"No, good lady. This deal is for the young man only." He motioned for his Vassals to back up. "You won't get a better offer."

Congratulations! *You have been offered a bet by a scion of House Friday. Beat him at a card game to keep your freedom, or lose and submit to capture.*

Accept/Decline

"Fine." Grant passed his pack over to Suki as he selected 'Accept'. "I'll do it. But if I catch you cheating, all bets are off."

"I wouldn't have it any other way." The man smiled and poured two glasses of a dark red wine. "Let us begin, shall we?"

"Sure. I always wanted to play a card game with my life on the line. I guess I can die happy after this is over," Grant sighed as he sat in the chair.

"Listen to you!" The Wielder chuckled as he handed over a deck of cards. "You sound like a proper Marchurian!"

CHAPTER FORTY-FOUR

"You never told me your name." Grant shuffled the cards while the man divided chips evenly between them. The Wielder was wearing fine silken robes, dyed blue, with thread-of-gold tigers sewn along the seams. His black hair and pale skin made a strong contrast, which was only highlighted by the precisely trimmed beard and mustache that covered the lower half of his face. "Considering the fact that I'm sure you know mine, I think it's only fair of you to tell me who I'm playing for my life."

"Oh, how rude of me! I'm Koshin Friday. It's good to officially meet you, Grant Monday." His green eyes flashed as he slid Grant his pile of chips, and Grant passed him the deck of cards so he could deal. "Or should I call you Lord January? Perhaps Lord February?"

"You seem to know a lot about me, Koshin Friday. Why don't you tell me about yourself?" Grant picked up the two cards that had been dealt to him, barely holding in a wince when he saw a two and seven. Suki had told him that was the worst combination to get. "Couldn't hurt to know who I'm dealing with, right?"

"Ha! Fair enough." Koshin laid out five cards face down,

and put in a single chip. Grant put in two, since he was the big blind, even though he could see perfectly. Such strange card terms. Koshin matched him by placing a second chip on the pile, then flipped over the first three cards.

None of which were a two or a seven.

"I'm the leader of House Friday here in March. Unlike most of my fellow Noble Houses, our branch doesn't have much debt. We're often used to track down the people who try to avoid paying their bills, meaning we're never short on well-paying contracts in a place like this." One of his Vassals came over and hung several lit lanterns around the underside of the awning. With the rain and the deepening night, the illuminated shelter made it seem like they were alone in a palace made of gentle waterfalls. Grant shook his head to clear it; the oddly peaceful environment was making him sleepy.

"Then why come after us?" Grant folded when Koshin put two more chips on the pile. "If you don't need the debt cancellation, why go through the trouble?"

"Why does a bird fly?" It was Grant's turn to deal, so he shuffled while Koshin talked. "Because that is the bird's purpose. It's born with wings; therefore, it must fly to become what it was meant to be. My purpose is to hunt down those who run. All I'm doing is fulfilling my purpose."

The man took a long sip of wine and cocked an eyebrow at Grant as he dealt each of them two cards. "Tell me, Grant Monday. What's your purpose?"

"My purpose?" He fell silent as he thought his answer through. Grant checked his cards, seeing a pair of fours. Not terrible, but not the best. He met the big blind, then laid out the next three cards face up. Two sixes and a five. "I'm trying to finish a quest I was given. If I complete that quest, things are going to change."

"I don't believe that is the correct answer." The man motioned off to the side, and Suki joined them under the awning. "Your friend, she's followed you on your quest. Is this her purpose as well? No? Good answer. You recognize that this is not her purpose, just what she's doing."

This time, the man folded, and Grant collected the few chips on the table. "Now, let me ask you again. What's your purpose?"

Grant puzzled over the question during the next two hands. He lost both of them, but he couldn't even remember what cards had been on the table. Figuring out the answer was really bothering him. What was his purpose? No one had asked him that before.

"Are you going to match my bet, or fold?" Grant didn't answer, instead tossing in four chips without thinking about it. The man matched the bet, and turned over the fourth card. "I check. It's on you, Grant."

"I check as well." Grant finally looked at his cards and realized that he was one card off of a straight. If the fifth card wasn't a nine, he basically had nothing.

"The last card is… a ten!" Koshin laid down two chips. "Fold or bet?"

Grant silently slid his cards into the middle of the pile. He was only one off, but close didn't count in poker. Suki was standing behind Koshin, and when the Wielder wasn't looking, she kept motioning toward Grant's wrist. He was confused at first, but then he remembered he was wearing the bracer that allowed him to hide a card or two.

While it was tempting, Grant didn't bother trying to cheat. Koshin had been nothing but upfront with him so far, especially since he could have just fought them. They might have gotten away, but it was far more likely that one or both of them would have ended up in chains. It felt wrong to cheat against such a man.

"Blinds go up this round. Two chips for the small blind, four for the big blind." Koshin laid out four chips in a row, and passed the deck over to Grant. "Your deal."

As Grant shuffled, Koshin turned to ask Suki a question about her hair. It gave Grant the perfect opportunity to cheat, one that even his poor sleight-of-hand skills could take advantage of. Even so, he just dealt the cards.

<An honest man can sleep at night.> Sarge's words made Grant feel better, for only a moment. <Even if that bed is inside a prison cell.>

"Your turn, Koshin. Bet, call, or fold?" He seemed surprised when he looked at his cards and put five chips in the pile. Grant had a nine and ten, so he matched him. The first three cards he flipped over were all Jacks, which didn't help him at all.

"Ah, what a flop! I'd say you're either very lucky, or very unlucky with such a hand." Koshin pushed in five more chips. "Which are you, Grant Monday?"

Instead of answering, Grant pushed in enough chips to match him. "A quiet man when Time is on the line, eh?"

"No, I just don't know what to say. I'm still trying to figure out what my purpose is supposed to be." Grant turned over the next card, showing a King. "Your turn."

"I'll check." Koshin took a long sip of his wine, taking his eyes off the table for a good bit of time. Suki was frantically motioning for Grant to do something, but he ignored her. Grant also tapped the table for a check, and turned over the last card. It was a six, meaning Grant had only the three Jacks on the table, with the King and his ten as the high cards. Not a very strong hand. "Hm… very interesting."

Koshin squinted at Grant, as if trying to discover his secrets. Grant felt like a lot of what was happening went right over his head. "What? Do you check?"

Koshin just stared at him for another moment, then tapped on the table twice, and flipped his cards over when Grant did the same. "I've got a full house, Jacks over Kings. I take it you have four of a kind?"

"Why would you think I've got four of a kind?" Grant flipped over his nine and ten. "I just have the three Jacks. You win the hand."

He shoved the chips toward Koshin, who carefully added them to his stack of clay disks. Grant handed over the deck of cards and placed his big blind on the table. The Wielder pointed to Grant's pile of chips, which were already down to a single stack of ten. "If you don't mind me saying, you're close to losing. You'd better start winning, if you don't want to end up in the Dokeshi's gallows."

"Thanks. I'm well aware of how bad I am at cards." Grant was gritting his teeth until he read the two aces that had just been dealt to him. "Usually."

The next three hands went by in silence, with Grant only winning once. He was down to just enough chips to make the big blind. His cards were a six and three, both the same suit. Koshin watched him carefully, silently flipping up the five cards on the table. Grant had nothing. Suki looked miserable, as if she knew that Grant would lose as soon as he flipped his cards over.

<Don't give up hope, Grant. You might be able to escape from prison and get to the Dokeshi before the month is over.>

"Well, I must admit that I'm surprised." Koshin stood up before Grant could even show his cards. He waved a hand and his men approached. Suki tensed, ready to fight. Grant just sat there, confused and wary. "I never thought I'd see one in person. An *honest* Wielder in District March. Men, pack this up. I forfeit."

It was hard to tell who was more stunned, Grant or Suki. Probably Suki. She looked like someone had bonked her on the head.

"Why would you forfeit?" Grant stood so one of Koshin's men could collapse his chair and pack it away. "I'm sure you know that you were about to win."

"First, it's getting late, and we run the risk of other people that are hunting you finding us. Second, this wasn't a game to see how well you play cards." Koshin handed over his empty glass of wine as the sounds of horses rose in the distance. "This was a test of character. One you passed."

"You just wanted to see if I was honest or not?" Grant

walked over to Suki and picked up his pack. "I thought you wanted me to answer your question about my purpose."

"Yes, that is true. I'd certainly like to hear your thoughts on the matter." A large carriage pulled up next to them out of the darkness, and Koshin waved for them to get in. "Why don't we talk about it some more, from the comfort of my ridiculously expensive carriage? Is there anything you need to grab out of your lovely little shack?"

"Nope, not a thing." Grant distinctly remembered the food bars soaking in water still inside. They definitely weren't worth the time to walk back and pick up.

"Are you taking us to the Dokeshi's palace?" Suki hung back, keeping under the protection of the awning. "Or do you have some other plans?"

"I assure you, my dear, I've no further plans other than those I expect you also wish to come to fruition." Koshin opened the door and waved for them to enter. "If you end up winning, *all* debts will be canceled, after all!"

His laughter was genuine, and Suki was the first person to get in the carriage. When Grant tried to step up, Koshin's hand on his shoulder stopped him. "You bring change to this place, Grant Monday. *Change* can be good, so long as you make sure it doesn't turn you into someone you no longer recognize."

He didn't know what it was about the word *'change'*, but when Koshin said it, Grant felt like he had been punched in the gut. All he could do was shake his head in agreement as his mind whirled. He took the step inside.

CHAPTER FORTY-FIVE

The trip to the center of March took the better part of three days, as they needed to bypass the second casino ring, but it was a far more comfortable and restful journey than he had been expecting his stay to be. Grant was reminded of a similar journey to the center of District January, but this time, there were no lavish meals or sycophants looking for attention, and Grant had to hide behind closed curtains during the day. The food shortage was affecting even the upper echelons of society, and no one was safe from the hungry mobs that only grew in size as time went on.

At least staying still during the day had given him time to heal, and Sarge was happy to have the chance to run through several training exercises after they stopped at night. They were less than an hour away from the casino where the semi-finals were supposed to be held, and their final meal of rice and wilted vegetables was already eaten. Koshin was amiably filling their last few minutes with idle chatter. "So, have you thought more about your purpose? I know it seems like a simple question at first, but it requires a man to truly know himself. If you want a real answer, that is."

"I've been thinking hard about it." Grant was reorganizing his pack, trying to make the weight distribution more even. For some reason, he just couldn't seem to balance it on his back correctly. "When I really think about it, I think my purpose is to bring change wherever I go. I mean, isn't that what my quest is really all about? Healing the world would be the greatest change the Districts have seen in more than a thousand years."

"It isn't just that." Suki was making sure the two healing potions they had left were well-padded, along with protecting their remaining food in waterproof wrappers. Not that it was needed, if Grant's attempts to boil it was any indication. "You've changed several things about yourself, Grant Monday. Think about what you looked like two months ago."

"Anyway… what I meant to say was that I think 'change' is the one thing I represent. It's more than just my purpose, it's who I… *am*." Grant gave Suki a mock glare.

"I see." Koshin ran his fingers over his mustache as he considered what Grant had to say. "It sounds to me like you're walking the Dao of Change. Pretty common, if any of the seeds can be called as such. Or… maybe the Dao of Transformation? Tell me, have you formed your Dao Seed yet?"

<Tell him no, and change the subject *immediately*. Any further discussion about this might ruin any chance of you gaining a Seed in the first place.>

"Um, no, I haven't formed any seeds." Grant was extremely confused and wasn't sure what to say next. Thankfully, Suki was there to step in.

"Koshin Friday, you *must* know that it's a terrible idea to speak of a Dao Seed before one is even formed." She arched an eyebrow and scooted forward on the upholstered bench seat. "You also know the reason. You're trying to sabotage him?"

"Oh, of course not!" Koshin leaned back, throwing an arm across the seat next to him. "It was an honest mistake. After all, if a young man like Grant was able to collect the Lordship of two Districts already, and is aiming for a third, you'd expect for him to have some form of trump card."

He motioned toward Grant, clearly trying to include him back in the conversation. "I mean, a Monday is a warrior and administrator, but that certainly doesn't mean powerful gear like a Wednesday, or massive resources like a Thursday!"

"My first name was Grant Leap." His proclamation was the first thing that came to mind, and he thought it would do a fine job of changing the subject. "I only became Grant Monday after… after defeating the former Lord January."

"You're a *Leap*?" Koshin seemed genuinely shocked. "Well, that would explain it, then. Have you inherited many of the Leap Sorcerer's abilities? Just a few, even? One or two would make you a force to be reckoned with in times like this."

<When I said change the subject, I didn't mean change it to something even worse!>

"Well, I wouldn't say I inherited their abilities. More like… I inherited their intent?" Grant was spouting nonsense now, just trying to distract Koshin. As soon as he had a chance, Grant was going to find out what a Dao Seed was. It sounded important, and he had a Plant Insight, so perhaps he could find his own information about these seeds.

"Their intent? How profound!" Koshin seemed genuinely excited, leaning forward and acting like a kid in a candy store excited to try something new and tasty. "Tell me, is it true that the Leap Sorcerers could see the future? Finding out any information about them in this District is almost impossible. As I'm sure you know, their headquarters was-"

"We have arrived, lady and gentlemen." They were so wrapped up in their conversation that none of them had noticed when the carriage had come to a stop. "The Vassals have already arranged for two rooms, as you directed, Hunt Leader."

Another servant set a step stool in front of the open door to make it easy for them to get out. "Registration has already begun for the semi-finals, and there are representatives ready to take your tokens."

"Thank you, good sir." Suki stepped down first and grabbed

both of the tokens from the servant's open hand. "I'll go register Grant and I, while you drop the bags off in our rooms."

She said the last bit to Grant, who could only smile in agreement. "Oh no, less work for me? *No~o.*"

"Before you go, I have one last thing to tell you." Koshin had grabbed Grant's shoulder as he started to walk off. "You need to understand that the Dokeshi will do his level best to end your existence. There's no time in this District that you should feel safe. He makes the rules, and his first rule is: The House Always Wins. Never forget that."

"Don't worry. I won't." Grant was genuinely surprised at the concern Koshin was showing for his well-being. "I've seen what his Vassals are capable of, and if they're just a shadow of him, then I know how serious this truly is."

"Good. Don't you forget it. Beat him soundly." He slammed a heavy hand down on Grant's shoulder. "Now, get some rest in an actual bed for once, and do me proud at the tables. I've got a whole lot riding on you, Grant Leap. Nine generations' worth of debt."

<I can't believe you told him you were a Leap! He just *had* to say it in front of half a dozen witnesses! It'll be all over the District by the end of the day.>

"Oh, Sarge. It isn't that bad. All the people that heard him were either his Vassals or his servants. I'm sure they'll keep it quiet." Grant inspected the room numbers stamped on the keys the servant had handed him. "Besides, why would that matter? Whether they know me as Grant Monday or Grant Leap, I'm still going to be the Calendar King."

<While I like the positive outlook, it's never a good idea to give the enemy more information. A mysterious opponent is a dangerous enemy, but a known opponent is a mere stepping stone on the path to victory.>

Grant didn't know what to say to that, so he just ignored the angry sword spirit. Finding their rooms only took a few more minutes, and Grant picked the one with the smaller bathroom attached to it. He was sure Suki would appreciate having more room to spread out, even though she was barely half his size.

"Talk about a nice place!" The voice behind Grant startled him, so he spun in place with his sword halfway out of the scabbard. Once he saw who was waiting for him, he pulled it out the rest of the way. "Whoa, none of that now! We wouldn't want to break the *rules*, would we?"

The person standing in the open doorway was dressed as a clown but otherwise seemed pretty unremarkable. As a matter of fact, it was the most normal-looking clown Vassal that Grant had seen so far.

"What are you talking about, evil clown?" Grant sidestepped, trying to angle the doorframe directly behind the Vassal as he turned to keep Grant in front of him. It would be harder for the clown to get away. "What rule would killing you break?"

"The *rule* that I'm talking about applies to anyone enrolled in the Dokeshi's tournament." The clown realized what Grant was doing and took a step back out into the hall. "Fear not, jumpy one. No one enrolled in the tournament can be captured, fought, or arrested. After all, how would a person be able to play for their freedom if they can't even get through the front door?"

"What are you talking about?" Grant lowered his sword, but he certainly didn't put it away. "Why would someone enter a tournament for their freedom?"

"Oh, that's one of the most common reasons for people to play!" The Vassal seemed to relax a bit, since it seemed that Grant wasn't about to try to cut his head off. "If you're a criminal, or too far in debt, you can enter the tournament for a chance to win! People try all the time. Some even manage to pull it off. You see, if a criminal wins, they can forgo the prize money and ask the Dokeshi for a pardon instead! He *almost* never kills them just for speaking to him!"

The clown laughed, and Grant saw a flash of crazy in his eyes for the first time.

"Get away from me before I decide your head is worth the price of admission." Somehow, the normal appearance had made Grant think this one was different from all the other Vassals he had come across. After he spotted the crazy hidden in his eyes, Grant was starting to wonder if this one wasn't the worst Vassal yet. Like a venomous spider hiding in the blossom of a lotus, this clown was dangerous.

"Ah, don't be like that! My name is Beans, and my brother Frank is around here somewhere." Beans snapped his fingers, and another clown skipped out of the bathroom Grant had *just checked*. "There he is!"

"Frank doesn't talk much; probably why he's so quiet!" Frank could have been Beans' twin, if he weren't clearly a few years older. The Wielder took a step back so the clown could walk past, and sheathed his sword.

"Anyway, we just wanted to stop by and say hello… and to make sure you understand what's waiting for you as soon as you lose." The clown's eyes narrowed, and his voice lost all veneer of sanity. "Tatters was my *friend*, and I'll be the one to juggle your eyeballs in my act after the Dokeshi has his fun."

Grant used Iaijutsu, only stopping his uchigatana once it was the slightest breath away from drawing blood. Grant didn't want the system to kick in, which might void the current hold the Vassals were under. Standing this close to him, Grant could smell the insanity coming off the clown; peaches mixed with ammonia.

"You're welcome to *try*, funny man." Grant waited for the clown to shiver in fear before taking a step back and sheathing his sword. "I won't run from you. In the end, it'll be me pulling you scared rabbits from a hat."

"We're *Jesters*, not magicians, fool!" The two Vassals backed up, clearly surprised by Grant's sudden outburst. They were probably used to intimidating anyone they felt like, and he hadn't responded the way they'd expected. As they slowly walked away, Grant stood in his doorway, hand on his sword and daring them to try anything. That was how Suki found him as she came up the hallway from the other direction.

"Grant, what's wrong?" Suki had been around him long enough to know that he was angry. "Is there something wrong? Do we need to fight?"

The garish outfits of the two clowns disappeared around a distant corner, and February Twenty Nine flashed into his scabbard. Grant answered with his eyes still trained on the empty hallway. "Not yet, Suki."

CHAPTER FORTY-SIX

They had arrived a day early, so the two of them made the most of their available time. Neither had been afforded a real bath in a long time, so they each took a long soak in their separate bathtubs. <Your training is coming along nicely, but I'm stealing Beans' idea and adding in some juggling exercises to help your hand-eye coordination. Oh, and we can't forget to have Suki play a few rounds of poker with you for practice. You need to work on your sleight-of-hand before the tournament starts.>

"I'm not going to cheat, Sarge. It just doesn't feel right." Grant was about to get out of the water anyway. It was beginning to get too cold. "Even if I don't mind the practice, just know that I won't be cheating during the tournament."

<You won't hear any complaints from me. An honest man is worth his weight in gold. Another thing… know what? A man who knows when to *hide* his honesty is worth his weight in jade.>

"Now I'm *sure* you're just making these sayings up. That one doesn't even make any sense!"

<What do you mean, it doesn't make sense? It makes

perfect sense! Knowing when to admit how honest you are is far more useful than just being honest all the time!>

"But that would mean-"

"Are you arguing with your sword again?" Suki's voice came from right outside the door, causing Grant to scramble for a towel to cover himself. "You know, it isn't polite to keep a lady waiting while you play with your sword in the bathroom."

"I'm almost done!" Grant quickly pulled on some clothes and opened the door while putting on his armor. "What are your plans for the day?"

"First, I thought I'd check out the gambling hall." Suki was holding a plate of food, most of which was some version of fruit he'd had before. "Then, I wanted to see what our competition looked like. You don't often get a chance to gauge the people you will be playing against."

"Sounds good, as long as you and I can have a few practice rounds before we start." Grant finished securing his armor back in place and belted his sword on. "It would also be a good idea to make sure we know where all the exits are. The rules say we can't be attacked while a part of the competition, but that doesn't mean they can't jump us the moment we walk outside of the casino."

"That's not a bad idea." Suki handed Grant the entire plate of fruit. "Just promise me that you will keep practicing sleight-of-hand while we play. I know you might not want to use it when playing cards, but you never know when it might be the time that you *need* to use it."

"I can agree to that." Grant quickly shoved down the food, then they made their way down to the gambling floor. It was the most opulent of all the casinos they had visited so far. The liberal use of gold, monster horn, and Utility magic was beyond anything Grant could have imagined to exist in one place. It also had some of the best security to match it. They counted an average of six guards per room, and there were at least two of the Dokeshi's Vassals roaming the building. That wasn't even counting the other Wielders and Vassals from the other Houses.

"Is it just me, or is everyone watching us?" Suki subconsciously swiped at her hair, making sure her ponytail was in its proper place. "I wasn't sure at first, but now I'm convinced they're paying entirely too much attention to us."

"Everyone must know who we are." Grant rested his hand on his sword hilt, and gave a woman covered in sheathed knives a glare. "All they have to do is wait for us to either lose or leave, and they can get the reward for capturing us."

"Well, they can certainly try." Suki clenched her fists, and a single purple spark shot out, causing a server walking past them to jump. Their reaction caused their drink tray to tip over and splash a table full of gamblers, eliciting more than a few screeching protests.

"Why don't we head back to the room and get some practice in? I think it'd be better than standing around here." Grant grabbed her hand and started to pull her back toward the stairs before they could get into a fight. "If we fight now, it might disqualify us from the competition."

They quickly returned to their quarters, and the two of them spent the next several hours training. Mostly, Suki just took all of Grant's chips over and over again, but he certainly learned a few things in the process. As they got closer to the evening meal, Grant finally got around to asking the question that had been simmering in the back of his mind. Suki was packing away all the cards and chips in her pack to take back to her room, so Grant stood up to help.

"Suki, what's a Dao Seed?" Her back stiffened, and she very carefully didn't turn to face him. "Seriously, what's the big deal? Sarge hasn't told me anything about it either. He always changes the subject, or throws something invisible at me."

"That's for a good reason, Grant." Suki finally turned to look at him, her expression rigid. "The number of cultivators that manage to create a Dao Seed within themselves is only a tiny percentage. That's even counting regular cultivators, not just Vassals and Wielders."

She placed a finger on the tip of her chin in thought. "I'd

say one in fifty actually form one, but only one in a hundred ever learn how to use it."

Grant was stunned by those low numbers. He tried to do the math in his head, but the numbers were too big. Just for Wielders, that would mean that out of the three hundred and sixty-six, only three, maybe four, actually had a Dao Seed they could use?

Whatever it even was in the first place. Suki seemed to anticipate his question and held up a hand to stop him from saying anything. "A Dao Seed is a cultivator's connection to the power behind reality. They have begun to comprehend the Laws of the Universe, and subsequently can use that connection to improve their cultivation speed, as well as the power in their bodies and spells. Even talking about it is supposed to ruin your chances for developing one, which is why you probably haven't heard about them. Also, probably why Sarge doesn't want to say anything."

<Leave it *alone*, Grant. Suki is right. Trying to force it into existence will have the opposite effect. You can't make the universe bend to your will. It'll fight you and close off any avenues to advancement.>

"Okay, I'll stop asking." Grant rubbed the back of his head. "I guess I'm sorry I asked?"

"It's understandable to ask questions, but you need to ensure you stay focused on the things you *can* control, like using that bracer I gave you to pull out an extra card or two when you're losing." Suki patted him on the shoulder before gently placing a finger over his mouth. He was getting tired of people stopping him from talking. "I know you don't want to cheat, but that may be the only way forward, Grant."

"Look, I understand better than anyone the importance of adapting to your situation, changing the way you look, or feel, or talk, or eat, or even *walk*." It was finally Grant's turn to silence Suki. "No, *listen* to me. I know when it's necessary to change, but I *also* know when it's important *not* to change. I will not compromise my values. If this is the rock I die on, then so be it. I'll die knowing that I stood for what I think is important, and that is *final.*"

Grant felt a stabbing pain in the center of his forehead, like something was trying to force its way inside his body. It made his mind fuzzy, like he had just downed three or four bottles of wine all at once. The sensation only lasted a few seconds, but he found himself breathing hard, like he had just run up and down several flights of stairs.

<Grant, are you okay?> Sarge's voice forced him to come back to his senses. <What's going on?>

"Sarge, did you just do something?" Grant was more than a little freaked out, and his grip on the hilt of his uchigatana made the wrappings creak under the pressure. "I thought I was being attacked."

"Attacked?" Suki immediately ran to the only door to the room and made sure it was locked. "I didn't see anyone. Do you think one of those Vassals is using a spell or ability to hurt you?"

<I didn't do anything, Grant. From my perspective, your heart rate and breathing spiked for no reason. I didn't sense any attacks or use of spells.>

"Sarge said there wasn't anything." Grant took a few more breaths to steady himself. "It must have just been my nerves. Don't worry about it."

"Are you sure? It wouldn't surprise me if those sneaky clowns find a way to hurt you that doesn't violate their stupid rules." Suki's gauntlets were back, and the purple sparks shooting out caused a burn hole in the nice rug by the front door.

"I'm sure, Suki. I probably just need some rest." Grant still felt like he had just finished a particularly difficult workout, and another bath and some sleep sounded like a very good idea. "I'm going to call it a night and get some rest before tomorrow. It's going to be a big day, one way or another."

"That's true. Make sure you bring your pack with you in the morning, just in case we have to run." Suki opened the door to check if anyone was waiting in the hallway. "We either win tomorrow, or fight our way to the Dokeshi."

She left, closing the door behind her.

"Suki's right, you know. Tomorrow we either qualify for the finals, or fight until we make it to the Lord of March." Grant patted his sword. "Either way, it should be an exciting day."

<You're absolutely correct. Which is why I've devised a training regimen that should utilize the next two hours perfectly, allowing you plenty of time for rest afterwards.>

"But…! Ugh. What's first?" This time, it was easy for Grant to hold in the sigh that wanted to escape his lips. Making sure he utilized his remaining time wisely was the best option, no matter how tired he was.

<Good! I like the attitude. First up, do one hundred squats while swinging your sword horizontally in front of you. Go!>

Grant could only smile. "At least *you* never change."

CHAPTER FORTY-SEVEN

Grant was awakened by the sound of shouting in the hallway. He looked toward the window to gauge the time, surprised to see the sun already well over the horizon. Sleeping in hadn't been a luxury he had been able to enjoy in a long time.

<I decided to let you get some extra sleep. For some reason, your energy levels are running out faster than normal.> That was concerning news, especially considering all of the health changes he had recently gone through. <Don't worry. We'll address it with more endurance training after you defeat 'the Mad Jester'. That is still your number one focus.>

It only took Grant a few minutes to get ready for the day, making sure to load everything in his pack in case he wouldn't be coming back. <It might be a good idea to split your valuables between your pouch and your pack, just in case you lose one or the other in a fight. It's an old soldier's trick, to make sure they at least have enough to survive if they lose something.>

"Makes sense. Thanks, Sarge." Grant had to take a few extra minutes to create more of a balance for his valuables. He split his Time evenly between the two, and then added a single food bar to his pouch. Just in case. As he was emptying the backpack, his fingers brushed against a shockingly cool item.

He pulled the game piece from his *Ties that Bind* quest and stared at it just as Suki started pounding on his door. Unsure where to put it to keep it safe, Grant decided to just tuck it in a small pocket that was between his breastplate and his leather cuirass. It wouldn't be going anywhere, and she had told him it was probably the most valuable item he had, besides his uchi-gatana. Now, even if he lost both his pack and his pouch, he would still have something valuable to trade.

"Grant, are you ready to go yet?" Suki was trying to open the door, and Grant was worried she might snap off the door handle, like she had the one to the building they had hidden in.

"I'm ready; just give me a second! I want to make sure I'm not forgetting anything." He gave the room a thorough scan, finally leaving after stealing a pillow off the bed. If he had to run, he wanted to have at least one comfortable thing to sleep on.

"Finally. Can we go now?" Suki didn't even wait for him to lock the door behind him as she took off for the gambling floor. "If we don't hurry, we'll be late. I figured you of all people would want to be early, so you could get some breakfast at the buffet table."

"Did you just say *buffet* table?" Grant quickly caught up and passed Suki going down the stairs, taking three at a time. "We better hurry!"

He was barely slowed down by the crowded floor and made his way to the line in the back. In a cruel twist of fate, the buffet table had been hit as hard as the rest of the District. The pickings were slim, making Grant think wistfully of the excess across District January. He made do with overcooked potato hash and some kind of gravy topping that might have had meat in the same pot sometime in the past week or two.

"Debtors, Bettors, and High Rollers, can I have your attention *please*!" The dull roar of the crowded room quieted instantly, and a well-dressed man adorned with the mask of a smiling clown appeared on a balcony overlooking the gambling floor. "Hello, and welcome! We're about to start the official semi-finals for Dokeshi March's Tournament of Champions!"

A brief round of applause filled the air, and the speaker waited for an awkward amount of time after it died off, almost as if he was expecting much more of an ovation. "As you all know, getting caught *cheating* is an instant disqualifier, and only the chip leaders from each table will advance to the final round, where they will play the Dokeshi himself!"

The man waved at a wall of windows on the second story overlooking the gambling floor.

"Wait, the Dokeshi is *here*?" Grant squinted at the windows to try to get a glimpse of the man he had been hunting, but the reflection of the lights didn't allow him to see inside. "I could have just gone up there and finished this by now!"

"No, you couldn't. Just take a look around." Suki nodded toward the single set of stairs that must be the entrance to the rooms overlooking the floors. When Grant focused, he noticed a slight haze over the stairs, as though they were putting off enough heat to cook an egg. "You see that? Those are House Thursday wards. Those are so powerful that they're *bleeding* magic. One step up those stairs without the proper pass, and they won't be able to find your teeth."

Grant raised an eyebrow in silent question, getting an eye roll and muttered explanation. "Because they would vaporize you, Grant."

"Oh."

"Yes, 'oh'. We have to wait for the crazed spider to leave its web before we can squash it." Sparks shot out from her closed fists again, but there was nothing on the hardwood floors to light on fire. "Don't worry. He can't stay up there forever."

"Without further ado, let the competition… *begin*!" Grant had missed the last few minutes of the speech, but he figured it wouldn't matter. "Players, please find your assigned seats."

<My guess is that Lord March wants to get a better look at the person coming after him.> Sarge's comment came on the

heels of Grant learning that his table was in the very middle of the floor, right under the view of the Dokeshi's balcony. Grant didn't answer, but Sarge could tell that he agreed. Suki was only one table over, and she was bracketed by guards.

They weren't making it obvious, but it was clear to anyone who was paying attention. Grant realized he was probably in the same situation and used the polished metal leg of his table to look for the guards standing behind him. <There's one by the door to the kitchens behind you, and one to either side of your table in the spectators. I'm pretty sure your dealer is one too.>

"Well, I don't know about you lot, but I like Lady Luck to decide my fortune. I'm all in!" The weaselly-looking man sitting at Grant's right elbow shoved his pile of chips into the middle of the table. Each person had started with one hundred chips, so it made quite a mess. "Anyone here brave enough to match me?"

"The cards haven't even been dealt yet! How can you go all in without even knowing what you will get?" A man who looked like he had been plucked straight from behind a food cart seemed genuinely shocked at the man's ostentation. He was in seat seven, so Grant had to lean forward a bit to see him. "I'm here to win enough to buy a vendor ticket so I can open up my stall in the inner zone, not lose my shirt to some half-baked loon!"

"I could totally eat a half-baked loon right now..." Everyone looked at Grant like a crazy person. "Did I say that...? You know what? So what? Am I *really* the only person who's hungry right now?"

"Opening bid is one hundred chips. Big blind is seat four, and little blind is seat three." The dealer brought everyone's attention back to the card game. "Blinds start at four chips for big, and two for small. Blinds will double every complete rotation of the remaining players."

The guard masquerading as a dealer did a poor job shuffling the deck, but it was passable enough that no one complained. Grant was in seat three, so he put out two chips.

"The game will continue until the timer expires, or there's only one player remaining. If the timer expires and more than one player is present at the table, the chip leader will be the winner."

He dealt two cards to each of the eight players sitting at the table, but only two people picked their cards up. The man who had gone all in, and the woman sitting at seat one.

"I'll match your stunt. All in." The white-haired old lady was clearly comfortable in the suede and velvet dress she was wearing, which made it likely that she came from a wealthy house in the District. "Let's see if Lady Luck is truly on your side, shall we?"

The man sitting next to Grant visibly gulped and carefully picked up his cards. If the color draining from his face was any indicator, the man was definitely regretting his decision. Since there were no more players or possible bets to be had, the dealer just laid out the next five cards face up and motioned for the two to show their hands.

"It looks like the Lady *wasn't* on your side today." The woman had two pair, which badly beat the boastful gambler's hand of King high. "Better luck next time, my dear."

A pair of very burly men came out of the crowd and plucked the gambler out of his chair before he even had a chance to say anything.

"Seven players remain. Blinds, please." The woman had already collected her chips, as if by magic. The neat stacks lined up in front of her spoke to years of experience. It was Grant's turn to gulp. The next few hands passed by in a blur, with Grant folding every time. He still had ninety-four chips after losing both his big and small blinds, but it was already his turn to chip in the small blind again.

<If you don't start betting, these people are going to clean you out in no time. Especially that old woman. She's incredibly lucky at this game.>

"I know, Sarge. I'm just waiting for something that feels right." Grant was mumbling under his breath so no one could hear him, but the person sitting in seat seven still noticed him talking to himself.

"Hey! He's talking to someone! That guy must be *cheating*!" The normal reaction of an entire group taking up arms against the accuser did not occur this time. Instead, two guards approached their table. One held up some kind of stone tablet and ran it over Grant. The other placed a heavy hand on the food vendor's shoulder. He seemed to curl in on himself when the man scanning Grant looked up and shook his head. "I swear I saw him talking to someone! He's a cheater! A cheater!"

The man was escorted away from the table, and his remaining chips were evenly distributed among the six remaining players. Now Grant was up to one hundred and twelve chips.

"A false accusation of cheating is a disqualifying offense, as stated earlier during the briefing. There are now six players remaining." The dealer collected the cards again, since they had lost a person from their table. While he was reshuffling to deal the hand for the second time, Grant turned his head just enough to be able to see how Suki was doing.

<It looks like she's already the chip leader at her table.> Sarge must have been able to make out what was in Grant's peripheral vision better than he could, because Grant had barely turned his head. <Focus on your game. Everything is down to this.>

"Right. It's all down to this." Grant picked up the two cards in front of him and noticed that the old woman was looking sharply at him. Maybe he wasn't as quiet as he thought.

The pair of nines in his hand felt right, so Grant raised the bid to five. The pot was quickly raised into the fifties before the bid made it back around to him. Grant had to take a moment to think, because these people all acted like they were wolves that had just smelled fresh blood. He folded and watched as two more people went all in before the fifth card was even turned over. The winning hand was a pair of fives. What was wrong with these people?

<They're playing the player, and not the game. Some are better at it than others.>

"Only five players remain. There are four hours remaining. Blinds are raised to ten and twenty." The dealer had gotten steadily better as they had continued to play, and the shuffling was much smoother.

That was the first thing Grant noticed, before it sunk in that they had already been playing for two hours. Was there some kind of time warp when you sat down at a poker table?

"Hey, she's cheating!" Grant whipped his head around at the declaration and was shocked to see Suki's arm being held out by one of the guards. He plucked a card from inside her sleeve, and she was escorted over to the spectators to the jeers of the crowd. Grant tensed, ready to come to her defense.

"What will happen to her?" Grant didn't ask anyone specifically, but the old woman was the one to answer him.

"Nothing." She waved her hand, as if swatting away an irritating fly. "It isn't against the rules to cheat; you just get disqualified if you get caught."

"Thank you." Grant made sure to sound sincere, considering he was genuinely pleased at her answer. She gave him a slight smile, then immediately pushed in a stack of twenty chips.

"No problem, young man. Now, I raise. Anyone willing to pay to see if I'm lying?" Grant most certainly wasn't, and the woman took the hand before the fourth card was even dealt.

The next hand was dealt, and Grant finally got a hand he liked. A Jack and ten, both with the red diamond symbol. He silently pushed in two stacks of ten, carefully not looking at anyone else as he did so.

"Ah, the shcaredy-cat finally deshides to bid, huh?" The man sitting next to the old lady had been sipping on a glass of wine while they played, but it never seemed to go empty. The servers here really were top shelf. "I shay hesh bluffing. I'll raish, by… that many."

He added another thirty to the pot, making the total bet half of Grant's chip total. Remembering what happened before, he silently matched the man. The old woman carefully looked at Grant before folding, which prompted the other remaining players to toss in their cards.

"The flop is a Jack, six and three." The dealer pointed at the drunk man, who had spilled wine down the front of his brown doublet. It looked like it wasn't the first time the shirt had seen such abuse.

"Ah, thatsh exshactly what I wanted!" He shoved in the rest of his chips, which was more than what Grant had remaining.

"The bet is for ninety chips." The dealer eyed Grant's smaller pile. "Do you have collateral to make up the difference?"

"Fine." Grant pushed his remaining chips into the pot. "This should make up for what I'm missing." He tossed in his coin pouch, which looked artificially inflated by the food bar stored inside. The dealer nodded in agreement, and turned over the next two cards. It was another three, and a ten.

"Ha! I got two pair!" The man tossed down two fours and laughed wildly. "Threesh and foursh!"

The dealer looked at Grant, who turned over his cards.

"The young man also has two pair, Jacks over tens. He wins the pot." The familiar faces of the two hulking guards removed the drunk before he could even try to argue. "There are now four players remaining, with three hours until the timer runs out."

The dealer backed away from the table after placing a small box over everyone's pile of chips. "We'll be taking a ten minute break before resuming."

Grant stood with the others, happy to stretch his back muscles. As he headed to the bathrooms, a strong grip grabbed him by the shoulder. Turning sharply, he was surprised to see Suki standing there.

"After all that grandstanding last night, here you are, shamelessly cheating to stay in the game." Suki crossed her arms with an eyebrow raised in accusation. "Tell me, how are you doing it? I didn't see you slip out a card at all! I mean, I know practice makes perfect, but wow! How much training did you do last night?"

"Suki, I'm *not* cheating. I'm just playing the game the way you showed me." She squinted at him, but all he could do was shrug. "Seriously, I've just been playing the hands that I've been dealt. Nothing more, nothing less."

"Fine then, don't tell me." She turned in a huff and headed back to the stands. "But don't think I won't figure it out!"

"Is it normal for a woman to constantly accuse you of cheating, even when you haven't done anything wrong?" Grant meant the question for his sword, but a man passing by just started laughing in reply. "What? What did I say that's so funny?"

CHAPTER FORTY-EIGHT

By the time Grant made it back to the table, he was the last one to get seated. They were down to the final four, and somehow he wasn't in the last position. The chip leader had been bouncing back and forth between the old woman and a middle-aged man dressed in the red colors of House Monday. His clothes looked a little worn around the seams, and more than one place on his undershirt had been patched. Overall, he came across as a Noble who had fallen on hard times.

The last person at the table was the one with the least number of chips. It was a woman only a few years older than Grant, dressed in chainmail that hinted at her being a professional Armor cultivator, especially since she carried no weapons to the table. Grant wasn't sure if she was a Wielder, Vassal, or just a regular cultivator. Without the customary tabard displaying her House colors, it was impossible to tell.

"Blinds are now twenty-five and fifty. They will double every time we make a full rotation of the remaining players." The dealer uncovered their chips, which had somehow been replaced with larger clay disks that each represented twenty five. "As you can see, your chips have been condensed to make counting easier. In the event that you didn't have enough chips to make a full twenty five, your chips were returned to the House."

The warrior woman opened her mouth to argue but closed it when the dealer kept talking over her. "These are the rules, as stated during the briefing."

"Well, looks like I might as well go all in just to get it over with." The warrior tossed in her three remaining chips before the dealer could even pick up the deck of cards. "Any one of you want to put me out of my misery?"

"Sure." Grant was already the big blind, so he just added another chip to match her. He somehow had four chips after this, meaning he had won more than he first thought. "I'll try my luck."

"Then I'll fold." The old lady put in her single chip for the small blind, but never picked up her cards. "I prefer to let the younger generations work things out on their own."

The dealer passed around the cards, and the nobleman silently folded as well after glancing at his hand.

"Let's turn 'em over and see what the Fates have decided." The young woman had an Ace and a Queen, while Grant had a six and an eight. "Ha! It looks like they like me better!"

The dealer laid out the next five cards, none of which were an Ace or a Queen. Instead of the expected outcome, Grant took the pot with a pair of eights. The warrior stared at the table open-mouthed for a beat before squinting hard at Grant.

"I don't know how you beat me, but I'll accept my defeat. I don't need a *license* to hunt beasts. I can still do it, even if it means I don't get the weekly stipend from the Houses." The woman stood and headed for the bathrooms. Grant most definitely didn't see tears brimming in her eyes.

"Three players remain, with two and a half hours until the time ends." The dealer briefly looked around the casino before starting to shuffle. "Only two tables are still in play. The other contestants have been decided."

"Blinds, please." All that meant was that more eyes were on

the remaining players than before, making it harder than ever to cheat. Grant was perfectly happy about that. He chipped in the small blind and carefully counted his chips. There were only forty on the table in all, and he was holding fourteen of them. The old lady was winning with sixteen, and the nobleman had ten. Unfortunately, it didn't stay that way for long.

Before he could blink, another thirty minutes had gone by, and he was down to five chips. The nobleman and old woman were mostly trading chips back and forth, with Grant losing his blinds each hand. He was also dealing with a strong itching sensation on his chest, and it was impossible to reach without loosening the straps of his armor. Finally, Grant got a good hand: an ace of spades with the Jack of hearts. Grant had good luck last time with one, so he decided to meet the big blind after the other two checked. They eyed each other, and Grant's chest started itching like crazy when the woman tapped her cards with a ring on her left hand.

The flop came out with a Jack, ten, and four. Grant did his best not to react, and waited for the other two to decide what they wanted to bet first.

"I'll bet two chips." The old woman's eyes flickered to the last two chips Grant had left. "Oh, I'm sorry, dear; that would put you all in, wouldn't it?"

"It's okay. All in." Grant shoved his last two chips in the pile as the nobleman folded. "I think I've got a good chance."

"I'm sure you do, dear." The old lady's smirk meant she was lying, but Grant was sure of himself. If only his chest would stop itching.

"The next two cards are… another Jack… and an Ace." The dealer flipped over the last two cards, and Grant barely kept himself from doing a victory dance. Grant immediately flipped over his cards, but he was shocked to see that the old lady was still smirking. "The gentleman has a full house, Jacks over Aces. And the lady…"

"As you can see, I've-" Her eyes bulged, and she seemed to choke as a pair of Queens came into view.

"The lady had two pair, Queens and Jacks. The winner is the gentleman." The dealer helped scoot the chip pile to Grant, who now had ten chips. He was suddenly in second place, as the nobleman had thirteen, while the old woman had just seven chips left.

"But, but, that-" The white-haired competitor took a deep breath and rubbed the ring on her finger again. "Never mind. Forgive an old woman her confusion. I thought I had different cards."

"That's okay." Grant nodded sagely. "I'm still confused as to why they call this 'poker,' when you don't actually have to poke anything at all. I mean, doesn't it seem like we should be playing this game with some kind of stabbing implement?"

Her eyes bulged out, and her already pale complexion grew even worse. The nobleman sitting across from Grant gave him a genuine smile and held his hand out for Grant to shake. "I don't think anyone has shocked Lady Wednesday in a long time. I'm Lord Thursday. It's a pleasure to meet you, Grant Monday."

"Ah, I guess you already know who I am." Grant looked around and was surprised to find that almost all of the spectators were watching him. "It looks like everyone does."

"Yes, I'm afraid so." Lord Thursday tossed in the big blind, which was now four chips. "Most everyone here would sell their own mother for a chance to capture you and your friend."

"Well, they will just have to wait until after I win the tournament." Grant watched as Lady Wednesday put in the small blind. "Them's the rules, after all."

"Indeed they are, young Monday." He stopped talking while the dealer dealt the cards. After looking at his hand, he glanced at Grant's pile of chips. "I've got a proposition for you, Grant Monday. In a hand or two."

Grant checked his hand and folded before the man could say anything else. He didn't want to bet on a three and four. "Sure; I'm willing to listen, at least."

He sat back while the two Nobles carefully tried to eke out as many chips as they could from one another. The Lady ended up winning the pot, which totaled up to twelve chips after she went all in and the Lord backed out. That made her the new chip leader.

Another three hands went past, with Grant winning only one of them. He was holding steady in second place while the other two kept swapping chip leader. Finally, the dealer collected up all of the cards and made an announcement.

"There's one hour remaining. The blinds will now move to ten chips for the big blind, and five for the small. Sir, you're big blind." The dealer indicated Grant, who had exactly ten chips remaining.

"Well, it all depends on this." Grant pushed in his stack of chips and wiped the cold sweat forming on his palms off on his pants. "Hopefully, Lady Luck smiles on me."

"I'm sure she will, Grant Monday." Lord Thursday leaned forward to speak with Grant. "Which brings me to my proposition."

Though he was curious about what this man could possibly want from him, Grant was ready to hear the offer. "The reward for your capture is quite substantial, and I'd like to give you a chance to choose how that arrest is made."

"…What?" Grant let a grin fly to his lips. He could choose how his arrest went down? "I'm not going to go quietly, if that is what you think."

"How about I sweeten the pot for you?" Lord Thursday pulled out a spell book and laid it on the table between them. "If you agree to accompany me without a fight if you lose, this spell will be yours if you win."

<I'd take it, Grant. You're going to fight your way out of here no matter what, aren't you?> Sarge's vote was all it took to decide the young man. In the spirit of District March, the precise wording was that he would accompany the Lord without a fight, not that he would submit to arrest without a fight.

"You have yourself a deal. I mean, I'm all in anyway." Grant leaned back in his chair, trying his best to exude confidence. "I might as well get all I can when I win."

"Sure, *when* you win." The Lord gave him another smile, this one a lot less genuine. "Are you staying in for this hand, Lady Wednesday?"

"You bet your shorthairs I'm in." She pushed in ten chips, leaving her with only one. Lord Thursday pushed in his nine remaining chips alongside the spell book, which Grant noticed was labeled with shifting Runes that read 'Apprentice Repair'. "Let's see what these cards look like."

She knocked her ring on the table, and Grant scratched at his chest. Lord Tuesday started rubbing a worn cufflink on his jacket, and Grant started itching even harder. "Yes, I'm excited to see what happens."

"Bets are placed. The only chip not in the pot belongs to Lady Wednesday, who has one remaining." The dealer turned over the first three cards, a four, seven, and Ace. Grant checked his cards. He had a three and a six. Not the best, but not the worst. All he needed was a five, and he would have a straight. "No further bets can be placed, so the next cards are… an Ace… and a five." Grant felt the tension in his shoulders leave in a rush. He got the straight!

"Well, it looks like I'll be taking this hand." Lady Wednesday turned over her cards, showing a three of a kind in Aces.

"Not so fast, my Lady! I've got a full house, fives over Aces!" Lord Thursday was smiling broadly, and it only grew when he saw Grant's face fall. He knew that a full house beat a straight. "Don't worry, son. I'm sure you can appeal to the mercy of Dokeshi March. He even grants it sometimes!"

"We'll see how far his mercy extends." Grant braced his hand on the hilt of February Twenty Nine. He tossed his cards on top of the pile and started looking around for Suki. She wouldn't know about his side bet, and he would need to warn her about the plan to fight once the man walked him to his supposed jailers. Instead, Grant was shocked by the spectators absolutely losing their minds all at once.

"The winner of the hand is Grant Monday, with a *straight*

flush." He could hardly hear the dealer make the announcement over the roar of the crowd. There were shouts and jeers in equal measure, but the combined volume caused the glasses and chips on the tables to rattle.

Grant could only plop back into his chair in shock. Apparently, he had forgotten how important the suits of the cards could be. Cards were weird. In a daze, he collected his winnings and put the spell book in his pack.

"There are two players remaining, with thirty minutes left on the timer." The dealer pointedly eyed the single chip remaining on the table in front of Lady Wednesday, who gave him a sour look.

"Fine. Let the boy have his victory." She tossed her last chip onto his pile. "I forfeit." As she stood up from the table, the crowd surged into the table area to congratulate him. As he was lifted up on their shoulders and carried to the winner's circle, Grant was filled with a sense of pride at the victory. He had won, and done it without compromising his morals or values.

It felt good to win. The cheering, though… that felt *great.*

CHAPTER FORTY-NINE

Grant placed second out of all the contestants, due to his table having the least number of exposed cheaters. For some reason, that meant his win counted for more of their imaginary points than the others. He was escorted from the gambling hall to a much better wing of the casino, where the seven winners from the different tables were all staying.

The manager of the casino had dropped off a large purse of Time and a finalist token, and escorted him personally to his new room. He told Grant that the final game would be played in two days, and Grant was supposed to stay inside the casino the entire time. Which he was perfectly fine with. His rooms were large enough to train in without worrying about bumping into anything, and they would be bringing meals straight to his room. Hopefully he could finally get some pancakes.

After getting settled, Grant immediately pulled out the spell book. He was dying to see what the new spell could do. What would 'Apprentice Repair' allow him to improve? Could he disable an enemy's armor in the middle of a battle? Could he build a house from nothing but sticks and stones? His brain was running with ideas.

<Why don't you just learn the spell and find out? Don't have to replace what you've got, since this is a Utility spell.> Grant could only grin as he sat down at a table near the door to read. He was absorbed by the words, and it took almost an hour for him to feel the knowledge seep into his Spell Slot.

Congratulations! *You have learned the Utility spell "Apprentice Repair." It can be used on everything from increasing an item's durability to lubricating hinges. Experiment to find out more!*

Grant was both happy and disappointed at the description. He checked his stat sheet to see if there was any further information.

Name: Grant Monday
Rank: Lord of The Month (January, February)
Class: Foundation Cultivator
Cultivation Achievement Level: 20
Cultivation Stage: Late Summer
Inherent Abilities: Swirling Seasons Cultivation
Health: 449/449
Mana: 23/23

Characteristics
Physical: 266
Mental: 92
Armor Proficiency: 141
Weapon Proficiency: 174

Spells:
Elemental Spell: Thundering Step.
Utility Spell: Apprentice Repair
Prerequisites: 80 Mind. Two hands. The ability to see or sense the targeted object.

Active Mode: Improve, combine, or repair the object or objects targeted by the spell. More complicated items require a higher-tier spell.
Mana cost: 7 per use.
Training Mode: If used when disassembling, reassembling, or cleaning an item, 50% chance of the user gaining a deeper understanding of how an item works.
Mana cost: 7 per use.

Well, that was… something. He would have to experiment to see if he could use it when fighting, but for now, he could at least patch up the few spots where his armor was starting to show some wear and tear. Getting blown up, shot, stabbed, and wrapped in chains hadn't been great for the durability of his gear, unsurprisingly. After learning the spell, Grant decided to do some training with Sarge.

The sword spirit had him focus on feints and counters, as well as using *Time is Space* to swap his sword from one hand to another in order to surprise his imaginary opponents. <I think this new trick will come in handy. Instead of you just using the skill at random, now you can start to think about using it *tactically*.>

"Yeah, I suppose I have been kind of… random with it." Grant got undressed so he could take a bath before his dinner arrived. Climbing into the tub, he felt muscles he didn't even know were tense starting to relax. He lost track of time and didn't climb out of the tub until after the water started to get cold. Then he spent the next hour going over his armor, using his new spell to repair any dents and dings, as well as a few outright holes.

"I think the best thing about this new spell is that it doesn't just repair items, it also cleans them a little more every time you use it." He sniffed the leather vambraces that had started to turn a little ripe, and was happy to find that now they didn't smell like anything at all. "It would have really come in handy when I was doing all that sweating in February."

He even found a better place to put his chess piece, using a dent on his backplate to hold it against the small of his back. He cut his shirt, pulled it into a pocket shape, and melded the fabric around the piece with his new spell. "I'm so glad that worked!"

<I'm *shocked* that worked,> Sarge grumbled, getting a chuckle in reply. After finishing with his repairs, they left the bathroom to see if room service had left him any food. Grant made sure to check the other rooms, but he didn't find even a single bite anywhere. <I think they might have forgotten to bring you a meal. Looks like you're going to have to go find someone to remind them.>

"I'd better get dressed. I don't want someone to see me by myself and think it would be easy to kidnap me." As Grant was going through the arduous process of strapping his armor back on by himself, he suddenly stood up straight. "Sarge, where's Suki?"

<Sword Saints! I haven't seen her since they picked you up and carried you to the winner's circle. She was in the crowd watching you the last time I caught a glimpse through your eyes.>

"Feces. I need to find her." Grant strapped on his uchi-gatana, grabbed his pack, and headed for the door. "She should have made it here by now, no matter who was standing in her way."

<I've gotta agree with you. There aren't many things that would keep her from helping us bring down the Dokeshi.> As Grant opened the door, he was surprised to encounter the shocked face of Beans with a fist raised to knock on his door. The young Wielder immediately took a half-step back and placed his hand on the hilt of his sword, ready to remove the head of the Vassal the moment he activated the sub-system. At this range, there was no way he could miss.

"Oh *my*, did I come at a bad time? I just came by to see if you had lost something recently." Beans obviously knew that he was within Grant's reach, but he was oddly confident. He put a finger to the lips of his mask. "Or, should I say, lost… some*one*?"

<Well, it looks like she's experiencing the true horror of the District. Clowns got her.>

CHAPTER FIFTY

"Get to the point, Beans, before I decide your skull would better serve the world as a plant pot." Grant wasn't an interior decorator, but he was sure he could find a skill for it.

"No need to be so hostile!" Beans took a step back, and Frank rounded the corner and came further down the hallway to be closer. Just in case. "All I wanted was to offer my services as a finder of lost persons. In fact, if you come with me, I can *guarantee* you will find her safe and sound!"

<You can't. They have a trap set up for you, and if they managed to capture *Suki*, they'll be able to capture you easily. *Su~uper* easily.>

"Let's say I don't go with you?" Grant had unconsciously pulled his sword a few finger lengths out of the scabbard, causing Beans to swallow hard and Frank to shift his feet uncomfortably.

"Well, if you can't find it in your heart to follow me instead of desperately and futilely searching for your companion, I'd hate to speculate about her fate." Beans fanned his face, as if he was overheated. "I'm sure it wouldn't be anything good."

<It doesn't matter. If you go now, both of you are done for. We'll come up with something else.>

"I understand." Grant sent the sword a feeling of acceptance, but didn't move beyond staying focused on the spot where the clown's neck showed a small pockmark scar. "Hey, Beans. You have a little mark right there on your neck. I'll let you know right now… if anything goes wrong for her, or me, that's where I'll slice to remove your head."

"Um… does that mean you will follow us?" The clown was wilting under Grant's killing intent, and he began to sweat furiously. "Or, should we come back later or something?"

"Go." Grant didn't know where his rage was coming from, but he could feel it coming off of him in waves. His forehead renewed that straining feeling, like something was trying to drill into him, but he was too angry to pay it any attention. "If he thinks I'll show him mercy after such cowardly tactics… ask him if he could have beaten Lord January, or bested Lady February."

The raging Wielder took a step forward, backing the clown against the wall. "Soon enough, he'll be nothing more than another tally on my kill sheet, feeding my cultivation and making me even stronger… all so I can take out the *next* petty tyrant in the *next* District!"

His heart was pounding, and at some point, he had unsheathed his uchigatana and pointed it at Beans' face. The blade of his sword was shimmering, like it did when it upgraded itself.

<Grant, you need to calm down. I don't know how you're doing this, but you're burning through your mana.>

He glanced at his sheet and saw that he was already down to only three mana remaining. It hadn't recovered all the way from his use of the Apprentice Repair spell, and now he could feel a headache starting to settle behind his eyes as the numbers ticked closer to zero.

"U-um, i-is there anything else y-you want me to s-say?"

Beans' mask was askew, and his fear-filled eyes were visible. "I don't know if I can remember all of that..."

"Get out of here." Grant took a step back into his room and slammed the door in the clown's face, immediately dropping to one knee and grabbing at his head. The sensation was reminiscent of the healer's drill boring into his skull; this was worse, though, as he was fully awake and cognizant. He forced himself to take deep breaths, and it faded into a dull ache. "What in the abyss was *that*?"

<I'm not sure.> Grant was surprised to see his health was still full, and felt even happier when his sword went back to normal. His mana dipped two more points, but leveled out while he still had one point remaining. <Whatever you just did, it was quite the show. I think that clown might have wet himself.>

"I need to be a *ruler*, Sarge. I need to be better than I am... I need to save her." Grant got back to his feet and put his ear to the door. Taking a moment to remove the pack that contained all of his recent winnings in order to lighten his footsteps, he cracked open the door to an empty hallway. "No time to worry about it now, anyway. I need to catch up to those two and find out where they're going."

Grant eased out, carefully avoiding a small, rancid puddle in front of his door. The clowns could only have gone one direction, so Grant moved as quietly as the hardwood floors would allow.

At the end of the hallway, there were two directions they could have gone, so he took the one that showed faint liquid drips trailing along it. That was the smallest, but apparently most useful, benefit for terrifying someone Grant had ever encountered. The trail led into a part of the casino that he hadn't been to before, where more of those wheeled games that took coins sat in long rows, cold and forlorn as they sat inert in the dark room.

There was no one in the room besides the clowns, and Grant was forced to duck behind a row of machines before he was spotted by Frank and Beans. They were talking to someone just out of sight through an open door marked 'Employees Only.'

"No, you don't understand!" Beans was visibly shaken, and his voice was a little higher pitched than normal. "He didn't seem to *care*. He just talked about killing the Dokeshi, and using my skull as a potted plant or something! The man is crazy!"

"*Heehee*... a potted plant, you say?" The voice of Cuddles made Grant's skin crawl. Now he knew how they had captured Suki. "Did he say anything else?"

"The Wielder stated that he would use the Dokeshi's skull as a vessel to drink wine from if any harm came to his female companion." The third voice must have been Frank, who had a surprisingly formal way of speaking. Grant scowled as he realized he was being complementary to the homicidal clown. "I believe there were statements made about his demonstrated battle prowess, which includes taking the Lordship from January and February."

"Oh, how glorious!" Cuddles sounded genuinely excited. "I do love an opponent that thinks themself a challenge! It makes it all the more delicious when the hope fades from their eyes... *heehee.*"

"What do you want us to do, Prime Vassal Cuddles?" Frank's voice came from farther away, as if he were already moving into the hallway.

"Stick with the plan. The Dokeshi knows what he's about." The sound of a slap rang out, and Cuddles' voice lost all sense of playfulness as he walloped Beans to the floor. "*You*, get yourself cleaned up. You're an embarrassment. Get out of my sight."

The sound of footsteps faded away, and Grant carefully made his way forward. The door wasn't quite closed all the way, letting a hint of light leak into the room from the glow orbs on the other side.

<You can't ambush them with the system in place, and the moment you walk through that door, you will no longer be

protected by the Dokeshi's rules. Are you sure you still want to go through with this?>

Warning: *You're about to leave the protected casino floors. Going any further will void the protections put in place by The Rules.*

"I don't have much of a choice, do I?" Grant pushed through both the doorway and the notification that popped up in his vision. "I can't leave Suki to these monsters."

<I'm not disagreeing with you; I just wanted to make sure you had considered all of your options.> Sarge was happy with Grant and let him know it. <I can easily say I'd have made the same decision, were our positions switched.>

"Thanks, Sarge. That does mean a lot." Grant moved deeper into the recesses of the building, still following Beans' trail the entire way. There were enough twists and turns in the bowels of the casino that Grant was almost convinced he was back in the Labyrinth. Finally, after over half an hour of sneaking along quietly in the dark, he spotted a light up ahead. As he silently slipped into the room, he instantly recognized its purpose.

<That is a *whole* lot of knives and saws.> Grant could only agree with Sarge. The row of sharp metal hooks along the ceiling proved that this was the casino's meat processing room. The abundance of large-grated drains indicated that they preferred to slaughter their animals on site. On the one hand, it meant they served the freshest meats possible. But on the other, it made for a very uncomfortable location for Grant to remain.

"I was beginning to wonder if you'd ever get here." Beans stepped out from a doorway across from Grant, and he wasn't alone. "Frank decided to bring some friends to the party. I hope you don't mind."

Frank and Beans were joined by a double-handful of men carrying meat hooks that had obviously come from the racks in the ceiling. Frank grimaced and took a moment to adjust his mask. "These fine gentlemen haven't eaten in quite some time, and they would like to show the Dokeshi why they deserve to join his ranks as a Vassal. There have been some new openings recently, and he needs replacements."

"This isn't going to end like you want." Grant pulled out his uchigatana and slashed it around the room in a dance that displayed both his skill and his prowess. He casually re-sheathed his sword and turned his attention to the men stretching out in a line in front of him. "Did they tell you that those 'openings' were created by *me*?"

"It doesn't matter. These men are ready to lay down their lives for the mighty Dokeshi!" Beans apparently hadn't taken a poll, because the looks on their faces said otherwise. "Attack!"

Combat initiated

Action: *Attack with Spell*

Result: *Damage of 92 increased to 101 by Lightning Attunement. Various levels of damage done to opponents. Abundance of steel surfaces causes additional damage based on target resistances. Three opponents defeated. Seven opponents stunned for nine seconds.*

Opponents remaining: 9

Actions: *Please select one option from the following list*

Attack: *Lethal, Non-lethal, Spell*

Defend: *With Weapon, Without Weapon*

Run: *Attempt Escape*

Grant decided that opening up with his trusty lightning spell was a good option, and he was instantly proven right. He had to fight off a wave of dizziness from using his mana again, even though he had completely regenerated his missing points during the search for Suki.

"Are you going to tell me where you put Suki, or do I need to use this room for its intended purpose?" Grant selected

'Attack: Lethal' and used Iaijutsu to remove the upper half of the head of a man just starting to climb back to his feet. "*I* don't mind slaughtering you… but maybe Suki wouldn't like that."

Action: *Attack: Lethal*

Result: Critical Hit! *Damage of 73 increased to 110. Opponent killed.*

Opponents remaining: 8

Actions: *Please select one option from the following list*

Attack: *Lethal, Non-lethal, Spell*

Defend: *With Weapon, Without Weapon*

Run: *Attempt Escape*

<Grant, I don't know what happened to you, but this is a level of being *ruthless* that I haven't seen from you before. Are you… well?> The rage shimmering in his chest was at a low burn, as the mantle of a judge and executor tried to fall on his shoulders once again. Grant shook his head in an attempt to ignore the distractions and selected 'Attack: Lethal' a second time.

"Y-you can't just-" The stuttering voice of Beans was cut off when Grant chopped into the upraised hand of another opponent, removing the offending limb and the metal hook clutched in its grip. The sound of the hook clanging off the ground seemed to snap the clown out of his daze. When his eyes met Grant's, he flinched, then dropped his scepter and backed against the wall. "I'll make a deal with you: spare my life, and I'll sacrifice my weapon and tell you where your companion is being held."

"*Now* we're getting somewhere." Grant used the flat of his blade to knock one of the cultivators still trying to achieve some form of battle formation into unconsciousness. "You?"

Grant was looking at Frank, who had separated himself from his brother.

"I'm of the strong belief that you aren't nearly as powerful as you seem." The well-spoken clown angled his scepter in front of his body like it was a sword and stood on the other side of a steel slaughtering table from Grant. "I don't wish to make any bargains."

"Fine. By. Me." As soon as a hook bounced off of his shoulder, Grant raised an empty hand to point at Frank while his sword was angled to protect himself from the cultivators behind him. "I prefer it this way."

Grant threw his sword, then dashed forward as Frank deflected it. Then he activated *Time is Space* as he got into position. When he had danced around in front of the clowns at the start of the fight, what he had actually been doing was ensuring his sword had been everywhere he could easily reach in the room. Frank was wide open, and February Twenty Nine slid home without resistance.

"*No!*" Beans dropped to his knees as the uchigatana appeared between Frank's eyes. The slain Vassal fell backward, his final breath escaping as he crumpled to the ground. "Not like this. It wasn't supposed to end like this."

Beans leaned over to close his brother's eyes while Grant dealt with the notifications trying to block his vision.

Action: *Attack: Spell*

Result: Critical Hit! *Damage of 73 increased to 110. Opponent slain.*

Opponents remaining: 0 (1 surrendered, 5 attempting escape)

Congratulations! *Your new battle count moves from* [8 Wins / 3 Losses] *to* [9 Wins / 3 Losses]. *Remember, the lucky rise to the challenge!*

"Where is *Suki*?" Beans must have been one of the lower-ranked Vassals, because his weapon merely cracked down the middle and fell into two equal halves as their gamble was enforced. Grant used his sword to lift the mask off of Beans, revealing a pockmarked young man only a year or two older than himself. "Tell me before I decide to find a nice plant to liven up my living room."

"She's inside the room with the number seven on the door. It's one floor up from this one, through there." Beans glowered at him with hatred in his eyes. "But you won't make it that far."

Grant ignored the helpless former Vassal and stepped through the door into a narrow hallway. He took two steps before he heard a click from the floor under his feet.

"You forget, Grant Monday. The House *Always* Wins." Beans' words followed him as the tiles under his feet disappeared, and he tumbled silently into the dark abyss below.

CHAPTER FIFTY-ONE

Grant sat up in a windowless room, the light cutting off as soon as the trap door above him slid closed. He took a moment to gather his senses and recover from the fall. He didn't think anything was broken, but he had definitely twisted an ankle when he came down. A solid minute passed as he berated himself for not wording his deal with Beans better. He *knew* that the man would try to trick him. Grant was supposed to be the kind of man who didn't make stupid mistakes like that by now!

His head ached, but he wasn't sure if it was from the new mystery problem he had been dealing with, or if it was just the pain of failure. A quick inspection of the room revealed him to be in a solid box just wide enough for him to take four steps in any direction, but the walls seemed to have no openings for a door.

As his eyes adjusted, Grant realized the darkness wasn't *quite absolute*. He limped over to a small rectangle on the wall where a faint, flickering orange light was streaming in. He couldn't be sure, but it seemed to come from a candle, and it was getting brighter. Suddenly, the bloodshot eyes of Cuddles flashed in front of him, causing Grant to jump back.

"Ah, welcome! Grant Monday, how I've *longed* to get another chance to meet you face-to-face." Cuddles took a step back, so Grant could see more of the overly-large clown. "I want to make a deal with you! Well, more of a game… but if you win, you can go free!"

"What kind of game, Cuddles?" Grant was practically scraping the words out of the bottom of his diaphragm. He knew nothing good was about to come out of the rotten Vassal's mouth.

"Oh, the game is simple, really." Cuddles took a turkey leg out of his pocket and pretended to take a bite out of it through his mask. "You see, all you need to do is guess how many days, hours, and minutes you can live without any food or water, and the door will open!"

The Prime Vassal took another pretend bite, even faking the chewing noises, and smearing grease all over the mouth of his mask. "Of course, to find out if you guessed correctly, you have to die first… *heehee*… but that's a gamble I'm willing to make!"

Grant only had a single food bar in his belt pouch which he could stretch for a few days, but the lack of water would kill him in only three or four days. Even if he did manage to escape, he had already voided his protection as a finalist. He would have to make it back to the casino proper, and he had no idea where he was. No matter what he did, he couldn't see a way out of this one.

"There it *is~sss*…" Cuddles slammed his face up against the slot, his bulging, bloodshot eyes boring into Grant's. His voice once again dropped into something raspy, showing what hid behind the thin veneer of his mask.

"The moment when you realize all hope is gone. The moment when you see there's absolutely *nothing* you can do, and death is the only outcome for you." Before Grant could stab the clown in the face with his sword, the slot slammed closed. "Goodbye, Grant Monday."

The faint scent of spoiled peaches and ammonia was the only reminder that the clown had been there a few minutes later, when any trace of light disappeared as the Prime Vassal walked away.

Grant wanted to rail against the unfairness of it all, to have come so close to victory, only to sample failure as bitter as the odor of insanity left behind by a jester. He wanted to smash his sword against the walls, over and over again, until either their stone gave way, or his muscles tore from the effort. "Why do I suddenly want tartar sauce?"

Despite the desire, Grant didn't do any of those foolish things. He was no longer a child, forced to bend to the wild mood swings of a teenager. No, instead of all that… he decided that it was a good time to train. He rubbed at his forehead, where the strange pressure was once again making itself known. "Sarge, do you have some kind of training plan for fighting in an enclosed space, in absolute darkness? I need something to center myself."

<I…! Hooray! Yes, Grant, I sure do! First, close your eyes and use your hands to measure out the space around you.> Sarge's Wielder did so, quickly making a mental map of the space. There was a small hole in the far corner, and the faint smell of human waste told him it was meant to be his toilet. Other than that, the room was completely empty. Perfect for training.

The next hour was a smooth lesson in transitioning between the stances already ingrained in his muscle memory, and included a few new tricks that Sarge taught him about using walls to push himself off of as a way to speed up his movements. It was an oddly light training session, but it still did the job of calming his emotions.

<I made it lighter than normal on purpose.> Sarge sounded strangely solemn, as if he was about to deliver some bad news. <The various movement techniques I was showing you were also a way for me to gauge any weaknesses in your cell. Sadly… I didn't find any. This place is as solid as a bank vault in District May.>

"That's okay, Sarge. It isn't your fault I'm in this position."

Grant sat with his back against the wall and closed his eyes. "My only chance is if they make a mistake. I've got to be ready to take advantage if they do."

<Hmm, a good outlook, considering your position.> They sat in silence for a time, before Sarge broke his contemplation. <Someone is coming.>

Grant didn't know how much time had passed since Cuddles had showed up to taunt him, but it didn't feel like it could have been more than three or four hours.

"I hope you aren't sleeping in there!" A loud boom hurt Grant's ears as one of Dokeshi March's Vassals slammed his scepter against the metal slot covering the viewport of his cell. "We came to ask about what you did to Lord January. You kill him? Is he imprisoned somewhere? What do we need to do to get the food shipments rolling again?"

Grant ignored the Vassal, not even bothering to learn his name. The Dokeshi had a whole bunch of them, and he didn't have the energy to bother asking for all of their identification.

They fell into a pattern, with Grant trying to conserve his energy and various Vassals returning every few hours to make sure he couldn't fall asleep for any length of time. Despite his best efforts, Grant's mind started to become fuzzy with fatigue. He didn't know if it was from the excitement of the last few days, lack of food and water, lack of sleep, or maybe even from the pain in his head and the odd mana drain he had experienced when his sword had started glowing. No matter the reason, he was beginning to feel intense fatigue.

One thing Grant never did was acknowledge the Vassals' presence. Unless they were willing to open the door, he wasn't talking. They *needed* to make a mistake.

Finally, something changed. He didn't know how long it had been, but one entire wall dropped into the floor, flooding his cell with light. His eyes watered at the sudden change, but he blinked through the pain and got a glimpse at what was on the other side.

"But... how?" Grant wasn't sure how they had moved him,

but somehow, he was looking out at the tournament area as it was being set up. They must have wheeled his cell to one of the windows overlooking the floor, where the Dokeshi watched as people gambled away their fortunes.

<They're taunting you by showing you that you'll miss the tournament. It's meant to kill your spirit.>

"Has it really been that long already?" Grant had lost all track of time, but he didn't feel like it had been long enough for the tournament to be starting.

<No, it's still the day before it's supposed to begin. They're just getting things ready.>

"So I still have some time." Grant tried punching the window, but all that did was hurt his knuckles. Next, he drew his uchigatana and stabbed forward with all his weight behind the blow. A miniscule crack appeared, and he instantly got excited. "I think I can break it!" A second blow at the same spot widened the crack, but the wall started rising back up from the floor to cut off his view. "No! I'm so close!" He pounded furiously at the window, but the crack only grew to the length of his finger by the time the wall covered it up.

<It was a good try, Grant. No one could ever accuse you of not giving it your all.> The defeat in Sarge's voice was almost too much for him to handle, but he wasn't willing to give up.

He tried to shove his sword in the paper-thin gap where the covering was rising from, but the blade of his uchigatana was too thick. Scrambling for an idea, he tried his spell, *Thundering Step*. It did nothing but cause him pain. As a last gasp of desperation, Grant used his newest spell, *Apprentice Repair*.

Warning: *Your spell level is too low for the complexity of this mechanism. Damage may occur as a result if you choose to continue.*

"Oh, do I *ever* want to continue!" Grant confirmed his choice, and the spell fired off just as the wall finished sealing back up.

Holding his breath, hoping for a miracle, Grant waited… waited… and waited some more.

Nothing happened.

CHAPTER FIFTY-TWO

After a few minutes of just sitting in the dark, Grant decided to try it again. Even though he couldn't see the mechanism anymore, he knew it was there. Thankfully, the knowledge was enough for the spell to continue to work. At least, the spell fired, and Grant continually got warning messages, so he *guessed* it was still working. There were no visible changes, but he wasn't exactly flush with options at the moment.

He had enough mana to use the spell three times back-to-back, but after that, he had to take a thirty-second break to allow his mana to regenerate. "Sarge, why am I taking so long to regenerate all of my energy? This isn't adding up."

<That's because your sheet is only showing you the maximum *potential for* your mana to refill. It doesn't take into account your true condition.>

"Explain?" Grant knew he could just look at his stat sheet to see for himself, but he was focused on using his spells the second they became available.

<You're hungry, dehydrated, and exhausted.> They didn't say anything for a few minutes as Grant routinely fired off his

new spell. <The good news is, this is steadily increasing your mental cultivation.>

For some reason, that struck Grant as extremely funny, and he started laughing. Before long, Sarge joined in, and the two of them were cackling like a couple of hens.

"Tell me, what could possibly be so funny?" Grant barely registered the voice of the most recent Vassal that had come to ensure he wasn't getting any sleep. "What could you possibly know that is so funny that a person in your situation could laugh?"

"I was just thinking of the stories they will tell about your death." Grant gasped out as he wiped a tear, thought better of wasting it, and put it on his tongue. The Vassal didn't know what to say to such an outlandish claim. "My guess is they'll use it for a horror story around a campfire, but some might find it as funny as I do."

"Well, I think he finally cracked. It's only a matter of time now." The Vassal was speaking to someone farther down the hallway. "I'm surprised, since the other one is still holding out."

<Don't react. If he thinks you're losing your mental faculties, they might lower their guard even more.>

Grant fought down the urge to stab the Vassal through the small opening in his wall, and continued using his spell on the hidden mechanism instead. It was harder than it should have been. Maybe he wasn't quite as mentally sound as he thought.

More time passed, and Grant got lost in the pattern of casting spells three times, waiting, and repeating the process all over again. His recharge time was slowly getting worse, meaning his physical condition was definitely not improving.

He was hungry, thirsty, and tired. The thought of eating the single food bar in his pouch was a tempting one, but Grant knew the dry food would only make his thirst worse. Remembering how they had refused to break apart in the pot of water, he couldn't hold in the shudder that passed through his body. It would definitely hasten his death by dehydration if he ate that thing.

<Grant. I heard something.>

"What, another Vassal coming to offer me an unspecified amount of food and water for information on how to restart the food shipments?" Grant was surprised by the volume of his own voice. It was shockingly loud in the pervasive silence of his cell.

<No, I think the wall is about to drop down again. It coincides with the proper time of the start of the tournament, if my calculations are correct.>

Grant sprang to his feet, regretting the quick motion instantly. He had to fight to keep from face-planting as the feeling in his legs came back with the stinging pain of pins and needles. It was a rookie mistake to let his legs fall asleep like that, and he needed to stop acting like he was brand new at being captured. The thought that he was a veteran at being held prisoner made him laugh again.

They were lowering the wall so he could watch his chances of confronting Dokeshi March vanish forever, but little did they know that he had the mighty spell, *Apprentice Repair*! "Fear my might!"

<I think you might need to sit back down for a second.>

"No, I'll be fine, Sarge. I just need to get my bearings." As light started flooding into the room, Grant closed his eyes to center himself again. His mind was fraying a bit, and he needed focus for what he was about to go through.

Opening his eyes, Grant saw the wall lowering. Until it hit the halfway point. Then one side of the rollers stopped working altogether. The door was stuck, but the crack Grant had made wasn't visible yet!

He pulled out his sword and started pounding on the half-dropped wall with the hilt. It shuddered, and Grant took a step back when a loud grinding sound started to make the floor of his cell start to vibrate.

When the mechanism hidden under the floor exploded, it was powerful enough to knock Grant to his knees. The crack he had formed was now a full spiderweb of lines that spread across most of the glass. As he got back to his feet, he looked out over the crowds of people. They had gathered to watch the final seven players sitting around an oval table try their luck against the ruler of their District. There was one empty chair, and it was time he filled it.

"What's going on?" The familiar voice of Cuddles came from the slot on the wall opposite the splintered glass. "What happened in there?"

Grant took a moment to give the bloodshot eyes of the insane Vassal a view of him smiling before sprinting for freedom. "Don't you do it! Don't-"

Grant couldn't hear the rest of what he was going to say, because he was falling with the sweet sound of shattering glass—like music to his ears—accompanying him to the ground. Shouts and screams came from the crowd, but Grant ignored them all. In his mind, he had planned to drop down from his confinement and say something brave, or funny, or even intimidating to his enemies.

"Ouch."

None of his grand plans came to fruition. His sore ankle gave out on him, and he slammed his knee on the ground. The spectators quickly calmed down when no more humans came flying out of any windows, and a dull roar of excitement replaced their screams of fear.

<I'm pretty sure they're now convinced that you're a part of some show, meant to entertain them.> Well, no time like the present. Grant might have messed up his landing, but the lack of Vassals in the immediate area gave him a chance to take control of the scene.

"Sorry about that, folks. I was almost late to the tournament. Thanks for waiting for me!" Laughter rang out, even though it was obvious they hadn't been about to start. The Dokeshi hadn't even come downstairs yet.

"There he is! Grab him!" Six men dressed as clowns came storming around the corner, and Grant was quickly surrounded. All of them brandished their scepters, and a row of casino guards were closing in behind them. He knew there was no point in fighting so many. As they closed around him, one of the clowns pulled out a set of shackles and placed them around his wrists. Grant didn't raise a finger to stop them.

"Hey, that's one of the finalists!" A member of the crowd was pointing at Grant, who held his shackled wrists up for them all to see.

"The House is trying to *cheat*! They aren't going to let him play!" The speaker seemed familiar to Grant, who took a moment to stare at the man. He finally recognized him as one of Koshin Friday's Vassals; dressed as a commoner.

"Yeah, the House is keeping one of the players from the table!" Another voice rang out, and soon the uproar was more than the six Vassals could ignore.

"*Enough*!" The Dokeshi finally decided to make his entrance, and Grant was surprised to hear that his voice sounded young. It was certainly higher-pitched than he was expecting. "This man and his compatriot have come from across the barrier of District February to incite rebellion and dissension in my District."

The crowd was silenced by the Dokeshi's mere presence, which was the perfect opening for Grant to step in.

"You think you can lie and cheat me out of participating? Let me tell you this just *once*. I am Lord January." Grant swapped his name using the fragment's power, which had set his name as 'Monday' for all this time. The shock on people's faces as they saw the truth with their own eyes almost made him laugh, which would undo the results of his theatrics. "I *alone* decide where the food from January goes, and I came here in an attempt to renegotiate the trade agreements between our Districts… only to be hunted like an animal since I arrived."

That revelation made the Vassals holding him flinch, but not as much as his next revelation and name change. "One *more* thing. I'm *also* Lord February. Besides you, *March*, I'm the only one that can control the barrier between your District and the one that gives you access to that food."

The Vassals holding his arms let go of him, and Grant took

the key for his shackles from the numb fingers of the clown standing next to him. "If you don't release my 'compatriot', I'll refuse to open the borders to allow food through the barriers into this District, and you will starve. If your Dokeshi doesn't face me in a fair and equal duel, then every person in this District… even more than you are now."

That revelation created a great outcry. Grant could feel the rage building in him again, as he once again changed the target of his emotions. "I don't care if I never step out of here. If she is harmed, this District dies."

The sudden silence in the building was deafening. The crowd practically bent away from Grant as he turned to look at them. The Vassals took the opportunity to scatter, and he could feel his head swelling with pressure. He strongly suspected that if he were to draw his sword, it would be glowing.

"My, *my*, what a showman! I must admit, I'm almost *jealous*!" The slow clap of the Dokeshi shattered the fragile silence that had held everyone in place. The Jester's eyes roved over the people who had heard Grant speak. "As I said, he comes here attempting to spark a revolution. I'll tell you now, no one here has a chance of defeating me. None of them would ever accept that gamble."

"Maybe not *one* of them does, but I'd be willing to bet that *all* of them could." Grant's head started to relax as he calmed down.

"Perhaps…? But I do have an alternative." The Dokeshi waved to the table where eight equal stacks of chips were already laid out. "Instead of all that bloodshed, why don't we make a wager? We play the tournament as was initially intended. If you win, it'll be as if you have beaten me in battle. My power and mantle will fall to you."

"If I lose?" Grant finally spoke, after a brief daydream that involved him forcefully removing the frail-looking man's head in an exceedingly violent fashion. He really needed some water.

"If you lose, you spend the rest of the year *personally* escorting food shipments between District January and District

March." The Dokeshi's eyes flashed with a brief moment of insanity, and his mouth twisted in a sneer. "They will be *full* shipments of food. No short-changing us in some petty revenge scheme as a way to get back at me for losing."

Grant looked around the room before answering. A familiar pink shock of hair appearing from the doors to the kitchen helped him to make his decision. "My companion and I both walk out of your District in perfect health, no matter the results."

"As long as you return with food shipments, I don't care *what* happens with the girl." The Dokeshi waved her forward, and Suki was led over to a chair off to the side of the room.

"Fine." Grant knew that it would be easier to just fight the Mad Jester in combat, but many people would die in the process. Plus... Suki didn't like seeing people get killed. "Deal the cards."

"Excellent." Dokeshi March smiled, but it never reached his eyes.

CHAPTER FIFTY-THREE

"Debtors, Bettors, and High Rollers, welcome to the Dokeshi March Poker Tournament Finals!" The casino manager was back on his small stage, announcing the start of the final round. Grant was doing his best to hold in his impatience. As soon as he had agreed to the Dokeshi's deal, everyone in the crowd had instantly switched from fearful to excited. For them, it was a no-lose situation. Either way, they would be getting food shipments soon. Now it was all about the entertainment provided by the game.

"The first of your finalists should be a familiar face. This is the third time in as many years that we have seen Fryer Puck at the last table. He still hopes to win the money needed to buy the cure for his sick wife, who has only gotten worse as time has gone on. Last year, he bet his business that produced turkey fryers. This time, his collateral for his entrance fee… is his life!"

The crowd roared at the announcement. "If he loses, he dies. If he wins, it means his wife continues to live. Now, that's some motivation to succeed, am I right?"

The crowd responded to his goading with roars of approval.

"I think I might be sick." Suki had joined Grant, who was

hurriedly eating a dry heel of bread and sliver of cheese between gulps of water. "What's wrong with these people? Thanks for not leaving me to their tender ministrations, by the way."

"It was no big deal." Grant only shrugged at her. He had seen similar reactions in both District January and District February, so he wasn't particularly surprised. He wasn't going to spend the next five minutes explaining to her what he had gone through to free her; he needed that time to eat.

"No big deal, huh?" The corner of her mouth upturned in a small smile before she took a bite of her own food. She had been kept in a similar situation as Grant, except her cell had been incredibly bright the entire time.

"Our second finalist is here for the first time. She's bet her entire life savings—including her family's ancestral lands—for a chance at finding out who killed her father!" The cheers seemed even louder this time. "That's right! The Dokeshi's Vassals have already identified the person responsible for his death, but she lost the game of chance that determined whether she could learn who it was! If she wins, this will be her chance at justice. If she loses, both her and her elderly mother get to live on the streets!"

"Okay, that one is pretty messed up." Grant was appalled at how the court system involved gambling like everything else in this District. Appalled, but not surprised. "This place needs reform worse than District January needs a thousand personal trainers."

"You can say that again." Suki tore off a bite of a loaf in a rather unladylike fashion. "Why did no one ever tell me how good *bread* is?"

"I know, right?" Grant took a bite of cheese, trying to keep the ratio of bread to cheese as even as possible. "You should really try pancakes and honey. It'll blow your mind."

"Our third competitor is none other than the son of Lord Monday, here to play for his father's freedom!" The expected roar of the crowd was somehow even louder. "That's right! You all remember last year, when his father gambled away his freedom in exchange for his son getting to continue the noble line. Well now, his son has gambled his entire lineage for the chance at freeing his father from bondage!"

The next three competitors were just as heart-wrenching, he was sure, but he stopped listening. Knowing that he was destroying these people by winning wouldn't help him sleep at night, but stopping the cycle that allowed their situations to even exist in the first place was more important. The sudden swelling in his head caused him to choke on his water, but he pushed past it and kept drinking.

He wasn't happy about it, but the responsible part of Grant knew he *had* to win, otherwise there would be a dozen new Fryer Pucks, grieving children, and imprisoned fathers every single day that Dokeshi March was in power. Grant was sorry for their loss, but he needed to win.

"Without further ado, let the tournament… commence!" The announcer was finally done introducing everyone. Grant had missed what they had said about him, but it didn't really matter. What mattered was taking first place.

Grant took the chair directly across the table from Dokeshi March and spent a few seconds making sure he hadn't been short-changed on his chips. It would definitely be something the Mad Jester would get a kick out of doing.

"I don't need to short you on chips to beat you, Lord January." Dokeshi nodded at the dealer to start shuffling. "Or do you prefer Lord *February*? No matter. When I beat you, I'll simply call you 'delivery boy'."

"I won't call you anything. You'll be dead." Grant was feeling the strain of being this close to the man responsible for all the suffering he had seen, and unable to do anything about it.

"We'll have to see, won't we?" The twisted smile of Dokeshi March made Grant's skin crawl.

"Blinds, please." The dealer was the same man Grant had at his last table. He guessed The Dokeshi wanted as many guards as he could get. The man quickly dealt the cards, clearly having practiced his card skills over the last few days. "First round of betting starts with Fryer Puck."

"I raise." The man pushed in half of his stack, making the bet fifty chips. He was visibly sweating, and Grant felt a sharp pang of regret. It still bothered him that he would have to beat a man trying to win medicine to save his wife's life.

"I call." His bet was met by three others at the table, but both Grant and Dokeshi March folded. The betting between the four was fast and furious, and before Grant could blink, the hand was over, and Fryer Puck was on his feet in indignation.

"I had pocket Aces! How could I lose with *pocket Aces*?" He had gone all in on the first hand and was already disqualified. Grant saw Dokeshi March give a slight nod to the hulking form of Cuddles, who had somehow squeezed his bulk into a throne-like chair off to the side of the table.

He stood up and pulled a massive hammer from off its resting place on the wall. "It isn't fair! Math doesn't lie, and I-" Before Grant realized what was happening, Cuddles swung the hammer into Fryer Puck's head, sending the man tumbling to the floor. He didn't get back up.

"You sick-" Grant stood, his sword already out of its sheath and a faint glow running along the edge of the blade.

"Now, *now*, Lord Grant, you agreed to play the game as it was meant to be played initially, before our little side bet." The Dokeshi had his scepter in his hand, its crystal glowing a clear, white light. "That poor soul bet his life as collateral to join the tournament. What did you think would happen when he lost?"

Speechless, Grant slowly sheathed his sword and sat down. It wasn't until the blood stopped roaring in his ears that he realized the crowd was also roaring. In approval.

"I assure you; the man knew the risks when he made the bet." The Dokeshi's smile did reach his eyes this time. "If that makes you feel better. He simply forgot my number one rule. The House *Always* Wins."

The other players at the table were all freaking out a little, but it was a blend of fear and determination that Grant could respect. He had been in similar situations several times. The dealer collected up the cards and was already shuffling them after wiping a few spots of blood off the two Aces that had been in front of Fryer Puck. "Blinds, please."

Somehow, the only person not nervous was Dokeshi March. Even though his life was on the line as well—possibly for the first time ever—he didn't seem to be bothered. Instead, the man was playing the crowd, and they were eating it up.

"Oh, you wish to check? Well, no man checks my cards for free, Lord Monday. I raise you twenty!" The crowd cheered at the by-play, and Grant was sickened by their heartlessness. A tiny voice in the back of his head weighed the pros and cons of letting this nest of sharks starve to death before snapping out of it. This group of wealthy people, in their silks and finery, were not a proper representation of the people who lived in District March.

"Oh, what a surprise! Lord Grant folds again. What a genuine *shock*!" Grant ignored Dokeshi March every time he tried to provoke him into playing. He would play the cards he was dealt and not react to the goading of the madman.

Grant ended up winning two hands by the time the blinds made their third raise, which was just enough to keep him floating at roughly where he'd started, at a hundred chips. Another two players were escorted out in chains during that time, leaving only five competitors at the table. He was having a hard time concentrating most of the time, due to an awful itching sensation in the small of his back.

"What's up with my clothes? Did I accidentally touch some itch-weed at some point?" Grant tried rubbing his back against his chair, but it didn't do anything to help. He was distracted from his misery by the definite sound of someone making a terrible mistake.

"All in!" The finalist was one of the two that Grant didn't listen to, but when he saw Cuddles stirring in his chair, he knew what was coming.

"Oh, so close, yet so *far*!" Dokeshi March laid out a flush that was exactly one card higher than the one the man had. "I'm sorry. Better luck next time!"

Cuddles used his chains this time, and soon the man was wrapped in endless metal links that were slowly increasing in weight. The crowd was loving it, and Grant was ready to burn the place to the ground. "Okay, folks! It looks like we're down to the final four. It's time to take a quick break, and then we'll be right back at it! Players, please be back in your seats in ten minutes. If you take any longer, you will automatically fold, but your blinds will still be removed from your chips."

Dokeshi March quickly stood and made his way to his private booth. Grant also stood and stretched, his ankle giving him a twinge of pain. All the catching up on lost water had quickly developed into a strong urge to use the bathroom, so he headed to the nearest one to the betting table, bypassing Suki, who tried to talk to him.

As he was relieving himself, Sarge spoke to him for the first time since he had reunited with Suki. <I hate to be the bearer of bad news, but I'm pretty sure four people are waiting for you to open the door of your stall. One of them is very big.>

"It's Cuddles, isn't it?" Grant quickly finished and buttoned up. "Cuddles in a public bathroom is never a good thing."

CHAPTER FIFTY-FOUR

When Grant opened the door to the stall, he was surprised to see six people standing there, not four. Two of them weren't wearing shoes, which explained Sarge's failure to hear them. Feet wrapped in rags were always extremely quiet.

"Do you want me to wash my hands first?" Grant looked to Cuddles, who had his scepter in one hand and his massive hammer in the other. "Is that a no? Because that's pretty gross, even for your crazy self."

Grant pushed past the people trying to block his way and started washing his hands. "Besides, did you all forget? The system won't let you fight me while I'm still in the tournament. All you lot can do is stand here and look stupid. Which, I mean, good job. You really are nailing it."

"I think you're forgetting one very important thing, Grant Monday." Cuddles held up his scepter, and the gem let out a brilliant light. "Deactivate the system in my presence."

<Well, that's new.>

The lack of screens popping up to acknowledge the order caused a slight delay in their reactions, and Grant was more than happy to use it.

"*Time is Space.*" He said the name of the spell under his breath, so it was a complete surprise to the man standing behind him when his uchigatana appeared in his hands, then slammed into the man's undefended guts. Grant tore it free as he kicked the knee of the man standing to his left, forcing him to fall in the way of Cuddles. The clown smacked the man out of the way with the side of his hammer, pulverizing him into man-burger.

"*Apprentice Repair.*" His next spell forced the sheath and dagger of the man to his right to meld together, making it impossible to pull the blade free. Grant smashed the hilt of his sword against the man's temple, dropping the ambusher to his knees.

"What are you fools doing? Kill him!" Cuddles shouted at the last two men, trying to get them to close on Grant as he lifted his hammer for a killing blow. If they could flush him to Cuddles, Grant would be easily dispatched. Instead, Grant rushed them. He was fully under the control of the rage coursing through his body, even with the pressure in his head being enough to make him want to double over in pain.

The high guard position of Kenjutsu flowed into the low guard, and his glowing blade passed through the two men like they were nothing but the wind. Grant spun just in time to deflect a hammer blow aimed at his head, his blade passing through the solid metal shaft of the handle as if it were water. The hammerhead spun off behind him, shattering a porcelain sink.

"You know, I think I like it better this way." Cuddles took a step back, and chains sprang up from the ground, wrapping around Grant before he could even use his blade to deflect them. "Doing things yourself is so much more… *satisfying.*"

The weight of the chains wrapped around Grant doubled, and he was driven to his knees. The clown leaned in, "I knew the first time I saw you that it was going to end this way. You tried to *change your fate*, but the world doesn't work like that. This is how it *always* ends with the strong ones."

"I'm glad we got to know one another, Grant Monday, but it's time for you to meet your ancestors." Cuddles turned to pick up the hammerhead. It still had a foot of handle attached to it, more than enough to do the job. The entire time Cuddles had been talking, the pressure in Grant's head had been building. It was coalescing into a point no bigger than the nail on his pinky, but it seemed to weigh more than the chains slowly squeezing the life out of him.

When the Prime Vassal spoke the words 'change your fate', it felt like a door he hadn't even known existed unexpectedly opened in his mind. Everything within himself seemed to settle down for an impossibly long moment, and Grant finally *understood.*

The Dao Seed of Change fully formed in his glabella, the center of his forehead, and he stood up. The weight of the chains felt like nothing in comparison to the weight of the universe, which now had an anchor in his soul. He called his uchigatana to his hand, the tool he now knew to be the catalyst for change unlike this realm had seen in a thousand years. Grant felt *right.* Maybe for the first time in his life, he was completely aware of his place within the cosmos.

"What are you doing? How can you even stand up right now?" Cuddles was backing up. For the first time since Grant had met him, there was no insanity in his eyes.

"I'm here to *change* things." Grant raised his sword and placed it against the chest of the clown, who was now backed up against the row of smashed sinks. It was perfectly clear to the clown what was about to happen, and Grant watched as hope died in his bloodshot eyes. A quick shove, and those eyes dimmed. "I'll change things for the *better.*"

He didn't know how long he stood there, but when he came back to his senses, Grant felt completely normal. His head didn't ache, but he could still feel the kernel of something *solid* resting between and above his eyes.

<*Finally*! Grant, can you hear me?> Sarge's voice caused Grant to shake his head, clearing it of the cobwebs. <It has

been seventeen minutes. You're already late. Clean off the blood, and get out there!>

"But what about the Dao Seed? What should I do?" Grant was automatically rinsing the blood off his face with the water spraying from the broken fixtures.

<There's no time! Get out there before they drain you of all your chips!>

Grant scrambled out of the bathroom, hurriedly locking the door and flipping the 'vacant' sign to 'occupied'. He had to elbow his way through the crowd, who slowly let him through once they realized he was one of the players. When he finally plopped down in his chair, Grant wasn't the least bit surprised that no one was happy to see him.

"Ah, Lord Grant, so nice of you to join us. You have already forfeited twenty chips from a big blind. It's now your turn for the small blind." Dokeshi March's eyes kept drifting back to the door where Grant had come from, a frown twisting his mouth.

"He isn't coming. Also, you might want to get someone to clean up that bathroom. Someone left *quite* a mess." Grant watched carefully, but Dokeshi March didn't give anything away. They got back into the rhythm of playing poker, and somehow Dokeshi March seemed to keep piling up the chips. Every time he would bet, the itch in Grant's lower back would only get worse.

"Woot woot! Hey guys, check this out!" When the player to Grant's right got down to just a single stack of chips, several people in the crowd started shouting, tossing things, and even flashing a very bright glow orb.

"I'll take that!" The man to his right scooped up the chips, finally bringing his pile back to three full stacks of ten. Unfortunately, most of those had come from Grant. Now *he* was the person down to a single stack of ten.

<The people in the crowd are causing a distraction, which is allowing the man to cheat. I'm pretty certain that Dokeshi March is allowing it to happen.> The next hand, Grant paid

close attention, and the next time the lights flashed in his eyes, he snatched the player's wrist. The man was caught with a third card in his hand, and immediately the crowd turned on him.

"So *sorry*, Lord Monday." The Dokeshi's tone didn't sound like he was sorry. "It looks like your father gets to stay in my little dungeon, and now you're just… Mr. Monday."

The man was led away by a pair of guards, and his chips were divided among the last three players: the woman wanting justice for her father, Dokeshi March, and Grant.

<At least you can meet the blinds.> Now that there were only a few players left, the blinds had already been raised to ten and twenty. Grant had twenty-two chips remaining.

"I believe the big blind is *Lord* Grant?" The Dokeshi smirked at him, forcing Grant to grit his teeth. He shoved his chips in, making the Jester's smile only grow larger. Grant was so irritated that he finally gave in and loosened the straps on his armor, just so he could finally scratch the itch that was driving him mad. That was when it all clicked.

"All in." Grant smiled, the swift change in expression making Dokeshi March feel a little uncomfortable. As the cards were dealt, Grant didn't even bother looking at his cards. The Dokeshi immediately folded, and the woman matched his bet.

"Winner, Lord Grant, two pair; sixes and sevens." The dealer pushed the chips to Grant, and he scooped them into a pile one-handed. The woman seemed more surprised than angry and looked questioningly at Dokeshi March. He simply ignored her and put in his big blind as Grant put in his small.

This time, Grant folded, not liking his hand. That put him down to thirty-four chips, just in time for the blinds to raise to thirty and fifteen.

"All in." Once again, Grant shoved his pile into the middle of the table, still using just one hand.

"Fine. I'll see if lightning strikes twice." The woman pushed in her own pile of chips, coming up two short from matching Grant.

"I'll spot you, my dear." Dokeshi March slid two of his own chips into the pot, this time not even bothering to hide that the two of them were working together against him. "I'm *sure* you're good for it."

Once again, Grant didn't even touch his cards. He just maintained eye contact with the ruler of the District and waited for the dealer to announce the winner.

"Winner, Lord Grant, with a Queen high flush." The woman was instantly furious, jumping from her seat and pointing a shaking finger at Dokeshi March.

"You told me this would be the last time! You said you'd tell me who killed him! I know you know who it is! *Tell me*! We had a deal; you *have* to tell me!" Her shrieks, or Grant's stare, must have finally unnerved the man.

"*I* had him killed, you insufferable woman! Your father was a cheat and a con man, and he tried not to play by *The Rules*. Now begone, before you join him in a shallow grave!" Dokeshi March was practically panting in anger. For the first time, the crowd was completely silent, and he didn't like it. He turned to the dealer and tossed the cards still on the table in his face. "Do your job, and deal the cards!"

Now that Grant had sixty-eight chips, he was finally in a position to fold when he had the small blind. Which he did, immediately. Since it was just the two of them, they had to rotate the big blind and small blind each hand. The next hand, Grant had fifty-three chips remaining, and the big blind was now forty. He pushed his whole pile in the middle, giving his fate to chance.

"All in." When Grant didn't touch his cards again, Dokeshi March seemed to become just a little bit more insane.

"You aren't even going to *look*?" The Jester quickly glanced at his own cards before matching Grant's bet. "Do you truly have so much faith in your luck?"

"I've got faith in the universe's demand for a *change* in leadership." The collective intake of breath from the spectators was noticeable, and it only incensed Dokeshi March further.

"Winner, Lord Grant, with a King through nine straight." If looks could cause a heart to stop, the poor dealers would have turned to stone after the look Dokeshi March gave him.

"That's it. You must be cheating!" There was an outright gasp at The Dokeshi's words. "There's no other explanation. The rule is: The House Always Wins. *I am the House*, Grant Monday! Do you hear me! I. Am. The. *House*!"

Now he was full-blown ranting, and his face had gone straight past red and into purple. "Guards! Take this man away. He's a cheater and therefore forfeits the game."

"Dokeshi March, you must prove Grant Monday is a cheater. That is the *rule*." Grant turned to look at who had spoken. It was Koshin Friday, and Grant could have kissed him. "*You* are the one who made that rule, Dokeshi March. Even you have to follow your own rules."

"I know the rules! I *made* the rules, and no one knows them like I do!" The Dokeshi stood, his hands throttling his scepter like he wished it was the neck of every person who had ever crossed him. He plopped down in his chair after unsuccessfully trying to stare down Koshin Friday. "I tire of this game, Grant Monday. What say you to one final hand, winner takes all."

"That's the game I've been playing the last several hands." Grant shoved his chips in the center of the table. "It makes no difference to me. Change is in the wind, and I like my chances."

"Yes, let's see about this *change*." Dokeshi March shoved his chips into the center, his much larger pile covering Grant's like an avalanche.

The cards were dealt, and the entire building seemed to hold its breath. Five cards were laid out, none of them higher than the number nine. Grant chose this moment to finally reveal what he had been holding ever since loosening his armor. The chess piece.

According to what he had learned about the item, it was meant to show troop movements on a living map. It was also *heavily* enchanted to prevent spells from shifting the truth within its range, a necessary precaution for a general planning troop movements involving the lives of thousands. Grant found it fitting that it would serve in a different type of battle, with thousands of lives still in the balance.

"Winner, Lord Grant, with… Jack high." The crowd still held its breath as Dokeshi March stood on his chair, pointing his scepter like it was a crossbow.

"You! It isn't supposed to be like this! You cheated!" Dokeshi March kept trying to make his scepter obey his commands, but it wasn't working. He had lost.

"No, Dokeshi. I *didn't* cheat. I just brought a tool that repelled your Utility spells and caused them to fail. We've only been getting the cards dealt to us. The *real* cards dealt to us." Grant's vision was flooded with notifications, and his sword started to grow hot in its sheath. He drew it slowly, letting the light from the blade wash over the people witnessing the end of the rule of the Mad Jester.

Do you, Grant Monday, wish to absorb the power of March 1: Let's Make a Deal? Accepting Let's Make a Deal will override any previous Wielded Weapon power absorbed in the current monthly series. If not overridden by another weapon of the same month, this ability will return to its current Wielded Weapon at the end of the year, unless the quest 'Heal The World' has been successfully completed.

Accept / Decline

"I accept." Grant agreed to the notification solemnly, and his sword flashed for a bare instant.

Let's Make a Deal: Set a binding rule, as well as the punishment for breaking that rule. The harsher the requirements of the rule, the harsher the punishment may be. There are three restrictions.

- *If you're the only target of the rule, you may make any rule and any punishment for breaking it.*
- *If you and another entity are bound by the same rule, the punishment for breaking the rule must be mutually agreed upon for maximum effect, else the punishment will be halved for the unwilling target.*
- *If another entity is the only target of the rule, the punishment for breaking the rule can only be pain. If the rule is deemed to be predatory, there's an 80% chance of backlash upon the Wielder making the rule.*

Violet fireworks erupted from the Dokeshi as the Fragment chose that moment to begin moving to its new owner. Soon the explosions were floating overhead... then reversed course and flowed into Grant.

Quest Update: Heal the World (Legendary)

Congratulations, Grant Monday, you have defeated the Lady of the Month, Lady March, and have been granted her Fragment. As the new Lord March-

Resonance detected!

You're the Lord of January, February, and March!

The Januarian Fragment of Life, Februarian Fragment of Vibrancy, and Marchurian Fragment of Festivity are resonating!

Power flooded through Grant as the Fragments began to rotate around each other, bands of pink, brown, and violet connecting and intertwining. When the process completed, Grant stared at something completely different from the fragments he had seen to this point. It was a set of three stars that slowly rotated around him, casting his form in a trio of soft, beautiful lights.

. . .

You have reassembled the Spring Constellation.

1. *You have partied your way into attaining the power of the Februarian Fragment of Vibrancy! You now have the ability to restore your energy and mana to full whenever the month you're a Lord of is in its ascendency.*
2. *You have gained the ability to temporarily open the boundary separating any of the Spring Districts, as well as the boundary to April.*
3. *You have gained the ability to send a message to anyone within the Spring Districts.*
4. *You can now step through space and arrive anywhere within the Spring Districts, so long as you are within a Spring District.*
5. *To always be ready to take part in festivities, you no longer suffer negative effects from lack of sleep.*
6. *Constellation Exclusive: You have the power to name a regent for any District you're the Lord of, granting them lesser access to a single Fragment's power.*
7. *Spring Constellation Exclusive: You have the ability to switch your name from Grant Monday to Earl Spring at will.*

"These are… stars?" Grant murmured at the mesmerizing lights that swirled around him for another moment before vanishing. "Like… *actual* stars? How powerful *were* the Leap sorcerers?"

"No. *No, no, no*!" The Dokeshi was whipping his head back and forth, causing his long gold hair to fly in his face. "*Fine*! If this is how you want it, then so be it! We can all die together!"

Grant was still coming down from the euphoria of becoming Earl Spring. He barely had time to focus and see the Dokeshi pulling his Scepter Wielded Weapon from a holster to lift it into the air. Light was building around the weapon, strobing frenetically between various colors.

Words were written in those colors, but they were being rapidly erased, as though displaying a scribe's scribble in reverse. As the thousands of lines of text fully vanished, the Dokeshi swung the ball of condensed power toward the ground. Grant launched himself forward in a desperate lunge, noticing that without the words in it, the power was the exact coloration and consistency as the barrier between Districts.

The tip of his sword met the jeweled scepter.

CHAPTER FIFTY-FIVE

The world froze for Grant as February Twenty Nine mingled with the collected barrier energy, and a glaring red notification took all of his attention.

Caution: a concentrated mana source has been detected. Left as is, this mana source will detonate with enough force to reduce ten kilometers to dust.

As Earl Spring, you have the authority to redirect this energy in one of three ways.

1. *Wielder option: You may redirect its current path, and dissipate the energy as a nova-explosion that will not touch you. This will count as personal kills against anyone that dies. There are an estimated 14 Wielders and 86 Vassals in the blast radius.*
2. *Cultivation option: You may attempt to absorb this energy into your Armor cultivation. There's a 20% chance of death, +/- 10%. If absorbed, your Armor cultivation will increase by approximately 10,000 hours.*
3. *Early Spring option: You may redirect the energy using any compatible Wielded Weapon ability so as to benefit any of the*

Districts you control. Compatible abilities include 'Sword Grandmastery' and 'Let's Make A Deal'.

As the three options populated within his mind, Grant found a path to saving March that he hadn't expected. The monsters here were far too powerful and too numerous, and the residents would no longer have the dubious benefit of the subsystem to keep them safe. He made his choice and redirected the power of over fifteen thousand erased laws into just one.

"I choose the Earl Spring option, Let's Make A Deal. First rule: Monsters in District March must remain below surface level. Punishment: constant pain." He could feel the world bending to his will as he declared his first and only rule for District March. Just like that, the frozen moment in time ended.

Dokeshi March slammed the Wielded Weapon into the ground with a wild scream of expectation... only for the jewel to bounce harmlessly off the plushily carpeted floor. "Why... why are you all *alive*? Die! I order you all to *die*!"

"There's no way I can let your presence and poisonous mentality infect this District for another moment." Grant's completed Dao Seed weighed on him like a heavy crown as he assumed the mantle of a leader tasked with judging those who had betrayed the people they had been obligated to protect. The choice was brutal, but it didn't feel wrong. "As justice for all the people of District March, I—Earl Spring—sentence you to death."

He didn't bother drawing things out. He made a hard chop into the side of The Dokeshi's neck, slamming his uchigatana down at an angle, all the way into his chest cavity. The Dokeshi's mask slid off and fell to the ground as Grant's sword dug through yielding flesh, the light fading from the eyes of the woman as the painted smile fell to the carpet without a sound.

Sarge's voice boomed into Grant's head a moment later. <Grant, it appears Dokeshi March sent a stand-in! I'm... sixty percent sure, but this *could* have been the Dokeshi. Huh. I thought that was a typo when you got the Fragment.>

Grant felt like he had just been punched in the gut. "How… when… is this some kind of imposter?"

"Earl Spring, I can answer that… if you're willing to make a deal." The speaker came forward from the crowd, a familiar pockmarked-faced man. "I only ask for my life, in return for the truth."

"Deal." Grant paused to close the woman's eyes, then turned to face the former Vassal, Beans. "Tell me, did I just kill the real Dokeshi March?"

"Yes, Earl Spring, that is the real Dokeshi March." Beans took a deep breath, visibly steadying his nerves. "Three years ago, the previous Lord March went insane and tried to kill his only child, a daughter named Joy. She managed to kill him instead. To avoid a panic, she wore his mask and a lot of paint to make others believe she was the real Dokeshi. Since all of the Vassals still called her Dokeshi, everyone else just… followed along."

"Why didn't she reveal the truth after securing her rule?" Grant could at least let out a small sigh of relief. He hadn't inadvertently killed the wrong person. "Wouldn't it have been fine after a few months, or even the first year? No… another thing. She *sounded* like a man. A woman, especially one this young, pretending to be a man? She should have sounded like someone playing pretend!"

"It wasn't that simple, though the voice was easy. Simply a Utility spell on her face covering." Beans pulled out a faded cultivation manual from his back pocket. He leaned down and retrieved the blood-splattered mask, pushing it on over his face. As he spoke, his voice was that of the Dokeshi's. "She followed the same mental cultivation manual as her father. We all did. It allows the user to tap into the power of the scepters at a level no one could have ever expected… but it also slowly drives you insane, the longer you use it."

<It must have been a deviant cultivation path. Short-term power with long-term side effects. I thought all of those had

been destroyed during the Wielder Wars... why would *anyone* recreate something like this?>

"So, what happened after she started going insane?" Grant suddenly felt very tired. This poor girl was shoved into a terrible situation, and life didn't pull any punches.

"After a while, she didn't even know who she really was anymore." Beans tossed the cultivation manual down next to the corpse, along with the mask. "All she cared about was playing games, so she turned the whole District into nothing *but* games. I never did like using the cultivation manual, not after I saw what it did to Joy. You saw how weak my scepter was, compared to everyone else's. I just wish Frank hadn't used it so much..."

Beans' voice trailed off, and he eventually walked away. Grant was fine with it. He didn't need anything else from the broken man.

"Grant!" Suki's voice brought him out of his stupor, and he gave her a long hug when she reached him. "Are you okay? That was a lot."

"I'll be fine." He looked up to find that they were the only two people still on the gambling floor. He noticed Koshin Friday standing by the bathroom that held the body of Cuddles, furiously whispering to a group of his Vassals. "What's going on?"

"The entire District is in an uproar. Most people don't know how to live without the system in place, and the food is almost all gone." She pointed at Koshin. "He's already trying to redistribute what stores there are in all of the casinos, but that won't last long. I... I need to go back to February. Someone has to coordinate the food shipments from January to March, otherwise thousands here will start dying of starvation."

"I understand, Suki. I never expected you to go with me the whole way to December anyway. Besides, *you* should be Regent February, not that unhappy Lord Monday." Grant had a new tight feeling in his chest, something completely different than his Dao Seed. He concentrated, and her status changed to reflect his wishes. "Now you can get through the barriers without a problem."

"You better make it all the way to December without me, Grant Monday." She wiped at her face, doing her best to not let Grant see her cry. "I mean it. You come back to me. When I see you again, I'll have our wedding all planned out. There will even be… I'll allow cake. I promise."

"Thanks?" Grant didn't know what else to say, so he gave her another hug instead. "I'll bring you back to February momentarily. I have a few small requests first."

"Earl Spring, do you have a moment?" Grant glanced over as Koshin waved him down. "I've taken the liberty of collecting your things and restocking some of your basic supplies. The storeroom was woefully short on potions, but I gave you what few we could spare. Please, follow me."

"Thank you, Koshin, I truly appreciate it." Grant and Suki were guided out of the floor and to a strategy room, where they stopped at a large table covered in maps. "What's all this?"

"It's meant for us to plan, my Lord. Your province is in anarchy, and we need to bring it under control." Koshin pointed at the northern section of the map, near where Grant had entered the Labyrinth. "This entire section of the District is being… dissolved… by some new, strange fungus. No one knows what it is, and this invasive species has no predator. It doesn't have any impact on people, but it eats through buildings like a Ravenous Termite Horde. If it isn't brought under control, the entire northern region will be nothing but rubble in a week!"

"Well, Koshin, it sounds like you just found the perfect location for the fields of crops that need to be planted." Grant concentrated again, and Koshin Friday became *Regent* Koshin. "Besides, as the new ruler of this District, I'd think you would want your people to be more self-sufficient. Growing crops is the first step!"

The man seemed to be filled with an equal mix of shock and fear when he saw his new title. To Grant, that was the proper attitude for a good leader to have. "Well, I'm off, then. Good luck!"

A slash of February Twenty Nine later, Grant and Suki were standing at the barrier to February. He pushed his sword through, and they stepped into the District. "Suki. I have a favor to ask of you."

"Anything, Grant." Suki's eyes were welling up, and her fists were flashing with purple lightning.

"The barriers are going to come down at the end of the year, and January will almost certainly be wiped off the map by the monsters alone." Grant took a deep breath and made a request that he knew would cause no end of hatred to be sent his way. "Can you mobilize the *entirety* of your Pacers for Trainers? If anyone is struggling in their health journey, and they need people to encourage and motivate them… it's District January."

"I can't even *begin* to tell you how excited I am to make that happen," Suki confirmed solemnly, her eyes shining with plans. "I'll bring the very best cultivation manuals. They won't be happy, but they *might* live through next year."

"I'll go warn them." The two exchanged one last tender moment, and he took three more steps. One to the edge of the District. One to return to his land. One to step into Castle January.

EPILOGUE

He could have never expected the sight that greeted him. Grant stared at a huge man that was running in place, his knees breaking and reforming with each huge bound up an oversized set of stairs that constantly descended. "Lord January… no… I don't know your actual name."

"You." The previous Lord of the Month didn't pause. "I recognize you, no matter how you've changed, Grant Leap."

"*Earl Spring,*" Grant retorted, causing the man to flinch back and almost fall.

"You actually did it…" The man swallowed harshly and focused on continuing to climb. "This District is pure anarchy. You left them to rot without a leader. At least, under me, people were happy."

"Happily *dying*, sir." Grant decided that there was nothing wrong with being cordial in victory. "I'm here to appoint a Regent, and warn that February is coming to help train our people in cultivation. The barriers will be falling at the end of the year, and the monsters… even in February, they're just too strong. I wish you well."

"I never meant to hurt them." The man's plaintive voice

called Grant back before he could vanish. "I had… I had good *reasons* for doing what I did. We had lost all purpose. This District went from feeding the entire world to a rotting, overgrown farmland. The land is *too* fertile. Food *will* grow. If we didn't eat it… monsters would. The entire District would have died and become utterly overrun with monsters."

"Why not burn it?" Grant turned back slowly, this history lesson something he had never heard mentioned in the slightest. "Something. *Anything* would have been better than this."

"*You* try telling a million people, who have cultivated the land, to destroy the fruit of their labors. That thought calls guillotines to mind." The ex-Lord shook his head. "I was the brightest mind in generations. I studied the monsters and created a cultivation method that could take those resources and put them to use. I did the *best* I *could*!"

Grant had no words. He merely nodded and examined the strange machine the man had clearly made himself. "Thank you for telling me. When I'm the Calendar King… I'll need a competent Vassal. Will you come with me and find a way to redeem yourself?"

"You'd… give me that? A new life?" The Lord's face was hard to read. Were those tears, or sweat?

"No. I'd give you nothing. You'd *earn* it." Grant stepped through the District to his old home. He knew where Randall's secret vault was, and he had the power to smash his way through it now. The farm was utterly abandoned, and he knew better than to go looking for his old cow friend. Moments later, he was once more in front of Lord January; this time, holding a book.

"Here. A shortcut to regaining your past self." Grant hadn't thrown the book; that would be cruel to the man.

A single glance at the grimoire in his hand, and the large man dropped to the ground sobbing. "H-his personal *resource draining* spell! No matter what I offered, he would never tell me where it was, or how to use it! Randall moved to the edge of the

District just to escape my badgering! I can be myself again… a thousand years later…!"

"I'll be back when the barriers fall." Grant decided to take the moment to escape the uncomfortable atmosphere. His plan had been to make a Regent, but he could just do that without all the legwork. He set his sponsor, Sir Friday, as the Regent, and vanished from the District.

Finally standing next to the border to District April, Grant looked back at the megatropolis that was District March, and noted huge columns of smoke rising from what was likely dozens of miles of burning casinos. "They'll be fine. I'm sure they'll figure out how to… buy and sell based on Time instead of gambling. Eventually."

Sarge ignored his concerns and launched into conversation. <I've been looking over the powers you got from March, and it turns out they've been using them wrong the whole time!>

"Oh?" Grant was feeling his way up and down the border, trying to find the best place to cross. "What's it really meant for?"

<The true purpose of the scepter was meant to be a tool to reinforce self-discipline. It's at its weakest when forcing others to follow rules, which is probably why they were reduced to using that deviant cultivation method.>

"What does this mean for us, then?" Grant finally found a place that didn't feel too strong, making sure all of his straps were tight before trying to cross over.

<It means we can use it to enhance your mental fortitude, which should increase your mental cultivation by leaps and bounds!>

"That's great news, Sarge!" Grant used his uchigatana to slice a hole through the barrier and stepped into District April for the first time. "Wait. That means this is really gonna suck, doesn't it?"

<Not for me!>

Grant looked over the rolling grassy plains of April, the first District of Summer. It was nothing but endless waves of green as far as the eye could see. Grant didn't spot a single building anywhere, and he was momentarily stunned by the barren beauty the new land provided.

"This place is incredible." For some reason, the sound of Grant's voice turned out to be a siren call for every monster within twenty miles. He had barely closed his mouth before a green-striped tiger the size of a horse sprang out of the grass, its metal claws aimed for his throat.

"*Bwaragha*!" The sudden ambush put Grant on his heels, and if it wasn't for his skill levels in Iaijutsu, his journey would have ended right there on the lonely plains. "Sarge, what's happening?"

Grant was having an impossible time cutting through the tough hide of the grass tigers, who had somehow multiplied from one to four in the blink of an eye. <Fall back! Get out of here; these monsters are too high of a level for you right now!>

The Earl spun in place, making a cut through the barrier just large enough for him to slip through. He leaned wearily against a nearby rock, trying to catch his breath after making his escape. "That was… just a bad place to cross. I'm going to try crossing over somewhere else."

He made another cut in space and walked through a spot in District March that was a hundred miles south of his previous attempt. "Let's try here."

This time, Grant made a much smaller cut, doing his best to stay quiet when he squeezed through the gap in the barrier, which was when he was swarmed by prairie dogs the size of *actual* dogs. As he made wide sweeping motions with his sword at knee-height, he had a moment to catch his breath. *Just* a moment, though, as the group of six he was facing had apparently only been waiting for a larger group in the distance to join them in their attack.

<Look at all of them! Monsters, one and all!> Sarge whooped as Grant's monster-kill tally began to rapidly climb. <I have a feeling that I'm going to *love* Summer.>

ABOUT DAKOTA KROUT

Associated Press best-selling author, Dakota has been a top 5 bestseller on Amazon, a top 6 bestseller on Audible, and his first book, Dungeon Born, was chosen as one of Audible's top 5 fantasy picks in 2017.

He draws on his experience in the military to create vast terrains and intricate systems, and his history in programming and information technology helps him bring a logical aspect to both his writing and his company while giving him a unique perspective for future challenges.

"Publishing my stories has been an incredible blessing thus far, and I hope to keep you entertained for years to come!" -Dakota

Connect with Dakota:
MountaindalePress.com
Patreon.com/DakotaKrout
Facebook.com/TheDivineDungeon
Twitter.com/DakotaKrout
Discord.gg/mdp

ABOUT MOUNTAINDALE PRESS

Dakota and Danielle Krout, a husband and wife team, strive to create as well as publish excellent fantasy and science fiction novels. Self-publishing *The Divine Dungeon: Dungeon Born* in 2016 transformed their careers from Dakota's military and programming background and Danielle's Ph.D. in pharmacology to President and CEO, respectively, of a small press. Their goal is to share their success with other authors and provide captivating fiction to readers with the purpose of solidifying Mountaindale Press as the place 'Where Fantasy Transforms Reality.'

Connect with Mountaindale Press:
MountaindalePress.com
Facebook.com/MountaindalePress
Twitter.com/_Mountaindale
Instagram.com/MountaindalePress

MOUNTAINDALE PRESS TITLES

GameLit and LitRPG

The Completionist Chronicles,
The Divine Dungeon,
Full Murderhobo, and
Year of the Sword by Dakota Krout

Arcana Unlocked by Gregory Blackburn

A Touch of Power by Jay Boyce

Red Mage and
Farming Livia by Xander Boyce

Space Seasons by Dawn Chapman

Ether Collapse and
Ether Flows by Ryan DeBruyn

Dr. Druid by Maxwell Farmer

Bloodgames by Christian J. Gilliland

Threads of Fate by Michael Head

Lion's Lineage by Rohan Hublikar and Dakota Krout

Wolfman Warlock by James Hunter and Dakota Krout

Axe Druid,
Mephisto's Magic Online, and
High Table Hijinks by Christopher Johns

Skeleton in Space by Andries Louws

Chronicles of Ethan by John L. Monk

Pixel Dust and
Necrotic Apocalypse by David Petrie

Viceroy's Pride by Cale Plamann

Henchman by Carl Stubblefield

Artorian's Archives by Dennis Vanderkerken and Dakota Krout

www.ingramcontent.com/pod-product-compliance
Lightning Source LLC
Chambersburg PA
CBHW051519250626
47156CB00001B/145

* 9 7 8 1 6 3 7 6 6 0 8 2 9 *